The
Angel
of Pain

Brian Stableford

PAN BOOKS
LONDON, SYDNEY AND AUCKLAND

First published in Great Britain 1991 by Simon & Schuster Limited,
a Paramount Communications Company

This edition published 1993 by Pan Books Limited,
a division of Pan Macmillan Publishers Limited
Cavaye Place, London SW10 9PG
and Basingstoke

Associated companies throughout the world

ISBN 0 330 32607 4

1 3 5 7 9 8 6 4 2

A CIP catalogue record for this book is available from
the British Library

Printed and bound in Great Britain by
Cox & Wyman Ltd, Reading, Berkshire

For my wife Jane,
in recognition of the influence
which she had on my thinking about pain

CONTENTS

PROLOGUE
The Secrets of the Grave

The wooden arch surrounding the gateway to the burial ground was ancient and weather-worn but still as strong as the day it was built. The oak from which the arch was made had been well weathered and was more solid by far than the kind of timber in use in Victoria's England. The only parts of the structure that had submitted to the ravages of time were the hinges on which the wrought-iron gate was mounted, which had rusted and become friable; Jacobean metalworkers had known nothing of the excellent steel from which Victoria's England built her empire and her Industrial Revolution.

Luke Capthorn watched Jason Sterling test the strength of the gate with his fingers. The gentlemanly hand which clutched the hooded lantern was not completely steady, and Luke smiled at his master's unease. The shadows which clustered here held no terrors for Luke; once, he had been afraid of the dark, but that was long ago. Nowadays, he felt far more comfortable at night than he did in the light of day. Sterling was not his only master, and the other was more powerful by far when night fell.

The same rust that had rotted the hinges of the gate had caused the original lock to seize up, and the gate was now secured by a padlock. Sterling pointed to the place where the crowbar should be inserted, and stepped back so that his servant could get sufficient purchase to break the chain.

Luke quickly found that his unaided strength was not adequate to the task, and called on Richard Marwin to lend a hand. Marwin had to set down the two spades which he was carrying in order to do so.

When the two of them heaved in concert, the crucial link in the chain was easily sheared. The sound of its breaking seemed to Luke as loud as a pistol shot, and he saw Sterling look nervously towards the darkened windows of Charnley Hall, fearful that a light might appear there.

None did.

Luke had told his master that they had little to fear from the inhabitants of the house: the doctor who owned the house was a widower in his seventies, and the servants were meek and frail. Nevertheless, Sterling had insisted that it would be better by far were they to complete their work without being discovered. Luke agreed: the Devil's work was always best done secretly.

The three men did not follow the overgrown path to the disused chapel. They had no interest in the building, which had been allowed to fall into dereliction by the present tenant of the hall; their business was with those who lay beneath the soil without, in the small, private graveyard where the old Charnleys had carefully accumulated their ancestors.

Sterling had to take the hood from the lantern in order that its light might fall upon the gravestones, but he kept it low to minimise the risk of being seen.

Sterling's face, eerily lit from below, seemed very pale and drawn; his moist eyes caught the light oddly. Nor were they the only eyes that reflected the sudden gleam, for Luke caught a glimpse of a yellow stare among the trees; that was a barn owl, which quickly turned and flew away.

There were numerous tiny bats flitting back and forth between the trees and the chapel, quite undeterred by the invaders. Perhaps that was because the lantern-light attracted the insects which they hunted, but Luke did not think so. Bats were the creatures most loyal to his second, secret master. Bats were the Devil's minions, able to fly in the dark despite their blindness by virtue of his gift of a special sense.

One day, Luke thought, Sterling – who was the Devil's man but did not know it – would extend his experiments to involve bats as well as worms and toads. Then they would see what miracles might be wrought by the Devil's alchemy.

'Which one?' said Sterling, when he could not find the grave he sought. His eyes glittered in the eerie light.

Luke could only shake his head. He knew that the grave was here, but he had no idea which one it was. Sterling turned away, cursing the difficulty of trying to read the eroded legends on the lichen-covered stones. In his own house – which was surely full enough of horrors – Sterling seemed for ever cool and composed and every inch the magician, but there was an anxiety in his eyes now that made him seem merely human.

A bat zoomed low over their heads and Marwin, who was the tallest of the three, ducked and cursed. Then he transferred both the spades to his left hand, and promptly crossed himself.

Poor fool! Luke thought. *That sign cannot protect you, while we are about such work as this.* He bathed in the luxury of the thought, which he found oddly comfortable. He had spent many years in the Lord's service, working for the nuns at Hudlestone, writhing and chafing under the pressure of their stern expectations. When he had changed sides in the great struggle, to become the agent of the Satanist Jacob Harkender, it was as if that weight had been lifted from his shoulders.

Luke did not fear the Devil at all; his faith assured him that the demons which lurked in shadows and stones, ever ready to erupt into the world and make play with its inhabitants, would not harm him. Instead they would shield him from harm and keep him safe from human enemies.

Sterling was a devout unbeliever, contemptuous of the very idea of the Devil – but Luke Capthorn knew that many of those who were Satan's servants were not privileged to know who their master was. In the reckoning of men, Sterling was cut from far finer cloth than Luke, but Luke had always taken satisfaction from the knowledge that in the reckoning of the fallen angels, Sterling was a mere instrument, less worthy than a true collaborator like him.

Sterling, in need of yet more light, paused to turn up the wick of the lantern. Then, holding it out before him, he continued to inspect the rank of standing stones. Most were simple and not too large, having been laid down long before the modern era arrived, with its grandiose notions regarding the propriety of monuments. No Charnley had been buried here since Victoria came to the throne, and there was not a single stone angel or mock mausoleum to be seen.

When this place of preservation had first been laid out, the Charnley family had been newly ennobled; in the building of a private chapel and the consecration of a burying ground large enough to contain twelve or twenty generations of their descendants they had expressed the hope that they would become and remain one of the great families of England. Now, with the graveyard only half-filled and virtually abandoned to the weeds, their name and title had been consigned to the pages of history; and the doctor who lived in the Hall had thought so little of the significance of this place as to bury a man here who had chosen his name upon a whim, for mere convenience.

Sterling let loose a small cluck of annoyance when he finally found what he sought, and Luke understood why. The grave they had come to find had no stone at all, but only a wooden cross – as they might easily have guessed. It was in a covert, close to the place where the wall of the chapel met the wall which marked the boundary of the Hall's grounds.

The name carved into the horizontal bar of the cross was ADAM CLAY.

Sterling pointed at the ground, and Luke took one of the spades from Richard Marwin. Because the big man hesitated, it was Luke who first thrust the blade of his implement into the rain-softened earth and began to turn it. Marwin joined in quickly enough and set to work with a will; he was plainly of the opinion that if the job must be done, it had best be done quickly.

Sterling held the lamp a little higher so that they could see what they were doing, but Luke saw him glancing anxiously in the direction of the house. A copse of trees blocked the direct line of sight, but it was impossible to judge whether any faint glimmer of light might be glimpsed through the branches if anyone in the attics should chance to wake.

The chapel wall beside the grave was brightened by the light, and the shadows of the two diggers danced against its background like players in a silhouette theatre. The stonework was surprisingly free of dust and grime, but signified its antiquity with its greyness and grimness. Its colours were by no means uniform, but there was nothing to be seen that had the extremity of whiteness, and the only blackness was the negativity of the moving shadows.

'I wonder whether there have been any here before us,' Sterling murmured, looking down at his perspiring servants. 'Austen is a doctor, after all, and of an age to have patronised resurrection men in the years when their trade was at its height.'

Luke did not dignify the teasing speculation with a response.

'But I suppose that sort preferred their carrion fresh,' Sterling continued, 'and the Charnleys were probably the kind who'd place a guard over their dead until they might be considered safely rotted. The only man who would have been easy to steal is the one we seek – and his interment was presumably unattended by any publicity at all.'

Still Luke said nothing, giving his full attention to the work. Marwin was digging so furiously that it was difficult to keep pace with him, and Luke did not like to be made to seem weak.

Again a quick-moving bat passed over their heads, and Marwin cringed away – but he did not pause this time for any futile ceremony. All three of them started, though, when the branches of a nearby yew tree rustled ominously. It was only the owl again, returning to its hunting ground, but it did not turn its pale face away from the light of the lantern. It was as though it had come to keep watch over their illicit labour.

They continued to dig, as fast as they could. They were down into thick brown clay now, compact and glutinous, but it yielded readily enough to the blades of their tools. There were no stones to make the going hard. It was, Luke thought, almost as if those who had filled the grave had known that their work would one day be undone, and had not wanted to make the undoing difficult. Was it possible, he wondered, that Austen had not quite succeeded in maintaining his unbelief in the face of his patient's astonishing assertions? Had even Austen been persuaded, in spite of himself, to entertain the possibility that Adam Clay might one day return from the dead, like Lazarus before him?

Luke could not yet believe that himself, and would not until he saw the task accomplished – and in the meantime, he had to live with the possibility that he would be shown up for a fool. Better by far to hope that Austen was the fool and had harboured the faint suspicion all along.

Sterling started again at the duller sound which Marwin's spade made as it penetrated the last thin layer of clay and hit the sturdy wood of a coffin. The two diggers moderated the power of their blows, anxious to avoid damaging the box, which they still had to carry back to the city in the cart that waited in the lane.

When they had cleared enough earth away, Luke bent down to test the weight of the coffin. It was not very heavy; it was a pauper's coffin, and its softened boards were thin.

'Be careful,' Sterling said, when Luke and Marwin began to lift the coffin out of its slot. Luke's heart had begun to pound with avid excitement, and he guessed that Sterling's heart was leaping likewise.

Sterling moved back to clear a space as Luke and Marwin raised the fragile coffin to ground level. When it was properly balanced, Marwin bent down to recover the two spades, and waited for Luke to clamber out of the pit before handing them up to him. Luke dropped the tools again in order to extend a hand to the big man, helping him to heave his bulk out of the deep hole.

When an angry cry suddenly cut through the silence, Luke froze. He felt Marwin's hand clutch at him, and he nearly let the man fall back into the open grave. Then, as if panic had lent him extra strength, he hauled again, and the big man was brought up to stand beside him.

They turned together, and Luke saw that there was a second lantern bobbing among the trees between the chapel and the house. Two men were hurrying across the lawn towards the arched gateway.

Sterling cursed, and it was obvious that he did not know what to do.

'The wall!' said Marwin, meaning the wall which separated the burial ground from the lane. But the wall was nearly six feet high, and Luke knew how difficult it would be to manhandle the coffin over such an obstruction. They could have climbed it with ease, had flight been their only aim, but Luke did not want to go without the thing they had come to fetch, and nor did Sterling.

'Pick it up!' their master instructed. 'Let it drop and I'll see you damned!'

Luke bent down, but Marwin was still uncertain, and Luke had to add his own urgent appeal to Sterling's. Marwin condescended to be told, and picked up one end of the coffin, but when they had lifted it they had nowhere to go. The two men approaching had almost reached the gate, and Luke's heart skipped a beat when he saw that one of them carried a gun. It was an ancient sporting piece, but it was nevertheless a gun and could kill any one of them. Luke recognised the man as James Austen and turned his own face away, hoping that he was too far away from Sterling's lantern to have been recognised in his turn.

'Wait!' Sterling called out, and such was the imperiousness of his tone that the two men did indeed stop running. Neither was dressed for an outdoor escapade, and once they had paused they seemed uncertain enough of their own objectives. It must have alarmed Austen to see that there were three men in the graveyard, for his gun had only one barrel, but the doctor raised the weapon regardless to threaten them all.

'Don't fire, Dr Austen,' said Sterling immediately, with what surely qualified as cool temerity. 'The law of the land would not condone the act, despite what I have done.'

But Austen, although as much a man of science and reason as Jason Sterling, was too frightened and angry to be cool. He sighted along the barrel of the gun, and Luke was certain that he intended to fire.

But he never had the chance.

Suddenly, the doctor was sent staggering backwards, his white nightshirt billowing out in a curious fashion, crazed with peculiar shadows. It seemed for a moment as though the nightshirt had been rent apart, but only for a moment.

Luke realised, to his amazement, that the black shapes which were materialising like shadows upon the garment were bats flocking out of the darkness to buffet and cling to the man. They fluttered about his upper body like moths about a candle flame, and some must have clung to his face and hair, for he dropped the gun instantly and tore at his face with his hands. The creatures were very tiny – hardly bigger than mice – but there were hundreds of them, mobbing him with a fierceness which belied their size.

Marwin let loose a small screech of terror, but did not drop his burden. Luke gasped, too, but his gasp was glad surprise: a vindication of that mysterious instinct which told him to love the cloak of darkness and trust the creatures of the shadows.

Austen cried out as he fell down. It was a thin wail of anguish, not a blood-curdling scream, but it was replete with shock and terror. The doctor's flailing hands beat at the little bodies which fluttered madly about his face, while all the muscles of his limbs seemed to be jerking convulsively against the horrid grip of those which clung to his nightshirt. The servant who had come with him fell to his knees and joined in the attempt to beat the bats away, but he too was all too clearly terrified by what had happened.

Austen's servant had dropped his lantern, and the light flickered uncertainly for a few seconds before the flame was snuffed out. The darkness was too much for the man, who rose to his feet and ran away in blind panic, abandoning his writhing master to the unexpected outrage of the hunters of the night. Austen did not cry out again, but as he thrashed about, trying to dislodge the bats, he emitted small hissing noises that would not have disgraced the wildest and most brutal of his one-time patients in the asylum at Hanwell.

The white nightshirt caught just enough of the light of Sterling's lantern to show Luke what was happening. Austen's antics put him in mind of a mad spectre, dancing on the border which separated the world of men from the great wilderness of Otherness.

Tear him! Luke cried in the silence of his thoughts. *Feed on his blood and suck him dry! Let his fate serve as a warning for all those who dare to interfere with the Devil's work!*

Sterling somehow retained sufficient presence of mind to say 'Go now!' to his servants. More importantly, he had sufficient courage left to lead them towards and through the gateway where the bats were wheeling in a flock about the fallen body of the old man. Luke followed, and even the superstitious Marwin allowed himself to be urged along.

They could not run because the laden coffin, though light enough to be carried easily, was awkwardly shaped and cumbersome. They could only walk, and that unsteadily.

As they went out of the cemetery, they kept as far away as they could from the fallen doctor, but they saw as they passed him that he was still threshing about on the ground, trying to dislodge the clinging bats from his nightshirt and his bare flesh, sobbing as he did so. But the bats were doing him no real harm; the lantern-light revealed no blood. If Austen's heart was not stopped by the surge of his terror, he would come to no harm.

The discarded gun lay beside the stricken man, and Sterling might have picked it up had he wished, but he did not bother. Instead, he hurried on into the waiting night, urging his staggering followers to increase their speed.

Somehow, the half-rotted coffin stood up to the strain which they put upon it. It was, Luke thought, as though the Devil himself had lent it strength.

All this, Luke felt sure, had been intended and planned by one who was far wiser and more powerful than Jason Sterling. Sterling was merely the means by which the scheme would be put into effect. The man who was made of special clay – immortal clay – was required by another, whose purposes were surely more ambitious by far than Sterling's quasi-alchemical quest for the secret of extended life.

Only show me what you need, Luke prayed silently, *only show me what you desire, and I will be a better servant by far than Jacob Harkender ever was or Jason Sterling ever will be. Only caress me with shadows, only bathe my heart in soothing darkness, and I will be the sharpest and the best of all your human instruments, asking less and giving more than any man of their kind ever could.*

ONE
Brooding on the Vast Abyss

1

*T*he surface of Hell is in turmoil still; the magma still flows beneath the charred and cracking surface, bubbling up in turbid pools and dazzling rivulets – but Satan is no longer stretched supine upon that blazing bed.

The nails which once pinned him down are gone, and the scars which remain in his hands and feet are mere stigmata, faint shadows upon his lustrous golden flesh. Satan is free to roam the fiery fields, and to seek what shelter he can from the incandescent clouds and their ceaseless rain of blood. He cannot entirely escape the ravages of his environment, but he is free, and he has long since grown accustomed to his agony. He still carries in his careworn heart, undulled by time, the chagrin of loss and despair, of bitterness and remorse, of anguish and misery, which has been his curse since the dawn of his existence, but he is free to make what use he can of his clever hands and his fertile mind, and he is by no means desolate of hope.

The Earth still hangs in the flame-filled skies of Hell, cocooned by protective darkness, but it seems infinitely more remote than it did when he was prisoned. No longer is every human sin made vividly evident to his lachrymose eyes; no longer does the world seem fatally injured by the myriad temptations which afflict mankind.

If Satan still numbers Tantalus among his many names, he is a Tantalus who has learned to live with hunger and *thirst, who is no longer tantalised by the mockery of his fate. He is more content now to be Prometheus, and to be proud of his Promethean role, channelling the icy fire of enlightenment to those men who are content to see with their eyes instead of their souls, that they may understand how to guard themselves from the destructive forces which threaten them.*

Satan is free now to be proud of the men whose souls he chilled with his mercy, free to hope that the fire of Hell will never claim them, free to dream that they may build a cool and placid empire whose bounds will extend from the surface of the Earth to the multitudinous earths of the multitudinous suns whose great milky halo shines ever more brightly in the dark cocoon.

Satan is free, and Eden – that tiny forest where temptation grew luscious upon every fruited bough – is forgotten now by man and angel alike.

It is a mercy, Satan knows, that Eden is no more – for Eden, as he remembers all too well, was the honeyed trap which snared him and made him the hapless instrument of man's damnation. Satan understands now that Eden existed only to supply an arena for the cunning treachery of God, which made Satan victim of his own ambition and Adam victim of his own innocence, and spoiled them both with dire punishment.

Satan can forgive much, for he is an angel whose nature it is to forgive, but he can never forgive what was done to him in Eden, and what he was forced to inflict upon the sons and daughters of the human race. Satan is generous with his forgiveness, but he can never forgive God for that particular trickery and that particular treason.

Satan is free now, and hope is alive in his breast. Satan is free now, and ambition is renewed in his intelligence. Satan is free now, and science has begun to dissolve the evils which afflict his heart.

Although the fires of Hell still burn, the world is well.

And why should it not remain well, now that the legacy of Eden has faded into the oblivion of myth and misremembrance?

More than twenty years after suffering the bite of a snake which was an angel's needle, David Lydyard was still afflicted by the dreams and visions which were the legacy of that pricking. No long interval of respite had ever been granted to him, save for a few gentle months before and after his marriage to Cordelia Tallentyre.

For David Lydyard, sleep was no rest from confrontation with the world, but simply a removal into another world, more vexing than the one in which he spent his waking hours.

He often dreamed of Satan, but he knew that Satan did not exist. The Satan of his dreams was symbolic of himself, and the Hell in which Satan was confined was symbolic of his own troubled body.

It was easy enough to liken his life to Hell, for he was never free of the pestilential fire of pain. In time, though, a man may become accustomed to anything, even to the fires of Hell; and a man who has courage, curiosity and determination may find a freedom to enquire, to make plans, and to act, even though he is beset by the fires of Hell.

David Lydyard had courage, curiosity and determination.

The world of Lydyard's dreams had not the same stability and familiarity as the everyday world in which he spent his waking hours, but it possessed him so vividly when he slept that it was every bit as real to him. It was frequently confused, and the helter-skelter flow of its events commonly refused to respect the constraints of rationality, but the sheer force of its presence commanded him to concede it the status of a real world of real experience.

He had long since lost the valuable art of forgetting his dreams before he woke; but there were certain aspects of his dream-experience which he was not allowed to remember. In his waking life he was a free man and a graceful master of servants; but in his dream-life he was himself the servant of a cruel and tyrannical master. In his waking life, he was a sceptic through and through; but in the world of his dreams he could not possibly deny the existence, the immanence and the wrathful demands of godlike entities, one of which held

him in thrall to be its pawn in all its dealings with the world
of matter and men.

The confusion of his visions and nightmares was not so
constant as to deny him recognition of certain locations
and landscapes, whose aspects and appearances seemed to
his sleeping self to be set in the permanent substances of
sand and stone, bricks and mortar. There were places in his
dreams to which he could return again and again, and persons
in his dreams whose faces and situations were continually
revealed to him.

Unlike his waking self, his sleeping self could float and
fly; there was magic in the power of his will. Even so, the
stone of his dreams was hard and cold, and the sand was
coarse and hot; that other world in which he often walked
and sometimes flew was as solid and unyielding as the one
which he confronted by day.

By virtue of this, David Lydyard had learned by bitter
experience the truth of what the philosopher Berkeley had
argued: that matter is the possibility of sensation. He could
not doubt the materiality of the world in which his waking
self moved; not could he doubt the materiality of the world
in which his sleeping self moved. Even though the world of
his dreams was a world which existed only as ideas in his own
secret consciousness, it nevertheless presented to his sleeping
self the same evidences of permanence and actuality that the
world of the everyday presented to his waking self.

He knew that other men experienced their dreams in quite
a different way; they found no permanence there and no
solidity, and therefore came to believe – quite rationally
– that the world of dreams was a mercurial phantom of
the imagination. For such men, the hardness of the world
of waking life was unique and quite independent of the
ideas men had of it. Such men found Berkeley's viewpoint
uncomfortable, and easily fell into the error of thinking
that they could refute it by kicking a stone and finding it
sufficiently hard to hurt them. For David Lydyard there
was no possible consolation to be gained from any such
experiment. Pain was not, for him, a route which led from
internal to external awareness; he was one of those upon

whom it exerted an altogether contrary force. He was one
of the unfortunates among the prisoners in Plato's allegorical
cave, freed from the chains which had formerly bound him to
watch the parade of shadows playing upon the wall.

He was able to turn his head and see the figures which cast
them. He could see the gods.

The gods were made in his own image. The faces which
they wore, human and unhuman alike, were borrowed from
the spectrum of his own ideas. Still he *saw* them. He was free
to confront the makers of the world, unable to cling to the
conviction that they were mere shadows, abstractions.

Once upon a time, he had been told, it had been the
common curse of all mankind to meet the gods as they walked
upon the surface of the waking world. But the world had
changed; and if, as some believed, there was a single Creator
supreme above all others, the fact that the world had changed
might be considered evidence that the supreme Creator was
merciful in his dealings with men. David Lydyard had been
born into a waking world from which the gods had been
exiled, reduced to the status of paradoxical phantoms even
in the manifold worlds of men's dreams. In his world, only
a very few men knew how the gods might be glimpsed, and
only a handful were mad enough or brave enough to tread
that way of pain.

David Lydyard had no choice but to follow that path. Had
he not been brave, he would surely have gone mad.

*The Angel of Pain has wings that are black and sleek, that
cloak her with darkness when they are furled, and open like
stormy clouds when she takes to the air.*

*The Angel of Pain has burnished skin the colour of bronze,
which glows with heat; and her eyes are like fiery embers,
which fade when she is sad to the colour and the texture of
ashes. The Angel of Pain is frequently sad, for she is, like all
the angels, a creature capable of love and fear as well as wrath
and pride, and she does not like to be hated for what she is.*

*The Angel of Pain has hands bedecked with black talons,
whose points are curved and polished. Her grip is exceedingly
powerful, but so sharp are her claws that even the most gentle*

of her caresses is likely to rend and lacerate. When she is at her most sincere, refined and delicate, the tracks of her affection are written in her lovers' blood.

The Angel of Pain has full lips, which seem to the observing eye to be soft and gentle; but their kiss is caustic and her tongue is a rasp which abrades as though it were dressed in diamond dust.

The Angel of Pain has flowing tresses, slivery in hue, which she combs most carefully to smooth perfection, but like the hairs which dress the leaves of stinging nettles hers are harsh to the touch; and the tears which she sheds to lament her loneliness are purest poison.

The Angel of Pain has a heart which beats like any heart, and a heart which harbours all the desires which angels have; and of all the angels there are, she is the most loyal to those who seek intimacy with her. She denies no one, and there is no other angel in Heaven who has such generosity in loving her enemies as dearly as she loves those who like her best.

Many are those who believe that the Angel of Pain is a creature of Hell, but there are some who learn to see her differently, who see purpose in her ministrations. For them she is instead the ruling authority of Purgatory, and the justification of her harshness is to be sought in the hope of eventual transcendence.

Those who hate the Angel of Pain say only this, that the empire of fear has the greatest of all despots set at its head, whose name is Death, and his consort is named Pain; but those who surpass hatred say instead that a spur is not an altogether evil thing, and that Pain may prove in time an enemy of Death, and in her fashion friend to hopeful Man.

The Angel of Pain did not exist. She was not a true angel, like the Spider or the maker of the Sphinx. She was only a symbol: a symbol of the manner in which the true angels dealt with their human favourites. She was only a courier: a courier sent by the true angels to summon their unwilling servants to the world where the true angels lived.

The way to the world of the true angels was as familiar to David Lydyard's sleeping self as the route from his house in

Kensington to University College Hospital was to his waking self. The journey always had the same stages.

He would find himself at first in the comfortable interior of a large house, unreasonably rich in dark and dingy corridors, whose rooms were cluttered with strangely obtrusive furniture. The dusty air was always dead and heavy, disturbed only by the exaggerated ticking of clocks whose echoless measurement of passing time seemed to emphasise the distortions to which the obstinately undomesticated spaces were subject. The walls were hung with ornately framed mirrors, in which nothing was reflected but the empty rooms, stretched and warped according to the particular whim of each mute glass.

His sleeping self would be confused by the combination of utter emptiness and menacing entrapment when he tried to leave the house; for a while it would seem that the corridors wished to deny him egress, intending to restrain him in that more commonplace and tolerable dream-realm whose solidity was false and evanescent, easily destroyed by the act of awakening. But he could not be so easily confined; he would break into a purposeful run, moving at a steady pace for mile after mile, while the ticking of the clocks grew ever louder. Finally, he would pass on into the greater dream-world, nakedly exposed to the fearsome starry eyes of the infinite sky.

He would invariably find himself in a night-lit desert where nothing was to be seen but rock and sand. The sand was gently stirred by a warm wind, its tiny motes sparkling with reflected starlight as they drifted in the heavy air. He would begin to walk across the derelict landscape, but would soon find that he did not need to exert his muscles in order to make progress, and that each step he took would carry him for thirty yards if he would only let it. Content to float, he would steer a course between ragged cliff-faces, following the meandering course of a great river of silver sand. As he did so, the cliff-faces to either side would become gradually higher and closer together, until he was following a narrow path along a twisting canyon, with only a slender ribbon of stars to light his way.

Enigmatic shadows would occasionally blacken parts of the
starry stream; it was impossible to say what shape they had,
but they might have been huge predatory birds leaving their
nesting sites. He was sometimes afraid that the canyon walls
might close above him, trapping him in a tunnel which could
only lead him to a blind end somewhere near the centre of
the earth, but they never did. Instead, the valley would begin
to open out again, exposing brighter stars in such astonishing
profusion that he could no longer believe himself to be on the
lonely earth he knew. Then he would see ahead of him, in
the distance, a great city whose buildings, though half fallen
into ruins, were greater by far than any of the petty edifices
of the waking world.

Here were columns a thousand feet high and statues six
hundred feet from top to toe. Some of the statues had human
heads, others had human torsos or human legs and feet, but
all of them were chimeras of one kind or another. Some
were like the gods of Egypt, but only some; there were more
bizarre compounds of the human and the animal here than he
had seen in the most extravagant representations of ancient
art, and every one was so huge as to preclude the possibility
that it had been shaped by the hands of human sculptors.

The city was vast in extent. It stretched from horizon to
horizon and far beyond, and though he flew through it much
faster than a swift horse could have carried him he was certain
that days rather than hours were expended in penetrating to
its heart. He knew that in the waking world the sun would
have risen and set half a dozen times while he moved through
the paved streets, but here there was only a glorious plethora
of fixed stars patiently wheeling their way across the sky.

Eventually, he would come to the very centre of the city,
where the white towers had been taller still before they had
fallen into ruins. Here there was a steep-faced pyramid which
had not been toppled by age and time, although most of the
crystalline blocks forming its smooth outer face were missing,
revealing ragged steps beneath. The apex of the pyramid was
a mile above the base, and each of its steps was taller than a
man. To scale it would have been an extremely difficult task
for a group of men, but David drifted lightly up its face as

though he were nothing more than a mote of sand tenderly carried by the capricious wind.

As he soared upwards, David sometimes thought for a few giddy moments that he would be carried all the way to the tip of the edifice, part company with the mass of the world and fly into the realm of the fiery stars, but this hope was always dashed when he saw a dark opening in the distance, which grew as he approached it into a great arched portal through which he entered the interior of the pyramid. He would begin to drift downwards then, through slanting corridors and vertical shafts, and into a great maze of catacombs. The darkness here was profound but not absolute, and by some mysterious means he could always see the pattern of the brickwork in the walls of the shafts and tunnels.

This journey into the darkness often became frightening, but the fear did not last long, for his mad flight always began to slow down, and he soon saw light ahead of him. As the light came closer, reassuring in its yellow brilliance, his movement gradually ceased, until he found himself standing once again on booted feet, at the threshold of a great lighted chamber.

As he stepped forward into the welcoming light, David always experienced a return of sensation which was not altogether pleasant. He felt the weight of his own body, the dry warmth of the air against his face, the grip of his clothes about his chest, the slow beat of his heart. He was uncomfortably material here, and distressingly alive.

The chamber was vast; its ceiling was more than two hundred feet high and its floor must have measured four or five hundred feet on either side. There was no obvious source of the light by which it was illuminated, but flickering shadows played about the walls, as though somewhere there ought to be a huge fire. In its centre was a throne, and there on the throne – fifteen or twenty times as tall as a man – the goddess Bast would sit, looking down at him with her huge green-coloured eyes. There were never any other human or semi-human figures to be seen in the carpeted chamber, but there were usually yellow cats, sometimes by the thousand, variously occupied in sitting, strolling, grooming or playing.

These cats were her creatures: fragment of her own soul, like the Sphinx which she had made to walk the earth.

It was David himself who had named her Bast and selected the form in which she appeared to him. That was how his delirium had shaped her when he had first encountered her in Egypt. In a way, she was his own personal deity, reserved for the sight of his inner eye.

He loved her, after a fashion; and he hated her, after a fashion; but he did not worship her.

He loved her, because his latent desires had spun her a fleshly garment of uncanny beauty. He hated her, because he was her victim and her pawn and she a conscienceless oppressor. He feared her, because she was an angel and he was but a man, and she could obliterate him on a whim. He was consoled by her, because she was an angel and he was but a man, and she might shield him from the whims of dire fate if she cared to do it. But he did not adore or worship her, because he needed no act of faith to know that she was real, and thus he knew that she was only a being like himself, and was no more entitled to the worship of men than men were entitled to the worship of insects.

Often, he went to her pyramid determined to tell her that she did not need to look down at him from such a lofty height, and did not need to show herself as an awesome giant as old as time itself. Often, he went with the intention of asking her to meet him face to face, as one being to another, so that he and she might talk frankly and openly as equals. But she would not permit that. She was jealous of her apparent godhood and of her secrets. She would not even allow him to remember what he said to her, and meanly deprived him of the certainty that he had ever said to her that which he intended to say.

She clung to the authority of her apparent godhood, of her absolute power over him. But still he would not worship her. Still he insisted that in spite of all her power she was only a being, like himself.

Even the Supreme Creator, whose face he had sometimes glimpsed in the intensest moments of his visions, did not seem to David an entity worthy of worship. If He existed, in the same solidity as the Pyramid of Bast or St Paul's Cathedral, he was but one more being; and if the present nature of the evolving universe proved anything at all, David thought, it proved that the Creator of Creators was just as prone to folly and error as any other god, or any man, or any insect.

The Sphinx is a creature of many forms, but when she stirs the dreams of men she wears the face of a beautiful woman, as befits a seductress and succubus. Her beauty, like all beauty, is a snare, but the lure of beauty is its own reward. What does it matter that the Sphinx has the wings of an angel, which carry her soaring through the worlds beyond the world? What does it matter that she has the talons of a gryphon, which might rend and lacerate a man, body and soul? She is kinder by far than her imaginary sister, the Angel of Pain.

What the Sphinx seeks, above all else, is to learn and to know. In ancient times she courted sophistry, but nowadays her fascination is for science. The first and most fundamental of her riddles is always the same, though foolish men once thought that mankind was the answer rather than the puzzle. Always she demands to know the what and how and why of man's creation, because the destiny of mankind and the destiny of the angels are entwined in a fashion so cunning that neither the intelligence of man or the vision of angels can penetrate its mystery. All her other riddles emerge from the one; they are different facets of the same problem . . . or so, at least, it seems to those she plucks from the highway of life to serve as her pawns and fellow enigmatists.

Even the oddest and most paradoxical of her questions is, in the end, a question about the nature and purpose of the world of men; and if she should ask, 'How many angels may dance on the head of a pin?' that too would be a question about the nature and purpose of the world of men.

Once, the dreamer feared the Sphinx, but he fears her no longer. If ever she meant him harm, that harm was done long ago. Now she is his protector; she needs his effort and she needs his mind; she needs his accumulated wisdom and all his desire to increase that wisdom. He knows that she might hurt him, and might well be the source of the hurt which constantly assails him body and soul, but he also knows that he is too precious to be cast carelessly aside, and far too precious to be made a hollow man, a mere slave of her will.

To serve her purpose, he must be alive and he must be free.

What more could a man demand of an angel, once destiny has decreed that he must meet the angels face to face?

David Lydyard and Sir Edward Tallentyre had become certain long ago that what Bast and her servant the Sphinx required from their pawns was the power of their reason and the accuracy of their educated sight. Bast could make a creature like the Sphinx, lending it the substance and the soulfire of her own being, but she could not put into the Sphinx's mind the knowledge and the intelligence that men had.

The Sphinx, for all her shape-shifting powers and all her magic, lacked something that men had, and could not easily acquire what she lacked. That, Lydyard and Tallentyre deduced, was why the angel and her creature had never let go of any of them. Tallentyre, Lydyard and William de Lancy remained prisoners and pawns of Bast, each with a different role to fulfil.

Tallentyre believed that without such aid as her human instruments provided, the angel could not hope to calculate her own course of future action. Unless she understood the changed world as thoroughly as she could, she might not be able to preserve herself against the predations of other angels; but if she became confident enough of the superiority of her understanding, she might then hope to turn her second-hand wisdom to good advantage in becoming an irresistible devourer of her own kind.

Believing this, David had learned to meet Bast's gaze as squarely as he could, and to go to her with the intention of speaking to her with all the cleverness which he brought to his conversations with Sir Edward Tallentyre.

It was not so easy to meet the gaze of the Sphinx's shadowy sister, the Angel of Pain; but even that, David schooled himself to do. He could not look forward to his meetings with her, and was never glad to enter that infinitely vivid garden of tortures which was her realm, but still he tried to face her, as bravely as he could.

After twenty years of close acquaintance, he felt that he faced her as well as any man could, and dared to find a perverse triumph in the conviction that he had begun to root out the secrets of her soul.

Although he endured the perpetual caresses of the Angel of Pain, David Lydyard thought himself a man more fortunate than most others of his kind. He had a loving wife and children, which he counted very precious. More than that, he had the excitement of enlightenment, which he won by making his tribulations into an object of study and enquiry.

When, soon after his marriage, the dreams and visions reclaimed their empire in his soul, he had decided that the study of pain must become his career. By this means he made the Angel of Pain his tutor as well as his torturer.

All the while, he knew, Bast and the Sphinx would be his examiners. And in spite of the fact that they meanly robbed him of the memories that would have been most useful to him, he was equally determined to be theirs. While they used him to discover the answer to the riddle of the world of men, he did all that he could to clarify the mystery of their existence and nature.

One day, David Lydyard thought, he might be in a position to explain the ways of the gods to his fellow men. Unlike Milton, he never imagined that such an explanation would also serve as a justification. He never imagined that any such justification was possible. Whatever the apparent gods really were, they certainly were not just.

2

David Lydyard listened to James Austen's story with mixed feelings. For a little while, he was lazy enough to allow himself to wonder whether it really mattered, but he could not in the end deny that it did. For twenty years the greater world had been untroubled by the angels; they had been content to study and not to interfere. Now, it seemed, one or other of them believed that the time had come to act.

David had often discussed with Sir Edward Tallentyre the possibility that something of this kind would happen. It would have been too optimistic to hope that the angels might eventually be content to return to their age-long sleep. What purpose could there have been in all his nightmare visions, save to prepare the way for a moment such as this? Even if the angel which they now called Bast had no wish to act, it had nevertheless to be on guard against the threatening actions of others.

David found himself oddly relieved that the moment had finally come. He discovered that he would not have liked to die feeling that his peculiar and painful life had been wasted in preparation for events he had not lived long enough to witness. But his relief was inevitably mixed with fear. He was fearful not so much for himself as for Cordelia and the children. He had grown accustomed to his own painful intimacy with the Creators, and had little left to lose, but the children still had everything before them which human life could offer.

While Austen brought his tale to its conclusion, struggling to find words adequate to describe his feelings as he fought against the astonishing attack of the bats, David stole a covert glance at his wife, trying to judge her reaction. Cordelia had been belatedly snatched up by the fantastic whirlwind of the events of twenty years ago, but her part had not been insignificant. She had killed a werewolf in her father's house, and then she had been abducted and taken to Harkender at Whittenton, so that she might be rudely thrust into a nightmare vision of Hell, to serve as bait in a trap.

David knew that she remembered it all quite calmly now. For her the horror of it had long since shrivelled into ashes; she did not dream as he did, and although he had no secrets from her, she could not begin to imagine what his dreams were like. Her sharpest memory of that first dizzy adventure was the fierce resentment she had felt of Sir Edward's determination not to involve her. It annoyed her still that it was not until she was dragged into Hell that anyone had consented to offer her an explanation – and not until then that her future husband had condescended to share the awful burden of his misery.

David suspected that she had never quite forgiven him for that. Despite the fact that she loved him *almost* as fervently as he loved her, she had never quite been able to put away her annoyance at the way in which he had capitulated to the demands of her father and tried to imprison her with ignorance. Even in the intervening years, he knew, she had thought herself disadvantaged. He had retained a means of pursuing further understanding of what had happened to them, and what bearing it might have on their understanding of the world. Like Sir Edward, he had become a man of science, a physiologist dedicated to the elucidation of the obstinate mysteries of life. Cordelia had been anchored down by motherhood and the management of the household.

David wondered whether she now realised that it was all beginning again, and that this time she was witness to its beginning, privileged to be present at the birth of the mystery.

'Of course,' Austen said shamefacedly, after he had finished his tale, 'it's susceptible of a rational explanation, but . . .' He put his gnarled fingers to his cheek, where there was a patchwork of unhealed cuts made by tiny claws.

The alienist was leaning forward in his armchair, his eyes agleam with reflected gaslight; it seemed to David that wrath and puzzlement had combined to bring Austen back to life, at a time when exhaustion and tedium had brought him to the very brink of oblivion. Ever since his wife had died, Austen had been fading away, but now he was ignited with indignation. David could see, too, that there was something he had yet to reveal: something that he was saving up for melodramatic purposes. There was a tiny note of triumph to be heard even in his confession of failure.

'I dare say,' said David, playing the reasonable man as he was bound by circumstance to do, although it did not reflect his true feelings, 'that there's nothing plainly supernatural in a man being mobbed by bats. I won't try to persuade you otherwise, if you insist upon the point. But whoever removed the body of your one-time patient must have had a reason, and you can't hope to persuade me that these were resurrection men in the service of some renegade anatomist. You're certain that you didn't know the man who spoke to you?'

'Perfectly certain,' said Austen, with a hint of smugness. 'I had never seen *him* before . . .'

Now it comes, David thought, shifting his position on the sofa and wincing at the pain in his spine and arms. *Here is the revelation.*

'. . . But when I first caught sight of them,' Austen went on, 'the light of his lantern fell briefly upon the faces of his two accomplices. I think, perhaps, that I can put a name to one of them. I'm not sure – I haven't set eyes on the man in twenty years – but I believe it was Luke Capthorn.'

Cordelia straightened herself, jolted by the name.

Austen, who had not seen her reaction, went on to add, by way of explanation, 'He lived with his mother at the Lodge when the nuns had Hudlestone.'

Cordelia, who could hardly help feeling that this comment was woefully insufficient, added, 'He was also the man who took me from your care, doctor, and carried me off to Jacob Harkender's house.'

David put his hand over hers, to calm and reassure her, but she did not seem grateful for the gesture. 'It might mean that Harkender is behind this,' he said, speculatively. 'It's difficult to believe that he isn't dead, after all these years, even if he survived the fire which destroyed his house, but . . .'

'The man who took the body away was certainly not Jacob Harkender,' Austen said. 'I don't think *he* can be involved. Magician he may have been, but I doubt that he had the secret of eternal youth.'

'Nevertheless,' said David, patiently, 'the men you saw might have been sent by him. When Gilbert Franklin first went to Whittenton on Sir Edward's behalf, Harkender was very anxious to know where the body of Lucian de Terre might be found. I can't think of anyone else who would have an interest in stealing it.'

Austen had relaxed slightly and was watching David and his wife, trying to judge their reaction to his tale. David knew that Sir Edward had felt obliged to offer Austen a full account of the strange events of 1872, but he did not know exactly what interpretation the baronet had suggested to the alienist, or what Dr Austen had condescended to believe in consequence. In all probability, Austen had not made up his mind, even now.

'If Jacob Harkender believed that Adam Clay was also Lucian de Terre,' Austen pointed out, scrupulously, 'then others may believe it also. And if they are able to believe *that*, they may also be able to believe that what Lucian de Terre wrote in *The True History of the World* was indeed a kind of truth. You believe it yourself, after a fashion, do you not?'

David chose to evade the question, because he did not want to become embroiled in what was to him an ancient and tired argument. 'I've never seen the book itself,' he said. 'Sir Edward's attempts to acquire a copy have never borne fruit. There can't be many men who have read it, and we know that Harkender was the last person to see the volumes which were once lodged in the Museum Library.'

Cordelia took leave to interrupt. 'What do you think, Dr Austen?' she said, quietly.

Austen looked at her and smiled, but without undue condescension. 'You will forgive me, Mrs Lydyard,' he said, 'if I take refuge in one of your father's favourite circumlocutions. I don't know what to believe, but I'm prepared to entertain any and all hypotheses for the sake of speculation. Perhaps, after all, there *are* such things as werewolves and immortal men. Perhaps, for the man I knew as Adam Clay, death was only a petty interruption of active life, and not an end. In truth, I've sometimes wondered why your father and your husband have been content to let his body remain where it was through all these years, while it presented such a tantalising enigma.'

They both looked at David then, and he recoiled slightly from their enquiring gaze, startled by the question. 'Because of Pelorus,' he answered awkwardly. 'Adam Clay was his friend, whose wishes he respected. He offered me his own flesh and blood to study, but the instruments of my enquiry have not been adequate to discover how his substance differs from ours. The science of life is as yet in its infancy – we've only just begun to understand the chemistry of living things.' He hesitated, then added another sentence in a more decisive tone. 'Pelorus must be told, of course. That's one thing I must do tonight.'

'I leave that to you,' said Austen. 'But what of Sir Edward? Shall I write to him myself, or would you rather . . .?' He left the sentence dangling.

'I'll do it,' David said. 'I'm very grateful to you for coming to us, and very sorry that Sir Edward was not in London to hear your story from your own lips. I shall write to him immediately, so that the letter will go out with the morning post, although it'll take some while to reach him in Paris. You'll stay the night, of course?'

Austen nodded, and David glanced at Cordelia. She came to her feet obediently, disguising her sigh, and went to ring for a maid to make up the bed in the guest room. As she passed her husband's chair, he looked up and saw how pale she was. He knew then that she saw the matter much as he did. Twenty years of anxious expectation had been coiled up within them both, waiting for this release, and it had marked her as indelibly as it had marked him.

As the hem of her skirt brushed past his chair, she lowered her hand to touch him, very gently, on the cheek. It was meant as a gesture of tenderness and reassurance, but for some reason which even he did not understand he could not receive it, and he moved away.

When Cordelia had gone, Austen settled back in his chair. His expression was unfathomable. The bats which had swarmed upon him when he threatened the grave robbers had unsettled him, and no matter how scrupulous he felt obliged to be in pointing out that a natural explanation was possible, he too was well aware that something ominous had occurred.

'Mrs Tallentyre is frightened,' said the doctor, half apologetically. 'I am sorry that I could not get here earlier, while the bright sunshine could have set my story in a better light.'

'The light doesn't matter,' said David distantly. 'She's her father's daughter, capable of feeling the excitement of fear as well as its threat.'

'For herself, perhaps,' Austen admitted. 'But she fears more for you than for herself – and the two of you have yielded your hostages to fortune.'

'The whole world is a hostage to fortune,' said David, trying to speak lightly, although he meant every word. 'That's what we discovered, twenty years ago. But still, as Sir Edward is overfond of saying, we must accept the world as we find it, and live in it as best we can. We must hope for its survival, if not its salvation, and must do what little we may to help preserve it.'

Already his attention was wandering from his guest; already he was trying to pierce the curtain of mystery; already he was trying to imagine what might lie in store for him now that the angels were unquiet again. He hardly heard Austen say: 'Amen to that.'

In the cave beneath the Earth the multitude of men still lie in chains, with their legs fastened to the stone and their faces fixed on the wall of cold, cold stone. The fire still burns behind them, and along the narrow path which runs before the fire there passes the infinite parade of all that the gods have made, not excluding the gods themselves.

The shadows of all the beings in Creation dance upon the walls as the firelight flickers. At one time they are sharp, at another they blur; the magnitude of their distortion changes from one moment to the next. The echoes of true sound which resound from the walls are likewise distorted and murmurous.

The multitude of men who are born and live and die seeing nothing but the shadows on the wall curse the frailty of their senses and the deceptiveness of the dancing shadows. They long to be free, that they may no longer be forced to look upon uncertain appearances of things, but might turn instead to look upon things as they are. But the few who have broken their chains, and have turned to see the gods as they are, know what a terrible burden those must bear whose naked faces meet the hot stare of the true angels, and the brightness of things as they are.

The dreamer has looked into the faces of angels, and the angels which make angels, and the gods which make gods. He has seen the riot of things as they are, in all its dazzling confusion, and knows very well what advantages there are in watching shadows.

The dreamer knows what it is to have his senses over-whelmed; he knows what the heat of the fire may do to a man's eyes, and the intelligence behind those eyes, and the soul whose instrument intelligence is. The dreamer knows how false the faces of the angels are, how deceptive their beauty, how terrifying their fury, how fluid their forms. The dreamer knows.

The dreamer knows, too, that a man may look into the faces of the angels simply by turning his head. While his legs remain anchored to the ground, a man might yet be cursed to see the light of the fire, and everything which passes by on that narrow road which winds between the fire and the place where the multitude of men are bound by the chains of their existence.

There is one thing more that the dreamer knows, and needs to know. The dreamer knows that there is a passage which reaches up from the firelit cave towards another and far more bright light. The dreamer knows that if he were truly free, he might cross the road on which the gods and their myriad creatures walk, and walk through the fire to the passage beyond, and climb the slope towards the farther and brighter light. The dreamer knows that a free man – if only he had the courage, and the strength of will to pass through the flames of the fire – might see what the angels themselves have never seen, by the true and brightest light of all.

If only he had the courage.

If only he had the strength of will to pass through the flames of the fire.

If only his eyes, and his mind, and his soul, could look into the brightest light of all, without fear.

He might see Hell, and he might see Eden . . . but he might instead see a Paradise which the gods themselves had never seen.

Until a man has truly seen the world, how can he hope to change it?

Later, Cordelia came to David's study, where he was writing the letters which he had promised to dispatch as soon as possible. The letter to Sir Edward was only half completed, but he had been forced to lay down his pen for a while. Even the penning of a dozen lines was an ordeal nowadays, and his handwriting had grown dreadfully untidy. The other letter had not delayed him long, however, and it was complete. Cordelia picked it up from the desk and scanned it briefly.

Pelorus, it read, *I have news of the Clay Man which may be important. The waiting may be over. Come when you can. Lydyard.*

'Need you be so mysterious?' she asked.

David flexed his painful fingers and leaned back in his chair. Cordelia put her hand on his shoulder. This time he reached up gladly to catch it and enfold it in his own. He felt her fingers grip his, very careful of their frailty.

'One never can be sure when or if a message will reach him,' he answered. 'We haven't seen him for nearly a year now, and the letter might lie for some time at the collection point. In any case, I hesitate to commit my darker suspicions to paper.'

Cordelia perched herself demurely upon the corner of the desk, gathering her skirt as tidily as she could.

'Will you reveal them to me?' she asked, softly. 'It's such a strange thing that anyone should rob the grave in Austen's grounds. I can't guess what it means.'

David looked into his wife's eyes, and he knew in spite of the tenderness which he saw there that this was a contest of sorts. He loved her very dearly, but there were circumstances which set them at odds and made them combatants. *She does not intend to be left out of it this time*, he thought. *She is declaring her intention to play a part, if she can. She hopes to protect me, as I hope to protect her, but this is one thing we cannot do together.*

'The thing which Harkender summoned from the depths of time is still here,' he said. 'I can't claim to know what it is, or what form it has, but it's somehow incarnate in the soil and rock of England in the same way that the other is anchored to the ancient rocks of Egypt. They've been content thus far to suspend their conflict, but it may be that the Spider now believes that it has seen an advantage. Despite the fact that I'm by necessity of the Sphinx's party, I'm not privy to her plans, nor to the scheming of her parent, but I feel in my bones that *they* will be disturbed by this occurrence, and if that's so, how can I doubt that I'll be involved in what follows?'

'It may not be a matter of such great import,' she said softly. 'It's not so very much, after all: the theft of a coffin and a corpse. Even if Harkender *were* involved, do you think he could rouse his fallen angel for a second time? Was it the bats that made you so anxious?'

David paused before answering, in order to gather his thoughts, then said: 'We can't fight fear with mere denial. We've been forced to see what a frail thing the world is, and we're fully entitled to be afraid. We've both seen . . . we were both there, in that little Hell which Harkender's fallen angel created. We've always known, in our hearts, that it would one day begin again.

'But there's no cause for despair. You saw that Hell which the ignorant angel made, and what a shabby thing it was, how full of fakery and pretence. It was a theatre and nothing more, and it told us that such angels as there are upon the Earth have less imagination and less vision than the best of men. We learned, as the angel itself seemed to learn, that such power as it has is futile, if it knows not how to pursue its ends in an intelligent way. When we saw that it could be defeated by the force of reason, we learned the very important lesson that we don't have to fear such things blindly and unquestioningly. Reason is a weapon which we can and may use against them. We cannot simply cling to the hope that they will let us alone, but we aren't entirely impotent, if they don't.'

'But if it does begin again,' said Cordelia, haltingly – as though the last thing in the world she could desire was to dent his confidence – 'Harkender's angel might snatch us up as casually as it did before. We have Teddy now, and Nell and Simon. We have far more to lose now than we had then, and

I fear what a return of that madness might do, not to me or to the world, but to you and to the children.'

'I've entertained my own fears on behalf of the children these last eighteen years,' he assured her. 'I've always known that they must brave all the perils of the everyday world. There's been fear enough in that, without thought of the wicked werewolves of London or the mischief of lurking demons.

'We're not alone in our knowledge that the world contains malevolent forces; the great majority of men have lived with that belief since time began. Still they manage to live, and to contain their fear; still they find room for much more ordinary anxieties; still they dare to hope. How else could they live in a world overshadowed by famine, war and plague? Should we be capable of less, simply because we understand more?'

When he had finished speaking, David released her hand, slightly discomfited. Its warmth lingered in his palm, an evanescent yet invaluable treasure.

'You're right, of course,' she said, looking down at his unfinished letter to her father. 'There's enough to fear in the everyday world, and if we can live with *that* fear, we should also be able to face the extraordinary with a stout heart. You're quite right.' Her hand remained on his shoulder, even though he had removed his own, and now she pressed harder to emphasise that she was with him.

'Sir Edward will set our minds at rest,' said David, offering further reassurance. 'He'll return from Paris as soon as he receives my letter. My hand is better now, and I'll finish it very soon. But it's late, and you mustn't wait for me.'

She hesitated for a moment or two, but consented in the end to be dismissed. 'I'll go up now,' she said, lifting her hand at last. 'Don't be too long, I beg of you.'

'I must finish the letter,' David told her, 'but it's nearly done. I'll join you very soon.'

He smiled at her as she turned away, but the smile was as much a mask as the reassuring tone in which he dressed his words. His inner thoughts were in a different vein. *I will come to bed*, he said silently, *to lie in your arms for a little while. But tonight, I will only be waiting there – waiting to see what my dreams may bring.* The force of that anticipation was like a hand clutching his heart, but there was as much thrill in it as fear, and as much hunger as dread.

Then the dawn will come, he added, scrupulously, *and I will go to my work and find solace in its routines, as I always do and always will. When I am needed, I will doubtless be summoned. Such is my fate.*

3

As the dull afternoon drew on, David was forced to light the oil-lamp which stood upon his desk, rearranging his papers so as to get the benefit of the light. The sun had not yet set, but London was blanketed by sullen cloud, and the narrow line of high-set windows which let daylight into the room had glass which was begrimed as well as frosted.

In this underworld beneath the hospital there were no plain windows; the activities that went on here – which included the dissection of multitudinous cadavers, human and animal – were of a sort which had to be shielded from the eyes of passers-by.

It was a difficult environment to humanise and make comfortable, but Lydyard had tried. The anatomical drawings and diagrams with which he had decorated his room were brightly coloured – the veins mapped out in blue, the arteries in red, the organs in shades of green and gold. Inside the door he had pinned a full-scale reproduction of a design from an ancient Egyptian mummy-case: a painting of a female figure dressed in royal robes, which stared at him with large, beautiful, open eyes as though to ask him some coquettish riddle. Sometimes, when he was forced to lay down his pen or his instruments, Lydyard would look across his room at the picture and imagine that it was a portal to the ancient past of legend, and that what lay behind it was a world of brilliant light, not a gloomy corridor at all.

It was cold in the underworld, although it was early autumn and the air outside was warm enough to raise a sickening fetor from the streets. Down here it was always cool, and the mingled odours of formaldehyde and Jeyes fluid overrode all others with their oppressive sterility. Lydyard had become so accustomed to the combination that he no longer noticed it at all, though there had once been a time when he found it horrible. Now the room full of books, manuscripts and specimen jars seemed no less hospitable to him than his book-lined study at home.

He often found that he could write here more easily than he could at home, perhaps because there were fewer distractions, and hence less temptation to abandon his work in favour of some pleasanter pastime. He tried to take advantage of this, forcing himself to work while he was here, no matter how hurtful the process of writing became. He was writing now, concentrating as fiercely as he could between the necessary pauses for recuperation.

When the door opened, David was so intent on what he was writing that he did not look up immediately, but continued doggedly until he had reached the end of his sentence, and the end of the thought that he was shaping in his mind. His tacit assumption was that the newcomer was one of the assistants or one of the students.

When he did look up, however, he was seized by a shock of alarm. The pen fell from his stiff and painful fingers as he tried to lay it down. He drew back his hand as though to hide and coddle it in the folds of his clothing, but he stopped and sat very still, perversely determined to hide his infirmity.

She was wearing a black cape, which hung slightly open as her gloved hands moved to push it aside. Her dress was black also, and fairly simple by the standards of the day, though it was buttressed beneath by a modest sufficiency of petticoats, and was shaped to lie over a thoroughly conventional corset. Her straight, gold-spun hair cascaded from the underside of her narrow-brimmed hat to gather neatly about her shoulders, and her violet eyes were very obvious even though her pupils had expanded to adapt to the dim light.

She was standing in front of the picture that was tacked to the back of the door, as though taking the place of the Egyptian princess. Her eyes were very beautiful.

For a crazily split second it seemed that he became detached from real time, as though his consciousness had been rudely fragmented. It seemed that somewhere in the recesses of his memory a spark ignited, and in a timeless interval the liquid fire of the visionary world poured out like a cataract to confuse and overwhelm his train of thought.

She looked at him, with her beautiful violet eyes.

The wolves are running across the field of ice to which they have been abandoned by Machalalel, beneath a deep black sky lit by countless stars. When they pause to howl at the moon, their cries seem mournful and mocking to the human ear, and the children who hear them shiver in their beds, for the children alone know the wisdom of the ancient rhyme, which bids them beware.

But the dreamer knows that the wolves are not really mournful at all, while they are wolves. While they are wolves at the hunt they are filled with the joy of the hunt, which is a purer joy than any that could ever soothe the chill of the human soul. While the wolves are wolves they are possessed and exalted by their emotions, because they are innocent of any but the slightest thought or conscience. While the wolves are wolves, even pain itself is merely a sensation, as pure and empty and ecstatic as any other.

The dreamer knows that it is only when the wolves cease to be wolves that they feel the weight of fate's cruel mockery. Mournfulness descends upon them with the frightful cloak of consciousness.

While the wolves are human, such joy as they can find is feeble and polluted. While the wolves are human, they are afflicted by their emotions, which tear and harry their awareness with anxieties. While the wolves are human, pain is their constant enemy, filled with foreknowledge of injury and extinction.

The dreamer knows enough to pity the wolves, and to understand that yearning which they have to surrender the burden of humanity, which was the curse of their Creator. But he knows enough not to envy the wolves, for his is a burden which he shoulders willingly, thankfully and hopefully, not as a curse but as his true nature. Though his joy is polluted, he treasures it; though his anxieties afflict him, he accepts their spur; and though his pain is ugly and unconquerable, saturating his soul with the threat of death, he faces his affliction with the calm, cold eyes of one who seeks understanding and not release.

The dreamer does not hate the shining wilderness of ice, or the infinite darkness which is the sky, and in the faint, frail light of the stars he sees a great milky river of hope.

Because he has listened to Satan's prayers, and learned to live with the Angel of Pain, the dreamer knows better than to lament the loss of Eden – and if by chance he might be returned to the garden where Adam delved, he would not be content, as the wolves would, to dwell there in the joy of innocence returned.

He would, instead, fix his eyes and his heart upon the prospect of the distant wilderness, and make his escape.

She had not changed at all.

To judge by appearance alone, she was twenty years younger than his beloved Cordelia. But for her, time stood still; her beauty was a mask which never need be put aside. Skin-deep it might be, but it was inviolable.

She said his name softly and warmly, as a lover might.

For a long moment, he could find no words. He did not want to speak her name, lest something of the same implication should somehow echo in its syllables. Finally, he managed to say, 'What do you want, Mandorla?'

She smiled and looked carefully around. 'What a dismal little den,' she said, dismissing all his attempts at prettification with deadly contempt. 'So bare, so very hard. And all these flayed and coloured men for company! For once I am thankful for this poor human nose which can hardly sense at all, though my keen eyes fare little better, surrounded as they are by so much morbidity. You are a doctor now, I believe?'

'A doctor of philosophy,' said David, glad to hear his voice so level, proud of his ability to remain still and find words. 'Although I work here, I don't practise medicine; I belong to the university. I'm an anatomist, of sorts: a student of human physiology.'

'A student of pain,' she said. 'I have read your work.'

'You, a reader of scientific journals?' he said sceptically. 'I would not have thought it.'

His tone was as level as he could make it, but she was looking at his face again now, and he watched a frown of perplexity form upon her countenance. He watched the growth of her realisation that the lines upon his face were not simply the legacy of age, and he tried to read her reaction. For one fleeting moment, there was an expression of pity in her eyes, but pity was a passion for which her kind had little capacity and less use, and he was not surprised to see it fade into something more akin to disgust.

Still, when she spoke again, it seemed that she might be genuinely concerned.

'Why, David,' she said, 'you are ill! I never saw a man so pale.'

He tried to smile, and hoped that it did not seem like a deathly grimace.

'I've been ill for a long time, Mandorla,' he told her. 'I've grown quite used to it. I can only apologise if the sight of human frailty appals you. Had I the power to change my shape, I might hide the signs of my distress, but I have not.'

Mandorla sat down in the armchair where students often sat to be instructed. He wished that it were less threadbare, the wood less chipped.

'What is it?' she asked, and now her concern was entirely convincing. Her voice was as beautiful as her eyes.

'Severe rheumatoid arthritis,' he told her. 'It has proceeded to the point where the cartilages of my joints have nearly been destroyed and the bones beneath have become deformed. My lumbar vertebrae are beginning to fuse but I can still walk, with difficulty. I feel it very badly in my fingers, but I hope to have the use of my hands for a few years more. Ultimately, I'll be crippled, but it's not a killing disease. I sometimes suffer fevers, but I've grown accustomed to delirium.'

'Is it very painful?' she asked.

'I've also grown accustomed to pain,' he told her, knowing that she would understand what he meant by that. 'Even a man can bear a deal of pain when it can't be avoided, and laudanum helps me to keep the worst at bay. I could bear the burden more easily if I were certain that the disease was an accident of fate, but even knowing that this might have been done to me by one whose interests are served by my pain does not make it impossible to bear.'

She nodded slowly. 'I think I understand your work a little better now,' she said.

He moved his fingers to ease them, no longer concerned to hide their infirmity. 'Have you really read my papers?' he asked, wishing that he did not find the thought quite so flattering.

'When we last met,' she said, as idly as she might had it been at some garden party or similar polite occasion, 'I had barely learned to read. I despised the written word because it was an invention of men, all the more so because the Clay Man and Pelorus had become such devoted scholars. I clung to the conviction that the way of discovery which I knew was better by far. But now I have read your work, and Sir Edward's. I have even read *The True History of the World*.'

'I wish I could say the same,' said David truthfully. 'Sir Edward's best efforts have never succeeded in locating a copy.'

'You should have come to me,' she said, with a small ironic smile. 'I can locate anything, given time.'

'What changed?' David asked curiously. 'What made you into a scholar?'

'The world changed,' she said, with a lightness which falsely implied that the statement was simple. 'You will think me stupid, I know, and I know now that you have grounds for thinking it – though I could not have understood that before – but you must understand that the world seems very different in the eyes of immortals. I have lived through many thousands of years, and I have seen changes which seemed to me far greater than anything which could be wrought by human hands. You think of the history of your own kind, in so far as you have any real knowledge of it, as a fever of change, but it appeared to me very differently: as a wilderness of changelessness, from which all but the very last drops of authentic creativity had been lost.

'Pelorus told me more than once that my view was wrong, but I thought that he was infected with the Clay Man's madness and deluded by the legacy which Machalalel forced him to bear. Now I know better. I understand that despite the weakness of the human hand and the blindness of the human eye, the great machine which is the collaborative labour of thousands of men is a power not to be despised, and the great instrument which is the collaborative intelligence of thousands of men has an insight of its own. The world changed without my knowing it, but now I too have begun to change. Do not mistake me, though. I am still a wolf. In my heart and soul, I am still a wolf.'

He stared at her, speculatively. He was a little surprised by his own temerity; he would never have looked at her in such a frank way had she been a true human being. He looked at her as if she were simply a work of art, like some pre-Raphaelite vision made flesh. In a way, that is what she was; that was why he felt that she might be stared at without reserve.

'What is it that you want from me, Mandorla?' he said again.

From a pocket inside her cape she drew out a folded piece of paper and leaned forward to drop it on his desk. He reached out and picked it up. It was the letter he had sent to Pelorus.

'How do you come to have this?' he asked stonily.

'Pelorus has been missing for some time,' she told him. 'It became a matter of concern to me, and I took the trouble to trace his last address. I made arrangements for any messages to be sent to me.'

'He must have moved on,' said David. 'If he found out that you knew where he lived, that would probably have been reason enough to make him go elsewhere.'

She shook her head slowly. 'I could always find him, given time,' she said. 'He is one of the pack, no matter how he has been estranged by circumstance. He is not in London; I know that. I am anxious for his safety.'

'I doubt that,' said David. 'I'll admit that I am hurt that he did not see fit to tell us when he moved on; but we are, after all, mere mortals. Perhaps he's gone to Paris. If so, he may have contacted Sir Edward there.'

'He is not in Paris,' said Mandorla. 'Nor do I think that he has suffered an accident which has sent him into the long sleep. I think he has been taken.'

'Were to? And by whom?'

'I don't know. Nor do I know where the Clay Man has been taken, yet.' There was a challenge in her gaze as she said it.

'But you can locate anything, if you want to,' he said, repeating her own words back to her. 'Surely you did not come here to ask for my help?'

'No,' she said, her equanimity quite unthreatened by his irony. 'I came here to offer mine to you. Don't be afraid, David; I sought to use you once, but that was in very different circumstances. I was afraid, then, of the thing which had warmed your soul; afraid, but also hopeful that I might turn it to my own purposes. I hurt you, but you understand why I did it, and *that* wound has long since healed.

'It is not the sight of your inner eye which interests me, but the cleverness of your mind. I know its value now, and I know that I have not yet mastered the art of seeing as you see, without the burden of habits of mind which were ingrained ten thousand years ago. You have nothing to fear from any of the werewolves of London, David; that I swear to you. But there are others from whom you may have a great deal to fear, and I doubt that Pelorus can help you at all. I will find out who has taken the Clay Man, and will tell you when I do. I cannot tell yet whether you or I will be in a better position to find out why.'

This long speech left David feeling numb and more than a little confused. 'Pelorus told me never to trust you,' he said flatly. 'Why should I go against his advice?'

'I do not ask you to trust me,' she riposted. 'After all, I am a wolf, and you are a man. I owe no more to you or your kind than you owe to the cattle which pass through your abattoirs or the birds which you shoot for sport. But I can gain nothing by hurting you, and I might obtain useful assistance by aiding and protecting you. The game has begun again, as I think you know. You and I have not magic enough to be players, but still we have the intelligence to understand the moves which might be made, and we are wise enough to fear what may become of us while we are pawns.'

'You have no need to fear,' he said. 'You are immortal, and death to you is only a temporary affair.'

'I have thought in those terms,' she admitted, 'and have told myself as often that to exist as I do, forbidden my own nature save for the briefest of intervals, is a kind of death worse than death itself. Even now, I am not yet sure that Pelorus and Sir Edward Tallentyre are right and that the Golden Age can never return, but I must be brave enough to admit the possibility. I must ask myself what future is possible for my kind if, in fact, we are condemned to be werewolves for ever.'

David shifted in his seat, conscious of the fact that it was becoming dark outside. Her pupils were very large now, but the rim of violet around them glistened in the yellow lamplight. Her golden hair seemed almost to be made of evening sunlight. Even in her glorious youth, Cordelia had never been as beautiful as this; but Cordelia had never hunted in the filthy alleys of the East End, killing little children for meat. Mandorla was not human, and that was why her beauty surpassed the merely human, capturing the very essence of dreams born of sensual desire.

'Is it the Spider?' he asked, in a low tone. 'Has it become unquiet again? Edward and I have always feared that it would, and that when it began to work once more upon the pliant substance of the world's appearances, it would do so armed with a better knowledge by far than that which it obtained from Jacob Harkender.'

'You could not hope that it would be content to rest eternally simply because you shocked it with your vision of its insignificance,' she answered. 'You and Tallentyre did what I would never have believed possible; you, mere men, set fear in the heart of a Creator. Did you think it would be grateful? Perhaps it was, after a fashion. But you are less to a being of that kind than a fly or its maggot is to you. Even bold Sir Edward is a mere microbe, and the fact that he once infected a fallen angel with a fever of doubt cannot make him master of the world. Now that you have come to understand the diseases which afflict your own kind, you are doubly avid to stamp them out, and only as patient as you are forced to be while you search for the methods and means. The Spider and the Sphinx have busied themselves for twenty years and more in a race to reach some understanding which would give one the advantage of the other. Now, they extend themselves again – as carefully, stealthily and secretly as they can. Neither will strike until it is certain of what it intends to do, and how . . . but now that they have been awakened, and have found the world so strange, I do not think either of them will dare to sleep again. Fear is a spur, David, as I think you know.'

Again she looked around at his books and papers, his jars and bottles, his drawings and diagrams. He wanted to tell her that it was not fear that had brought him to this and shaped his life, but only curiosity; but he was not certain of that himself, and knew that she would not believe him. Why should she?

'What have you seen in your dreams, David?' she asked, when he did not reply to her speech.

'Only the stuff of dreams,' he lied. He would not – could not – tell her about the Angel of Pain which had been sent to ride the unruly tide of his nightmares, nor about his fancies of being Satan no longer chained in Hell, nor about his encounters within the great pyramid of Bast. All such matters were private, not to be spoken aloud to her.

He wondered, though, whether the visions which her not quite frigid soul cast into the glass of her magic mirrors were much different in kind.

'You have not seen me?' she said, feigning reproach. 'I have let *you* into *my* dreams, David; I had hoped, I confess, that you had allowed me a similar courtesy. I had always thought that I had an advantage in gaining access to the dreams of men. Try to find me in your dreams, I beg of you, for I do not care to be undesired. I have glimpsed you in my mirrors, but you are always cloaked in shadows, and I have never known the future so dark. I could almost begin to believe what those foolish priests say about the imminence of the world's end: almost, but not quite.'

She smiled as she added the last phrase.

'It's strange,' said David, uneasily trying to turn the conversation in a new direction, 'that one doesn't hear so much nowadays of the depredations of the werewolves of London. Twenty years ago, there were always whispers. I see my fair share of mutilated bodies in this place – I don't carry out postmortem examinations for the court, but am sometimes asked for my advice by those who do – and I've observed, over the years, a change in attitude among those who handle them. The old willingness to believe in you is fading; but here you are, alive and well! Have you followed Pelorus' example and forsaken the eating of human flesh?'

'Yes, I have,' she said, neither proudly nor defiantly. 'There is no matter of principle involved, I do assure you, but I have lost my taste for human meat, for the time being. You may take it, if you wish, as one more reason for believing me when I tell you that I mean no harm to you, or to your wife and children. But the fact that we no longer hunt as we once did is not the only reason for the fading of belief. The world is changing, as I have acknowledged. Our actual existence was never really necessary to sustain belief in our kind, nor will it be a barrier to the extinction of belief.'

David watched her, puzzled by her defensive attitude. He wondered whether it was some cunning ploy to make him believe her. Pelorus had warned him that she could be very deceptive. For all her protestations of ignorance, she had lived among men for a very long time, and had known them intimately enough to have learned the art of manipulating their trust.

'Are you married now?' he asked her, guardedly.

'No,' she replied, 'I am not. But Siri is, and so is Arian, though his wife thinks him cruel because he cannot make love to her as she would wish. We are comfortable. You are welcome to visit my house at any time.' As she spoke she took out a card – a perfectly ordinary visiting card – and leaned forward to lay it on his desk. He did not pick it up.

'I would be afraid to enter a den of werewolves,' he said lightly, 'unless I had a pressing reason.'

'I am not sorry to hear it,' she told him. 'I would be disappointed if you were not a little afraid of me. But you are not a coward, and I am glad of that, too. You are afraid of the Spider and the Sphinx, because you are not a fool, but you are not so afraid that your mind will break, nor will you bow down to them in craven adoration. I know that much about you, you see! If you can find the truth in your dreams, you will not flee from it in terror, nor seek release in forgetfulness. You are forearmed and forewarned by what happened to you before. You are stronger, I think, than Tallentyre could be, now that he is old. Still, you will need help. If Pelorus does not come, and Tallentyre does not come in time, remember that you may call on me. Trust me or not, as you please, but remember that I have resources which you have not. I will come to you again, when I know where the Clay Man has been taken.'

As she stood up, he stood too, pulled upright by the gravity-defying force of politeness. She gathered her cape more closely about her and looked up at the darkened windows.

'You need not be anxious for my safety,' she said, with a certain gentle levity. 'I like the night, and have no fear of darkness.'

'I wish I could say the same,' he said.

'You are more fortunate than most men,' she assured him. 'For you alone know that should you hear the footfalls of the werewolves of London moving in the shadows around and behind you, they are there to protect you and not to hurt you.'

'But I also know how impotent such protection is, against such beings as the Spider,' he pointed out.

She only smiled at that, and turned to go, closing the door behind her. When she had gone, he sat back down again, suddenly aware that his heart was racing, though he honestly did not know why.

Forgive me, Cordelia he said beneath his breath. *Forgive me for my sight, and for my dreams, and for the helplessness of the desires inbuilt into my nature. Though I know what she really is, I cannot help seeing her as she appears, and it is so difficult to reject entirely what the unwary poet said about the identity of beauty and truth. What a terrible thing the treachery of appearances is!*

He took up his pen again and made as if to write, but he could not do it. His fingers were too stiff, and the ink had dried on the nib.

He dropped the pen again and stood up, gritting his teeth against the pains which raked his legs and lower back. Then he walked, lamely but hurriedly, into the gaslit corridor, as though he could no longer bear to be in a room which Mandorla Soulier had called dismal.

4

On the next day, which was Sunday, the dull weather cleared and the sun shone from a clear blue sky. After breakfast, David and Cordelia went into the garden to sit at the oaken table. They each took a book to read, but the books remained unopened while they watched their two younger children at play among the apple trees.

Nell was nearly twelve years old now, and studied during the week with her governess. Simon, who was eight, would soon be going away to school, following in the footsteps of his older brother. The two of them had little time left to be together, but they had not yet grown apart; despite the difference in their ages they enjoyed one another's company. Theirs was a world as tightly closed, secured and comfortable as moderate wealth could contrive.

David watched the children with fond eyes. While they were free to play hide-and-seek among the bushes, everything seemed right with the world. When he was able to relax, his pain eased, and the tenderness of his feelings seemed to dissolve it entirely.

The normality of the occasion was sufficient to banish all anxieties, just as the bright sunlight had banished the crowded shadows of the night.

He had dreamed during the night, as he always did, but he could not now remember the substance of his dreams. This he took, rightly or wrongly, as a sign that his dreams had been naught but the fantastic and illusory produce of his own brain. His sleep, aided by a now customary draught of laudanum, had been as restful as it ever was.

David knew that the laudanum sometimes exaggerated the vividness of his dreams, and that he had become physically dependent upon it to an unfortunate degree, but he did not regard the drug as an enemy. To the contrary, he believed that the effect of the laudanum was an effective shield against the ravages of the Angel of Pain, who was ever avid to turn his nightmares into visions. He knew that he could never be truly free of the godlike being which used his inner eye, but laudanum gave him a defence – a way to blur and distort visions which could not in any case ever be clear and precise.

He could not remain relaxed for long. There was a duty which he was neglecting, and although he knew that it would shatter the harmony of the moment he could not put it off indefinitely. Last night, following his late return home, it had been easy to find excuses for postponement, but there were none now. He had to tell Cordelia that he had seen Mandorla.

He dared not withhold his news from his wife, because he knew only too well how deeply hurt she would be if he did; but the prospect of describing the meeting was not one which he could relish. It was so much simpler to sit quietly and watch the children ducking in and out of the bushes, each pretending that they could not see the other in order to make the hunt more thrilling.

The sound of their laughter was as soothing as any drug.

Finally, David plucked up sufficient courage to break his news. 'I had a visitor last evening,' he said, 'while I was at the hospital.'

Cordelia looked at him sharply and shrewdly, but said nothing about the delay in telling her.

'It was Mandorla Soulier,' he said, biting the bullet. 'The letter I sent to Pelorus had come into her hands.' Without pausing, he continued to give an abbreviated account of Mandorla's explanation of her possession of the letter, and her suspicions regarding the disappearance of Pelorus. He also told her about Mandorla's offer to find out where the Clay Man had been taken, and by whom.

'What does she want?' asked Cordelia, when he had finished.

He repeated some of what he had already told her in different words, expanding it slightly to take in a little more of what the wolfwoman had actually said to him. Cordelia's only response was to say, 'But what does she *really* want?'

'How can I tell?' David complained. 'Unless some magical sight enables me to share her consciousness for a while, I have only her words to rely on. If what she says is intended to deceive, how can I judge what her true motives might be?'

Cordelia turned away to watch Nell and Simon, with her lips slightly pursed. Then she said: 'It's disturbing to think that something may have happened to Pelorus. Do you think, perhaps, that it may have been a mistake to ask my father to return here? Perhaps we should have gone to him, in Paris.'

'We can't run away,' David said. 'The Spider and the Sphinx can reach out to touch us wherever we may be. I suppose that we're uncomfortably close to the Spider's physical presence here in England, but we don't know that we would be any safer elsewhere. We couldn't expect to be safe even if we were in Egypt, where the Creator of the Sphinx is. In any case, I wouldn't flee to it for succour, even if I believed that it cared sufficiently to listen to the prayers of men.'

'That's my father speaking,' she said, though not as a rebuke. 'He's the man who would be too proud to pray to God, even if he thought that God existed.'

'It isn't pride,' he said. 'Even Sir Edward is no longer as

certain as he once was that God does not exist. Now that we have been forced to recognise that Acts of Creation are possible, it seems far more reasonable to see the universe entire as a created thing. But the kind of God that Sir Edward could believe in – the kind of God which might have shaped and plotted out the destiny of the universe as he knows it – is not some paternal figure obsessively interested in the moral affairs of mankind, but something extremely remote and essentially uninvolved in earthly events.'

'Perhaps, in that case,' she said, 'we should be prepared to address our prayers to those pettier godlings which do take an interest in earthly affairs, and which hold the power of life and death over us. Perhaps the pagans were right to hold their rites of propitiation and to make their blood sacrifices in the hope of keeping the favour of the demons which they worshipped.'

'I doubt it,' David answered, although he took it for granted that she was being ironic and could not mean what she said. 'I think your father would argue that even if it could be proven – which it could not – that prayers and sacrifices were effective in winning the approval of such invisible tyrants, the brave and moral man would refuse to do it. I'm sure that he would speak of courage and right, and not of pride at all. You're entitled to be sceptical, if you wish, but I must take his side.'

'Of course,' she said, but not resentfully. After a pause, she went on: 'Did your handsome wolf venture any guess as to why the Clay Man's body was stolen, or what the Spider may be about, if it is indeed becoming active again?'

'She did not,' said David. 'I don't think that she is much given to forming hypotheses. She has not taken as much trouble as Pelorus has to cultivate the arts of reason – which, after all, she is eager to give up for ever in favour of the instincts of a beast. Perhaps that's why she proposed an alliance. Perhaps she thinks that Sir Edward and I are better equipped than she is to unriddle the mystery, despite her supposed cleverness in being able to discover who has done what. She confessed that she had read my work, and Sir Edward's.'

'And what had she to say about your studies in the physiology of pain?' asked Cordelia.

'Nothing,' he admitted.

'No doubt there'll be time enough to hear her views. No doubt, too, there'll be time enough for her to hear yours, if you are in fact to forge this alliance. What will you tell her, do you think, about the nature and designs of the fallen angels? Will you trust her with the conclusions of all the long discussions that you have had with my father and Gilbert and Pelorus? And will she be properly grateful for your reasoned insights?'

David smiled ruefully at the mockery. He could not count the hours which he and the others named had spent in debates of the kind to which she referred – certainly there had been thousands, possibly tens of thousands. But in the matter of conclusions, they had reached too many or none at all. They knew too little, and could find far too many possibilities.

'You've been party to many such discussions yourself,' he pointed out to her. 'Despite your thin pretence that we despise your contributions because they are issued by a mere woman.'

'Oh yes,' Cordelia admitted, 'you'll always condescend to ask my opinion, as if you thought it mattered. Even Sir Edward is not too proud to do *that*. You're polite enough to pretend that you don't find my simplicity amusing, but I'm not deceived.'

'That's not true, and you know it,' he told her, still smiling.

It was not, and she did know it. She could not maintain her pose, and so she continued in a different vein. 'If my father were here,' she said, more seriously, 'you and he would be sitting here now, trying to fathom the changed situation – including Mandorla's motives – by analysis and speculation. Should you and I do otherwise, simply because he's away?'

He felt that he was being accused of something, but she was speaking earnestly, and he had no need to flinch. He lifted his hands, palms open, to signify that he had no quarrel with her.

'Very well,' she said. 'I suppose we should take for granted the conclusions which you and my father have already reached. We accept that these Creators left over from the ancient world are like the piece of shagreen in Balzac's fable. They may have all their wishes granted upon a magical whim, but each indulgence loses them a little more of their substance; thus, they're on the horns of a dilemma. They have survived so long only because they've exercised the most careful conservation of their creativity, becoming almost inert. Some of them are now willing to use their power again – modestly, at least – because they believe that by so doing they may gain an advantage over those of their kind which are still inert, perhaps enabling themselves to prey upon those others and hence increase their own power. But they're very wary, lest they should have mistaken their situation; they fear the possibility of weakening themselves in wasted action, and thus becoming vulnerable to the predations of others.'

'We're all agreed on that,' said David – meaning Sir Edward, Pelorus and himself.

'Then we already know,' she argued, 'what the resumption of their activity must signify. These beings became quiescent in the first place because of a stalemate in their ongoing war, but the world has changed out of all recognition since then, and the awakened ones must at all costs discover whether the stalemate still holds. The Spider, which obtained its initial understanding of the new world from Jacob Harkender, was convinced that it had an advantage over its rivals, but Harkender's understanding was badly flawed. The Spider's actions only succeeded in awakening a rival and causing it to begin its own investigations of the new world of appearances. Since then, the two have been in covert competition, each hoping to discover a means to win a new advantage, each wondering when the moment might become ripe for a resumption of their conflict. It has always been probable, has it not, that one or other would renew the conflict, if and when it became convinced that it could win?'

'An admirable analysis,' David conceded. 'But the conclusion may be premature. If Bast and the Spider are indeed going to war, it seems peculiar that one or the other should begin by raising the Clay Man from the dead. What purpose might be served by such an action?

'One problem we have is that we have no idea what kind of advantage might conceivably be gained by one or other of the fallen angels, or what conditions could force or tempt one or other to use its powers. Nor do we know whether it's conceivable that Bast and the Spider might prefer to join forces, collaborating in the victimisation of others of their kind. We don't even know how many fallen angels there are, dancing upon this infinitesimal pinhead which is the surface of the Earth. We don't know where they are, nor what they're made of, nor the true scope of their power to transform the world of appearances. It's possible that they're less powerful than we imagine, having changed along with the world to become creatures more fitted to an age of iron than an age of gold.

'I often wish that I might be allowed to put such questions to Bast herself, or to the Sphinx, which is wandering the Earth with de Lancy in its thrall, but it seems that such beings as these will not deign to enter into honest discussion with cold-souled men. Perhaps they're ashamed of their own ignorance and are too proud to expose their slender powers of reasoning. That has always been our best hope – that these things are so blinded by their ignorance that they'll never know enough to act, and will leave the progress of the world undisturbed.'

'In that case,' she said, 'might one of them have concluded that it needs the insights of clever immortals to complete its understanding? Might that be why Pelorus has been taken and the Clay Man exhumed?'

'It's possible,' he agreed.

'And Mandorla, too,' Cordelia proposed. 'Perhaps she is now an instrument.'

'It's by no means impossible,' David said, 'that all the creatures made by the Clay Man's Creator have always been instruments of that kind. Pelorus has never believed that his Creator was destroyed; he has always assumed that Machalalel became inert with the other angels. Perhaps Machalalel has also awakened.'

It was always the same. There were too many possibilities, and always would be. It was small consolation to know that the Creators themselves must be similarly confused. Even the angels were not omniscient.

Nell ran up to them then, interrupting the debate. David had to stand up hurriedly as she hurled herself into his arms, quivering with an excess of laughter and excitement. Simon ran after her, as fast as he could go. As he ran, he stumbled and fell face forward on the lawn. The turf was still softened by moisture, and it was not a particularly hard landing, but he had been running so freely and recklessly, oblivious to the possibility of an upset, that he bumped his knees and his elbows, scraping the skin in three or four different places.

He began to cry, perhaps more with shock than pain, but loudly nevertheless.

Cordelia ran to pick him up, lift him high in the air and hug him tight, quite careless of staining her dress.

Leave the child alone! David cried silently, with a vehemence which surprised him. The instruction was not addressed to his wife; he had fallen into the habit of addressing silent speeches to the Angel of Pain, despite the fact that she was only a phantom of his own imagination, designed to give shape to the paradoxical demands made upon him by the Creator which used him as a pawn, which hurt him in order to open his inner eye. To make pain an entity – something outside and independent of his own being – somehow made it easier to deal with. This was not the first time that he had vented his spleen upon the Angel when one or other of his children had been in sore distress, and he was not ashamed to infuse his silent cries with such spontaneous and unthinking anger.

He hugged Nell to him, soothing the agitation which echoed in her because of her brother's hurt. David knew that a man was supposed to love his sons more than any mere daughter, and that Teddy would have been the apple of Sir Edward's eye whatever name he had been given, but Nell was much more like her father in appearance and temperament than either of the boys, and David felt a tighter bond with her than with them.

Meanwhile, Cordelia pressed Simon's face into her shoulder, smothering his sobs while she whispered in his ear that everything was well, that the hurt would go away and that the injuries would soon be mended.

And then, over her other shoulder, David saw something move among the bushes – something which had no right to be in a place where the boy and the girl had been playing only minutes before.

It was a wolf, and he could not help leaping to the conclusion that it was one of the werewolves of London.

Mandorla had promised him that he and his family had nothing to fear from her kind, but he knew that the promise was meaningless. Even if she had spoken the truth, it was a promise she might not be able to keep.

David lowered Nell to the ground and pushed her towards her mother. 'Go inside,' he said, his voice cracking like a whiplash.

Cordelia must have seen the alarm in his eyes as well as hearing the urgency in his tone, because she glanced behind her before reaching out to take Nell's hand and doing as she was told, but she did not panic. They had ten or twelve yards to cover before they reached the door, and David did not dare turn to go with them. Instead he stepped forward, fixing the animal with his stare, hoping to see it change to human form.

The wolf was unnaturally large, slate-grey in colour. David could not recognise it. He had seen Mandorla in wolf guise, and Pelorus too, but only briefly. He could not be certain that this was not one of them, but he thought it unlikely.

Unlike Cordelia, who had stood firm against Calan's attack in the distant past, David had never stood face to face with one of the werewolves in a situation pregnant with danger, but he judged from the way the beast came stealthily forward that this was no friendly meeting. The wolf's eyes were fixed upon him, devoid of expression but not of menace. He had to fight the impulse to panic, but forced himself to remain quite still, challenging the creature with his own stare.

To his relief, he heard the door open behind him, and close again.

The beast was now no more than six or seven feet away, and seemed even larger at such close quarters. Its eyes were yellow, and it crouched slightly, as though undecided whether to spring. David, knowing that he had no weapon and that there was nothing near to hand which could be pressed into service, could only raise his empty hands defensively.

'Who are you?' he asked, loudly and aggressively. 'Why are you here?' He did not know whether a werewolf in wolf form could understand such questions, because he had never found Pelorus' accounts of what it was like to be in that state entirely clear, but he hoped that the mere fact of his having spoken so resolutely might give the beast pause.

It took another pace forward, and crouched again. David, knowing that Cordelia and the children had reached the safety of the house, took a pace backwards; but he dared not turn his back on the wolf.

'Get out!' he said, baring his teeth as though in a snarl. 'You have no right here!'

It was the wrong thing to do. The wolf met his snarl with a snarl of its own, emitting a strange sound more like the purr of a cat than the bark of a dog, and it launched itself forward. It took one great bound and then shot up from the earth with astonishing speed, aiming for his throat. David could do nothing but bring his raised arms together so that the forearms crossed, forming an X in front of his face and neck.

Help me! he cried inwardly, forgetting that he was too bold and proud a man to pray to fallen angels. *For the love of God, save me!*

He felt the daggerlike teeth of the wolf clamp tightly about his right forearm, scything through the flesh and grating on the bone. Agony flooded his body as he stumbled and fell, bowled over by the weight of the animal's lunge. He landed heavily on his back, unable to use his arms to break his fall because his one thought was to keep them before him, to keep the furious beast at bay as best he might.

He heard a scream, but it was not his own. It was Cordelia, who had remained outside while she shut the door on the children.

David felt the clawed feet of the wolf scrabbling at his abdomen as the animal tried to get on top of him, still thrusting with its huge head at his face. His right arm was free of the jaws now, but the animal was snapping at the left, and though it could not get a grip he felt the nip of the teeth in his flesh and knew that a ribbon of skin had been sliced away. David felt that his one chance of survival was to reach out and grab the wolf by the throat, and hold those vicious jaws at bay with every last vestige of his strength, but his right arm was powerless. It had lost all capacity for action, although it continued to flood him with pain.

He groped with his left hand, but the beast's head knocked it aside, and he saw the great yellow eyes flare as the animal ducked inside his guard, ready to tear him apart.

Then, seemingly less than a second before his appointed end, the beast's head exploded into a great cloud of gore and pulverised flesh.

David had to shut his eyes as the deluge of blood and tissue splashed him, covering him with hot, noisome fluid. The horror of it was almost too much to bear, even though he knew that he had been saved from certain death. As he rolled sideways he was already vomiting convulsively, and the fingers of his left hand tore jerkily at his eyes, trying to wipe away the filth so that he could open them.

As he rolled over on his right arm, he was agonised all over again, but somehow he staggered to his feet and looked down at the twitching, headless body of the wolf.

He half expected it to resume human form, as dead werewolves were supposed by legend to do, but it did not. It lay there as though it were the corpse of a real wolf. Nothing was left of the creature's head; nothing at all. It had been blasted by a magical thunderbolt hurled from beyond the world's edge, and turned to vapour.

As Cordelia ran back to him, and he looked down at the dead animal, David had already begun to realise that he owed no thanks to his saviour. The creature had been *allowed* to hurt him. It had been *sent* to hurt him; its destruction was a token gesture. His protector was playing with him, as it had always done, since first he had envisaged it as a thing with the soul and manners of a cat. He bitterly regretted the way he had called out to it in his extremity, and wished that he had had the courage to stand alone.

'Dear God!' Cordelia cried, seeing what had been done to him and to the wolf; but she too must have known that she was wrong. She must also have been able to see that this was the work of one or more of those pettier godlings whose predicament she had described so clinically only minutes before. The only question at issue was whether the one which had sent the wolf had also destroyed it, or whether this was a shot fired in the course of a combat in which two were involved.

Either way, the summons had come; David could not doubt that he was now a part of whatever game was unfolding. As he looked down at his horribly wounded arm, seeing the white of bone within the lacerated flesh, and feeling the brutal thrust of an agony which even laudanum surely could not dull, he could not but wonder what fiery poison those savage fangs might have delivered into his simmering soul.

5

The delirium took hold of him even before the servants had brought him into the house, and while they tried to remove his clothing his senses were reeling so madly that he found himself struggling against them. The world was already dissolving before they brought laudanum to calm him, and there were a few brief moments when he felt as though his body were being consumed by fervent flames, before . . .

He saw the face of the cat: the face of Bast. It filled the field of his vision, and there seemed to be no distance separating the stare of its green eyes from the sight of his own inner eye. He did not seem to be inside the pyramid to which she was fond of summoning him; he did not seem to be in any place at all. There was only the face of the cat, filling everything: the face of the angel which aspired to be a goddess.

She spoke to him, saying: 'I have a thing to ask of thee, my beloved. There is a thing which thou must do, and do willingly. Be certain of my love and my protection, but be *ready*, I beg of thee. All is altered, all is changed, all is in hazard. Thou must serve me well, beloved, lest all be lost.

'*Serve me well!*'

The face faded into darkness, and while it dissolved David wondered whether it could have been anything but a hopeful phantom of his own mind. The angel had never appeared or spoken to him that way before, and the implications of it, if it were real, were very difficult to grasp . . . and, in any case, he had no time.

He felt the talons of the Angel of Pain raking his soul, though he could not see her face. He could not see anything at all, until his inner eye opened and showed him the world of men. He saw, as he had sometimes seen before, through the eyes of another person. He shared the other's sight and hearing, the other's thoughts, and the other's inmost soul. His sensibility rebelled against the shame of such an intrusion, but he had no choice; he was forced to share the inmost secrets of the imprisoning soul, whether he liked it or not.

'May I sit down?' said the man in grey, speaking very softly. The room was dim, but there was a limelit stage to one side, visible from the corners of the eyes whose sight David was sharing.

David felt his host frown slightly as she – it *was* she, though he could not yet sense a name – looked up at the newcomer, puzzled by the fact that he had come to her table when one or two others closer to the stage had empty chairs. She had never seen the man before, but that was not so very surprising; her house was famous now, and its regular patrons took a pride in bringing guests to see her dramatic entertainments.

David was in no doubt as to the implications of the word 'house'. He knew that he was in a brothel – a brothel with a theatre.

Somehow, from rumours encountered in clubs and smoking rooms, David guessed precisely where he was even before shared self-consciousness leaked the name into his thoughts. This was Mercy Murrell's house; these were Mercy Murrell's eyes through which he looked.

Like the bawd, David had no idea who the man in grey might be; unlike her, though, he was uneasy in his ignorance, for there was something about the man which disturbed him.

Mrs Murrell nodded her head, and the man sat down. He was tall, and the grey in which he was uniformly dressed was peculiarly suggestive of soft shadows. His face, by contrast, was was not soft at all; it was pale and angular, the features sternly set, as though he were in pain.

Mercy Murrell did not share David's insight; she was content to assume that the man was possessed by ordinary awkwardness. She knew how long it took for newcomers to her little world to learn to relax. This, she guessed, was a man of law – an experienced barrister, perhaps even a circuit judge.

David could not agree with this judgement, but he could not quite decide why.

Mrs Murrell did not mind in the least that the visitor might be a lawyer or a judge; her establishment was on good terms with all the agents of the law. She watched him while he finished arranging himself and turned his attention to the little stage. His stare was curious but not avid; it gave every indication of being clinically studious. Mrs Murrell permitted herself a small ironic smile. What pains some men took to hide their lusts, even in a brothel!

Again, David thought that she was mistaken. The man did not seem to him to be in the least lustful, but only curious and uncertain. It was as though he, like David, had been *sent* here to see something significant, without knowing what to look for.

Mrs Murrell returned her attention to the stage, having missed only two or three lines. It did not matter; she knew them well enough. She took a great pride in the fact that she wrote the scripts for all her own productions, just as Shakespeare had done. Her stare, as she watched the actors, was incurious. That of the passenger which she entertained unawares was not.

David was witness to Mrs Murrell's pride in being an unashamed opportunist. She had not hesitated to name the play which was currently in performance *The Lustful Turk* after one of the most widely circulated of naughty books, despite the fact that her plot bore little resemblance to the story told by the anonymous author of the book. The subject matter was similar: the capture, seduction, and spoliation of a modest English girl by a strutting Mohammedan; but in adapting the tale for her particular audience Mrs Murrell had embellished it greatly, liberally developing the image of the harem, which her establishment was so well equipped to duplicate. All this David understood at second hand, from an attitude which made it seem even more bizarre than it was.

On the stage, the heroine of the play, confined within the harem against her will, was about to experience for the first time the rigour of its discipline. The former favourite of the Dey, fearing displacement by this new and charmingly reluctant jewel, had tempted her to the violence of a slap, and was now about to see the lawful penalty for that reckless act exacted upon her enemy. That penalty was, inevitably, to be a flogging. Every one of Mrs Murrell's melodramas included a pivotal scene in which one of her beauties would have the privilege of appearing to castigate another.

The part of the heroine, in this instance, was played by a girl identified by Mrs Murrell's thoughts as Sophie; she wore a honey-coloured wig which was intended to signify innocence as well as Englishness. Her wrists, tied with obscenely thick rope, were secured to a hook mounted high on the painted wooden boards at the back of the stage.

The flagellator wore a brightly coloured turban, but the remainder of her costume made no real effort to conceal the fact that she was a girl pretending to be a castrated slave. The whip which she carried was similarly obvious in its artificiality, its cords resembling those of a plush curtain-sash rather than an authentic cat-o'-nine-tails. No doubt it could still have stung, had it been plied with any considerable force, but the girl who laid it on was not actress enough to imply any real violence in the way she swung it.

The screams of the victim provided a better show, all the more effective for the effort which went into controlling their volume without compromising their apparent vehemence. The scene was stolen, however, by the offended party, whose darkly stained skin and jet-black raiment were beautifully set off by her mimicry of ranting jealousy and blood lust – here, perhaps, there was just a teasing hint of authenticity of feeling – and the audience joined in enthusiastically with her pantomime of avid encouragement.

Mercy Murrell's own attitude, the lens through which David's understanding of the proceedings was necessarily focused, was partly clinical and partly contemptuous. She measured the performances of her players very scrupulously, weighing the effect of their every gesture; at the same time she bathed in the luxury of her contempt for the young bucks and stern hawks who threw themselves far more enthusiastically into the effort to believe in this fiction than they ever would have deigned to do when they took their luckless wives to see some time-hallowed tragedy in Drury Lane.

In other circumstances, David might have been amused by the way in which Mrs Murrell played the misanthrope, affecting even in the privacy of her secret thoughts to despise the clients whose expensive appetites supported her in moderate luxury; as things were, sheer astonishment precluded any possibility of amusement.

Why am I here? he asked of himself. *What purpose can there possibly be in this?*

Crowded into Mrs Murrell's claustrophobic thoughts, he shared her knowledge of the fact that the coldness of her common sense was tinged with envy, and that the all-consuming hatred which she had for the male of the species was based in the resentful frustration of her own femaleness and the lack of potency which went with it. He saw also that she forgave herself for that particular weakness. Had she been a man, she believed, she might have made a very fearsome warrior and a monstrously devoted spoiler of virgins; as things were, she could only pander to vainglorious soldiers and play the procuress for rape-pretenders.

It was a poorer way of life, she knew, but it had its compensations.

David felt ashamed to be here, even though he knew that he had not brought himself and could not get away even if he chose. There must, he thought insistently, be some reason for his being here – that, at least, was something on which to focus his attention, and excused the steadiness of the gaze which he was forced to share.

The flogging scene was followed by a quiet interlude when bewigged Sophie, weeping and lamenting, was comforted by the lowest and most despised of the harem slaves, who was played by a shambling, hunchbacked figure which Mrs Murrell's thoughts named Hecate. Hecate seemed virtually inarticulate, which handicapped her capacity for delivering lines, but the alchemy of the theatre – which applied even to such stages as this – seemed to turn that to her advantage. Her dumb show of good will and helplessness, conveyed mainly by the agitation of her strangely discomfiting eyes, was surprisingly effective.

David's attention was briefly caught and held by Hecate, but could not persist in its curiosity because Mrs Murrell's gaze refused to linger on the girl's deformed body.

Those members of the crowd who had but a moment ago been howling their encouragement to the whip-wielding torturer were now content to pause, to let their hammering hearts slow down again. Nor, Mrs Murrell knew, were they simply gathering their resources in order to take a full measure of satisfaction from the impending defloration scene; there was something in the pantomime of tenderness and reassurance which touched a chord in the paradoxical morass of their own feelings.

While it seemed that awkwardness possessed the entire auditorium, Mrs Murrell glanced sideways again at the man who sat opposite her. He was leaning forward now, not quite lasciviously but certainly intent with curiosity. In the dim light Mrs Murrell could not tell what colour his eyes were, but she had no difficulty in perceiving that they were fixed upon Hecate's ugly face.

Mrs Murrell was not overly surprised by his fascination. She had discovered long ago that men did not always value prettiness in whores. She knew that there were those who took a perverse delight in ugliness, and cherished deformity in their victims. She thought that she understood such perversions in a distanced, quasi-scientific fashion. Some men, she knew, had been taught too well to fear and despise their own sexuality, and sought peculiar ways to punish themselves in its exercise.

From the calm confusion of Mrs Murrell's mental activity, David picked up the intelligence that after every performance in her little theatre, the services of the actresses were auctioned, and that although the auction of poor twisted Hecate would always be attended by much false laughter and many derisory offers, she never failed to attract a bid of some sort. He sensed Mrs Murrell place a silent wager with herself that the man in grey would bid for Hecate tonight. The man seemed raptly attentive as he watched the cripple comforting the desolate heroine.

Then, just as the quiet scene was about to end, a crashing sound emanated from the wings, abruptly breaking the mood. It was followed, comically, by a smothered oath from one of the actresses waiting there. A ripple of laughter ran around the room, and Mrs Murrell frowned angrily as she looked back at the stage. The scene lurched through the final few seconds to its allotted conclusion, and the curtain was hurried across the makeshift proscenium to conceal the scene-shifters.

The gaslights in the brackets around the walls were turned up, and girls scurried back and forth with bottles of wine. Mrs Murrell looked at the man in grey, who had no glass before him, and said: 'Would you care for a drink, perhaps?'

She could see his eyes clearly now. They were as grey as his suit.

'No, thank you,' he said, still speaking softly, though there was now a low hubbub of conversation in the room. 'You are Mrs Murrell, I believe?' David got the impression that the man in grey was trying not to frighten her, though why he should think it likely that he might was not altogether clear. Mrs Murrell was not in the least frightened.

'I am,' she admitted. She did not ask for his name in return; some of her callers did not like to give their names.

'Where did you find that girl?' he asked. It was an impolite question, but it was not asked rudely, and Mrs Murrell was not in the slightest doubt which girl he meant.

'Her name is Hecate,' Mrs Murrell said, well aware that it was not an adequate answer.

'Was it always Hecate?' asked the other, without any hint of amusement.

'It was once plain Cath,' Mrs Murrell admitted, 'but she lived among fools who treated her like an idiot, which she is not, and charged her with bringing them bad luck, which she could not. They called her a witch, and said she was attended by an invisible imp, so I named her Hecate.'

'And is the name apt?' he asked, without any obvious irony.

'People are sometimes clumsy when she is nearby,' said Mrs Murrell, 'but that's only because she makes them uncomfortable. I don't believe that she has any mischief-making imp to serve her, nor any magic of her own, but you might prefer to make up your own mind.'

The man in grey nodded and permitted himself a slight, thin smile. 'I might,' he admitted.

David could read the implication easily enough. If the girl did have an invisible imp in attendance, she must be an instrument of the fallen angels, like himself. Perhaps she was one of their creatures, like Gabriel Gill. But if so, what was she doing here? And why had he been sent to watch her?

Mrs Murrell saw no reason why she should not be permitted a little irony of her own, since her companion had none to offer. 'Perhaps,' she suggested, 'you're a member of the Psychical Research Society in search of phenomena?'

'Are you a medium, then, as well as a brothel-keeper?' the man in grey asked in return, not wittily, but still so very softly that she could not take offence.

'I'm acquainted with one or two,' she admitted. 'I know one who's an expert at materialising very pretty ghosts, if your tastes run to the supernatural. Or do you merely wish to be reassured that your mother is safe in Heaven?'

'If only she were,' said the pale man, in a voice hardly above a whisper. If she had not been watching his lips as they moved to pronounce the words, she would not have been able to make them out, and she doubted that they had been intended for her. She would have said more – and David wished that she had – but she was distracted by one of the serving girls, and by the time she had dealt with the girl's difficulty the next act was ready to begin.

Mrs Murrell knew that the defloration scene which followed the withdrawal of the curtain was one of the weaker parts of the play, and the attempts of the actresses to build it up by putting more feeling into the acting of it merely added a touch of the ludicrous. The problem with the scene, she supposed, was that it pretended falsely to be a climax, and the entire audience knew it. Had the story been shaped in parody of the domestic melodramas on which the semi-respectable theatres depended so heavily, an orthodox rape might indeed have provided an entirely natural conclusion, but the oriental setting guaranteed a different pattern, in which the conventional penetration could only be a prelude to another. In the curiously deceptive language of pornography, Turkish lust – or any other exotic kind of lust – must perforce go beyond the desires honoured by more homely euphemisms. After poor Sophie had protested and fainted her way through one ravishment, she had then to rise to the challenge of portraying deeper outrage and more awful horror while her sister whore pretended to bugger her.

David did not know whether or not to be glad that he was forewarned of all this, and he would have been very glad to be released from the uncomfortable trap of his own fascination. Alas, he had no alternative but to watch, through the critical eyes of the author of the scene.

Mrs Murrell knew, as she watched the first of the two key scenes and gauged the response of her audience, that it was not working as it should. She had done her best with it in many trials but had never contrived to bring it to perfection. Like the other onlookers, she found herself on edge, wishing that the actresses would hurry up and be done with it instead of contentedly drifting with the pace of events. She had experimented with the use of a male actor and with authentic rather than simulated penetration, but the scene had then lost the *frisson* which it gained from the implications of perversity contained in its artifice, and, if anything, had made the audience even more impatient to witness the authentic climax.

When the scene ended and Hecate came on to the stage again to lead poor ravaged Sophie away, the mood of the audience was by no means as receptive as before, and someone shouted a half-articulate item of petty abuse from the back of the room. Mrs Murrell could not see who had called, and though she was not certain of the precise words she was sure that they had been more ribald than insulting, but the deformed girl seemed to wince almost as though she had been struck.

For a moment, Mrs Murrell thought that the girl might fail to play her part, and drew in her breath; but then the scene continued to unfold as she had planned it, with the Pathetic Grotesque leading the Spoiled Beauty away to her bed of grief.

The curtain was drawn across while the scenery was changed, but it drew back again without undue delay to reveal the ranting, leering Dey, who laid his final plans very audibly before his servants and co-conspirators. The transition to the harem was smoothly achieved, and there the stained houri made her final speech, full of deceptive contrition and thinly veiled ironies, while the excellent Sophie was obliged to pretend belief in the absurd contention that the Dey had fallen in love with her while plundering her maidenhead.

Some laughter was heard in the restless crowd, but now that the last act was properly unfolding, its members knew exactly where they were and what pitch of excitement they should have attained.

Despite the fact that such incredible contrivance had been used to set it up, the final dialogue between the two leading players was delivered with authentic panache, as though the two whores had fallen so completely under the spell of their own performances as to be capable of entering into the true spirit of the play. Mrs Murrell studied them as they delivered their lines, pleased by their efforts. Not until the time for talk was done and the script expired in a welter of horrified screams and groans, did she turn away.

This might have been a release for David's shame-soaked consciousness, had he not been party to her memory-laden reasons for turning away, which were that she had been witness to too many acts of authentic anal intercourse to have any interest in such a farcical pretence. She preferred to watch the faces of the men in the audience, where the true comedy was. Most were laughing, to be sure, but their laughter masked real excitement and fierce imagination. The fact that it was all pretence seemed actually to enhance their enjoyment, allowing fantasy a freer rein.

The man in grey, by contrast, seemed lost in thought, as though his interest in the performance had ended with the final exit of the girl with the twisted spine.

Mrs Murrell stood up and moved through the crowd to join her cast on stage. Her aim was not to answer demands that the author of the masterpiece present herself to be applauded, but only to move on to the next phase of the evening's entertainment: the auction of favours.

David understood that there were cynics who still occasionally took the trouble to tell the bawd that her plays were merely an exercise in drumming up business – devices for seducing the poor deluded members of the audience to pay three times as much for bedding the actresses as they would on another night – but he also understood, as she did, that they were fools who did not properly understand what was going on. Mrs Murrell knew that the play was a magical incantation, which really did add to the worth of those who had taken part in it for those who desired to play the games all over again.

Oscar Wilde had once told Mrs Murrell, as she supposed he must have told virtually every host and hostess in London, that a cynic was a man who knew the price of everything and the value of nothing. She wished that she had had the presence of mind to counter with the observation that a realist must be a man who knew that everything had a price and that nothing was truly valuable, but she had not thought of it until it was too late.

The auction was, from Mrs Murrell's point of view, a disappointing one. The minor players were knocked down at prices somewhat below her expectations. The eunuch with the whip fetched a higher rate, and the dark-stained coquette even more, but not sufficient to satisfy Mrs Murrell's ever optimistic hopes. The Dey, despite a satirical parade, fetched only half as much as the price Mrs Murrell considered her due; only Sophie excited such spirited bidding as to draw gasps of amazement from those who had come to ogle rather than to bid.

By the time she ended the ceremony by inviting bids for the favours of her pale Hecate, Mrs Murrell was no longer giving her full attention to the business of trying to whip up trade. If the audience would not play its part to the full, she saw no reason why she should make any special effort to pander to their taste for vulgar amusement. Amid the obligatory gale of laughter she acknowledged the shillings offered by three or four desultory bidders, and wasted no time in closing the auction at half-a-crown. That, she thought as she did so, was five times what the girl had cost. It was not until she stepped down that she remembered the bet she had made with herself, which she had lost.

The man in grey had not bid for Hecate or anyone else, and was now no longer to be seen anywhere in the room.

David Lydyard, embarrassed by what he had seen and sorely puzzled by it, found himself drifting out of the mind whose privacy he had temporarily shared, and into velvet darkness. But there was to be no rest for him, and the darkness soon gave way to the garish light of a fever dream, where the cruellest and loveliest whore of all, the Angel of Pain, was waiting to earn her fee.

6

For some time, David hovered on the brink of the world he had left. He was conscious, but not awake; capable of sluggish thought and dim feeling, but only in a curiously spectral fashion. It was as though his soul floated free of the material world, unable to engage with it in any way at all. He was not quite blind, but everything he could see was so badly blurred that he could not find any sensible shape in it; and all that he could hear was a faint susurrus like that obtained by placing a large conch shell close to one's ear.

Sometimes he thought he heard the sound of voices in the murmurous current of noise, but no words could be discerned.

He had been in some such limbo before, and knew what a strange spectrum of exotic sensations was available to those whose souls were agitated by donated heat. He was not terrified, nor was he desperately impatient to return to the presence which he had lost, for he knew what pain awaited him there. But still he felt that he had been abandoned, left to lie while events unfolded elsewhere.

Eventually his thoughts began to clear and he was able to form them into trains, submitting them to the calm command of intention and logic. As soon as he could, he took leave to speak to the thing which was using him.

If you have aught to ask of me, he said silently – not knowing whether she could hear – *then you must approach me honestly and make a proper contract, as befits two thinking beings. How else can I give you my best? How else can I join my will to yours in a common purpose? If my rebellion would be inconvenient, you must earn my amity.*

There was no reply.

He could feel his body again now, as though it were coalescing out of chaos around him in order to imprison and torment him. With the returning sense of physical existence came a new confusion of thought and feeling. His powers of reason inherited an oppressive and cloying burden from the laudanum which Cordelia had given him to damp down his pain. Nevertheless, he contrived to force his eyes open and look about him.

He was in his bed, with a wan nightlight burning on the table beside him. There was a chair drawn up close to the bed so that someone might sit and keep watch on him, but it was not Cordelia who presently maintained that vigil; it was Nell. She seemed tired, and her expression was uncommonly grave. He was very glad to see her, and to see the loving concern writ plain upon her face.

He spoke her name, and tried to smile.

'Mama said that I might take my turn here,' she told him, defensively. 'I wanted to.'

'Good girl,' he whispered. He tried to raise his head so that he could look down at his arms, which lay upon the counterpane, but he could not find sufficient leverage. Nor could he lift his right arm, which was heavily swathed in bandages. The left, though its own wounds stung more than a little, was just about movable.

She must have seen the strain in his face, for she said: 'Does it hurt a lot?'

'I can bear it,' he told her, hoping that it was true. 'The medicine makes it dull.'

'Why does it hurt when we bleed?' she asked, with an ingenuousness typical of her years. 'Teddy told me that you know, because your work is to find it out. Why do we have to hurt?'

'Pain is what teaches us how to avoid things that damage us,' he said, all too well aware of the inadequacy of the answer. 'Pain is what makes us draw our hands away from a flame or a cutting blade.'

'But why did it hurt when I had the scarlet fever?' she asked. 'And why did it hurt for so long? Why do your fingers always hurt, when you already know what not to touch?'

'I don't know,' he said, ashamed of the fact that he had no better answer to offer. He tried to move his head again, and this time managed to raise it a little while he turned sideways, trying to face her.

'The wolf died,' said Nell, unaware of any incongruity in having seen a wolf in an English suburban garden. 'Mama put it in a trunk, and locked the lid. It had no head.' Her voice was quite matter-of-fact. She was still a little too young to know exactly how odd and inexplicable the attack upon him had been. For her, the world was still a constant source of novelty, and she was used to events which she could not entirely comprehend. She had not yet learned an adult capacity for astonishment and unease.

'Has Grandpa returned yet?' David asked, realising that he did not know what day it was, let alone what hour.

'No,' said Nell, and added, apologetically, 'Mama said I was to fetch her when you woke up.' She hopped down from the chair and went to the door. As she reached it, David heard the distant sound of the doorbell, and leaped to the hopeful conclusion that it must be Sir Edward, returning in time to lend his stabilising influence to a world which had tilted out of his own control.

David hauled himself into a semi-sitting position. The room was very dimly lit by the single broad candle, but its light was eerily distributed by courtesy of the large oval mirror which was set into the door of the wardrobe and its tall rectangular counterpart which was mounted, at a right angle to the first, on the wall. David could see himself in the wall mirror, so pale of face that he might easily have fancied himself a ghost.

Sir Edward did not appear; nor, for quite some time, did Cordelia. When she finally did come, she was not alone and she was carrying a gun.

Mandorla Soulier was with her, dressed in the same black cloak which she had worn before, but with her pale hair bound up in a black scarf. Her eyes seemed less radiant, but that was probably the effect of the poor light.

Cordelia had found his old revolver. It was the one with which she had shot Calan twenty years before. David assumed that she had gone hunting for it after the attack, fearing that the visitation might only be a beginning, and urgently desirous of having some defence. It seemed, though, that the second werewolf had come in more orthodox fashion, by way of the front door.

While Mandorla waited, Cordelia came forward to touch David's forehead and reassure herself that he was as well as could be expected.

'She begged leave to see you,' said Cordelia, pointing at the wolfwoman with the barrel of the revolver. 'She insisted that it would be a dreadful mistake to send her away. I've warned her that I'm more than ready to use the gun. She admits that the creature which attacked you was one of her kin, but insists that she was not responsible, and that she's as anxious as we are.'

While all this was being said, David looked first at Cordelia and then at Mandorla, trying to fight off the deadening effect of the drug. When Cordelia had finished, he indicated with his left hand that she should sit beside him on the bed, and then he beckoned to Mandorla to take the chair.

'It was Suarra who attacked you,' said Mandorla quietly. 'But it was the will of another which made her do it. She was as helpless as Pelorus, or more so. Still, I must ask for her body; she is not truly dead, despite what was done to her.'

'Is that why you came?' David whispered.

Mandorla shook her head. 'I came because I need you,' she said, 'and because I may be able to help you. We are both in dire danger, and we need to find out why. If we act in concert, there may be something we can do.'

David studied her carefully, and knew that Cordelia was doing the same.

'It makes no sense,' he said eventually. 'If one or other of the fallen angels wanted me dead or hurt, it could have done it in any one of a thousand ways. Why use one of your kin?'

'Perhaps because I promised that you would be safe,' Mandorla replied. 'I think the angels fear us, firstly because they do not understand what we are or why we were made, and secondly because I interfered in their plans once before, and tempted them to use their power. They would like to render us impotent, but they wonder whether we, too, have a protector.'

'Why come here?' The question came from Cordelia.

'To forge an alliance,' Mandorla replied curtly. 'If I am to be sucked into this struggle, I must make myself useful. We must all do that, if we are not to be too lightly discarded. What was done to Suarra could as easily be done to David, or to you, and *your* flesh is of a kind which permits no return from the grave.'

'I can't believe that the wolf will return,' said Cordelia sceptically, 'given that its brain was blown to atoms.' David was content to let his wife speak, while he fought to regain complete control of his befuddled senses.

'In times past,' said Mandorla coldly, 'I have been burned to ashes, and had my ashes scattered on the wind. I can assure you that the pain brought little reward in the way of enlightenment, but it did not destroy me. How the habitation of my soul was built again I do not know, and whether the memories I have now are truly those which were burned out of me, I cannot say for certain. But I live now, and I am certain that I lived before, and still I remember the life I had before Machalalel cursed me with human form. Perhaps your human hopes of resurrection are not without foundation – that is not my concern – but I take leave to doubt that David will accept death gladly on account of such a hope.'

'And I take leave to doubt,' said Cordelia stubbornly, 'that you are rather to be reckoned a friend than a foe. I've heard nothing to dispose me to believe it.'

'Agreed,' said Mandorla. 'Shoot me, then, if you wish. If the world into which I awake is very different from this one, I will learn its ways soon enough, and shed no tears for what is gone.'

Cordelia was silent, though she seemed half minded to accept the invitation.

'What do you want me to do?' asked David, hoarsely.

'Tell me your dreams,' Mandorla replied promptly. 'I know far more about the Creators than you do, perhaps more than Pelorus or the Clay Man. Together, we might discover what is happening, and be better able to do what we can and what we must.'

'I fear,' said David, drily, 'that my dreams may not be so easy to fathom. What the wolf did to me broke through the laudanum's protective wall, but what I saw was so puzzling that it would take a cleverer mind than yours to see significance in it.'

'What did you see?' asked Mandorla warily.

'As a matter of fact,' said David, 'I saw a brothel, through the brothel-keeper's eyes.'

Mandorla was impassive, but Cordelia had to close her mouth in order to quell some exclamation which had sprung to her lips.

'As in all dreams,' David continued, 'it was difficult to separate the significant from the irrelevant, but there was a pale man with grey eyes who did not seem to fit the surroundings, and a strange girl with a twisted spine, whose name has been changed from Cath to Hecate. I believe that I have seen the brothel-keeper once before, and I know her by repute; it was Mercy Murrell, who was once an intimate of Jacob Harkender's.'

'Harkender again,' said Mandorla softly. 'First Luke Capthorn and now Mrs Murrell. Did you know, by the way, that Harkender did not die in the fire which destroyed his home?'

'I knew that his body was never found,' David said. 'How did you know about Capthorn? I did not tell you that he was one of those who took Adam Clay's body.'

'I told you that I could discover anything, if I needed to,' said Mandorla equably. 'The note was enough to set me searching. I have discovered the name of his master, too, if you would like to know it.' Her violet eyes challenged him.

'I would,' said David.

'Luke Capthorn is now in the service of a man named Jason Sterling. He was the one who supervised the removal of the coffin from the grave; the third man was another of his servants, by the name of Marwin. They took the Clay Man to Sterling's house in Richmond. He is infamous in the neighbourhood, because he is reputed to have an alchemist's den in his cellars, where he makes monsters by magical means. Have you heard of Sterling at all?'

David realised as she spoke that perhaps he had. 'Sir Edward has mentioned someone of that name,' he said reflectively. 'A man with unorthodox ideas on the subject of evolution. The issue is one which is dear to Sir Edward's heart, but I must confess that I have not read the man's work. I doubt *that* Sterling can be a magician, though; perhaps this is a different man.'

'I doubt it,' said Mandorla. 'You pride yourself on being a man of science, having no truck with magic, but in the eyes of ordinary men there is no difference between a scientist and a magician. Had you not been hurt, I would have suggested that we should pay a call on Jason Sterling, as you seem to have the means of making an introduction, but I see that you are not well enough to travel.'

'Do you think that Sterling is an instrument of the Spider, as Harkender once was?' David asked.

'As Harkender still may be,' said Mandorla, 'and Luke Capthorn and Mrs Murrell, too.'

'But not you or I, or . . .' David hesitated over the nomination of a third candidate, then said instead: 'Do you know where Harkender is?'

'He was taken after the fire to a private asylum somewhere in Essex. It is said that he was blinded, barely able to move or speak, and perhaps insane. I have not sought to do him any harm, despite the fact that he was my enemy once. Physically, he is quite helpless, but he once had powers remarkable in a human, and it may be that the damage done to him has not cancelled them out. Whether or not they were donated by the Spider, the Spider may have continued to use him, as the other has continued to use you.'

'What of the Sphinx?' asked Cordelia. 'Where is she?'

Mandorla shook her head. 'I don't know. But whether she is far away or close at hand, David can probably communicate with her, if the Creator who is master of them both cares to allow it.'

David struggled to sit up straighter, and achieved this end without bringing too much distress upon himself. He was now able to look down at his bandaged arms.

'They say that a man who is bitten by a werewolf and lives may become a werewolf himself,' he said. 'I suppose you'll tell me that it's not true.'

'It is not true of *our* kind,' said Mandorla calmly. 'There were others, once, but I have not encountered one for a very long time. If you are glad to hear that, you are wrong. I do not like what I am, but it is better to be allowed to be a wolf sometimes than never at all.'

David was not disposed to quarrel. His throat was dry and he felt very thirsty. He reached out with his left hand to touch his wife lightly on the arm.

'Could you fetch a cup of water?' he asked. 'I fear that I have a slight fever.'

She looked at him oddly, and he realised that she was doubly anxious. She was reluctant to leave him alone with

Mandorla, not only because he might be in danger from her, but also because she thought that his request might be a pretext to dismiss her. She reached out her hand to touch his brow, though, and found it hot.

'I can't believe that she has come here to do me harm,' said David softly. 'Nor can I believe that she would be allowed to do it, if she had. Whatever my possessive angel wants from me, she has not yet obtained.'

Cordelia nodded. 'You must eat, too,' she said. 'You've been asleep for nearly twenty-four hours.'

'Give the gun to David, if you are anxious,' said the wolfwoman. 'I dare say that he could fire it left-handed, if there was any need. Or, if you prefer, I will call one of your servants so that you can make whatever arrangements you wish without leaving the room.'

Cordelia might have accepted that offer, but David raised his left hand and flexed his fingers to show her that he had control of all the muscles. She gave him the gun.

He laid it down beside him, as though to say that he was perfectly confident that it would not be needed, but he let his hand lie on top of it, to satisfy his wife. She would not leave until she had that reassurance, and when she did move towards the door she looked back at her husband with such a dire anxiety that he felt ashamed of his own lack of fear. He wished that he might be horrified by the sight of Mandorla, but he could not, even though he knew what she was.

She had feasted on human flesh. She had plotted to turn the world of men upside down. He did not know how he could possibly trust her word when she said that she had become a scholar of sorts, but he did.

'She is more afraid for you than for herself,' said Mandorla when Cordelia had gone, leaving the door ajar. 'And for the children, of course. I saw your daughter – she is a very handsome child.'

'I dare say you have eaten prettier ones,' said David darkly. 'I would rather you did not favour her with your compliments.'

She smiled at that. 'You would not like me half so much if I were truly meek and mild,' she said. 'And I would be less tender in my feelings towards you, were it not for the fact that once I had the pleasure of hurting you. Let us not pretend to be more reasonable than we are.'

'I am not Pelorus,' he said, 'who's bound to you by his instincts while he fears you with his reason. There's no wolf in *me*.'

'No wolf at all,' Mandorla agreed readily enough. 'But also less reason than you dare to hope. The world has changed its appearances, and men dare to think that they have become civilised; but solidity is not as secure as you would like to suppose, and when men set aside their careful manners and those ugly clothes with which they imprison their avid flesh, they are what they have always been. Wolves are less violent and more honest.'

'I'll remember,' he promised wryly, 'not to trust you *too* much.'

'You will *remember*,' she conceded, in a self-satisfied fashion, 'but I have found in all my dealings with men that they can often be persuaded to discount their memories in favour of their appetites. You are no different from the rest. All men can be seduced if they are only tempted with sufficient care and tenderness.'

It was not a threat, only gentle mockery; but when she said it he could not help recalling the ominous way in which the cat-goddess had played with him as his dream began, and how she had called him 'beloved'.

There is a thing which thou must do, she had said, *and do willingly.*

He did not doubt that the velvety tone concealed an iron-fisted force, but still she had condescended to woo him, and he could only wonder why.

He was quite certain that when the time came for him to find out, he would not like the answer at all.

7

By the time Cordelia returned with food and water, David's fever had increased. Ignoring the bread and meat, he seized the mug of water and drained it greedily. Although his hand was shaking, he did not spill a drop. Cordelia put down the tray and placed her hand on his forehead.

'I must call for the doctor,' she said, looking at Mandorla as if to accuse her of increasing David's distress. But David, whose eyes felt unnaturally large in their sockets, and whose vision now had an unnatural brightness and clarity, could see that the wolfwoman was no less disturbed by his condition than his wife.

'The doctor will not be able to help,' said Mandorla quietly. 'It is no natural heat which is flooding into him.'

'He wasn't like this before,' Cordelia complained angrily; but her manner made it plain that she remembered only too well that she had not been a witness to all that David had gone through twenty years before.

'Something is happening which I do not understand,' said Mandorla, 'but I do not think that he is in mortal danger. Whatever protects him will surely preserve him from any fatal harm, however much it has to gain by hurting him.'

While she spoke, it seemed to David that her golden hair became incandescent with light, and when he looked at Cordelia, she too was glowing with some strange radiance. The flame of the nightlight which burned by his bed was as faint as ever, but in the sight of his oversensitive eyes it seemed to burn like the tropical sun. The two mirrors which reflected it seemed to have been transformed into magical windows, which looked upon some strange and unbelievably bright alternative world.

While David looked desperately from side to side, and tried unthinkingly to raise his right hand as though to protect his eyes, a cataract of light erupted into the room from every direction, dissolving the furniture and drowning the faces and forms of the two watching women.

He had only one weapon with which to fight the deluge of light, and he used it. He grabbed his right arm roughly with his left and forced it upwards, not as a physical barrier, but as a wall of pure pain.

Suddenly, as he had known that he would, he found himself falling away from the angry light, floating free into a whirlpool of darkness which snatched him away from where he lay and sent him soaring through an empty void.

He could not tell how many minutes or hours passed before the Angel of Pain condescended to release him from her keen embrace, but he knew that he and she had outlasted the effects of the laudanum which he had earlier been given. He knew it by the temper of her caresses and by the contentment of her loving whispers. He knew it by the way she hugged him, which she did with all the satisfaction of one whose dominion is utterly secure.

Finally, she spoke to him, saying: 'You are mine and mine alone, my only beloved. Surrender to me, and I will shower you with gifts which no man before you has ever earned. Only pledge your soul to me, freely, and I will show you all the worlds of the universe. Only cease your fight against my empire, and I will share with you the deepest secrets of Creation. Only sacrifice your pride, and I will teach you to hear the rhythm of the Heart Divine.'

He knew that she was not the Devil, trying to deceive him into signing his soul away. He knew that she was no creature of Hell, because he knew that Hell was only an estate of the mind. He knew that there was hope even in suffering, that there was in life something worth doing, and being, and seeing, even though the torment might never end.

He had given form and face to the Angel of Pain, and had made her beautiful, just as those who could give form and face to themselves chose beauty for their mask when they confronted men. Although she had trapped him long ago, still he was free, still he had the power to choose.

Even so, the answer he gave to her now was in no way defiant. It was merely a question to counter hers.

'Why should I give you anything at all, *unless you will let me understand?*'

When he asked her that, in spite of the fact that she must have been annoyed, she took her talons from his ravaged flesh and let him fall into a deeper darkness, as cool and peaceful as the grave, where he stayed until he was thrust into the mind of another man, to look upon a room which was very different from his own.

The steel screws which sealed the lid of Adam Clay's coffin seemed to have rusted in the course of the thirty years in which it lay in the tomb, but the slots in their heads had not decayed so far that they would not turn. Luke Capthorn watched while Jason Sterling removed them one by one, in patient fashion, and set them down on the tabletop. David Lydyard, an undetectable prisoner in Luke's consciousness, watched with him.

When he had finished, Sterling looked up at Luke, smiling to see his discomfort. Sterling was a handsome man, with black hair and dark eyes. He was no older than David, and might have been taken for a younger man by those who judged only by the softness of his features, and not by the glint of wisdom and curiosity in his eyes.

Is this an alchemist? David wondered. *Is this a necromancer, successor to Harkender in the Spider's affections?* He wished that Luke would not concentrate so sharply upon his master's face and hands, because he caught tantalising glimpses of strange items of apparatus and huge glass tanks at the periphery of his borrowed vision, but Luke was no stranger here and all his attention was absorbed by what Sterling was doing.

'Help me lift the lid, Luke,' said Sterling. 'It's not heavy, but we must set it down carefully beside the box.'

Luke looked apprehensively at the unsecured lid. In the secret arena of his imagination, which only he and David could see, the coffin lid slid away of its own accord, allowing a partly decayed hand to emerge, sluggishly searching for a throat to grip. Then, instead, the lid was drawn aside to reveal a vast horde of white maggots and blind grave worms, jealously guarding their empire of putrefaction. In the meantime, the real lid waited to be hauled away.

Luke was not coward enough to be terrified by his own morbid fantasies. He did as he was told and took hold of the board, applying leverage in concert with his master.

The lid clung a little, but it required no great force to dislodge it, and the two men carried it away without undue difficulty. As they set it down, both were already looking into the coffin. Luke's images of horror dissolved in the face of actual evidence. The body was enshrouded, and there was nothing to be seen but a clean white cloth shaped by the form within into the merest approximation of human semblance. There was no sign of any invasion by worms or other vermin.

Sterling fetched a scalpel and lifted the cloth to make it taut before cutting it. Luke moved back half a pace, in anticipation of inevitable unpleasantness, although there was no noticeable reek of decay.

Sterling slit the cloth from head to toe before folding back the edges to reveal the corpse within. Luke's fascination had not diminished in the least.

The naked body within seemed to be perfectly preserved. The flesh was very pale and somewhat meagre, but it was certainly not flesh which had been more than twenty years dead. The man who wore it was not tall, but he would have been handsome enough had his face not been so white.

So that is the Clay Man of whom I have heard so much, David thought. *Were he not where he is, he would seem very ordinary. Small wonder that Austen could never quite believe that he was anything but a madman.*

Sterling emitted a slight sigh, but what combination of emotions the sound might signify neither Luke nor David could judge. Luke's dominant emotion was relief, first because his fears had erred on the side of alarmism, and secondly because the information which he had given his master had not been entirely without foundation.

David, sharing Luke's thoughts, realised that the servant thought of Sterling as his 'master' only in an ironic fashion. David saw that it was Luke who had suggested that the body be stolen, believing when he did so that he had done it for the sake of a very different master. Nor was David prepared to think that Luke was a fool for believing that, although he supposed that what Luke took for the Devil was really the being which he had always called the Spider.

Sterling took up the hand of the recumbent man and tested its texture. He indicated that Capthorn should do the same, which the younger man did, gingerly. The flesh was quite cold, and firm. David knew from long experience, though Luke only guessed, that the firmness had not the feel of ordinary mortal rigour.

After setting down the hand, Sterling reached out to lift one of the dead man's eyelids. The blue-grey iris and dilated pupil of the eye within were visible, and he touched it very gently, presumably to make sure that it was not glass. Letting the eye fall closed again, Sterling took from his waistcoat a small speculum which he held to the dead man's lips. After thirty seconds he showed the mirror glass to Capthorn, who saw that it showed a very slight trace of condensation.

'He's still breathing!' Luke exclaimed.

Sterling shook his head. 'Austen would never have committed the body to the ground had there been the least sign of life. He's breathing *now*, but he wasn't breathing before. He's already returning to life.'

Luke stepped back, reflexively.

'Is that not what you promised?' Sterling asked. 'Or did you not dare to believe?' He was not angry; his voice quivered with barely suppressed excitement. Until now, David judged, Sterling had *not* dared to believe – but in the face of evidence he had become avid in his conviction. Luke, on the other hand, was not so sure that he wanted to face this strange revenant, and could not but dread the moment when those eyes would open of their own accord.

For the first time, Luke looked at one of the glass tanks arrayed beside the table. His gaze met another pair of staring eyes. There was nothing in that stare to disturb Luke, who must have met it with equanimity a thousand times before, but David was startled. The eyes belonged to a creature which seemed to him to be utterly strange and sinister: a homunculus no more than a foot or fifteen inches tall, which stood erect on a leafy branch, grasping another with the little fingers of its right hand. Its skin had the colour and texture of a common toad's, and the face was unmistakably batrachian, save for the fact that the eyes were set close together in the front of the head, like a man's.

Luke looked back at his master.

Sterling lifted the dead man's hand again, and this time pricked it with a needle. He kneaded the flesh gently, and when no bead of blood could be made to appear on the back of the hand he made a second attempt on the inside of the wrist, directing the needle into a vein whose blue trace was evident from without. This time, when he withdrew the needle, a tiny leakage of fluid was obtained. It seemed that the fluid was ordinary blood, reddening on contact with the air.

'Either he was not embalmed,' said Sterling thoughtfully, 'or the process of embalming has somehow been undone while he rested in his grave.'

Luke contented himself with a nod of acknowledgement, having nothing substantial to say in reply.

Sterling now took up a syringe and carefully inserted it into a vein higher up the man's arm. With considerable care and patience, he sucked fluid from the vein. The sluggish blood did not emerge easily, but the pressure of the vacuum was adequate to draw it off, and the bulb of the syringe was slowly filled with dark-red liquid.

Sterling carried the full syringe to a second table, which was liberally bedecked with apparatus. Here there were already three sealed glass cylinders of blood, their contents varying in quantity from a gill to a quart, each one containing a pair of electrodes connected by insulated wires to copper sulphate batteries. Sterling carefully decanted the blood he had taken from Adam Clay's body into a fourth such cylinder, which he evacuated by means of a pump and sealed. He took care to check that this cylinder too was electrified before returning to look at the dead man. He took up the scalpel again, and studied the corpse in a contemplative manner.

Luke merely watched and waited, but David's thoughts leaped ahead, wondering what the effect of a cut would be. Would any flesh that was cut away be regenerated?

Sterling must have been too anxious to take the chance. After a moment's pause, he laid the scalpel down again. He moved the heavy lid from where it lay beside the coffin, sliding it across the tabletop and lowering it to the floor.

'Help me take him from the coffin,' he said to Luke. 'Take his thighs while I lift his shoulders.'

Luke moved uneasily to do as he was told. It was not until he lifted the naked body that he and David realised how very light and frail it was. Adam Clay had never been a tall man, nor a stout one, but he was thin enough now to seem half-starved.

When the body was laid out on the bare wood, Luke removed the coffin from the table, lugging it across the stone floor to one of the few uncrowded corners of the laboratory. He glanced around, as uninterestedly as before, his gaze unthinkingly glancing over the glass tanks stacked against the wall.

David wished that Luke would focus his eyes and his attention on the contents of the tanks, because it was very difficult for him to concentrate his own attention on something about which his host did not care at all, but he could not exercise any influence upon his host. David was very interested in the inhabitants of the tanks, but he could catch only the vaguest impressions from Luke's mind as to the nature of the creatures confined there.

There were glasslike insectile things which Luke called 'acari'; there were huge worms of various kinds; there were astonishing grotesques, including the manikin at which he had earlier glanced, which had grown from toads' eggs; but to Luke these things were no longer strange or fascinating. He had grown accustomed to them over the years, and though he could never quite put out of his mind the knowledge that they were monsters – unnatural beings designed by man and not by God – that only encouraged his eye to pass over them quickly and inattentively.

When Luke returned to the table, Sterling had used the shroud as a blanket to cover Adam Clay's nakedness, and he was rubbing the man's slender wrist between his hands, as though trying to stir the circulation of the blood.

'Can you wake him?' asked Capthorn, anxiously curious.

'I hope so,' Sterling answered dubiously. 'I must be careful, for there is some risk that I might unwittingly damage the capacity he has for awakening, but it seems that he went gently enough into the deathlike sleep and it may not be so very difficult to quicken him again. Go ask Mrs Tolley if she would heat up some oxtail soup before she goes up to bed. You need not tell her why. Bring some brandy, too.'

'Perhaps you should not try to wake him just yet,' said Luke hesitantly. David could sense the confusion of the younger man's anxieties, and knew how half-hearted a Satanist he was. Of all the people whose sight he had been forced to borrow, Luke must have been the least intelligent, and David was annoyed that his laziness of eye and his vagueness of mind combined to make him such a poor instrument.

'Why not?' asked Sterling silkily. 'What is there to be afraid of?'

'I don't know,' Luke replied slowly. 'But I know what Jacob Harkender was, and it didn't save him from destruction when he delved too deep into things which he might have let alone.'

'Harkender was a mere magican,' Sterling told his assistant. 'I'm a better breed of man than that, despite the rumours which say that I've sold my soul. You've seen what I have so far achieved in playing the game of Creation; this man is but another player, who possesses as a matter of nature what I've sought to achieve by artifice. He's not a demon but a man, and the fact that his nature is better than ours doesn't mean that we can't hope to understand it.'

'Harkender thought something similar,' Luke answered, a little resentfully. 'But it came to naught but fire and ashes in the end. There's danger in this; I know it.' David could see well enough, however, that Luke's dutiful caution was tempered with hope for more than one kind of reward.

'Do you fear that he'll be wrathful when he awakes, and will curse us?' asked Sterling mockingly. 'I doubt that. Perhaps he'll be grateful. At the very least, he should be intrigued.'

'He has friends who may not like our taking him captive,' Capthorn muttered, 'You've read the book and know what they are. I never saw them, but I know that it was the werewolves that damned Harkender, by stealing away his precious wonder-child.'

Even as he spoke, Luke knew that it was far too late for second thoughts. He had been glad enough to win the approval of his master by telling him about the book and the buried man, and content to believe that he was simultaneously serving his other master; he knew full well that there could be no drawing back from the threshold. He knew, also, that Jason Sterling was not the kind of man to be intimidated by tales of the werewolves of London. That was not because he was not prepared to believe in them, but simply because his interest in their unhuman nature was far more powerful than any superstitious fear which lingered in the depths of his soul. Were the werewolves to come howling in the grounds, Sterling would probably go out to meet them, and beg leave to take a sample of their blood, and ask if he might photograph their metamorphoses.

From these fleeting thoughts, David thought that he had learned a good deal about Capthorn's master, but still he wished that Luke might pay more attention to the shadowy recesses of the laboratory and the creatures confined there. He wished, too, that he could figure out exactly what was going on here, and why he had been sent to witness it on behalf of his own tutelary godling. If Sterling was an inquisitive instrument, like himself, what was it that he hoped to learn from the Clay Man, and why was it so important?

'If what you've told me is all you know,' Sterling said to Luke Capthorn, 'you have but half the tale at most. I don't know what started the fire which gutted Jacob Harkender's house, but I will not take it for granted that it was the vengeance of God or Satan upon one who dared too much. If you were truly afraid of that kind of wrath, you would never have gone to Charnley with me. Go to Mrs Tolley, then fetch the brandy. And a suit of clothes, too, from my wardrobe.'

Luke shrugged his shoulders and went to do as he was told. He had calmed his fears by voicing them, but there was no curiosity in his calmness. David cursed silently as the uncaring gaze swept over the tanks yet again without pausing to look at what was within.

The maker of monsters is a key element in all of this, David thought. *And so is the ugly whore. Bast fears them both, or she would not have sent me forth to spy on them. Something is brewing here, but I cannot tell what it might be. That is surely what she needs me for, and why she begs the full indulgence of my curiosity and my reasoning. There is a new riddle here, more urgent by far than the ones I have been set to solving during these last twenty years. She is afraid . . . and when those who would be gods are forced to be afraid, what comfort can there be for the mortal men who are their pawns?*

As soon as Luke Capthorn's hand touched the handle of the door and began to turn it, David fell again into the darkness and was whirled away, like a dead leaf caught up by a cruel and random wind.

8

While Lydyard had shared the thoughts and sight of Luke Capthorn, he had not doubted for a moment that all that he saw was quite real. Not for a second had he hesitated over the possibility that it might all be a mere dream or figment of his own imagination.

Now, by contrast, he felt utterly uncertain of what was happening. Again he was conscious of being part of another's consciousness, but he could not find any sense of identity in this man's mind to assure him that it was not his own self that he had returned to inhabit. He was conscious of a body, and of certain impressions of sight. The body was racked with pain as his own so often was, but this pain felt somehow wrong, and the sight which he had was blurred and distorted. All this could easily be taken as evidence of unreality, but he was not *sure* that it was not happening, and he knew that in his present condition of bewitchment he could not possibly identify a boundary between the subjective and the objective.

The only thing of which he could be certain was that something wanted him to see all that would be revealed to him, wanted him to know all that would be told to him, and wanted him to feel all that he would be subjected to. Dream or reality, this was the rhetoric of the angels, and must be heeded if he were to have any chance of understanding what was being done to him and why.

It was raining, very hard. The twilit streets, washed by the deluge, were almost deserted. Though darkness had not yet fallen, the cloud which filled the sky was so grey and gloomy that the city seemed to cry out for light.

He did not know what city he was in. He was running. He ran past an ancient church, which he was sure he should have been able to recognise, but could not. The sound of his footfalls was drowned by the hiss of the rain upon the pavement and the splashing of horses' hooves as carriages sailed past.

As the man ran, he glanced behind him again and again, as though searching for signs of pursuit. He found them, too, to judge by the continuing urgency of his flight, although David's connection with the stream of his host's consciousness was so slight and so peculiar that he could not tell what the man might have seen or heard, or even what it was that he feared.

Although the running man's legs were strong enough to bear him along, he carried himself awkwardly, and though the colour of his coat was darkened by the rain which had soaked into its fibres, it was still possible to see a darker stain which spread from the left sleeve to the line of buttons crossing his breast; in the midst of all the greyness it seemed black, but David, feeling in a dull and distant fashion the heaviness of the arm, did not doubt that it was in fact a bloodstain. Beneath his coat the man was nursing a bloody and hurtful wound.

David tried to sense the pain of the wound. He found it oddly dull and distant, as though the man whose pain it was had contrived to mask and blur it. He was amply familiar with the manner in which laudanum dimmed pain, but this was different, and quite in keeping with the general haziness of the man's mind. David wondered whether the lack of sensation might be the result of an imperfect connection between their two souls; if not, his host's lack of feeling was very puzzling.

The running man looked back again; David, sharing his sight, still saw nothing. But it seemed that the man could see something that the passenger in his mind could not, and David picked up a shadowy impression of what it was that the man imagined he could see: wraiths within the rain, creatures of shadow which need not fear its force. The running man imagined them as great grey wolves, but even he knew that they were not really beasts at all, not even werewolves. The running man knew that they were things without substance, sent to haunt as well as to hunt him . . . sent to mock him as well as hurt him. He did not know, even while he ran, whether their intention was to catch him before he reached his destination, or to force him to it all the faster. He knew only that he was afraid, as he had hoped never to be afraid again, and that he did not dare to stop and bid the ghostly hunters to do their worst.

But the man who knew – or imagined – such strange things as these did not know much simpler things. He did not know who he was, or where he was, or where he was going. Nor were his emotional reactions anything like as intense as David might have expected.

It came into David's mind that the running man was not in full possession of his faculties because he was being guided by another, and he wondered whether he was the only ghost possessing this faulty machine. Perhaps this was yet another act of the enigmatic angels, unfathomable to mere humans.

At a junction where he turned a corner, the running man nearly slipped and fell, but he caught himself on the firm stone of a wall and thrust himself off it in such a way that he regained his balance and kept all but a little of his impetus. The monsters which bounded along behind him could not have seen him stumble, had they had eyes to see at all, but he did not doubt that they *knew* of his momentary peril, if they were capable of knowing.

David tried to remind himself that the pursuers were only phantoms, mere appearances without mass or solidity, but there was nothing reassuring in that for a man who knew as much about appearance and reality as he did. He knew what a phantom he was himself, in spite of his substance, and how uncertain was the world which contained him.

The man began to look about him as well as behind, as though searching for a particular side street. There drifted into David's mind an image of a gated courtyard. This was not something the man knew, but something that was being intruded into his mind by another. Along with the image came the information that the courtyard which he sought was an impasse, blind at its further end, and that once he turned into it he would have cornered himself, but there came also the stern admonition that he could not run much farther and must not try, and that he had a mission of sorts to perform. He could not escape the ghostly wolves, if they did not intend him to escape. If their objective was to trap him and slaughter him, he could not avoid his fate.

When he saw the gates which he was commanded to find, however, the runner felt a surge of energy which gave him greater capacity for effort, but made him pay with a surge of the pain from which he had so far been protected. His breathing was already ragged, and the shock of it made him cry out hoarsely, but the pace of his steps increased as he hurled himself across the road behind a coach-and-four.

The shadowy wolves, which could not be touched by the rain, increased their pace too. Their glistening eyes were as dark as jet, and their fangs gleamed with an unearthly whiteness. Although they existed only in the imagination of his host, David felt the hostile pressure of those dark, glaring eyes, and the threat of those pointed teeth.

The gates protecting the court had been drawn back into the shadow of the arch, and for a moment the man was tempted to pause, in order to close them against the enemy at his heels; but he knew how absurd such a gesture would be, and he ran on, past the shuttered shops which crowded the alleyway, towards a flight of steps which ran up to the apartments above.

He stumbled at the foot of the flight, and fell on his wounded arm. Pain ripped through him like a saw blade, and through David too, and their minds melted together, so that David *became* the other as he imagined his wound opening up to release a great gout of blood from his bursting heart. But it was only pain; only pain, without the ecstatic escape of oracular vision.

Up the steps he went, half thrusting with his heels, half dragging himself, grappling at the railing with his one good hand. When he looked over the side, he saw the ghost wolves gathering in the court, turning and leaping as though with laughter and the thrill of the chase . . . as though the game were over, and they had won.

He stumbled again at the top of the stair, but reached out with his good hand to hammer on the door with all his might. He did not pause at all, for though his legs had done their work he still felt the convulsive need to drive himself to action, and an awful fear of what might become of him if he allowed himelf to be still.

He was still hammering when the door was thrown back and an aged concierge stared out, her brow thunderous with ill temper.

'For the love of God,' he said, though the agony of his breath threatened to tear the words apart as he spoke them, 'bring Sir Edward! Fetch Tallentyre, I beg you!'

When he heard the voice, David suddenly realised who it was that was speaking, and whose mind it was that he had shared, but it was too late for the knowledge to give him any extra purchase on the man's mercurial thoughts. Again he slipped into the darkness.

This time it was as though a net caught and held him, suspended in the void, while images bombarded him from nowhere.

There was a ship, lurching and heeling in a heavy sea, and a howling storm wind . . .

He was inside a cabin, clinging to the railing at the end of a bunk, trying in spite of the movement of the ship to stand up straight. The very walls of the stateroom were beginning to deform. It was as if, David thought, he were trapped in the belly of some dreadful living creature.

The lamp brackets began to writhe like snakes, and the chair was transformed into some monstrous hydra.

There was someone lying on the lower bunk, but David caught no more than a glimpse of her as she turned. She was trying to get out, to escape, but her slim body was trapped as the two bunks came together like enormous jaws, crushing and chewing her . . .

He let go of the rail and staggered away, trying to find some other purchase by which to steady himself.

Blood trickled from the blanketed lips, which were set tightly together. She had not uttered a sound as she was caught, but he wondered if she had changed her form. At least, *someone* wondered, though the fugitive thought was quickly overtaken by an urgent desire to get out, to escape being seized and mutilated in his turn.

The door would not open, and he knew that it was sealed around its rim, where the steel had become soft and seamless. He hammered upon it and cried for help. One of the gas brackets slashed at him, the hot glass scything through his clothing and his flesh. Then the porthole opened like a great sphincter in the side of the vessel, and he was sucked out as though by a great wind.

He thought that he would be cast into the raging sea and drowned, but he was hurled like a missile through the wind-torn night, dragged for mile after mile through the storm, slashed and battered by raindrops which would have stung like bullets had he not been gripped by some icy force which forbade him to feel, forbade him to think, forbade him to dream . . . until at last he was set down in the city streets.

Then the ghost wolves came, and he began to run.

Paris, David thought, as the torrent of disjointed memories released him. *The city is Paris. The man is Adam Grey, who used to be William de Lancy. And the woman who was killed, destroyed by that awful, avid magic . . .*

The woman was the Sphinx, Bast's creature.

The Sphinx had been destroyed!

Suddenly, alone and bodiless in the desolate darkness, David Lydyard felt an awful fear growing inside him. The angel which he called Bast was the creator of the Sphinx, and if the Sphinx had been trapped and killed – perhaps not destroyed, given that her kind was very difficult to destroy, but at least condemned to the same long sleep which sometimes claimed the werewolves – then Bast must indeed be embroiled in a deadly war.

De Lancy, if what David had seen could be believed, had been saved. But de Lancy was the least of all Bast's instruments, and perhaps he seemed hardly worth killing; or perhaps he was in danger still, and because he was now with Sir Edward, would increase the danger which *he* was in.

David could not help thinking that the balance of fate was tipping against his arrogant mistress. It seemed all too probable that the would-be goddess who had chosen him to be her reluctant oracle was losing her fight.

'I don't *know* that the Sphinx is dead,' he said to himself. He would have said it aloud had he had a voice with which to speak, but he had not. 'This may be the tale of a nightmare, not a memory of any actual event. It may be nothing but illusion, and though it may signify something, I can't assume that it is the literal truth.'

Sir Edward would have been proud of him for being so scrupulous in his doubting, but he could not hold the sceptical thought for long, because light blazed up around him yet again, and sight returned.

Alas, he realised with a pang of anguish, the sight was another's and not his own. Still his urgent odyssey was not to be permitted to end.

She was looking into a mirror, and so he saw her as she saw herself: her hair greying but still dark; her face gaunt and surprisingly unwrinkled, save for the corners of her eyes and mouth; her eyes pale and penetrating, more grey than blue.

She studied herself carefully, searching minutely for new signs of advancing age, knowing her face well enough to recognise every crease. David saw her differently, as a stranger, weighing the echoes of former beauty against the austerity of her expression, the pitilessness of her features, the harshness of her eyes. She was sixty, at least, but she had preserved herself by the power of her will and the pressure of discipline, striving with all her might to import the hardness of stone into her frail flesh.

And all for what? To deny and defy, after her particular fashion, the pressure of time and fate. She felt that she had been robbed by cruel circumstance of the kind of life which she would have wished, and which others had by virtue of a lucky birth. She had been born poor, with no inheritance but the soft youthfulness of her flesh, and that she had traded for what advantages she could.

Now, with her initial capital exhausted, she traded the flesh of others, but all to the same end: to fight back against the cruelty of circumstance, which had given her nothing, and to which she, in her turn, was determined to yield as little as possible.

David saw this, and understood it, in the space of a silent minute when nothing happened save that Mercy Murrell confronted herself, squarely and without deception.

At the end of the minute, she was interrupted by a sound from the room above. It was a heavy, dull sound, as though of a falling body, and it was swiftly followed by a long howl of anguish. Muffled as it was by the intervening floor and ceiling, neither Mrs Murrell nor David could tell whether the voice was male or female.

Mrs Murrell moved with calm efficiency. She had often heard screams before, and the sound of bodies falling or struck down. Violence and abuse were commodities in which she dealt, and it was sometimes difficult to maintain the boundaries of licence.

She did not look for a weapon before leaving the room, having confidence enough in her own authority and strength. Nor did she feel, as yet, the need to call for the burly manservant she kept as a guardian.

She gathered her skirts and ran lightly up the stair to the third floor of the house. It was Sophie's room to which she was going, and she saw as soon as she reached the stairhead that the door was open. The room was lit, but not as brightly as the corridor, where the gaslight still burned. Another door on the landing was opening, too, but the face which peeped out had no intention of coming farther, and ducked back as

Mrs Murrell moved along the corridor. Despite the lateness of the hour, there were still a few clients in the building, who would not leave until morning.

As she came to the doorway, another person – who must have been standing just inside – stepped towards her from the side and seized her arm. She saw who it was from the corner of her eye, and was as surprised as David was to recognise the man in grey who had spoken to her several hours before; but she did not look at him for long, nor did she react angrily to the way he had set his hand upon her, because her eyes were drawn to the scene inside the room.

Sophie had been cast down upon the floor, or perhaps had rolled from the bed. Her hands were tied and there was a handkerchief stuffed into her mouth, secured there by a knotted ribbon. Her back had been liberally and ungently scourged, and blood was flowing from more than a dozen cuts.

David remembered the scene in Mrs Murrell's play where the blonde-wigged girl had suffered a pretended flogging; she had no wig on now, and there had been not the slightest pretence about what had been done to her. But Mrs Murrell's thoughts had no horror in them at what had been done to the girl, only a certain fugitive anger that it had not been properly contracted and paid for. Her horror was reserved for the remainder of the scene.

Crouched beyond the fallen whore was the hunchback, Hecate, whom Mrs Murrell persisted in labelling, in her private thoughts, 'the grotesque'. Hecate's attitude was strangely confused, for she seemed to be reaching back with her hands as though to release poor Sophie and comfort her – as she had done in the course of the play – but she was not looking at her groping hands. Her eyes were fixed on the last member of the tableau: a man, not young, fully and expensively dressed, who had in his hand a thin birch rod some four or five feet long. He was bolt upright and absolutely rigid . . . and he was hovering in midair, with the soles of his polished shoes at least eight inches above the faded carpet.

Very slowly, his body was rotating; but his head was not.

His frozen features remained where they were, the sick stare of his unbelieving eyes fixed on the face of the deformed girl as though no power on Earth could be sufficient to tear them away.

His body continued to turn, very slowly. Neither Mrs Murrell nor David could believe that the turn would be interrupted; they both expected that the process would continue until the man choked to death, or until the head and body were torn apart by the torsion.

Mrs Murrell, although she did not like to be touched by men, made not the slightest attempt to throw off the hand which gripped her. She was content to accept imprisonment, so that she need not take another step into the room.

In the hand of the suspended man the birch rod came uncannily to life, twisting like a snake.

It seemed that the living rod drew up the hand which held it, until it came to lie over his heart. Then the rod slid smoothly around the twisted, tortured neck like a noose, and began to draw tight.

What agony the man was in with two separate forces tugging at his throat, David could not imagine. The expression on the man's face could not change to reflect it; only the eyes showed the strain, bulging out as though they were under a terrible internal pressure.

Cry out! David urged his unheeding host. *Stop her, for the love of God!*

Mrs Murrell did not cry out, nor even think of crying out. She watched as though mesmerised; as though she did not want to stop what was happening, even though she knew well enough that she would be in dire trouble if any murder, ordinary or extraordinary, were to be committed under her roof.

The body beneath the imprisoned head continued to turn, having rotated now through a hundred and eighty degrees. The sinuous birch rod continued to draw its choking clutch ever tighter.

David knew that the man must now be dead, because there was no way that mortal flesh could sustain that dual assault, but the hugely bulging eyes continued to stare in apparent fascination, and the remainder of the victim's features might as well have been carved out of stone.

Time passed, and there was nothing to do but wait. All thought was so completely suspended by the horror of the moment that David could not even wonder what was happening, or how, or why. He could only watch the garrotte of living wood tighten and tighten, while the body continued to rotate, until – after what seemed an impossibly long time – the head and body parted company.

The man's neck had been sheared clean through.

The head remained where it was, but the body fell. The great gush of blood which David and Mrs Murrell both anticipated never came; the man's heart had been stopped for some time, and there was no pressure at all in the arteries. The huge open wound, where the head had been severed, leaked very sluggishly upon the carpet, staining Sophie's naked thigh as she tried to scramble away.

The head remained exactly where it was, defying gravity and all other kinds of change. The birch rod had torn itself free from the dead man's hand as the body fell, and it clung to the head like a serpent, slowly moving its coils up and around in search of firmer purchase.

Mrs Murrell still would not have moved had not Sophie thrust herself to where she stood, groping with her captive hands at the hem of the bawd's skirt. That pressure served to remind her that she could still act, and she used her free arm to help the injured whore to her feet and draw her out into the corridor. Sophie must have been profoundly glad to get out, and Mrs Murrell had a sudden impulse to follow her, but the hand which had restrained her before now held her where she was. Someone else ran along the corridor to receive the staggering Sophie, but Mrs Murell did not turn to see which of her girls it was: her eyes were still fixed on the suspended head and the serpentine rod which caressed it.

Then, although the head remained exactly where it was, Hecate looked around.

Mrs Murrell's grotesque looked her mistress straight in the eye, and David felt a scream rising in the old woman's breast as she was stabbed by a mortal fear of what that gaze might do to her. The scream was suppressed by a constriction in her throat, but David did not believe that the suppression was anything but a reflex action. Hecate's stare was not hostile at all, but somehow amused and coquettish, as though the witch girl were inviting approval in a half-mocking fashion.

Hecate's face was cruelly misshapen; the eyes were set too wide and the nose between them was too flat; the mouth was sharklike, thin-lipped and downwardly curved at each end. In spite of that, though, it did not seem particularly ugly. It was quite symmetrical, and it seemed to David almost as though it were a perfectly normal – perhaps even beautiful – face seen in a convex mirror, and thus misfortunately distorted.

The eyes, because they were so far apart, seemed to have difficulty focusing on Mrs Murrell's face; indeed, they seemed not to be focusing on Mrs Murrell's face at all, but on some imaginary point within and beyond her. Hecate seemed to be looking through her mistress rather than at her, and David was inevitably seized by the paradoxical idea that she was looking at *him*.

As soon as the idea had taken hold of him, he realised that it might be less than absurd. Hecate, to judge by what he had just seen and was still seeing, was almost certainly a creature of the same kind as the Sphinx and Gabriel Gill. It was another that had sent him here to witness this, but Hecate might well be aware of his presence.

Although he had no eyes to use but those of Mrs Murrell, which he could not in any way control, David looked back at the grotesque, certain that she was an Other if not an angel, and equally certain that whatever mysterious troubling of the waters of reality had caught him up in its restless tide, she was at the very heart of it.

This is what Bast fears, he thought. *This moment of awakening – for the witch girl is certainly awake now, and all too well aware of her power – is what has tipped the balance in the affairs of the angels. Whatever it is that I must do, it is a response to this revelation. Sterling is part of it, too, and the man in grey . . . but the Sphinx is destroyed, and whatever advantage Bast may have had after her first encounter with the Spider is lost . . .*

As if she had heard the thoughts buzzing inside his head, the witch girl drew back her lips in a ghastly parody of a smile. It seemed to David that it was she, and not Bast, who threw him contemptuously back into the infinite void.

9

Davd awoke to a strange sense of infinite peace. The air in the bedroom was thick and cloying, and the dimensions of the room were somehow odd. It was as though the ceiling were too high and the walls too remote. The tiny flame of the nightlight beside his bed was uncannily steady, not flickering at all.

Mandorla Soulier sat in the armchair by the bed; Cordelia was not in the room.

David moved in order to bring himself to a half-sitting position, unthinkingly using his right arm for leverage. When he looked down at the arm, which was naked, he could see not the slightest indication of any injury.

He looked Mandorla in the eyes, and said: 'Is this, too, a dream?'

'No,' she replied. 'This is real.'

But it did not feel real. The air was too heavy and too still, and the room quite unfamiliar, although everything was in its proper place: the wardrobe with its oval mirror, the washstand, the chest of drawers, the chair, the other mirror on the wall. The mirrors caught the light of the little candle, and bathed in its gentle glory.

'Where is my wife?' he demanded, feeling hurt that she had gone away and left Mandorla alone with him. There was no sign of the gun which Cordelia had earlier pressed into his hand because she did not trust the wolfwoman.

'She stayed with you for nearly twelve hours while the fever raged,' Mandorla said. 'The doctor was with you, too. It was not Franklin or Austen, but a younger man. He was ready at one point to pronounce you beyond help, but the crisis did pass, in the end. When it had, the doctor decided to change the dressing on your arm. When he removed the bandages, all trace of the wound had gone. Whatever moved within you was powerful, David, but it is quiescent now.'

'Cordelia allowed you to stay?' he said, sceptically.

'She needed sleep. She is convinced, I think, that I mean you no harm.'

'You've been here all the time?'

'I have. I helped to bathe your brow and to make you take water. I can go without sleep for long periods, if the need arises. I can sleep for long periods, too, when the need is gone.'

She spoke softly, the flow of the syllables curiously cadenced. Her violet eyes caught the feeble radiance of the nightlight in a remarkable fashion, so that they seemed almost luminous. Her gaze was not threatening at all, but had in it some glamour – which might indeed have a hint of magic in it – which radiated innocence and kind affection.

Perhaps, he thought, she was only trying to put him at ease, but he did not believe it. It appeared to him that she had the mind to take a greater advantage than that.

'I think I know what's happening,' he said, after running his tongue around the inside of his mouth so that he would not sound hoarse.

She leaned forward, her gaze becoming even more intense, but no less soft. 'Tell me,' she said.

He had to take a deep breath, because the heavy air seemed reluctant to enter his lungs; but when he had drawn a full measure, the space within the room seemed to grow vaster still, and his unease multiplied.

'There's a girl named Hecate,' he said, 'in Mercy Murrell's house. She is deformed by a twisted spine. I think she's the kind of creature that Gabriel Gill was, made by the Spider. I don't know whether the Spider made her from its own substance as its rival made the Sphinx, or whether it stole her soulfire as it stole Gabriel's, but it has taken care to provide her with an education very different from that which Gabriel received. Now, like Gabriel before her, she's coming into her inheritance of power, but I think she is far better prepared to use it in the manner that the Spider desires.

'I think that the Spider has tried to destroy the Sphinx, and may have succeeded, though de Lancy was allowed to escape and driven to seek sanctuary with Sir Edward in Paris. Sterling has the Clay Man, and has awakened him, but I think he too – though he does not know it – draws on power which the Spider has granted him, for its own reasons. If all that I saw is real, then whatever web the Spider is spinning is already well advanced, but I can't tell what part I'm supposed to play, unless I'm merely the eye through which Bast is examining her predicament.'

He looked again at his uninjured arm, which had no pain in it at all. Then he looked back at Mandorla, suddenly uncertain of all his conjectures, imploring her for aid.

'Perris is watching Sterling's house,' she said softly. 'After what happened to Suarra I am anxious for him, but if nothing prevents him he will do what he can to discover what Sterling is doing. As for the Sphinx, her kind is not easy to destroy and I dare say that she will be safe enough. Still, the fact that she was attacked at all suggests that the Spider is very confident of its own strength. What did you see this Hecate do, which told you what she is?'

'If it wasn't a dream,' he replied, with a faint shudder, 'she killed a man, holding him in midair and twisting his body away from his head as though . . . as though she were a glutton tearing apart a crayfish. But it may have been a dream.'

'Do you think so?' asked Mandorla.

He shook his head. 'No,' he admitted. 'When I saw through other human eyes before, what I saw was real. This was the same. I saw what others saw, and it's difficult to doubt that I saw it. I could more easily believe that *this* is a dream, for my own senses seem distorted and my own room seems direly strange to me.'

'This is real,' said Mandorla. 'Even if it were a dream, which you and I were allowed to share, it would be real enough. Never doubt that. All this is real, however strange it may come to seem. Whatever you see, David, *believe it!*'

He could not tell why she was so insistent about it; but the light was wrong, and the air was wrong, and space itself had been wrenched out of true.

If the world should take on the form and substance of a dream, he quoted to himself, *still we must live in it as best we can. That is what these fallen angels can do; that is the very essence of what they are. Their dreams have the power to remake the appearances of the world.*

How could his arm have healed, though? Whose healing magic had accomplished it, and why? Was something trying to cancel out his power of vision by cancelling out his pain?

'What is the Spider trying to do, Mandorla?' he asked. 'What plan has it formed while it has studied the world that now exists? What has it learned?'

She reached forward to touch his forehead with her slender fingers, as though testing for renewed signs of fever. Her fingertips stroked him very gently, and he knew that she was quite conscious of the effect her tenderness might have. She was playing with him, as she had always played with the feelings of men, casually assuming that what he knew of her true nature would not interfere at all with his response to her beauty, her voice and her seductive gestures. He swayed away from her hand, uncomfortably, but she only smiled.

'You have nothing to fear from me, David,' she told him, as though by frequent repetition she could make him believe it. 'I will make a better ally than anyone while this mystery deepens around you – better than Pelorus, even if he were here, and better by far than than your loyal Cordelia.'

He could not imagine that she seriously intended to seduce him in his own house, nor did his suspicion that this might not really be happening encourage him to modify his own behaviour. Again he tried to move away, and he put up his right hand to grip hers and hold it back.

The contact of his fingers upon her flesh was electric. The pain which had been so mysteriously banished from the arm, along with the injury which the wolf's teeth had caused, now flowed back into the flesh like a consuming fire, and the skin along his forearm erupted as though it were being crushed all over again by invisible jaws. He felt the bone crack and the broken halves grind together, and his hand convulsed about Mandorla's wrist like a vice.

Within his grip, her wrist began to change, shrivelling in size and changing dramatically in texture as coarse hair sprouted from the smooth skin.

Mandorla was dressed conventionally, petticoated and corseted beneath her black shift. Her mode of dress had seemed reassuring to David before because he could not imagine how she could extricate herself from her entanglements were she to change, but he realised now that he had been quite wrong to foresee difficulties on her behalf. She must have experienced such changes before, and while her flesh flowed and her form was indeterminate she somehow contrived to wriggle free of the greater part of her encumbrance. She might have won entirely free had he not retained for a few seconds more his grip upon her forelimb, preventing her from shuffling off that sleeve.

Then the pain which had sealed his grip weakened it again, and he found that he could not hold her as she wrenched away from him, falling backwards on to the floor, writhing free of the clothing as she found her true form. While he sagged back on to the bed, the blood from his right arm drenching the eiderdown, she bounded up on to the bed to stand over him. She was unnaturally huge and pale, but her violet eyes were still shining brightly, seeming now to be full of baleful menace.

He tried, impotently, to raise his arms against her, but there was no strength in him. The heavy air, which was becoming more glutinous with every second that passed, clogged his lungs and choked him. With her forepaws straddling his recumbent form, she brought her great pale head slowly forward. Her jaws gaped slightly to show the shape of her pink tongue. He could feel her hot breath upon his face.

He knew that while she was in wolf form she retained only the most rudimentary echo of her human intelligence, but he had no idea whether the instinct which drove her now could be held in check by the vestiges of her conscious motives and purposes. Were she to tear his throat out, he knew, it might be only because she could not help herself.

But she did not attack. Uncertainty possessed her. She swished her long tail madly, and she cowered back as though from some invisible threat emerging from the wall behind the bed.

As it had been before, the room was suddenly flooded with light. The light came not from the curtained windows but from the huge oval mirror on the wardrobe doors and the mirror on the wall beside the washstand. The sluggish air into which these rivers of light poured was set alight by them, glittering and gleaming of its own accord. The tiny nightlight beside the bed flared up like an exploding star.

The light flowed over the bedclothes and over David's ravaged skin, moving like quicksilver. It bathed his eyes and all but blinded him, but he felt Mandorla move, turning upon the bed to face the wardrobe. Then he heard her cry out. She made a curious mewling sound, more like a cat than a dog. The pathetic sound was full of bewilderment and fear.

This is not her doing, David thought. *She is being taken, as Pelorus was. She is to be held prisoner, so that she may not even try to interfere.*

David raised his broken, bleeding, pain-racked arm, with the fingers splayed, as though he might instruct the light to be still, to be calm, to submit to control.

And the light yielded.

As he extended the gesture of command, the intensity of the mood abated and he found that he could see through the glare again. The light *fell* from the liquid air, settling into a swirling lake of luminance, which filled the room to the level of the bed and extended through the wardrobe's mirrors into some fabulous land beyond, where he could see its distant shores.

Although the light within the room remained pure, the light in the mirror world dissolved into a mere sheen, reflected from water whose waves lapped gently at a sandy beach. Beyond the beach David could see trees with twisted boles and vividly luxuriant foliage. Among the branches of the trees, tiny shapes moved, but he could not see what manner of creatures they were.

Mandorla too was looking into that looking-glass world. She was perched at the foot of the bed, with one paw raised as though to keep the unearthly light at bay.

For a few moments they both remained quite still, frozen by amazement. Then Mandorla dropped her paw and gathered herself for a leap. David felt the pressure of her hind feet on the blankets, near his own feet, and then he felt the force of her projection as she launched herself forward in a mighty bound. Her leap took her clean through the oval mirror, as though it were an unglazed window.

He saw her land in the shallows, sending up a silver spray as she scrambled on to the sand. Without a backward glance, she hurled herself into the trees and was gone.

There was a split second when he wondered whether he ought to follow her, but then his brave attempt to command the tides of light was frustrated by the weakness of his ravaged arm. He could not hold it up any longer, and his hand fell. As it fell, it brought darkness to the room. Night fell upon the other world beyond the magic mirrors, and it was hidden from his view.

He had no sensation of awakening from sleep; the transition was instantaneous. Suddenly, there was only the flickering flame of the nightlight to disturb the darkness, and he saw that the person sitting in the chair, keeping watch over him, was neither Mandorla nor Cordelia, but his darling Nell.

She seemed very tired, and her expression was uncommonly grave. He was seized by a sudden rush of love which welled up inside him and nearly overflowed in tears.

He spoke her name and tried to smile, but his attention was caught and held by the bandages which swathed his injured arm.

'Mama said that I might take my turn here,' said Nell, choosing her words carefully, attempting the inflexion of an adult. 'I told her that I could.'

Were those, he wondered, the same words that she had spoken before? He could not remember, and did not know whether this was happening for the second time or the first, or whether it was all part of the same interminable dream.

'What day is it?' he whispered.

'Monday,' she told him. 'You slept a long time. You were very ill, Mama said. You moved about in your sleep. The doctor said that you were dreaming, and that your dreams were bad.'

Monday! He could not believe it.

'Did I do this yesterday?' he asked, hoarsely, meaning the wounds on his arms.

Nell nodded. 'You slept a long time,' she said again, obviously mistaking the reason for his surprise. 'You had bad dreams. Why do we have bad dreams, Daddy?'

It was not a dream! he told himself, urgently. *It is the world that is perverse, and not your mind. It was all real, and not to be doubted!*

That was futile; he could not but doubt. He could not but ask himself, sceptically, what evidence he had that any of this was aught but a figment of his delirious imagination, except perhaps for the wolf which had bitten him. The wolf, at least, had surely been real, unless his memory of receiving the injury to his arm was false as well.

'The wolf died,' said Nell. She had said the same before; he was certain of it. 'Mama put it in a trunk, and locked the lid. It had no head.'

And what headless thing did Mrs Murrell hide in her trunk last night? David wondered. *It must have been last night that the murder happened – and the Clay Man's awakening too, and de Lancy's flight through the rainswept streets of Paris. It was all last night. I have had to play tricks with time to see it all, but it is easy enough to play such tricks when one dreams.*

'Has Grandpa returned yet?' he asked, knowing that she would say no. He listened, instead, for the doorbell, but there was no sound. There was no sound at all.

'I had a dream last night,' said Nell reflectively. 'I dreamed that I was a wolf: a baby wolf. Simon was a wolf cub too, and Teddy was there. It was dark and warm, and there were other wolves who looked after us. It was very peaceful. We ate little men with eyes like frogs. We ate them raw but they were warm, and the blood in them tasted wonderful. It was all so warm, and I didn't know who I was, not until I woke up and found that I wasn't a wolf at all. Why do we dream, Daddy?'

He realised, belatedly, that she had asked a similar question before, and that he had ignored it. He was tempted to ignore it again, because he had no answer to give her, but he did not like to do that. A child's curiosity was a precious thing and should not go unanswered, even when there were no answers to give.

'Nobody knows,' he said. 'People have searched their dreams for hidden meanings ever since men first began to think, but we simply don't know.'

It is a lie of sorts, he thought, *and she deserves better from a loving father. But how can I tell her that our dreams are things which can be captured and possessed by uncaring angels? How can I tell her that they are, or may become, a sixth sense, and that they only produce random illusions, until the hateful angels decree otherwise? May merciful chance protect her from that!*

If that were not troubling enough, he had also to wonder whether her dream of being a wolf were really a random illusion, or whether her dreams had been made captive and her inner eye forced to open. He wished that Tallentyre would arrive; now that Mandorla was gone, he felt dreadfully alone.

'I'll fetch Mama,' said Nell, slipping demurely from the seat and walking to the door. David looked at the mirror in the wardrobe door, and saw the reflection of the foot of the bed and the wall. The air was stale and slightly warm, but not heavy. The flame of the nightlight flickered in the updraught.

I am not mad, said David to himself, as firmly as he could. He remembered, though, that the Sphinx had once told Sir Edward that the angels lived in time like common men, and could not easily pervert it to their pleasure. If time were bending now, the contortion could not be cheaply bought – unless he were dreaming still!

Perhaps it is the Spider that is playing with me, he thought. *Perhaps I am trapped in its web and tightly trussed, and it has shot its poison into my body to dissolve my soul and make it fit to drink.*

Then Cordelia came in, full of solicitude, armed only with a mug of water. He was so glad to see her that his anxiety began to abate. He knew when he looked at her that he was not alone, and never would be. But her face was wan and worn by lack of sleep, and she was deeply concerned for him. For the first time, he wondered whether he might die if his illness could not be contained.

'Has Mandorla Soulier been here?' he asked, uncertainly.

'No,' his wife replied. 'We've had no callers since the fever began. I wouldn't have admitted her if she *had* called.'

David felt that he ought to be more surprised by this news than he was. He felt that he was almost beyond the reach of surprise. It seemed to him that the gods were taunting him, teasing him with their ability to alter the past as well as the future. Perhaps they were trying to persuade him that nothing was beyond their power, and that he could never be equal to the task of understanding them.

But he had not given up. If this was not simply a further stage in his dream – if he really had been returned to time and the material world – then the time had come to act.

'You must send a message for me,' he told Cordelia, when she had pressed the mug to his lips and taken it away again. 'There's a man named Jason Sterling, who has a house at Richmond. Your father has mentioned him to me – he's published papers on evolution. I don't know his address, but he has a certain notoriety, and I don't think it'll be difficult to find him by enquiry. Write a letter begging him to come here as soon as humanly possible; tell him that it's a matter of the utmost urgency. Send John to carry it, and make him understand that the note must be delivered as quickly as he can. Give him money for the train, and thirty shillings for himself.'

Cordelia was understandably perplexed. He tried with all his might to impress upon her the seriousness of his request, knowing that he could trust her if only she could be made to understand his urgency.

'Please,' he said, intensely. 'I will explain, I promise you, when I can. But it must be done *now*. Whatever is happening, time is of the essence. I'm sure of nothing else, but I am sure of that. The war of the angels has already begun, and any truce which they declare is likely to be brief.'

10

David insisted on getting up, although Cordelia tried hard to persuade him to keep to his bed. He knew that what had happened to him during the curiously extrapolated night had nothing to do with the bed or the room, and that leaving it would in no way lessen the probability of further distortion of his sensibilities, but still he felt that he would be in better control of himself if he dressed and came downstairs. It was a way of asserting that he was not content to remain passive, that he could and would comport himself as though he were a player and not a mere piece in the convoluted game which had been joined.

Cordelia, eventually seeing how determined he was, helped him to put on his shirt. He could not fasten it properly at the cuff, but it was neat enough. He contrived to don a jacket, although he had to be content to leave the right sleeve empty, so that he could support his bandaged arm in a sling.

John, his manservant, returned at three o'clock, having successfully concluded his eccentric mission. Sterling was not with him but had promised to come within the hour. David was pleased with the boy; resourceful servants were harder to find with every year that passed, because their resourcefulness usually discovered more promising ways of employment. John could read and write, and would not long remain in service once he attained his majority.

When Sterling arrived, David was not in the least surprised to find him exactly as he had seen him through Luke Capthorn's eyes: dark, handsome and bold. He had the air of one whose guesses and hazards had run so consistently to his advantage that he believed himself inspired. It was easy to see that the bubble of his confidence would not readily be pricked, and David was by no means certain what he should say to the man.

David received Sterling in the library. He did not attempt to send Cordelia away, knowing that she was very curious to hear whatever might pass between them.

'Thank you for coming,' said David. 'My request must have seemed very unusual.'

'That was one good reason for accepting it,' said Sterling politely.

'You've heard of me, I suppose?' David found himself forced to sit awkwardly, unable to assume the same calm posture as his guest. His arm was giving him a good deal of pain, but he did not fear to be swept into some new vision. He suspected that this meeting would be of sufficient interest to the angel which had him in its grip to be allowed to proceed uninterrupted.

'I know your work,' Sterling agreed. He added, with a brief nod in Cordelia's direction: 'And your father's work, of course, Mrs Lydyard.'

'You know more about us than that,' said David levelly. 'I dare say that Luke Capthorn has said more to raise your curiosity about the purpose of my summons than you've found in my published papers.'

'He knows very little about you,' Sterling replied off-handedly. He glanced again at Cordelia, but this time more furtively. He knew, obviously, what dealings his servant had once had with her.

'But he knew where to find the body of Adam Clay,' David retorted, intent on coming swiftly to the point. 'And he knew enough to persuade you that there was something to be gained by raising him from his grave.'

Sterling met David's gaze quite openly. 'You speak as though I had done something wrong,' he said. 'In fact, I've done something which anyone would be bound to do, were he persuaded of the possibility that a man consigned to the ground was not dead at all. The Society for the Prevention of Premature Burials would proclaim me a hero, I have no doubt. The man I took from the grave in Austen's grounds is alive; what kind of man would I have been, had I let him remain where he was?'

David could read the veiled accusation which lurked within the casual defence, but he did not want to explain himself yet.

'You have read *The True History of the World*, I suppose?' he said.

'I have,' said Sterling. 'As you have also, I presume.'

'Actually, no,' said David. 'Despite Sir Edward's best efforts, we've never succeeded in finding a copy, and had begun to suspect that none still existed. But I have a friend who knows the text thoroughly. Do you believe the story which the book tells?'

'If your friend knows the text as thoroughly as he claims,' Sterling replied, 'he must have told you that the title is ironic. One of the arguments of the book is that no *true* history of the world can ever be inferred, remembered or divined. It tells us that the world's course through time is like a traveller's tale, its former stages being constantly reconstructed and embellished by the imagination which works upon our memories. The text claims that the world in which we live is mere appearance, and what each of us thinks he knows about the past – whether one is an historian and archaeologist studying artefacts or an immortal consulting one's memories – is merely part of a pattern of shadows cast by those appearances.'

'I didn't think that he put it quite so strongly,' David said. 'I believe he argued that although memory is fallible, it is preferable to inference, and that the history he knew by his experience was closer to the truth than the history deduced by men of science from the record of the rocks.'

'True enough,' Sterling conceded. 'No doubt your friend agrees, if you're speaking of the werewolf Pelorus. But I fear that he has mistaken the true logic of the argument, as the author himself may have done. I doubt that you, Dr Lydyard, would have made such a mistake, had you ever had the text itself to study. Sir Edward Tallentyre, I'm certain, would agree with me, even though he has modified his opinions to admit a far greater measure of uncertainty into the scientific image of the past. The book is a fantasy, though its author believes sincerely that what he remembers is very near to the truth.

'I'll let you see the book, if you wish – and Adam Clay too, of course. I have nothing to hide, Dr Lydyard, nothing at all. Perhaps you've heard rumours of my reputation as a monster-maker, but I dare say the ignorant regard your own work in the catacombs beneath the hospital with superstitious unease. I'm a man of science, like yourself – and if you summoned me here to berate me as a necromancer, I fear that you've made an error of judgement. I'm prepared to consider myself, in metaphorical terms, as an alchemist, but the alchemy which interests me is the alchemy of the flesh. It is not gold that I obtain by my transmutations but new species. Your father-in-law thinks that my ideas are unorthodox, but I can assure you that I'm as good a Darwinian as he is.'

'I didn't bring you here to accuse you of anything,' said David. 'I asked you to come here in order to warn you that you may be in danger.'

'From whom?' asked Sterling, raising a sceptical eyebrow.

'I've been told,' said David carefully, 'that your house is under observation by the werewolves of London.'

The dark man did not contradict him, but neither did he seem alarmed by the allegation. He simply said: 'Go on.'

'Normally,' said David, 'I don't think that they would harm you, in spite of what they are; but circumstances are no longer normal. Something has taken control of the werewolves and is using them to carry forward a scheme whose purpose I can't fathom.' While he spoke he moved his injured arm so as to catch Sterling's attention.

'Was it one of the werewolves that wounded you?' asked the scientist.

'It was,' David told him. 'But I have every reason to think that it was sent by one of the beings which Lucian de Terre calls Creators. They may not be what he thinks they are, and I doubt that they are what the Order of St Amycus thinks they are, but they exist, and it doesn't matter whether we call them Creators or gods or fallen angels. They have the power to disturb and destroy the world, and men in whom they become interested may find their interest difficult to bear.'

'I can see that you have difficulties of your own,' said Sterling lightly. 'I've read your work, and have found it all the more interesting in the context of what is written in the *True History*, but I'm not sure that I'm yet ready to believe in the visionary inspiration of pain. Nor am I ready to accept that pain-induced visions can put men in touch with fallen angels, in spite of Luke's account of the adventures of his former master.'

David knew that Cordelia's eyes were on him as well as Sterling's, and felt uncomfortable because of it. He felt that he was at a greater disadvantage in this debate than he had anticipated.

'Last night,' he said, 'I watched you take the lid from Adam Clay's coffin. I watched you while you put the mirror to his lips to catch his breath. I watched you draw off blood and place electrodes in the vessel to inhibit the clotting process. I saw the staring eyes of one of your homunculi, grown from the egg of a toad. I heard you send Luke to your cook, Mrs Tolley, for oxtail soup.'

Sterling seemed not in the least dismayed by this news. 'You might have been told as much by someone who was watching through a window,' he pointed out. 'Perhaps it was one of the werewolves who is watching my house.'

David had no way to persuade him otherwise. 'The evening papers will be published soon,' he said. 'They'll carry news of a murder committed in the early hours of the morning, too late to be reported by the morning dailies. I saw that, too, in my dreams. I don't ask you to take everything I say on trust, but I must implore you to humour me, if you think me a madman. Will you hear me out?'

'Of course,' said Sterling, still very courteous but seemingly not yet convinced that there was anything in what David was saying to him which he desperately needed to know.

'What did Luke Capthorn tell you about Jacob Harkender?'

Sterling did not seem offended by the abruptness of the question, but he countered it with a question of his own. 'What should he have told me?'

'However unlikely it may seem,' David said, 'Harkender really did school himself to the acquisition of unusual powers. He went searching for supernatural beings, and found one, or was found by it. He entered into an uneasy alliance with that being, which had lain dormant for a long time, and tried hard – but in the end unsuccessfully – to persuade it to exercise its power to intervene in the world of men.'

'Yes,' said Sterling. 'Luke has told me all that, and more.'

'But you don't believe it.'

'I believe that he believes it. I suppose that his interpretation of events might be reckoned as good as another, if all histories are similarly false. I have not yet encountered any such being, and can't form any sensible estimate of what such a being might be. You say that you have.'

'I have,' said David. 'I've encountered the one with which Harkender associated himself, and one other. If you wish to argue that their appearances are likely to have been deceptive, I will certainly not dispute the fact. Sir Edward and I have fallen into the habit of calling the being which Harkender found the Spider, and I see the other in my dreams as the Egyptian goddess Bast, but the fact that they ever presented such appearances has more to do with our crude attempts to see and understand them then any innate identity of their own. I think you also may have encountered one of these beings without quite realising it. I think it may have been involved in guiding your work for some time, and I feel sure in my own mind that it helped you to escape with the Clay Man's body when Austen tried to fire his shotgun at you.'

For the first time, Sterling paused for a moment before replying. Then he said: 'You disappoint me, Dr Lydyard. I'm used to the blind and stupid men who jump to the conclusion that I must have sold my soul to the Devil in order to have achieved the kind of mutations which I have produced in my laboratory, but I hadn't thought that a man like you would agree with them, when you haven't seen what I've done or heard my account of it.'

'I haven't accused you of making bargains with the Devil,' David said, with mild impatience. 'I only say that this being

– *I* don't call it a demon or fallen angel, though the priests of St Amycus would, and Luke Capthorn believes it to be Satan himself – is interested in your work, and that the fact of its interest may place you in danger. It may feel protective towards you, but the protection of beings such as these is sometimes as much to be feared as their enmity. Do you know a woman named Mercy Murrell?'

Sterling glanced reflexively at Cordelia, whose eyes were now on him again and not on her husband. Clearly, he had heard the name. It would have been surprising if he had not.

'I've never been to her house,' he said, perhaps more guardedly than his tone confessed.

'Nor have I, in the flesh,' said David. 'But I have twice been given a sight of events taking place there, just as I've been given a sight of events in your own laboratory. I'm a more practised visionary now than I once was, and I know that the gift of sight is too precious to the giver to be wasted in mere voyeurism. Something connects your house with hers, and within the last twenty-four hours there has been a very strange murder committed there. Mrs Murrell is harbouring a powerful magician, who is only now discovering what she is and what she can do. I've encountered something similar before, and so has Luke Capthorn, but neither the Spider nor Jacob Harkender knew quite what to do with Gabriel Gill. This time, I think, the Spider will not be unprepared.'

Sterling looked at David wonderingly, but without disdain. He accepted, it seemed, that David really was trying to help him.

'What would you advise me to do, Dr Lydyard?' he asked. 'Indeed, what could any man do, if he were solemnly assured that what the Church mistakes for a fallen angel has involved him in its schemes? David slew Goliath, I know, but if your testimony is to be trusted, this is a giant of a very different order. How would you have me protect myself, given that mere humans have no magic with which to fight such beings?'

'We can't fight them with magic,' David admitted. 'We have no resources to bring to that battleground. But their powers of reasoning are no greater than ours, for all their ability to usurp the sight of our eyes. They have fears and anxieties of their own, and what they fear most is their own ignorance and the possibility of being drawn into fatal error. Nor will they seek to hurt us simply for the pleasure of doing so; when they seek to use us, it's because we are of some use, and if they have better reasons to preserve us than to destroy us, they will certainly try to do it. But they're in conflict with one another, and the instrument of one may easily become the target of a second, so there's always danger in being involved with them. Believe me or not, as you wish, but please remember what I've told you. I don't understand why, but these beings need us, and the ways in which they use us are apt to hurt us.'

Sterling looked again at David's injured arm. 'I haven't been hurt yet, Dr Lydyard. If I've been used, I haven't been used as you have, and I remain uncertain how the *True History* should properly be read. I deny nothing of what you've told me, mind, and I thank you for your trouble, but you will understand that my sending Luke to fetch oxtail soup is not so dark a secret that it couldn't have been divined by entirely orthodox means. If your warnings have forearmed me in any way at all for what may happen today or tomorrow, I'll be duly grateful, but I see nothing yet but a sea of confusion in which my work remains the star by which I must steer my course.'

As he finished speaking he looked from David to Cordelia, including both of them in his apology.

'You're very like my father,' said Cordelia, drily. David saw that Sterling accepted it as a compliment and did not care about the irony which she had injected into it.

'May I ask what the direction of your work is?' said David, changing tack again.

Sterling favoured him with a brief but unenthusiastic smile. 'Old wine in a new bottle,' he said. 'As I've said, I am an alchemist. I seek the elixir of life. But my methods are rather different from the alchemists of old. I'm following in the footsteps of Andrew Crosse in searching for the key to the creation of new life forms. I'm trying to harness the process of mutation, which is the source of the variations upon which natural selection works. Tallentyre accuses me of the heresy of vitalism, but he is only half right; the fact remains that Darwinism can't be true unless there's a source of variations, and it is to that source rather than the business of selection that we must look for the real motor of evolution. If that force can be amplified and controlled, we might sidestep the untidy processes of selection altogether and become masters of our own flesh. That's what I aim to do. The fact that there are shape-shifters and immortals already in the world proves that it can be done, if only we can find the way.'

'That's why you exhumed the Clay Man,' said David. 'You want to find the secret of his immortality: the difference between his flesh and ours.'

'You've had your own chance to do likewise,' Sterling pointed out, 'if you have friends among the legendary werewolves.'

'I believe that the method of maintaining the liquidity of the blood which I've seen you use was first devised by Crosse,' said David. 'I suppose it's not surprising that you should find him an inspiration for your exercises in the creation of life.'

'I don't *create* life,' said Sterling pedantically, 'I merely remake it. That's what Crosse did, too, although he did not realise it. The microscopes of his day were inadequate to make it clear to him how elusive the seeds of life are. I'm sure that his equipment wasn't sterile; that's why others trying to repeat his work had little success. What he achieved was not spontaneous generation but unusual evolution. I've done the same, and I remain adamant that I haven't needed any aid or inspiration from your mythical angels and monstrous spiders. I wish you'd come to Richmond to see for yourself what I've done, and to see Adam Clay, if you desire to reassure yourself that I've done him no harm. Your friend Pelorus would be more than welcome to come with you, and Sir Edward, too.'

'Pelorus has disappeared,' said David flatly. 'And Sir Edward has not yet returned from Paris. I have no information from any source which suggests that he will be prevented from so doing, but I confess to a certain anxiety in the matter. I will be pleased to accept your invitation if I can, however, and will bring Sir Edward if circumstances permit.'

Sterling nodded. 'Have you anything else to say to me at present?' he asked, implying with his tone that he would be glad if David did not.

David was tired and tense, and saw no point in prolonging the interview. He had learned what he wanted to learn, and had said what he felt obliged to say. 'Thank you again for coming,' he said. 'I fear that you may be correct in your judgement of the uselessness of my warnings, but still I felt obliged to offer them. If anything untoward should happen, you are forewarned. Will you forgive me if I don't stand up to see you out?'

'Certainly,' said Sterling, as he rose himself. He turned to Cordelia, who had risen with him and now went to the door in order to show him out. David remained where he was, deep in thought, until she returned.

The first question she asked was: 'Why do you think that something has happened to Father?'

'Because,' he said, without any comforting circumlocution, 'something has happened to all of us. Don't be deceived by this little oasis of sanity in which we find ourselves for the present. We're already entrapped, and I'm in a maze whose walls may shift at any moment.'

'What has Sterling to do with it?' she asked.

He shrugged his shoulders slightly. 'If my guess is right,' he said, 'Sterling has been set the task which the maker of the Clay Man and the werewolves once set himself: the task of examining the nature of man, to illuminate the mysteries of his creation. I think he may have come very close to success, and I think that what he has found out has some bearing on the fate and fortunes of the angels. It may be that there is something in his understanding of the world which is more valuable than anything I, or your father, or Jacob Harkender, ever discovered. At any rate, the approaching climax in the affairs of the angels is somehow focused on him, as it is on Mercy Murrell's witch girl.'

As he finished speaking, he heard the doorbell ring. Instantly, he leaped to the conclusion that it was Mandorla, and that the folds of time were once again closing around him.

'If that is Mandorla, admit her,' he said. 'It'll do no good to try to keep her out with mere refusals.'

Cordelia looked at him very strangely, but did not ask him what he meant. She went to the library door to look out into the hallway, keeping watch while the maid answered the door. She turned back quickly to say: 'It's a man, not a woman.'

David furrowed his brow, but quickly decided that he had no right to be surprised by anything. He waited, forming no hypotheses, until the visitor appeared beside Cordelia in the doorway. In spite of his resolve, he started in astonishment when he saw who it was.

It was the man in grey who had been in Mercy Murrell's brothel and witnessed Hecate's two performances. His face was as pale as ever, and he moved as though he were perpetually in pain. There was something familiar about him, and David almost managed to put a name to him, but then he realised that what he found familiar might only be the other's attitude of suffering.

Dear God! David thought. *Is that how I appear to all who see me? Is this another who is carefully abused by some inquisitive angel, as Bast has long abused me?*

'Who are you?' he asked.

'That,' said the man, in a strained voice, 'doesn't matter. I can't be sure that I'll be granted the time to explain. Lydyard, you must come with me now, else you will endanger everyone who is in this house. I dare not promise that you'll save them by leaving them behind, but it's the one chance you have. Come away!'

11

Cordelia stepped forward, ready to issue a protest, but the visitor turned his bleakly compassionate gaze upon her and said: 'You have no reason to trust me, I know, but I beg you to believe that I mean your husband no harm. He is not safe, wherever he may try to flee, and nor are you, but if he is elsewhere when they take us, the danger to you will be less. I have a carriage waiting.'

David tried to draw his wife to him to comfort her, but she would not be drawn. She was angry as well as alarmed, but the tall man met her wrathful gaze so meekly and so sorrowfully that she hesitated to give voice to her feelings. In the end, she simply repeated David's question: 'Who are you?'

'I think you know well enough *what* I am,' he replied evasively. 'I'm an instrument, like your husband. His fate and mine are linked now, whether we like it or not.'

David stared at the pale man, fascinated by his appearance. Now that he saw the other with his own eyes, by the light of day, it was easier to see what a wreck of a man he was. The flesh on his face was unnaturally white and strange in texture, almost as though it were not real flesh at all. The grey eyes were equally alien. What tortures, he wondered, had been visited upon this oracle? How courageously had he borne them? And how much had he been allowed to understand of what had been done to him and why?

'I will not let him go,' said Cordelia.

'You must,' said the man in grey. Again he spoke with such tender desperation, looking into her eyes as though he knew her and had the right to speak to her as a father or a friend.

'You must tell us your name,' said David. 'And the name of the one you serve.'

The glare which the visitor turned on David then was so venomous that it was difficult to believe his earlier protestation that he was not an enemy.

'It wouldn't matter if I served the Devil himself,' he said. 'You're obsessed with naming, as though it gave you some authority or power to speak of Spiders and Sphinxes, of Bast and Hecate. In the realm of the gods, names are but delusions, which produce false images and blind you with distractions. Man, there is no time! We are given as hostages, and if we don't deliver ourselves as easily as we can, others may be hurt. Come!'

David felt the force of this appeal, and though the speech held many implications which were disturbing in the extreme, his impulse was to obey and to let the other – who seemed to know far more than he did – lead him. He struggled to his feet, and the man in grey came to help him rise. As soon as the other touched him, David felt the pain of his wounds fade. The man's touch was more gentle and more powerful than any dose of laudanum; there was magic in him.

'No!' said Cordelia; but David was quick to shake his head.

'I must go,' he told her. 'I'm sorry, but I've seen enough already to know that I'm in danger wherever I am. While I'm near you and the children, you may be in danger, too. Forgive me, but I can't stay, and whatever else befalls us you must stay with the children.'

'I would rather we were all together,' she replied, but her defiance was undermined by uncertainty.

'We must go,' said David, knowing that he must be decisive. He kissed her lightly on the cheek and did not pause to look for a coat or a hat, but hurried as fast as he could to the front door. The man in grey came with him, having somehow contrived to interpose himself between Cordelia and David, to complete the break between them.

The day was sultry, and the air outside the house was warmer and more humid than the air within its shadowed confines. Even here, on the edge of Kensington, the stink of the streets was offensive.

The carriage to which the man in grey had referred was little larger than a hansom, but it was closed in front and had a pair of horses rather than just one. David barely glanced at the coachman, who was mounted at the rear, before hauling himself up into the interior with his good hand. The seats within were darkly upholstered but clean and free of dust, with a pleasant, leathery scent which almost contrived to drown out the stench of the street.

As soon as the man in grey had closed the door, the coachman cracked his whip and the horses broke into a rapid trot. The carriage lurched as it swerved away from the pavement and dashed into a gap in the traffic. David noted that they turned south, towards the river, but he paid little attention to the route which they followed. Instead he looked at the calmly austere face of his companion.

'Now that you've achieved what you came to do,' he said acidly, 'I suppose you might consent to tell me why.'

The man in grey was slumped against the side of the carriage, as though the effort of what he had done had cost him dearly. He seemed drained of strength. 'I told you the truth,' he said. 'There is no escape for either of us, but meek surrender might save others from being taken. I owe nothing to you, nothing at all, but I will give you honest advice: *whatever is asked of you, consent*. If you resist, the being you call Bast will do what it must to compel your choice.'

'What do you know about Bast?' asked David resentfully. 'What gives you the right to advise me?'

The pale eyes looked back at him from the shadows, but for a half a minute there was no reply. Finally, the thin voice said, 'The right? I've kept watch on you for nearly twenty years. I *know* you, Lydyard. I've heard all that has passed between you and Tallentyre. I know your theories and your thoughts, your delusions, your doubts and your disappointments. I know your pride and your courage. If I know now what's happening, while you do not, it's because I've used the gifts which were offered to me far better than you've used those which were offered to you. If you want to know what lies before you, ask your questions of the Angel of Pain.'

The voice was cold and hostile, with more than a hint of a sneer in it. David did not take the trouble to challenge the other's earlier assertion that he meant no harm. There were too many other uncomfortable questions crowding into his mind. He did not doubt that the other meant what he said: that for a very long time he had spied on the discussions which the Lydyards and Edward Tallentyre had conducted, and that he had heard enough of what had passed privately between David and his wife to have heard him speak of the Angel of Pain, which had lately become far more than a metaphor.

Whose eyes had he used to do that spying?

'If your achievements are so much greater than mine,' said David carefully, 'it's no wonder that the balance of power has tipped towards the Spider, and no wonder that the Sphinx has been destroyed.'

'Is that what you think?' the pale man countered, his voice grating harshly. But he seemed to be recovering now, and the pain in David's arms had been renewed.

'I don't know what to think,' said David bitterly. 'As you've taken pains to make clear, I am but a poor fool, who has failed to earn or win the trust of his tutelary spirit, while you seem to have earned and won the trust of the Spider. You won't even deign to tell me who you are, although I could make a reasonable guess. And yet you came to fetch me from the house. You came of your own accord, because our fates are linked. I've seen you before, through Mrs Murrell's eyes.'

He thought, just for an instant, that the man in grey was startled by that news; but the other was quick to curl his lip in contrived disdain.

'So you've seen Hecate for yourself,' said the pale man. 'A pretty creature, is she not? I've studied her for some years, and Jason Sterling too. Have you seen his laboratory? I suppose, if Mercy is open to you now, Luke is too. How do you like my seers? They're a sad and sorry pair, in their fashion, but I like them very well. I haven't always had a tender heart, and I never would have thought that a soul in Hell could learn compassion . . . but I've learned better. Do one thing for me, Lydyard, I beg of you. Consent! Don't make the angels force you to do what you must do in any case.'

'You have more riddles in you than the Sphinx,' said David, unable to contain his anger. 'But if you know me as well as you claim, you'll know that my consent can't be won except by reason. Tell me what it is that I must agree to, and tell me why. Otherwise . . .'

The man in grey sat upright, having regained some of his strength. His coat hung upon his spare frame as though he had too little flesh to clothe his bones.

'There can be no more compromises now,' he whispered. 'There's no more time for unruly oracles. The angel which made you her prize in Egypt needs your best efforts now. Nothing short of absolute commitment will do. The likes of Sterling and Capthorn have no defences – they're easily deluded – but you and I know what we are and whom we serve and how. You're a poor thing, more stupid by far than I, but it is your sight that the angel has chosen to train, not de Lancy's, nor even Tallentyre's. Only you can serve her now, and if she thinks it necessary or politic she'll make hostages of your wife and children. Spare them, Lydyard. Do what you must, willingly. If you fail, let your failure be yours alone. I ask no more of you than I'm prepared to do, and I think you know how intimately *I* have known the Angel of Pain.'

David was beginning to understand. 'For twenty years,' he said, 'the game has been stalemated. Bast and the Spider didn't know themselves – let alone each other – well enough to form a plan of action. In time, they might have formed an alliance; but now their complacency has been rudely disturbed, has it not? Now there are three awakened angels. The balance of their power is completely lost, and their sense of danger has become excessively exaggerated.'

The man in grey was still expressionless, save for his icy, staring eyes. After a moment's pause, he condescended to speak.

'That being which you call the Spider,' he said, evenly, 'I call Zelophelon. It has no name and needs none, but you and I are creatures which rely on names in order to exert the feeble powers of our reasoning. I would not plunder a name from the turbid pool of myth, and so I found one of my own. I have served Zelophelon far better than you have served Bast, but not because I was content to be its worshipper. We're more alike than I once thought, you and I. There's nothing in either one of us as powerful as restless curiosity.

'It was always inevitable that the balance of opportunity would break. When Hecate's Creator brought Sterling to the brink of success, and Hecate's own powers began to expand, Zelophelon and Bast no longer dared remain quiet. Then Pelorus was taken and the Clay Man resurrected. I don't know whether the other which we have to face is truly Machalalel, but if it is, then Zelophelon and Bast are themselves in dire danger. They had to act, and act together. We're hostages, you and I, not because of these frail and feeble bodies that we own, but because of the powers of sight which have been donated to us. The angels are determined to *see*, Lydyard. They intend to bare their very souls to one another. The only honesty of which they're capable is the sharing of oracular revelation, and it's the only way they know by which their knowledge may be rapidly increased. They've been patient with us, Lydyard, but they dare not be patient any longer.

'You must understand that they do not want war. They have no desire to risk destruction. The only thing they can do together – the only project they can sensibly share – is a mutual search for enlightenment. It's not enough that they can force us to see. For what they now intend to do, they must have our wholehearted collaboration. We must desire to see as much as they do, and they will do what they need to do to compel our desire.'

'They intend to hurt us,' said David, as unemotionally as he could.

'And we must agree to be hurt,' the pale man agreed. 'It's not so very difficult, for such men as you and I. We're no strangers to pain. Far more will be expected of us than the others, for we know far more than they. Which one of us will see more clearly, and understand more fully, the angels can't tell; but you and I are the precious ones, who have been tempered by the fires of Hell and schooled by the Angel of Pain in the arts of oracular wisdom. We must play our part willingly.'

David swallowed, but the lump that was in his throat refused to be cleared. He felt dizzy and dehydrated in the aftermath of his fever. He could see the absurdity of it all, though the tide of strange occurrences had carried him away to such an extent that almost any news had become expectable. He knew that he could refuse to believe any of it and accept instead that he was a mere madman, adrift on a sea of delusions.

This might not be real, he said to himself. *I thought I had awakened when Nell spoke to me for the second time, just as I thought I had awakened when I first saw her waiting by my bed, but I might easily be wrong. At any moment I might wake again, to find my arm throbbing yet again with opium-dulled pain, to hear the voice of my little girl.*

He could not convince himself. Indeed, he could not convince himself that there was any sensible distinction to be made between waking and dreaming, now that he had come so far into the labyrinth of visions and nightmares. This was his existence, however perverse and uncertain it might be, and he must do what he could to make himself safe within it.

'You may not be my enemy,' he said softly to the man in grey, 'but you're certainly not my friend. I can't trust your advice.'

Again the pale eyes glared at him with something very like hatred, which served only to emphasise the truth of what he had said.

'I can't save you from your folly,' said the man in grey, 'but it's possible that I might save your wife. If we should live through this, there will be punishment enough in your knowledge that it was I, not you, who preserved her from harm.'

This seemed, in the light of everything David now knew, to be a particularly nasty threat. Alas, he had not the least idea how to reply to it, or what to do in order to thwart it.

As soon as he had spoken, the man in grey leaned forward to look out of the window of the carriage. He did not seem to be relieved by what he saw, and the pallor of his face intensified as though with dire anxiety. David leaned forward to look out of the window on his own side of the carriage, to see what had alarmed him.

The streets of London were still visible, though David did not recognise the one along which they drove, but they had taken on a peculiar quality which he remembered only too well. When he had 'escaped' from the cellar beneath Caleb Amalax's house, where Mandorla Soulier had imprisoned and tortured him, he had found himself curiously disconnected from the world, which had faded into a kind of phantom existence, all but devoid of substance.

Now, the world had again become a kind of phantom. It had lost its colour and some of its solidity, so that the buildings to either side of the street looked like sets in a theatre, and the people on the pavements like mere wraiths. Only the carriage in which they rode seemed thoroughly solid; the others which passed by were as ghostly as their inhabitants.

It could have been worse, David assured himself. *This is familiar. Even if I sink into the fluid earth, into the cold underworld, I will merely be recapitulating experiences I have undergone before. Nothing will happen to me which has not happened before, and there is no cause for fear. Even if I dream of death, I may be permitted to hope that such deaths as I can die here are mere delusions.*

He contrived, courageously, to smile, and it seemed for a brief moment that his companion answered him with a similar change of expression. Then David saw that the appearance of a smile on the other's face was the consequence of the rapid dissolution of his flesh, which had exposed the horrid grin of a mouldering skeleton.

It was as though the man in grey had shrivelled upon the instant into the ultimate stages of desiccation, with nothing left to dress his bones but a thin film of dark dust. His clothes were quite unaffected, though they clung a little more closely to his narrowed frame. He remained sitting, though David did not know what force there was to hold the parts of his skeleton together.

David looked down at his own hand, half expecting to see that he had suffered a similar metamorphosis, but he had not.

The carriage slowed to a halt, and he felt the shift in its weight as the coachman jumped down – or perhaps fell – from his station. David opened the door and stepped out. While he did so, the vehicle and its two horses remained perfectly solid, but as soon as he released his grip upon the door it became as ghostly as all the other carriages. Although there was no coachman to be seen, the horses moved off again, and the carriage was soon lost to sight.

David realised that he was on Waterloo Bridge, and he turned to look at the Houses of Parliament, which seemed oddly graceful in their new-found insubstantiality. He looked at them for half a minute, then turned back again and went to the parapet of the bridge to look down at the turbid waters of the Thames, where ghostly boats skimmed across a surface as slick as oil.

He looked up at the colourless, empty sky. Despite its greyness it seemed quite cloudless, and he felt that he was looking up into a vast, starless void. He wondered for a moment why it was not black, but then he saw that the greyness was not quite uniform, and that a spectral face of unimaginably huge dimensions was staring back at him, as though from the very edge of the immense but finite universe.

He had seen the face before, in the vivid dreams of his poisoned delirium. It was the face of the ultimate God, the Creator of the Creators: an utterly helpless God who was naught but the boundary of His own Creation, impotent to interfere in that which He had shaped and set in motion. The face stared into the core of David Lydyard's soul, without pity or apology, as if to emphasise the utterly enigmatic nature of mankind and the world.

'Am I supposed to wait here for ever?' asked David aloud. 'Have I been brought here for some purpose, or simply cast out of the world so that I do not get in the way?'

The mouth of God opened, as though to reply – which would in itself have been evidence enough that the apparition was a mere hallucination – but no words came out. Instead, a tiny spark of colour blossomed in the greyness, whirling chaotically and growing in size as it hurtled towards him like a gobbet of divine spittle.

At first it was simply a dancing rainbow, but as it acquired shape and substance, he knew who it was that had been sent to claim him and bring him into the next phase of his purgatory dream. She had great wings as black as the night, eyes like brightly glowing embers, vivid red lips, and silver hair which streamed behind her in the wind like the tresses of a huge comet.

Her talons were extended, gleaming like fresh steel.

He could not help being afraid, but he did not turn to run.

For the moment, at least, he gave his consent. He opened wide his aching arms to receive the fond embrace of the Angel of Pain.

12

His seizure by the talons of the Angel of Pain ripped him away from the fabric of the ghostly world. Had such a shock of agony possessed him while he was incapable of magical vision, it would have driven him into insensibility, but he knew from bitter experience how difficult it was to become unconscious of the sight of the inner eye. For one such as he had again become, there could be no release. He soared, therefore, with the dark angel of his imagination, high into the brilliantly lit sky.

As they flew together, locked tightly in their fierce embrace, he was pierced and raked in every fibre of his being by her loving and untender clutch.

David had lived longer in Hell than most men. Once, identified in his own mind with Satan himself, he had been pinned to its fiery floor. His Satanic self had won free of that imprisonment, but Hell had come to him again, creeping furtively into his bones and sinews, patiently extending its dominion through his fingers and limbs, stretching its claws towards his warm and beating heart with its venomous chill.

He had fought that inner Hell with all his might. He had made its conquest the labour of his life and fought against it with every weapon that science brought to his aid: with laudanum, morphine and cocaine.

He had won his battles, but never the war.

Nor was he entirely free of the more intimate sense of threat which the idea of Hell conveyed. He had never quite been able to shed the burden of the faith which had been instilled in him in childhood: the faith which promised eternal life in Hell to unrepentant sinners. At the level of the intellect he had discarded the dogmas of the Church in their entirety, but at the level of rebellious emotion there was still a furtive and fugitive shadow in his heart: a shadow which mutely pointed the downward way to the abyss.

At the level of intellect David knew that the notion of eternal suffering was logically incoherent, that pain was in part a matter of contrast, and that eternal pain must ultimately become dull and void of meaning, but the skeletal shadow could never be quite convinced of that, and there was always a certain knowing mockery in its death's-head stare.

Now, he felt certain, all his doubts would be resolved. Now that the Angel of Pain had finally claimed him for her own, and was free to carry him away to the unimagined heart of her frightful realm, the truth of the matter would be made plain to him at last.

The pain did not die, nor was it diminished by infinite extension; but it did change. It changed *him*, or at least his sense of himself.

It seemed to him that he ceased to be a tiny, black-clad thing of flesh and bone, dangling like a rag doll from the Angel's claws. As they ascended together into the sky, which was leaden no longer, to a region where the rays of the sun were like cataracts of light, David's pitiful human soul seemed somehow to flow out of his body into the infinitely stronger and more gorgeous body of the Angel, where it fused with her soul and her sight.

There was no end to pain in this, for the Angel of Pain *was* pain, but it was a kind of transcendence which restored to pain the meaning it should properly have had, if the world had been sanely made and purposively planned. He was taken outside time and space, far beyond the limits of that mote of dust which was his body, and far beyond the limits of that mote of dust which was the Earth.

He was permitted to share the vision of the ultimate Creator, watching His Creation from without.

There was pain in that vision: all the pain of all the worlds of all Creation; and all the agony of all the grief and helplessness of all the creatures there had ever been and ever might be.

But there was something more than pain, there was a sharpening of perception which brought all possible perceptions into focus. In that one indivisible moment of vision, David saw everything: all actuality, all possibility. Had he cared to say, at that moment, *cogito, ergo sum*, he would have referred not to that infinitesimal flutter of sensation confused by the blur of human consciousness, but to a thought sufficiently vast, complex and crystal-clear to contain the whole of Creation.

He shared that single thought which was in God's mind, which was the universe.

And, being outside time, he shared it for a single instant which lasted for ever.

Or so it seemed . . .

'You see,' said the voice, 'that I am honest. I do not ask you to make a bargain without knowing what it is you pledge. I ask you to endure great pain. I will not try to trick you or delude you. As the other said, you are too precious for that.'

He was in the pyramid, looking up at the colossal figure of the goddess Bast, seated upon her towering throne. She was leaning forward, gazing down at him with an intensity that he had never seen before.

He had not been forced to undergo the arduous journey across the desert and through the streets of the ruined city, but still she faced him as god to man, giant to insect; still she intended to force him to acknowledge that all the power was hers, and none his; still she desired to crush him with awe of her sublimity.

'You might have been honest with me long ago,' he answered. 'You might have deigned to speak with me, to ask and answer questions, to share with me your secrets and your hopes.'

'You need not be jealous of the other,' she told him. 'I have used you more gently than he has been used. But you have been spied upon as he never was, and secrets shared with you would have been shared with others.'

She spoke to him as god to man, but her words betrayed her. She spoke in the manner of a cunning and crafty thing, whose reasons were as petty as a man's. There was no concealing the fact that she sought to make a bargain with him. She needed the consent which the pale man had advised him to give her. She needed his agreement to pass through the fires of Hell, not for himself but for her, and to commit his every effort to the task of seeing whatever it was that she needed to see.

He could make some guesses at what it was she needed to know and could not find out without his help.

How many angels might dance on the head of a pin? How many more are asleep in the substance of the earth? Precisely how remote are the others which inhabit the more distant reaches of a universe which seems to have grown almost to be infinite? Might a bond of amity be forged as easily between three as between two, in order to constitute a crew of predators whose assaults could not be withstood?

'I will be your eyes,' he said, knowing well enough what it was that he was promising. 'I have reasons of my own for wanting to see. Whether I can pay the price of sight, I don't know, but I will try. I'm afraid, but I will do what I can. But afterwards, all this will be different. You are not a god, and the pretence will be over. I'll know what you really are.'

The huge green eyes stared into his, their pupils narrowing to mere slits. In her right hand she held an oval mirror, much larger than the one which was mounted on the door of his wardrobe. She held it up now, so that he could see what was reflected in it.

David saw his elder son wake from sleep to stare at the phantasmal figure which waited by his bed. He watched Teddy smile at the beautiful pale lady who extended her slender fingers to take him by the hand.

The first verse of an ancient rhyme which he had known since childhood echoed in his mind:

> *Beware the days of the year, little man,*
> *When the moon hath a face like a silver crown;*
> *Cleave if thou may'st to the home of thy clan,*
> *And hide from the werewolves of London Town.*

He saw Teddy's body begin to flow and change, in that curiously graceful fashion which he had seen before. He saw Teddy become a wolf. Then the pale lady changed and became a wolf in her turn. Together they moved off into the shadows of the night.

He saw Nell, who had been reading a book by candlelight, look up into the face of a handsome young man with piercing eyes. She should have been afraid, but she only smiled.

The song continued to echo in her father's frightened thoughts:

> *Beware the coverts and courts, little maid;*
> *Where walks the man with the coat of brown;*
> *Though thou art abandoned, be not waylaid,*
> *By the hungry werewolves of London Town.*

He saw Nell change, and the young man too. He saw them both swallowed up by the darkness.

He saw Simon, fast asleep and dreaming, quite unaware of the violet-eyed creature which leaned over his cot, dangling her silken sleeves upon his coverlet. The little boy never opened his eyes, but he seemed to welcome her touch, and he adjusted himself to her embrace as though she were his mother.

And the words proceeded to their inevitable end:

> *Beware the starlit nights, my child,*
> *And the pretty lady in the sleek white gown;*
> *Though thou art forsaken, be not beguiled,*
> *By the charming werewolves of London Town.*

He saw the infant transformed into a wolf cub, nipped by the nape of the neck in the teeth of a huge white wolf, which carried him away into the gloom.

David was possessed by an appalling bitterness and anguish. He had not expected this. Somehow – though he understood now that he had never had any reason to hope for it – he had expected justice and honour. But this goddess that was not a real goddess was jealous, malicious, tyrannical and cruel, and she could not bear to let him think that he and she were free agents, entering into a contract as any equals might.

'And Cordelia?' he said harshly. 'What of Cordelia?'

'She is safe,' said the goddess, putting away her mirror.

This, too, he understood, was meant to hurt him. This, too, was cruel, because the man in grey, whose name he had guessed, had promised that he, not David, would preserve Cordelia from harm. He had promised, too, that David would always live with the burden of that knowledge. Bast had listened to him, and had not been too proud to take the hint.

'You didn't have to do this,' David whispered, as his soul writhed in the burning acids of his own bile. 'You had my consent!'

She leaned further forward, and in her great cat's eyes he thought he glimpsed a fugitive tear of pity.

'You know better than that, my beloved,' she said, very softly. 'Only think, and you will see that I had no choice. You have taught me something about pain that I did not know before, and I have learned it. It is to Hell that you must go for me, my only beloved; but Hell is not truly Hell, if there is comfort still in the hidden corners of your secret heart. I do this not to win your consent, which is already given, but to cause you hurt: hurt which you have sworn to suffer.

'Do not blame me for this, beloved, for it is what *you* have taught me about the nature and meaning of pain, and I dare not show mercy to you now, when you must see for me more clearly than you have ever seen before. I do not understand, any more than you do, why pain is necessary, but I know that it is, and so do you. And so, my beloved, I must hurt thee, as cleverly as I can.

'Forgive me, beloved, for I know not what I do, or why, but only that it must be done.'

David never lost consciousness, and so there was no awakening, but he did become lost in the further reaches of his stressful delirium, and there was a sense in which he had to find himself, when the Angel of Pain had brought him to his place of rest and set him down.

He found himself, by slow degrees, in a forest. The air was hot and humid, but the multitudinous leaves of the trees shielded him from the direct light of the sun, whose rays appeared to him as a vast mosaic of tiny brilliant pinpricks in the canopy. Although the ground was shaded, it was not bare; lush grass grew there in profusion, cushioning his supine form, and there were delicate flowers all around him. The trees too were in full flower, but the pendulous blooms which hung down from the trailing branches were very different from those which grew amid the grass, being huge and gaudily bell-shaped.

He could hear the sound of water gently falling into a pool.

When he tried to sit up, to see where the water was, he was racked from top to toe by renewed pain. He could feel the grating of every swollen joint, the strain in every ragged muscle. He wished, fervently and desperately, for the strength to ignore it, or at least for the strength to do what he must in spite of it, but more than a minute passed before he found the strength to force himself up into a sitting position.

The pool was half a dozen paces away, in a hollow. It was fed by a fast-running stream which tumbled over a little moss-dressed cliff to make a fall of no more than a handspan's depth. Its outlet was wider and shallower, half clogged with weed.

He had the idea that the water might be cool, although there was no real reason to think that it would not be as warm as the moisture-laden air. He had a fierce thirst to quench, and the only thought which he permitted to invade his troubled mind was a determination to reach the edge of the pool and drink. He did not yet ask himself where he could possibly be, or how or why he had been brought there; he concentrated his will on the single task of reaching the pool.

The air which he dragged, effortfully, into his lungs seemed glutinously thick. For a moment, when the pain stopped him in his tracks, the temporary failure of his will took the form of a perverse assurance that he did not need to drink – that the thirst might as easily be slaked by swallowing the wet air – but he forced himself on. He did not ask himself what he could possibly do next, given that he could hardly crawl; he only fixed his eyes upon the waterfall and the pond into which it tumbled, and dragged himself towards it inch by inch.

Eventually, at the cost of a great deal of merciless effort, he reached the edge.

He bowed his head to the water like an animal and tried to drink, but he could not do it. Instead he had to bring his arm forward and use his gnarled hand as a cup, lifting the water to his mouth and sipping a little at a time.

The water was not cool, but its warmth was as delicious as its purity, and as it leached into the tissues of his inner being – which it seemed to do with remarkable rapidity – it soothed away the pain that racked him.

Wonderingly, he felt a miracle unfold.

The pain abated by degrees. It was as though he had been wrapped about with many layers of barbed wire, which were now peeled away one by one. Each layer of release was precious balm, and each one went deeper to the heart of him than the last. Long before the end, he became acutely conscious of the fact that he had not known for many years what it was to be truly free of pain. He realised that the state of feeling he had come to accept as normal and bearable was no more than a level of pain which he had schooled himself to find tolerable.

As the end approached, he began to wonder whether all human life was like that, and whether any man who had ever lived had ever been truly free from pain.

He sipped more water, easily able now to move his arm and his fingers. What he felt was no mere absence of discomfort, but a sense of health and wellbeing which he had never felt before, even in the full flush of youth, before he had become ill and before he had been bitten by that magically treacherous snake in the Egyptian wilderness.

After a while, he stopped drinking and let the water which had been agitated by the dipping of his hand calm down again. Because it was some distance away from the waterfall, it soon became calm and glassy, and he was able to see a dim reflection of his face in its shallow, turgid ripples.

He recognised himself, but barely.

He might have been twenty years younger; all signs of stress, strain and aging had been smoothed from his features. Nor was it illusion, for he could look directly at his hand and the part of his forearm which projected from his sleeve. The ravages of his illness had been clearly marked on his flesh, but now they were gone. His skin was smooth and lustrous; his joints were no longer swollen.

He had drunk from the fountain of youth.

At first, his slow mind refused the thought, even as a metaphor, but the truth was manifest and he had to accept it. He knew, of course, that he must be dreaming, but to be free of his afflictions, even in his dreams, seemed to him an achievement of incalculable value. He had never ceased to dream these last twenty years, but his dreams – even when they were fed by laudanum's deceits – had never for an instant succeeded in freeing him from his pain as completely as this. The ability to dream in such a fashion was, he knew, in no way to be despised.

He came to his feet, smoothly and easily. Then he stood still, looking up at the boughs of the forest and the myriad chinks through which the sunlight flooded, bathing in the luxury of his own being. He threw his arms wide in celebration and opened his mouth to cry out in joy – but the cry did not escape his lips.

Some distance away, more than half hidden by the undergrowth, was the body of another man. Like him, the other was dressed – absurdly, given the surroundings – in the apparel of a gentleman: coat and trousers, waistcoat and tie. The suit was a sombre grey, which contrasted oddly with the greenery that surrounded it.

David could not see the man's face at first, but had guessed even before he began walking towards the unmoving form that it must be the pale man who had brought him away from home, and who had brought him, knowingly or not, to his rendezvous with the Angel of Pain.

The pale man's eyes were closed and he lay perfectly still, but he was breathing. He was alive.

David knew what to do. He went to the pool and cupped his two hands together, very carefully. Then he scooped up as much of the miraculous water as he could contrive to carry, and took it to the stricken man. It was not easy to manoeuvre the liquid to his lips, but he managed to wet them a little, and they parted reflexively in response. With some difficulty, David poured a little of the water into the open mouth; the rest was spilled.

He returned to the pool to fetch a second load. This time, when he returned, the man's grey eyes were open, and he was able to adjust his position so as to take a greater proportion of the precious fluid.

Even before the man raised himself to his feet, he had begun to change. It was not merely the legacy of the years that flowed from his face; it was as if the flesh which he had worn had only been borrowed. It was as if it were only a makeshift substitute for flesh which had long ago been scourged away.

David had only been renewed by the water of life; this man seemingly stood in need of reconstitution.

With David's help, the other man stood up, and David supported him while he made his way to the water's edge. They knelt down together, and David used his hand as a cup to carry water to the other's lips, over and over again.

With every mouthful the other took he seemed to grow bulkier. He had been thin, but now he became sturdy. His eyes, once lifeless, became darker and far brighter. His features, once pinched and extraordinarily pallid, became much fuller and softer. His clothes, although they had fitted him loosely, must have become uncomfortably tight as he grew stouter.

David, concentrating on the task in hand, did not take time to study his companion's face until the metamorphosis was very nearly complete. Then he stood back, to let the other stand up and rejoice in the gift of true health. His delight in the other's rejoicing was only slightly undercut, and not at all spoiled, by the shock of recognition. He had, after all, already guessed who the man must be.

It was Jacob Harkender.

Harkender looked down at his hands for a while, then touched them tentatively to his cheeks and chin, as though he were a blind man testing the contours of an unfamiliar face. Eventually, he looked up.

'Where are we?' he asked uncertainly.

'I think we're in a parody of the Garden of Eden,' David told him, 'but I suppose that it's just one more threshold on which we must wait for a while. I dare say we won't be here for long.'

FIRST INTERLUDE
The Pain of Finite Hearts

So far as we can tell from our investigations of the nervous systems of animals, that kind of information which we call 'pain' is transmitted by the same neuronal channels as other kinds of sensations. But what, given that this is so, serves to distinguish the painful from the pleasurable? All our sensations consist of electrical impulses transmitted through these neuronal conduits; why, then, are some such transmissions apprehended in a violently unpleasant manner, while others are welcome?

One hypothesis is that painful and pleasurable transmissions excite different regions of the brain, but even if the ludicrous failures of phrenological analysis had not cast doubt upon all ideas of this type, we would still have to account for why one kind of transmitted excitation should be received at one location and the other routed to another.

At present we can only sidestep this puzzle, acknowledging the existence of some unknown kind of natural mechanism. Although we do not know how it achieves the trick, the brain must be able to 'translate' certain patterns of electrical excitation in such a way that the active mind is encouraged to ameliorate the signal or avoid the source, while certain others are translated in such a way that the active mind will seek to sustain or repeat the stimulus. Pain teaches us to avoid its causes; pleasure is a physiological bribe which seduces us to seek out its external sources.

The utility of pain is, in a rough and ready way, quite obvious. Natural selection has necessarily endowed complex organisms with the means to cultivate habits which promote survival; it is entirely logical that that which has the capacity to injure us should cause us pain, in order that we may learn to avoid injury.

On first consideration it seems also to be logical that the greatest dangers should threaten the greatest pain, but in fact the logic of the case becomes dubious and uncertain if it is pursued. One might easily argue that pain which is too great is likely to prevent action instead of stimulating it, and that a grave injury which has already been sustained may have less chance of healing if the organism which sustains it is incapacitated by an excess of pain. Moreover, if one accepts that the function of pain is educative, it is not at all clear why there are certain degenerative diseases which the sufferer cannot take any steps to avoid, which are nevertheless intensely painful.

However one extrapolates the logic of the case, it is undeniable that there are several peculiar aspects of the various phenomena of pain. There is certainly no simple correlation between the extent of an injury and the pain which it causes. Soldiers wounded in battle sometimes report that very serious injuries pained them hardly at all when they were first sustained; on the other hand, they sometimes report that even when a wound has healed completely it continues to be associated with the kind of fierce burning sensation which Mitchell calls 'causalgia', and which he believes to be the most intense species of pain. Also to be considered in this context is the remarkable phenomenon of 'phantom-limb pain', whereby a limb which has been amputated may seem to the unlucky amputee to hurt badly even in its absence.

The pain associated with disease is similarly paradoxical. Some internally generated pain may be deemed educative; for instance, stomach aches may instruct us to avoid certain kinds of food. But it is very difficult to understand how the severe pains which may be associated with gallstones, kidney stones and cancerous tumours can have any good result of this kind. To argue that the natural function of toothache is to move its sufferers to invent dentistry, or that the innate merit of appendicitis lies in persuading its victims of the virtues of surgery, is surely to render the argument absurd. Natural selection can only simulate the intentions of a designer, and must have formed the nature of our ancestors long before there was the remotest possibility of their acquiring such skills.

We cannot reasonably dispute the manifest reality of the fact that much of the pain we suffer has no constructive effect at all, but merely serves to add to the burden of irremediable debilitation. If this seems to the majority of men to be entirely natural, that is merely because they have long been accustomed to such a state of affairs. The lack of any rational explanation for it is clearly exhibited by those religious myths which go to extraordinary lengths in order to account for the fact that human life seems to be lived under the curse of eternal punishment.

The simplest argument by which we might hope to provide a reasoned account of the problematic aspects of pain is one which hypothesises that those pains which cannot inspire us to useful action are merely a by-product of an apparatus which was favoured by natural selection solely because of the advantage of 'useful' (i.e., educative) pains. But this simply will not do, given that the apparatus which transmits pain – the nervous system – is not solely dedicated to that purpose. The electrical signals generated by an internal cause might, in principle, be experienced either pleasantly or unpleasantly according to the artifice of the brain; why, therefore, should the brain be so organised by natural selection that it regards certain signals as painful, even when there is no conceivable action which might be taken to diminish them or avoid their repetition? Why should not the capacity of the brain to feel be organised in such a way that the effects of irremediable illness are experienced neutrally?

Accounts given by hunters in Africa suggest that the pain mechanism in animals may work differently. Antelopes and zebras pursued by lions or hyenas will make every effort to avoid being seized, but once pulled down will often become completely acquiescent to their fate, as though they were incapable of further feeling. Similarly, trappers in Canada have reported that animals will sometimes perform an amputation by gnawing through a limb caught in a snare. Such an operation would be enormously difficult for a human equipped with a saw or a set of scalpels because of the effect which the pain would have on the mind and the hand directing the blades. In this context we must, of course, be prepared to distinguish between the physiology of pain and the consciousness of 'hurting' – which animals may or may not experience – but the introduction of that distinction does not resolve the enigma.

If we invert the problem, we might be disposed to wonder about certain capacities which the brain does *not* have, though logic suggests to us that natural selection might have provided them. If we approach the question from that unorthodox angle it surely seems very strange that we are so completely at the mercy of pain, and so easily incapacitated by it, when its purely educative functions would be compromised very slightly, if at all, if it were a more controllable phenomenon. When the pain of a burn has caused us to snatch our hand from the flame it has surely served its purpose; the persistence of the sensation of having been burned certainly reinforces the lesson – but could not the function of reinforcement be more gently served? Why must the informing signal be so intensely and irredeemably unpleasant? Why have our brains been so formed that the conscious mind has no capacity at all for merciful intercession in the face of agony?

It is worth re-emphasising here that those who believe in a supernatural providence have no better answers to these questions than men of science. If there really were a cosmic plan in which toothache was incorporated as a necessary spur to inspire men to devise dental care, why should it not also take the trouble to include some kind of natural anaesthesia, so that we might escape the worst hazards of ether and chloroform? And if pain, as some believe, is a visitation from God intended to punish us for our misdeeds or for the sins of our forefathers, how does it come about that the good seem to suffer its ravages to exactly the same extent as the wicked? (If there is any advantage at all, it surely lies with the the wicked, whose wickedness often consists of inflicting unnecessary pain upon their meeker brethren.)

Further puzzles are introduced when we consider the variety of individual responses to injuries and illnesses of apparently similar magnitude. There can be little doubt that our response to pain is to some degree a matter of attitude. The stoic bears with fortitude that which breaks the will of his fellow men. The coward finds unendurable that which his fellows take in their stride. The kind of man which Dr Krafft-Ebing has labelled a masochist may actively seek out certain painful experiences, and reckon them pleasurable. The rites of passage which mark the acceptance of adult responsibility in many primitive societies often involve trials by ordeal, and it is not so very long ago that such trials had their place in the procedures of European law; such trials are obviously based on the tacit assumption that endurance of pain can and must be a test of resolve and honest conviction.

It would undoubtedly be false, however, to argue that either stoicism or masochism could be taken to its logical extreme. It simply is not the case that sufficient courage and determination can enable any man to withstand torture, or that a man could so comprehensively renegotiate the terms of internal experience as to derive pleasure from any and all painful experiences. The experiences from which masochists derive their rewards seem invariably to be charged with particular and highly idiosyncratic meanings, usually religious or sexual; it is not the pain *per se* that is pleasurable but the situation of the pain within a particular social or psychological context. Neither the existence of stoics nor the existence of masochists can undermine the contention that pain is a curse for whose worst afflictions we have no adequate explanation, and to whose worst depredations we can mount little or no effective response.

It is tempting to speculate that this deficiency in human nature might yet be made good, not by some supernatural redemption which will deliver us into a Heaven free from pain, but by the further operation of natural selection, or by means of the cunning of practical science. Perhaps natural

selection, in favouring those individuals whose control of
their own pain is slightly better than their fellows, might
eventually produce a race whose experience of pain is in
stricter accordance with the principle of utility. Perhaps the
increase of our knowledge and understanding will free us
from the necessity to wait on such a gradual process, and
will provide us with some chemical or mechanical means to
alleviate pain quickly, easily and specifically. The imperfect
opiates with whose use we are already familiar – laudanum,
morphine and cocaine – may be supplemented in future by
other and better compounds.

But if we are to indulge ourselves in speculation, perhaps
we should follow a different line of thought, and ask whether
nature is not, after all, such a fool as this argument has
made her out to be. Is there, perhaps, some other utility
in pain which lies beyond and apart from the educative
function, and which we have somehow overlooked? Is it
possible that our ancestors, whose nature was formed by
the processes of Darwinian selection which operated for
hundreds of thousands of years, obtained some advantage
from pain which we have only recently lost, or which we have
as yet been unable to bring to the level of consciousness?

If the particular way in which human beings experience
pain is not merely a casual accident of nature – an unfortunate
by-product of the evolution of self-awareness and the power
of rational thought – then we must of necessity search for
functions and utilities which go beyond the merely educative.
If we do this, we are surely forced to take seriously, at least
as a hypothesis, the proposition that pain might be a kind of
spur or goad which urges men to efforts which go far beyond
mere avoidance of specific stimuli, and perhaps far beyond
a general quest for comfort, shelter and efficient medicine.
Perhaps we should be prepared to entertain the notion that
the intellectual progress of the human mind – both in terms
of individual self-development and in terms of our collective
wealth of understanding – benefits in some way from the
particular experience of pain with which human beings are
afflicted.

*

There is another issue which must be introduced into this discussion, which further complicates the business of analysis and speculation. We have already been forced to observe that there is a distinction to be drawn between the physiological phenomena of pain (i.e., the transmission of certain electrical impulses through the nerves to the brain) and the subjective experience of pain (i.e., the awareness of being 'in pain'; the hurtful feeling apprehended by the conscious mind).

To this observation we must add that the knowledge of the flow of causality is sometimes reversed. Sometimes we refer to being hurt by things which are very unlike fires that burn or thorns that prick; we also call 'hurt' the sensations of grief which follow the loss of a loved one or simply the loss of the love of a loved one. We often speak of being 'sick at heart' or of the injury done by an insult, and there may indeed be physical symptoms to accompany what is originally and essentially a mental experience.

What is more, these kinds of 'emotional pain' are often more powerful in their effects upon us than mere physical pain. The tears which a child sheds after grazing a knee are often less prolific than those which follow a scolding; adults learn to hold back their tears when they are literally wounded, but may well continue to shed tears of anguish when they are metaphorically wounded, and tears of sympathy for the wounds of those they love.

This difference of effect is nowhere more clearly seen than in the phenomenon of suicide. It is certainly not unknown, but it is relatively rare for men to kill themselves because they are in agony; grief and disappointment in love are far more common motives for self-destruction. One must note, too, a curious but common way of speaking which some people have, whereby they may report that, although they are suffering considerable pain from wounds or illness, they nevertheless feel quite well 'in themselves'. We may infer from this that the feeling of wellbeing which is associated with the sense of being emotionally right with the world is sometimes considered more valuable than the feeling of not being in pain. Men under torture can, almost without exception, be forced by their agony to betray their loved ones; but the guilt of having done so may curse them with a burden of emotional pain which lingers long after their physical wounds have healed.

Although it may seem unduly sentimental, there is much merit in the argument that the best antidote to the effects of pain is not a chemical palliative like laudanum but the ability to feel that life is worthwhile and rewarding even though one is suffering. The value of laudanum should not be underestimated, and a man in dire pain would be a fool to refuse it, but his need does not end when the laudanum is swallowed. The fact that a man may love his wife and children, and be loved in return, may make physical discomfort much more easily bearable in the long term.

There is no doubt that a man will often accept a very considerable risk of injury, and endure considerable physical pain, if he knows that his wife or his children are under threat. He may, indeed, be forced to yield up his principles by ruthless torture, but that does not lessen the significance of the fact that he may also sacrifice himself to save others. How could armies exist, and wars be fought, were it not for the power of a sense of duty to others to override the threat of injury and pain?

Such observations as these lend considerable credence to the hypothesis that pain has a complex function as a goad or a spur in addition to its simple educative function. Experience of emotional pain does not educate many men into a lack of feeling for those they love; the majority of men do not respond to their first experience of grief by becoming uncaring, however painful that first experience may be, and only a very few of those who are driven to temporary madness by disappointment in love become utterly hard of heart. Natural selection has *not* given us the power to feel emotional pain in order that we should learn to avoid its causes; if emotional pain is not merely a cruel accident of emergent sentience, it must serve another end which similarly adds to our capacity for survival and the survival of our descendants.

Whatever philosophers and men of science have to say about the phenomenon of pain, we will never succeed – nor, indeed should we even try – in convincing ourselves that pain is something to be cherished and welcomed. It is inherent in the very concept of pain that it is something that should be resisted and resented. By rational examination, however, we might hope to come to a better understanding of its necessity, and that better understanding should certainly aid us in our endurance of pain, and in the decisions we must sometimes make as to when the risk of injury can be justified.

Suffering does not ennoble us, as some hopeful philosophers have argued. Nor is it true, as other optimists have sometimes declared, that whatever does not kill us makes us stronger. Nevertheless, good consequences as well as evil ones do stem from our experience of pain, and we owe it to ourselves to try as hard as we can to discover what they are. If we are to win our war against the slings and arrows of outrageous fortune, we must learn everything we can concerning the nature and operation of those slings and arrows, and the precise configuration of the wounds which they can and do inflict upon human flesh and the human soul.

(Passages from 'On the Natural Utility of Pain' by David Lydyard, *Journal of the Physiological Society*, spring 1889.)

TWO
Adamantine Chains and Penal Fire

1

There was once a man who was caught in a terrible fire, and would have died had he not been preserved by an angel whose devoted servant he had been, which still had need of him. The angel, ever careful of its own magical power, used the fire very artfully to remake him in such a way that he became the perfect instrument of its need.

At first, the man did not understand what had been done to him, and he raged against the imagined injustice of his fate; but in time he became reconciled to his condition. He learned that what he had taken for Hell might instead be deemed mere Purgatory, and that he – who had always thought himself damned – might legitimately hope to be set upon the pathway of salvation.

Until he had passed through the fire and been cleansed of all sensation, he had not truly known what it was to feel.

Until he had passed through the fire and been blinded by its light, he had not truly known what it was to see.

Until he had passed through the fire and been destroyed by its heat, he had not truly known what it was to be.

There was a long interval, after the fire, when Jacob Harkender could feel no pain. The neural termini beneath the surface of his skin had been burned away so that his nerves were immune from stimulation.

During this interval he was disconnected from the world more completely than he had ever been in all the slumbers and trances which had previously been his hard-won escapes from the tyranny of the real. It was then that he learned the incontrovertible truth of what Berkeley had argued: matter is the possibility of sensation; when the possibility of sensation no longer exists *there is no matter*.

For this perversely fortunate man, the world disappeared for a while, and he tasted freedom. For that brief span he was like God: alone in his own being, outside Creation.

But like that God in whom his father had so stupidly believed, Harkender found in time that he could not bear the vacuity of isolation. As that God had been condemned by loneliness to do, he cried out in the end: *Fiat lux!*

Light there was, when he demanded it: light, and life, and all the unformed appearances of a world in the making. And in that glorious explosion of light, which was really nothing more nor less than the return of sensibility to his body and his brain, he beheld the Infinite.

The nerve ends which had been burned away eventually began to grow again in the outermost layers of Harkender's flesh. Receptors were regenerated where they had been lost, becoming wide open to renewed sensation, and into these naked apertures of possible experience sensation poured in an overwhelming cataract. There was a kind of light and there was a kind of sound; there was heat and there was pressure; there was a confusion of bitter-sweet-saltness on his tongue, and in the crevices of his nose dulcet scents were insanely alloyed with the reeks of decay and putrefaction.

Above all else, there was pain.

The light which blazed inside his mind did not emanate from the world without. His outer eyes, scorched by the flames and melted by the heat, would never see again unless some generous miracle could turn back the tide of time. But the inner eye of his soul, which he had laboured so long and so hard to open, in order that he might perceive the worlds beyond the world and savour the possibilities of sensation which were denied to the common human herd, was granted such sight as he had never imagined.

In that first flood of light he saw the great flare of creative energy in which the universe had begun, and the great cloud of stars which that outburst had become, and all the habitable worlds to which the stars gave birth.

Written across the face of the sea of stars he saw the loving features of that most glorious of all the creatures of light: the wild and beautiful Angel of Pain; and she in her turn saw him. She lashed and tore him with all her accumulated fury, and wrung out of him all the screams of which his scorched lungs were capable.

She was not real. She was only a delusion, which he conjured up in order to give form to his experience; but how could he help learning to see her, and to know her?

Would not any other man in his situation have done the same?

Jacob Harkender had earlier believed that he had already come to terms with the Angel of Pain and made her his dutiful mistress. He had believed, in his pathetic vanity, that he had suffered, and had come to terms with suffering, and had turned it to his own advantage. He discovered now that he had been very foolish to think so. His first tentative efforts to pay court to the Angel of Pain had served to introduce him to that other, more real angel, which had condescended to possess him; but that had been mere playful dalliance by comparison with the intercourse which was forced upon him now.

Now, he discovered the extremes of pain which the human soul could suffer; now, he discovered the extremes of pain which it was possible for the human body to bear.

At first, he thought that he could not bear it, but he soon discovered that he must. That was when he decided, for a while, that he must be in Hell, damned to eternal torment.

In time, however, he adapted to his condition.

The pain did not release him, nor relent in its torment, but it became a circumstance of his existence and he learned to exist within it. He learned that the embrace of the Angel of Pain, however fierce, is not impossible to endure. There was such strength in him, and such valour, that he would not even condescend to hate her. Even in the depths of his desperation, he resisted despair; even in the extremes of his agony, he courted the bright light of vision.

In his former innocence, Harkender had believed that he had trodden the path of pain well enough to reap its rewards. He had believed that he knew how to soar to the heights of vision, to see as the gods themselves might see. In the aftermath of the fire, he discovered his folly. As the layers of flesh which had been burned away were regenerated by degrees, he learned how woefully inadequate his imagination had been to the task of envisioning the pastures of Heaven, the ignominies of Hell, and – above all else – the enlightenments of Truth.

For a while, the light of his inner vision was dazzling; it showed him little but the ecstatic face of the Angel of Pain. But in time, he adapted his inner eye to its intensity, and began to see more clearly. Then, he began to understand why his possessor had saved him from the fire. He began to understand what uses his master had for the cunning vision of his inner eye.

The fire and what it had done to him was, Harkender knew, a punishment of sorts for the sin of hubris. He had dared to play the part of sycophant to a fallen angel, had dared to lay before that angel his eyes and his intelligence, offering to its use his hard-won understanding of the world; and what he offered had been inadequate. He had failed; he had betrayed the trust for which he had so devoutly prayed, for which he had gladly made a sacrifice of himself. It was only just that the angel should seek to punish him by making a gift of him to the untender Angel of Pain, who would keep him and tend to him throughout his season in Purgatory.

But this season in Purgatory was not only a punishment. There was mercy in it also, for it offered him an education which few of his race had ever been privileged to receive. The angel which had consented to use and possess him seemingly held itself equally accountable for its error and dismay, and so it sought repair instead of revenge. It elected, in passing its instrument through the fire, to temper as well as punish him. It chose to improve him, so that he might in time become a better and more trustworthy instrument. It set out to teach him properly that which he had learned badly by trial and error. It gave him into the loving clutches of the Angel of Pain so that he might be improved by torment.

Or so, at least, he came to believe.

What else could he believe? Had he believed otherwise, he would surely have died; but he did not die. He lived; and he persuaded himself to believe that he thrived. In his own estimation, he became a better man than he had been before.

Harkender could not take proper account of his physical condition. Because he was blind, he could not see himself. In the feeble sight of ordinary men, he supposed that he must be horribly disfigured, but there was no way he could judge the extent of his disfigurement. Although his fingers could once again feel pain, they no longer had the sensitivity of touch to measure the contours of his face. He believed that he still had some power of movement in his limbs, but he could not move them purposively because he could receive no sensation from them, except pain.

He had only the vaguest notion of where he was. He was in a bed, but where the bed was he did not know. He was moved on and off the bed while its soiled linen was changed; he was incontinent, and the changes were presumably frequent. His whole body was occasionally bathed with damp cloths, but he was never immersed in water. He was fed at intervals which were presumably regular, mostly on porridge and various kinds of soup which were spooned into his mouth by careful attendants. He could not speak to them sensibly, because his injured tongue and scorched vocal cords were no longer capable of forming coherent words, and they did not often speak to him; when they did speak, their words seemed to be coming from a vast distance, muffled by the ever present curtain of pain, and he found it difficult to respond in any meaningful way.

Still, they cared for him. He had, after all, been a reasonably wealthy man. The managers of his estate could easily afford to serve such primitive needs as his wrecked and stubborn carcase still had.

He did not care about any of that. He made no strenuous attempts to communicate with those who cared for him; he had no boons to ask of them or complaints to issue. He did not think that he owed them any thanks for keeping him alive; he knew well enough that their role was purely mechanical. He knew that he had no further business to transact with their world; his only concern now was with the world of his possessor and saviour.

Under the tutelage of the Angel of Pain the sight of his inner eye became much sharper than it had been before. It gave him access to the infinite reaches of the cosmos of the mind, which had formerly been hidden from him, and he slowly learned the skills of discernment which were necessary to life in that world. He did not know at first why his possessor required him to be schooled in this way, but he applied himself to his task as earnestly as he could. He soon learned to see the Angel of Pain for what she really was, and understood that his possessor, in its turn, saw him more clearly than it had before.

Harkender and his possessor learned to love one another as well as they might had they been siblings born of the same dark womb.

Or so, at least, Harkender believed. He could not have believed otherwise, because he needed the love of his possessor far more than he had ever needed the love of any merely human being.

By the time sensation had fully returned to him, and his body had recovered as much of its ability to function as it ever would, Harkender was reconciled to his fate. He knew that he would always be in pain – that the brief fire which had burned away the former surfaces of his physical being had lit a lingering conflagration inside him which could not possibly be quenched – but he also knew that this inner fire was not without purpose, and that the incessant heat of it could warm his soul, if only he could master its energy. He was comforted by the knowledge that he was not alone and never would be. The angel which had put him through the purifying flame was with him still, and would never leave him.

Possession had been his salvation, and he was profoundly glad to have been possessed.

He hoped for a while that the closeness of his relationship with his saviour would permit a dialogue between them, but this hope was disappointed. The angel which had saved him would not speak to him, though he had no doubt that it could hear all the prayers and questions which he formed within the silence of his skull.

At first, he wondered whether this was a further dimension of his punishment, but he eventually decided that it was not. He decided that his possessor would not speak to him directly because the use which it had for him would somehow be spoiled if it did. He was an instrument, despite that he might be loved and cherished, and not yet a collaborator in its schemes. He supposed that he could not properly serve his purpose if his possessor told him what that purpose was.

One day, he hoped, his loving master would speak to him; but in the meantime, he resolved to be patient.

Even in the absence of any perceptible answers, he continued to address his questions and his prayers to his possessor. As his outer blindness was compensated by inner sight, so his outer dumbness was compensated by inner speech. For a while, he was anxious because he did not know his master's name, but he decided in the end that in the absence of a known name, any one that he cared to invent would do.

So he named his possessor Zelophelon, thought of it thus, and addressed it thus.

Sometimes, he thought of himself as Zelophelon too, forgetting that he had once had another name. There did not seem to be any good reason to continue thinking of himself as Jacob Harkender, now that he no longer had Harkender's face or presence in the world of men; it seemed more reasonable to think of himself merely as an aspect or an avatar of Zelophelon. The invented name came to serve not only as a label but also as a bond: an affirmation of unity with his saviour.

While he was in the process of being reshaped for that mysterious purpose for which Zelophelon had remade him, Harkender could not gauge the passing of time. He could not count the days which passed his body by while it lay in its bed, for he had no awareness of the cycle of day and night; he could not perceive any significant difference between the states of dreaming and wakefulness. He might have counted the meals which his attendants fed him, but he did not even try. It seemed irrelevant, at the time, whether his schooling would take days or months.

When he was finally reconnected to the stream of time, he found that more than three years had passed since the day of the fire. He was neither astonished nor alarmed by this discovery. He was not, even then, incapable of astonishment or alarm, but the mere knowledge that he had spent three years in the sole company of Zelophelon and the symbolic Angel of Pain did not seem to warrant a response of either kind.

He was eventually able to infer what the principal purpose of his continued existence must be. He had no way of checking his deduction, but the logic of the case seemed unassailable.

He had been saved in order to be a master of seers.

Oddly enough, he could not tell whether it was some effort of his own which began to forge the necessary connections of sentience, or whether the links were made for him by his possessor. It did not matter; the day simply came when the truth was self-evident. He had been saved by Zelophelon in order that he might see, not through his own blind eyes but through the eyes of others. This was an ability which the inner eye had, and which he had once hoped to bring to oracular fruition in Gabriel Gill because he had not thought himself powerful enough to be his own oracle.

He was powerful enough now.

Uncertainly at first, but with growing competence and confidence, Zelophelon-in-Harkender built ties which bound him to certain other persons, whose eyes and intelligence he used parasitically, gleaning therefrom a kaleidoscopic image of the world as it seemed to be: comprising all the possibilities of human sensation.

The number of his seers might presumably have been legion, but in fact there were only three. Why Zelophelon had limited himself thus he could not know for certain, but he presumed that there must have been a danger of madness and confusion had he been further divided. Nor could he know how or why Zelophelon had selected the three whose sight he would share and whose inner thoughts he would hear. All three, he remembered, had been at the house in Whittenton shortly before its destruction by fire, but Zelophelon was surely too powerful a being to be limited by such a trivial coincidence; he preferred to believe that the significance of the choice lay in the future, and that each of his three seers would one day be uniquely useful for reasons which were not yet clear.

One of the precious lessons which Zelophelon-in-Harkender had learned from his passage through the fire, and from his intimate association with the Angel of Pain, was that patience and humility are greater virtues than they seem. He was humbler and more patient by far than the man he formerly had been, and was content to use his seers without knowing the ultimate purpose of his seeing. But he was free to speculate and to guess; to draw lessons from what he saw and to formulate hypotheses. He knew that Zelophelon must have a goal, to which his study of these three people must somehow be essential, and he was determined to be scrupulous in learning what he could from them. Though years might pass before the crucial revelation came, he had perfect faith in the inevitability of its coming.

One day, he felt certain, his second-hand sight would reveal what Zelophelon needed to know, and then . . . Then the time for watching and waiting would end, and

Zelophelon-in-Harkender's Purgatory would end too. Then, Zelophelon would act.

What Zelophelon would do, Zelophelon-in-Harkender did not know; he could only speculate. But of one thing he was absolutely certain; this long quiescence which they shared was merely a prelude to action, a process of preparation.

In due time, those Acts of Creation which had been stifled and deflected would be resumed and carried to their appropriate conclusion. It could not be otherwise, for the universe was changing, and Zelophelon had been forced to see how utterly inimical to its own ends and desires the processes and patterns of change had become. Zelophelon the angel had been forced to know and understand, beyond the shadow of a doubt, what utter futility there was in eternal waiting; everything which it saw and understood through the agency of Zelophelon-in-Harkender must therefore be directed to the end of discovering what it might reasonably do when the waiting was finally over.

2

The first and least of Harkender's seers was his one-time servant Luke Capthorn.

Harkender and Capthorn had first been drawn together by coincidence and convenience. Harkender's early adventures in magic – aided, though he did not know it then, by Zelophelon – had led him to attempt the experiment of stealing creative power from a slumbering angel, incarnating that soulfire within the embryo of a child which was to be carried and birthed by a whore named Jenny Gill. Unfortunately, Jenny Gill had not long survived the birth, and there had been a danger that those of his neighbours who thought Harkender an evil man (and there were few who thought otherwise) might build the accident into a scandal and succeed in having him thrown into prison. To hide the matter, he had placed the child in a foundling home at Hudlestone, which was supervised by the Sisters of

St Syncletica. Luke Capthorn's mother had been employed by the nuns to keep house for the orphan children in their care, and when Harkender sought an informant in that house to keep watch over Gabriel Gill, Luke seemed ideal for that purpose.

When the werewolves of London had stolen Gabriel away from the orphanage, Harkender had been sorely annoyed, and had taken Luke Capthorn into his employ in the hope that he might be of use when the time came to recover the boy. That hope had come to nothing, but Capthorn had served his new master loyally enough when he had been sent to Charnley to bring Cordelia Tallentyre to Whittenton, as a pawn for Harkender to use against her fiancé, who was an instrument of Zelophelon's adversary.

After the fire, Luke had returned briefly to Hudlestone, but had very soon left to take up a position as coachman in a house in London. Although he knew the work well enough, he was too lazy to be entirely satisfactory, and often lacked the foresight to make his many acts of petty dishonesty undetectable; for these reasons he had changed his employer twice before Harkender became a regular observer of his thoughts and habits, and was soon forced to seek new employment yet again.

At first, Harkender could find little stimulation or satisfaction in the use of Luke Capthorn's eyes and mind. Servants' quarters offered a view of the world which was both narrow and lowly; at times Harkender thought that he might have done better to be an insect busy behind a skirting board. Luke was not without curiosity – indeed, he was an inveterate eavesdropper – but the matters which most readily engaged his interest were of little or no concern to his user.

To Luke, information was a source of gossip and, very occasionally, a means to petty blackmail. His ambitions hardly extended at all beyond the pecuniary and the prurient, and the way in which he handled money was no more skilled or productive than the way he handled the servant girls he was perennially anxious to cajole or bully into his bed. He drank bad gin, he gambled without an atom of understanding of the principles of probability, and his conversations with those he thought of as his friends were as empty of sense and purpose as they were full of casual obscenity.

During his early days as a sometime passenger in Luke's mind, Harkender struggled unsuccessfully to find some merit or significance in the link which bound him to the man. He could not doubt that Zelophelon had some purpose in binding him thus, but he could not then imagine what it might be. As a lesson in humility it quickly exhausted its potential; Harkender had been born to the class of employers rather than that of servants but he had known his share of miserable servitude at school, and there was nothing he could learn about wretchedness from the likes of Luke Capthorn. As a character study, too, Harkender's new association with his former servant had limited potential; there was a certain initial fascination to be reaped from the contemplation of Luke's utter unsophistication, but it was after all a mere absence rather than a phenomenon in its own right. To see with Luke's eyes was to recover a primitive kind of vision informed by the most rudimentary understanding of the world, but once he had marvelled at its crudity there was little left in it to savour. If Zelophelon had intended it as some kind of antidote to the false sophistication which had been Jacob Harkender's undoing, it was a nostrum that failed.

Harkender considered for a while the possibility that Luke might have been presented to him as a medium of experiment. Given that the man's own desires were so brutal and his intelligence so mean, Harkender wondered whether he might not be susceptible to control by a higher mind. For a while, he explored the possibility that, in giving him access to Luke's inner being, Zelophelon might be offering him a body which he could possess and make his own. But try as he might, he could not even make himself heard or felt within the sordid theatre of Luke's self-awareness, let alone exert the power of his own will upon the young man's mind or body. He could share Luke's perceptions, but he could not begin to guide them.

Although he could not exert any conscious control over any of his seers, Harkender wondered nevertheless whether his occasional presence in the secret recesses of their sentience might have a subtle influence. For some time he looked in vain for signs that Luke might be changing, however slowly, to reflect the inquisitiveness of his mental passenger. But there was nothing; in fact, there was less than nothing, for Harkender could measure in his other seers the progress of natural processes of mental growth and sophistication which seemed quite impotent to affect Luke Capthorn's stubborn dullness.

Eventually – some time before any event which could be construed as confirmation – Harkender concluded that the part Luke was to play in Zelophelon's unfolding scheme would be determined not by what he was but by where he was destined to go. When he reached this conclusion, Harkender ceased to treat the tedium of Luke's daily routines as a puzzle, and simply used them as a way of marking time, extracting from them such tiny morsels of satisfaction as they were able to offer. He reckoned Luke the worst of that trinity of souls which had been opened wide for his inspection, and usually preferred to use the eyes of either of the others, but he accepted with patience and forbearance the apparent necessity of occasionally sharing Luke's being. It *was* necessity, for he could not choose which of his three seers to use at any particular point in time; it was Zelophelon's will which dictated that, just as it was Zelophelon's will which dictated that he should occasionally surrender the power of sight entirely, returning to the prison of his own blind self and his nightmarish dreams of the Angel of Pain.

After all inadequacies were recognised, though, there remained one great advantage which the sight of Luke Capthorn's eyes gave to Harkender while he used them; they were, after all, *eyes*; they were not blind. While he used them, he was not confined to the tight orbit of his own misery. The pain which gave him the power to use other eyes was not obliterated by the sharing sentience, but it was usually eased. Sometimes, to be sure, he could feel pain which his seers suffered as well as his own, but however bad their pains seemed to his seers to be, they never seemed to increase his own burden very significantly.

Agony, it seemed, could easily deny the logic of simple arithmetic.

Luke suffered few agonies of his own, beyond the occasional hangover or toothache; he was a sturdier man than most and a sufficiently devout coward to avoid courting injury. If only his enjoyments could have been more successful in compensating for Harkender's pain, the association between the two might have been reckoned usefully profitable, but they did not. Luke was the kind of drunkard who rarely paused to court elation, but pressed on hard to virtual obliviousness, and, on the fairly infrequent occasions when he persuaded some other to receive the gift of his semen, his thrusting was urgent and inartistic, calculated to win relief rather than savouring sensation. Harkender, who still thought of his earlier self as a connoisseur of good wine and unorthodox sexual intercourse, could find nothing in the sharing of Capthorn's pleasures which qualified as a distraction from his woes.

Ironically, the best palliative Capthorn's consciousness had to offer his unknown companion was a kind of numb lassitude which crept upon him when he was bored with his work, which he very often was. The ennui which Capthorn suffered and resented – and which Harkender would also have hated in his former incarnation – was experienced by Harkender/Zelophelon as a gentle balm.

Luke's devout Satanism was of some small interest to Harkender, even though he knew how foolish and misguided it was, and was irritated by the fact that his teaching had been misunderstood. It would have been more amusing had Luke sought out other heretics of a similar stripe, and given himself over to the fanciful dramatics of the Black Mass, but Luke was a Protestant Satanist rather than a Catholic one, and his relationship with his imaginary master was essentially private, unmediated by any but the most rudimentary of rituals. Nor was the devoutness of Luke's belief translated into any particularly avid penchant for evil works. He sinned continually and consciencelessly, but it could not be said that the religiousness of his self-indulgence was in any way heroic. Even the habits of sodomistic child abuse which he had cultivated at Hudlestone, long before he turned to devil worship, fell into decline once such opportunities were not so easily come by.

As Harkender's relationship with Luke Capthorn lengthened and deepened, he found an opportunity to observe the workings of nostalgic disease upon a vulnerable mind. As an objective observer he could see and understand the way in which Luke transformed and perverted his own memories, reconstructing his past into a benign and comforting presence.

By slow degrees, Luke's time at Hudlestone became a mythical Golden Age of glorious idleness and unlimited sexual opportunity. Harkender could agree that his labour had indeed been somewhat less burdensome in those days, and that the orphan children in his care had been far less able to withstand his various threats and temptations than the young servants who were now perforce the targets of his lusts, but Harkender could also understand – as Luke could not or would not – that these advantages had meant very little to him at the time.

Luke had been as miserable and sullen then as he was now, equally unappreciative of the bird in the hand by comparison with the two in the bush, identically frustrated with his own powerlessness, similarly convinced that he had been unjustly treated by fate and fortune. And yet, the drab dereliction of the experienced past was slowly transformed by the alchemy of false memory into an authentic buried treasure. How right Lucian de Terre had been to reveal the essential falseness of history, and how clever to recognise that only those who had sloughed off all delusion could ever begin to believe him!

Nostalgia was a disease to which Harkender considered himself immune, because he saw his own childhood, measured from the day that he had been sent to school, as a special Hell from which time had rescued him. He was therefore rather intrigued to see the magnitude of its effect on a true victim, and to speculate about the probable parallels between Luke Capthorn's misperception of his past and the grander misperceptions of history. But witnessing Luke's involvement in the unthinking business of forging an imaginary Golden Age made him suspicious of Lucian de Terre as well as helping him to recognise de Terre's genius. He could not but wonder what role nostalgia might have played in de Terre's attempt to offer a better history of the world than the one contained in the distorting lens of Victorian science.

This question was important because of its relevance to the enigmatic nature of his possessor Zelophelon, and for a while Harkender wondered whether that might be the sole reason why Luke had been given to him as a seer, but he concluded that it was far too trivial a matter. Still, such adventures of the imagination helped him to while away the many hours which he spent as a rider on the steed of Luke's consciousness, while he waited for Zelophelon to show him where that steed was destined to go.

Luke had been Harkender's seer for seven years when that moment of revelation finally arrived. Suspicion had fallen on him once too often in respect of one of the many small thefts which plagued the house where he was employed. Nothing could be proven to the point where he might be delivered to the processes of the law, but he had outstayed his welcome in yet another place of employ, and was forced to move on again. As was his wont when misfortune (as he reckoned it) caught up with him, he enquired among his acquaintances for news of any available position, and was referred by one of them to a certain gentleman whose servants showed a marked reluctance to stay with him, and who was therefore disinclined to worry about such niceties as references.

Luke went immediately to see this man, who looked him up and down, dismissed with an airy wave his attempts to explain why he was embarrassed by lack of employment, and demanded to know whether he had any objections to the sight of blood or the practice of vivisection. On being told that he had not, the gentleman asked whether he was host to any silly superstitions about man's right to tamper with nature. These enquiries could not but catch and hold Jacob Harkender's earnest attention, and he was triumphantly glad when Capthorn – having answered in the negative – was welcomed into the employ of Dr Jason Sterling.

Until this crucial moment in his new affairs, Harkender had been bitterly disappointed that his possessor had not given him direct access to a man of real mental achievement. He had gone so far as to lament the fact to his unanswering master, and to complain that admittance to the thoughts of such a man would surely be more valuable as a means of furthering Zelophelon's understanding of the world. Sir Edward Tallentyre and David Lydyard, upon whom he was enabled to spy by one of his other seers, provided some such supply, but Harkender's opinion was that both were and would always remain hamstrung by Tallentyre's keen scepticism. While he listened to their scrupulous dialogues he had often longed to insinuate himself into a mind more fertile and more daring than theirs, whose speculations could boldly go where theirs would not.

Sterling, he saw immediately, might be reckoned a partial answer to this prayer; from the moment of their first meeting he was convinced that Luke Capthorn's sole purpose as a seer was – and always had been – to confront him with Sterling. He would far rather have used Sterling himself as his seer, or a man who could ask more intelligent questions of him than Luke ever would, but he understood that the truly vital thing was that Sterling had been found. Zelophelon had discovered the man, perceived the importance of what he was trying to do, and had brought Harkender's seer into a position where he could observe the pattern of Sterling's experiments and the measure of his successes.

Jason Sterling had Sir Edward Tallentyre's power of reasoning and imagination, but he also had a practical turn of mind which made him active where Tallentyre was content to be contemplative. Tallentyre had never been an experimenter, and though his protégé Lydyard had gone a little way towards making up for that deficiency, Lydyard was a mere dabbler by comparison with the energetic Sterling: a painstaking analyst, not a bold contriver. Lydyard's powers of imagination were castrated by his father-in-law's stubborn orthodoxies but Sterling's knew no constraint at all.

Sterling shared with Harkender's former self a hatred and contempt for all established faiths, especially in science. He was realistic enough to recognise that many of the things which other men believed were undeniably true, but that only made him all the more anxious to find out some lie or folly with which to assault their complacency. He was a man who devoutly desired that every orthodoxy might be wrong, and that he might prove it; but he was never cowed by disappointment whenever he found out, to his chagrin, that what was commonly believed could not be much improved upon.

Sterling's laboratory seemed to Luke to be a place of dark magic; to him it reeked of the unholy. He was convinced that he had been guided there for a purpose, and was all the more enthusiastic in his work because of it. Harkender could appreciate the differences between Sterling's practices and his own, but he too recognised a kind of kinship in them. The studies in ritual magic which he had pursued in the days before the fire had been a quest to penetrate the appearances of the world, to go beyond the ordinary possibilities of sensation. His aim had been to lacerate the veils of illusion which confounded the five senses, dissolving them in the acid bath of self-torture in order to gain what glimpses he could of the higher powers which were capable of true Acts of Creation. Sterling was a hardened empiricist who would have been very impatient with talk of a world beyond experience, but still he was an adventurer, utterly unafraid of the extraordinary. He was ever avid to try something new, in a spirit of pure exploration. Nineteen in every twenty experiments produced nothing, but he was a man of indefatigable energy, more buoyed up by rare success than downcast by frequent failure.

Harkender's own interest in the progress of science had naturally drawn him to those ideas regarded as heretical by the vain peacocks of scepticism. Unorthodoxy had always attracted his attention. One of the matters which had fascinated him most had been the experiments in elec-trocrystallisation carried out by Andrew Crosse at Fyne Court, which had caused his superstitious neighbours to think him an authentic version of Mary Shelley's fictitious tempter of providence, Victor Frankenstein. Harkender had always considered the imaginary Frankenstein a great hero in spite of the doubts of his creator, and had deemed Crosse a hero too. When Crosse had inspired widespread curiosity and vitriolic criticism by his claim to have produced living 'insects' from inert materials while attempting to precipitate crystals of silica, Harkender's natural instinct had been to trust Crosse rather than the scoffers who stated confidently that the claim was unworthy of serious consideration.

Jason Sterling's scepticism had been rigorous enough to allow him to doubt Crosse's doubters; in his view the claim had been sufficiently intriguing to warrant thorough testing. Nor had Sterling, like so many others, been content to accept that a single failed experiment was conclusive disproof. By the time that Luke Capthorn was taken into his service he must have tried a thousand times, employing many different materials and many different sets of conditions, to create life using Crosse's methods. He had not succeeded in creating life from inorganic materials – and had eventually concluded that Crosse had not done that either – but his work had not been without rewards. He had discovered that the electrical stimulation of fertilised ova from various metazoan groups could, albeit rarely, result in remarkable deformations of the embryo developing therefrom, and the resultant organism. He had carried forward this work in electrical mutation, broadening its scope very considerably as his skills increased.

Luke Capthorn was at first a mere pair of hands for Sterling to use. He fed Sterling's creations, without thinking them any more peculiar than odd creatures which he had seen in Regent's Park Zoo. Such assistance as he rendered in vivisections and other experiments was initially minimal, but his stolid stoicism in the face of operations which might have sickened more squeamish eyes made him useful, and as time went by he slipped naturally enough into the role of Sterling's confidant. Sterling began to issue commentaries on what he was doing, and while Luke's attitude was no more than dutiful, Harkender's was much keener. In time, the sheer bizarrerie of Sterling's activities prompted Luke to increasing curiosity, and he learned to ask questions which were not completely stupid.

Many of Sterling's new species were insects, almost indistinguishable in Luke's eyes from their natural relatives, but some were more spectacular; some had been derived from the spawn of frogs and toads, others from various kinds of worms. A few of these were remarkable, not only in their oddity of form, but also in their habits.

In time, while Luke Capthorn helped him, Sterling contrived to produce adult amphibians which retained the powers of metamorphosis implicit in their normal development, so that they became different in form when they took to the water, and recovered a shape better adapted to crawling when they returned to the land. Some he schooled to stand upright, and these acquired the useful power of binocular vision. He also produced huge flatworms which fed in a manner entirely alien to their former nature, attaching themselves like leeches or lampreys to mammalian hosts and nourishing themselves on blood sucked through the wound made at the point of attachment. One of Luke Capthorn's duties was to keep these creatures regularly supplied with mice which they might use in this manner.

Harkender was fascinated by all these experiments. To him they seemed to comprise the first steps on the road to a scientific understanding of the power of Creation itself.

To Sterling, who could not know that the werewolves of London were not a legend, and did not share Harkender's knowledge of the Creators slumbering within the earth, his triumphs had a very different pattern of significance. When he had taken Luke fully into his confidence it became clear that Sterling's main interest was the possibility of transforming flesh in such a way as to overcome its essential frailty. Like all great alchemists he was not content with miracles of transmutation; he sought the secret of eternal life.

As soon as he learned of this quest, Harkender became enthusiastic for its success, for it went to the very heart of his own ambitions. He saw how wise Zelophelon was to have taken an interest in Sterling; and he came to understand that even angels might not be ashamed to learn from the enquiries of men.

3

Harkender's second seer was the brothel-keeper Mercy Murrell.

Harkender had known Mrs Murrell for many years, having first encountered her when she was a common whore, but it was not until she set up her own house and turned procuress that he took the trouble to cultivate a particular relationship with her. He had offered her an entry into certain strata of society which she could not otherwise have penetrated; she had supplied him with necessary services. In serving her ends he had served his own; while he insulated her from the worst consequences of her notoriety, his own image of calculated wickedness was nourished by the association. She had been his apprentice in magic for a while, but had been unable to make the slightest progress in liberating her spirit from the chains of naïve realism; he had interpreted this failure as proof of her irremediable dullness of mind, she as proof of his self-delusion.

Harkender and Mercy Murrell had been bound more tightly together by the unfortunate death of Jenny Gill, though the procuress was far too sensible to use what she knew of it as an instrument of blackmail. She did not need his money, being clever enough to make her own and invest it wisely; she only needed the unorthodox publicity which his acquaintance guaranteed. She had been in his house at the end, with one of her girls, whose function it had been to supply the stimulation which Harkender needed – or found convenient – in order to exercise his mediocre magical powers.

Mrs Murrell's independence of Harkender's charity by the time their first relationship came to its end was demonstrated by the fact that her career had continued to develop without his help. In the years which passed before Harkender made contact with her again, she had not merely survived but thrived; she had acquired a better and far bigger house, and had augmented its money-making potential with a very shrewd eye for the principles of trade and marketing.

In earlier times Harkender had despised the procuress,

though she was so frequently in his company. There had been no shred of affection between them, and neither had thought that they had anything in common with the other. Now it was different. Now that he could share her eyes and her intelligence, and move within the space of her very soul, Harkender gradually came to realise that he had misjudged Mrs Murrell.

What he had taken for dullness of mind he could now perceive, as she did, as a kind of strength. Far from being bound and imprisoned by the authority of worldly appearances, as he had thought her to be, Mrs Murrell was a past master in the art of penetrating a certain species of appearances: the masks which men wore in order to sustain and improve their everyday intercourse with others of their kind. While his other female seer provided Harkender with a telescopic outlook on the stars of scientific idealism, Mercy Murrell served to provide him with an insight into a gutter of covert desire which he found hardly less intriguing. In their notions of what men were and might be, his two female seers had views which were polar opposites, one seeing the great even in the downtrodden, the other seeing the bestial even in the grandiloquent.

Like Luke Capthorn, Mrs Murrell had escaped unscorched and unscathed from the fire at Harkender's home, but her exemption from harm had been the more remarkable because she had been on hand at the moment of outbreak; she had witnessed (as Luke had not) the tragically wasteful metamorphosis of Gabriel Gill. Her lack of reaction to that incident, Harkender came to understand, demonstrated the true extent of her obstinacy; the vision had not touched her soul any more deeply than the fire had touched her body. She had not believed in angels, and her unbelief had proved unconquerable by what she had seen, which she counted mere illusion. She still believed, resolutely, that the fire which had consumed the house had been started by a lamp overturned by Harkender in a fit of mad excitement.

That strength of conviction still served the aims and ambitions of its owner, and was clearly reflected in the way she ran her house. During the years that Harkender used her as a seer, hers became one of the most successful and fashionable brothels in London. This was no mean feat in a city whose population of prostitutes was estimated by the magistrate Colquhoun at 50,000 and by the bishop of Oxford at 80,000. Mrs Murrell considered – and Harkender could not doubt it – that her success was entirely due to her understanding of the true rationale of prostitution: its courtship of illusion and fantasy, its theatricality.

The success of Mrs Murrell's establishment was partly assured by the care which she took to cater to the full panoply of fetishisms, which the strict repressions of Victorian moralism had brought to a fuller and more gorgeous flowering than had ever been seen or imagined before. But this did not exhaust her ambitions and affectations, for she was keen to provide these services in a very particular environment. She built a stage in her new house and became a playwright of sorts, devising entertainments for her customers which owed as much to the inspiration of Drury Lane as to the music hall.

There were a dozen other establishments in London which made equally elaborate provision for simulation of the untender caresses of the Angel of Pain, and there were half a dozen others which had their own stages for the mounting of lewd shows of various kinds; but Mercy Murrell was fervent in her belief that only her productions could be trusted for true and poignant artistry. Her vanity in this matter was not without a certain absurdity, but the flow of money into her establishment gave her adequate cause for self-congratulation.

Harkender found Mrs Murrell a far more satisfactory companion in his private Purgatory than Luke Capthorn. Her view of the world was just as narrow, but it was infinitely more colourful. Harkender had been conclusively neutered by the fire which obliterated his earlier self, but an uncertain flame of sexual desire still flickered eerily within him. When he peered through Mercy Murrell's eyes at one of her dramatic productions, he could easily imagine himself as a eunuch in a harem, deliciously tempted and tantalised by sight and thought but quite unable to produce any meaningful physical reaction. Nevertheless, he did not dislike the experience at all. Indeed, he revelled in it; he loved the paradoxicality of it, and quickly became a connoisseur of delicate frustration.

The pleasurable quality of this experience was enhanced by the peculiar nature of Mrs Murrell's own reactions as she devised and consumed her own entertainments. She never indulged in sexual intercourse of any kind; the possibility seemed to her to be on a par with the idea of a self-made factory owner condescending to join the labourers in his own sweatshop. Indeed, she took pride in having exorcised from her soul all potentially enslaving feelings. Her voyeuristic interest in what went on in her house was, she believed, abstractly aesthetic and clinical. She was sufficiently proud to compare her pleasure with that of the architect or the scientific student of human behaviour, fondly imagining that it had nothing of the animal in it.

Harkender, sharing her consciousness, could see a measure of self-delusion in this, but for the most part the mere effort of representation was enough to make it true. Mrs Murrell was an eccentric connoisseur of lewd exoticism, a gourmet of sexuality. By a remarkably happy coincidence, this cerebral exercise of controlled lust was exactly tailored to the requirements and restrictions of Harkender's situation as an impotent sharer of her thoughts and sensations. He could not have envisaged a more satisfying partnership.

Harkender could no more direct the course of Mercy Murrell's thoughts and actions than he could control Luke Capthorn, but when he used her eyes instead of the servant's he felt less of a stranger. Mrs Murrell had been more profoundly marked by her acquaintance with Jacob Harkender than Luke had; she had known him far longer, and had shared his crimes as well as his intrigues. Of all his seers, Mercy Murrell was the one who thought most frequently of Harkender; her gaze was more often caught and held by sights in which Harkender would once have been interested, and she would sometimes silently say to herself on such occasions, 'How Harkender would have loved that!'

Almost invariably, he would have; almost invariably, he did.

There was so much solace and entertainment to be obtained from his sharing of Mrs Murrell's experience – despite the fact that his own body continued to burn in the grip of phantom flames – that Harkender was initially inclined to accept it as a gift instead of questioning its purpose. During the early years of his renewed association with Luke Capthorn he was for ever asking why and searching for a clue which would justify the tie which bound him to the man; but although he knew, at an intellectual level, that his renewed association with Mrs Murrell was equally problematic in terms of Zelophelon's interests, he did not allow the enigma to preoccupy him. He was content to let the question rest. This did not mean, however, that the relationship was incurious and unthinking; just as Mrs Murrell set out to be an objective, calculating connoisseur of her own productions, so Harkender set out to become an objective, calculating connoisseur of Mrs Murrell's feelings and philosophies.

To compare Mrs Murrell and Luke Capthorn was to embark upon a study in contrasts. While Luke was driven, sometimes uncomfortably, by the pressure of semen production to continual prurience and frequent masturbation, Mrs Murrell enjoyed such a carefully cultivated control over all such feelings that they could not even echo in her being. Such discomforts as she had when she bled each month were purely physical; her mood was quite unaffected. She and Luke were fiercely acquisitive in respect of money, but Luke's greed was basically a greed to consume, while hers was a greed to possess. Luke was as avid to spend as to acquire, and money had no meaning to him beyond its power to purchase instant gratification; Mrs Murrell, on the other hand, was a true capitalist, who valued money for its own sake and for its miraculous powers of increase; her spending was all calculated as investment, even when it seemed superficially to be wasteful and self-indulgent. While Luke tended to dwell nostalgically in a past which he repainted in softer colours to make it more inhabitable, the thrust of Mrs Murrell's thoughts was usually futurewards, anticipating triumphs yet to come.

Harkender, of course, had infinitely more sympathy with Mrs Murrell's turn of mind than Capthorn's. He was a product of the aspiring middle class, and, whatever other ideas had been beaten into or out of him at school, his commitment to the principle of deferred gratification remained inviolate. He too had a far heavier emotional investment in the future than he had in the past; hope was more dominant in him than fear, even now. He could see, however, as an objective observer, that there was a certain falsity in Mrs Murrell's attitude, for her anticipations of future gratification must inevitably be betrayed and destroyed – as all future hopes had to be – by death. He came to understand that there was a certain logic in Luke Capthorn's attitude to money which neither he nor Mrs Murrell could fully appreciate; Capthorn would die having had a full measue of gratification from every penny he ever earned or stole, while Mrs Murrell would die with the bulk of her fortune in store and unused. She had not even the excuse of wanting to enrich an heir which the majority of capitalists employed as a saving rationalisation for their habits.

In perceiving this absurdity in Mrs Murrell's attitudes, Harkender was forced to see an even greater absurdity in his own. He was a man as near dead as any could be; such sensation and emotion as he had was entirely second-hand, save only for the pain which racked and rent him. And yet he laid claim to be a hopeful man, whose mind was oriented towards the future. How ridiculous it would seem to Luke Capthorn that he refused and despised nostalgia, refusing to seek delight in his memories of a time when he had been whole and hale and capable of feeding his sensual appetites! But Harkender persisted, nevertheless, in believing that he and Mrs Murrell had the right of it. He was content to say, defiantly, that if he and she were to be reckoned perverse, they had every right to be proud of their peversity. He was a man who had never been ashamed to oppose the values and verities of others.

*

Although he could find no particular urgency in his consideration of the problem of why Mrs Murrell had been appointed by Zelophelon to be his seer, Harkender remained aware of it. Once or twice his attention was caught by some event which might provide a clue. When Capthorn found Jason Sterling, there followed an interval in which Harkender fully expected Mrs Murrell to make some equally valuable acquaintance, during which he watched every new client of her establishment with a speculative attitude. As the months went by, though, the clients came and went, and those who seemed potentially interesting remained firmly in the background of her life.

Harkender had recovered his former patient equanimity by the time she bought Hecate, but as soon as she had done it, he became convinced that this was her allotted role in Zelophelon's convoluted scheme.

It was by no means uncommon for Mrs Murrell to buy children for her house from their parents; she regarded it as a kind of charity. She paid a token sum – as little as a shilling or as much as half a guinea – to take girls from families which could not feed them, assuming responsibility for the task of saving them from starvation. No other future but whoredom was possible for the female jetsam of overpopulation, and it was to their great advantage that they might be launched into the higher echelons of that profession rather than take to the meaner steets, where gin and the pox would ruin them in a matter of half a dozen years. But Cath was very different from the common run of tradeable maids, and there was not another whoremistress in London who would have looked twice at her. Those who sold her were unashamedly gleeful to be rid of her; her price was sixpence, and they thought that they had made a wonderful bargain. Even Mercy Murrell did not think that she had got the girl cheap, but she did understand, as many others did not, that male sexual desire sometimes defied such notions as beauty and prettiness.

Mrs Murrell's customary practice was, of course, to hunt for attractive girls who might, with time and proper encouragement, become more attractive. She rejected dozens who would grow too dull or too lumpen, though it sometimes took a well-schooled eye to see the sleek woman within the starveling child. But she had an eye, too, for the unusual, and she understood the value of grotesquerie. Cath-who-became-Hecate was a grotesque: her spine was twisted and she had a club foot, uncompensated by any comeliness of face. But she had about her eyes a certain perpetual anxiety which was in its way hypnotic. More intriguing than that – much more, from Harkender's point of view, which was shared to a degree by Mrs Murrell – was the fact that she had a reputation as a witch. No one accused her of brewing potions or casting spells, or even of any particular evil intent, but it was said that in rooms through which she passed no ornament was safe, that chairs might fall and tables might rock uneasily. Those who knew her unhesitatingly proclaimed that she was accompanied wherever she went by a mischievous imp, the mocking and spiteful spirit of her deformity.

Mrs Murrell paid sixpence willingly enough, knowing that it would not be a foolish investment.

Harkender's thoughts, which ran in parallel with Mrs Murrell's as they contemplated her discovery together, soon diverged to follow a different track. To him, the rumours of her constant attendance by trivial misfortune spoke of possession and of poltergeists, and he knew from the very beginning that there was a possibility – however slim – that she was only partly human. He began immediately to speculate whether she might be one of those Others of whom Lucian de Terre had spoken in his book, which still had fugitive sparks of Promethean heat in their souls, or whether she might even be a creature like Gabriel Gill, carved by Zelophelon from its own soulstuff.

Although Hecate was as ugly as Gabriel had been beautiful, it was not difficult for Harkender to imagine that there might be something bound up inside her which, if and when it was permitted to unwind, might transform her as profoundly as Gabriel had been transformed. Harkender was not ashamed to nurse hopes that this might be true, despite the fact that the clues were slight and that he had been so direly disappointed by Gabriel. After all, he thought, Zelophelon had appointed Mrs Murrell to be his seer; what better service could she possibly render Zelophelon's cause than to discover and tend some latent power of Creativity which an angel might eventually direct to serve its ends?

Harkender also began to hope and fervently desire that Hecate might prove to be the means of repairing his own mistakes in respect of Gabriel Gill. In his foolishness he had delivered Gabriel into the hands of nuns, mistakenly unafraid of their influence because he knew how cowardly and hypocritical they were; but that mistake had spoiled the plan which he had woven around the boy. Now that Zelophelon itself had taken charge of their collaborative scheming, Harkender was confident that there would be no further mistakes of that kind. He was content to believe that Mrs Murrell's whorehouse would be a far better training ground for the kind of creature which Hecate might become than Hudleston Manor had been for Gabriel.

So, from the moment that Hecate was brought into Mrs Murrell's house and given her name, Harkender became intensely interested in her every action and all that went on around her. Here was a slender hope for the end of his punishment, and for his redemption from the pit of pain into which he had been cast. One day, he thought, he might be allowed by his possessor to renew the fleshy envelope that had been burned away in the fire, and walk abroad in the world again, so that he might tutor Hecate in those arts and skills a witch might be required to cultivate.

Even in the painful extremity of his private Purgatory, therefore, Harkender retained his faith in the marvellous providence of the being which possessed and kept him. From what he saw through the eyes of his seers, he took assurance that Zelophelon was gradually perfecting its methods of dealing with the world of men, taking from that world the best of what it contained, husbanding precious resources of knowledge and power.

Could its rival, he thought, possibly do as well, with only the likes of Tallentyre, Lydyard and de Lancy to aid it?

He thought not.

Zelophelon, he remained convinced, was more cunning than the Creator of the Sphinx, and shrewder by far as a judge of men.

4

The third, and the most precious, of Harkender's seers was Cordelia Lydyard.

Cordelia was the only one of the seers whose usefulness to Zelophelon seemed obvious from the very first. Being the daughter of Sir Edward Tallentyre and the wife of David Lydyard, she was intimate with both the men who had been responsible for the failure of the scheme which Harkender had hatched for the recapture and exploitation of Gabriel Gill following the seizure of the boy by the werewolves of London. The two men in question had been – and presumably still were – linked to the consciousness and cause of Zelophelon's adversary in much the same way that Harkender had been bound to Zelophelon. In Cordelia, therefore, Zelophelon had a spy in the heart of its enemy's camp. There was no way to know what the angel which Lydyard called Bast might be thinking, or planning, but through Cordelia it was at least possible to keep track of David Lydyard's reactions to his continued possession, and Tallentyre's attempts to deduce the true nature of the universe and the relative places of men and angels within it.

When Harkender had first encountered Cordelia, she had been unmarried. He had sent Luke Capthorn to kidnap her when it seemed to him desirable to obtain some leverage over Zelophelon's human adversaries. He had not liked her then, and had taken pleasure in frightening her. Had things worked out differently, he might have taken equal pleasure in causing her real harm, and not just because he hated her father with a particularly bitter virulence.

By the time Harkender began to use Cordelia as a seer, though, such petty malices had to some extent been burned out of him along with his flesh. He could still gloat over contemplation of the horror which Lydyard and Tallentyre would certainly feel if they only knew that a man they loathed had access to her inmost thoughts and secrets, but he had no particular animosity towards the woman herself.

When Harkender became an unsuspected parasite of her sensations, Cordelia had been married to David Lydyard for over a year, and she was heavily pregnant with her first child. Cordelia's mother died soon after the birth of that child, and her father spent as much time thereafter in Lydyard's house as in his own. Cordelia, at her own insistence, was party to all their discussions and speculations, or at least to those which took place in her home. She was sufficiently intelligent and interested to make her own contribution to their attempts to understand David's predicament, and their attempts to anticipate what the beings whose existence they had recently discovered might do, once they had properly acquainted themselves with the changes which had overtaken the world of appearances while they slept.

Cordelia was as precious to Harkender as she presumably was to his master by virtue of the fact that she had access to these discussions. Until Luke Capthorn met Sterling, Lydyard and Tallentyre were his main source of intellectual stimulation. He knew that everything he saw and heard at second hand through Cordelia's eyes was avidly consumed at first hand by the Creator of the Sphinx, and his association with Cordelia was therefore sharpened from the very beginning by the sense of being involved in a contest, in which his task was to wring more enlightenment from Lydyard's intellectual progress than Lydyard and his own silent passenger could.

He quickly found, however, that there were other facets of this particular association which were equally engaging, and perhaps equally important.

Strangely – and, in the beginning, somewhat against his own inclinations – Harkender found himself more easily able to sympathise and empathise with Cordelia Lydyard than with his other sometime hosts. In a matter of months, a special bond of community was forged between them. It was not a tie which Harkender set out deliberately to make, and Cordelia would have been utterly appalled by it had she had the least consciousness of it, but the simple fact was that she and the passenger in her thoughts were much more similar in outlook and feeling than either of them might have supposed. Harkender had far more in common with Cordelia, both in terms of the questing nature of his intellect and the hot intensity of his emotional life, than he had with either of his other seers.

Harkender and Cordelia Lydyard were both well-educated by their reading; and the knowledge which they had thus acquired had served to nourish and refine their native intelligence in broadly similar ways. In addition, they had both been drawn by their different philosophies and experiences into a dedicated opposition to the prevailing values of the society in which they lived. Harkender, having been made an outsider by the calculated exclusion of his peers, had become greatly embittered against those who considered themselves his superiors in social status; while Cordelia, cursed with having to meet the expectations embodied in the popular image of femininity, had become fiercely resentful of the status of her sex. Although Cordelia was less inclined than Harkender to embrace every possible heresy in reaction against her discontent, at least she had become very sceptical of every received wisdom, including those which her supposedly ultra-sceptical father never thought to question.

The growth and development of these seeds of resentment in their characters had equipped both Harkender and Cordelia with a tendency to suppressed wrathfulness, whose energies were frequently deflected into the expression of other emotions. Although the pattern of Harkender's former passions had been quite different from the pattern of those which Cordelia Lydyard cultivated, the fact remained that they were both passionate people. Harkender had little option now but to contrast his own former nature with the coldness of Mrs Murrell and the carelessness of Luke Capthorn, and he quickly understood that Cordelia was just as acutely aware of the difference between her own inner warmth and the temperamental coolness of her father and her husband.

All this was general, but there were specific and more intimate sharings which seemed to Harkender to be even more significant. Cordelia's life was not an eventful one – convention bound her to her home and to the homes of her close friends once she was a mother – and it was very different from the life which Harkender had lived, but it was punctuated by moments of intensity which reminded him very strongly of his own intensest moments. Over time, as more and more episodes of this kind accumulated, his identification with Cordelia's feelings and frustrations became far more profound.

There were, inevitably, two aspects to the empathy which made these moments infinitely precious to the man who savoured them at second hand: sexual excitement and pain.

Harkender was easily able to maintain a quasi-clinical attitude while he shared the lubricious voyeurism of Mercy Murrell and the perfunctory intercourse of Luke Capthorn. Their experiences offered little enough satisfaction to them, and hardly any to their patient observer. In the eyes of moralists and alienists Harkender's own sexuality, when he had been capable of indulging it, would have seemed no less perverted – probably far more so – than theirs, but Harkender had been capable of an intensity of feeling far beyond anything that Luke or Mercy Murrell could attain, which could bear comparison with what men were supposed to feel when in the throes of ecstasy. Compared with Harkender, Luke Capthorn and Mrs Murrell were emotional cripples, devoid of inner warmth.

Cordelia was not given to the kind of loud orgastic fervour which featured so extensively in pornographic fiction, and which Mrs Murrell's whores were carefully educated to pretend, but when she was touched, caressed and penetrated she was drawn into a long and thrilling crescendo of feeling which Jacob Harkender had not the slightest difficulty in likening to his own experiences.

In Cordelia Lydyard's couplings Harkender was able to find both delirious joy and luxurious solace. These were infinitely precious sensations which he could not find in either of his other seers, and certainly not in the disposition of his own wrecked body. Much to his gratification, the involvement of Lydyard as an instrument in these experiences, which meant nothing at all to him, also meant surprisingly little to Cordelia.

In his former life Harkender had cared very little, if at all, about his sexual partners – their role had always been mechanical, facilitating his escape into a private and perfectly self-enclosed world of pure sensation – and he could have schooled himself to be selective in paying attention to those of Cordelia Lydyard's sensations which best served this purpose. In fact, though, Cordelia was much less aware of Lydyard's identity and the particularities of his behaviour than Harkender would ever have dared to suppose. It was not that she did not care who it was that made love to her, nor that her feelings for her husband were not loving; but she too, when she made love, was cast by the animal spirits which stirred in her soul into an essentially private and personal realm in the secret depths of her self-awareness.

How different it was for Lydyard, Harkender could only guess. There was no way to judge whether Lydyard was perpetually and acutely aware of the specific physical presence of the woman he loved, or whether his sensations carried him away like a restless tide into some secret theatre of his own, populated by fantasy figures like those which strutted and fretted their fakery upon the stage of Mercy Murrell's whorehouse. Harkender did not know and need not care. Cordelia did not know either, but she did not know that she need not care, and there was always an intriguing edge of doubt about the love which she felt for her husband: a small measure of perceived risk, about which she could not but be anxious.

Harkender had no difficulty at all in separating Cordelia's diffusely joyous feelings from the object of her love. She most certainly did love Lydyard – though not quite as wholeheartedly as Lydyard might have hoped – but

Harkender felt not an atom of compulsion to do likewise simply because he shared the sensations of their copulation.

Harkender, in fact, learned to translate his empathy into something very different: a deep, abiding and passionate love for Cordelia herself.

More than once Harkender reflected wryly that this might qualify as a perverse narcissism, given that he shared Cordelia's consciousness, but that was unfair to himself. He did not *become* Cordelia while he used her as his seer; he always remained an observer, separate and in a curious way distant. He felt entitled, therefore, not to doubt the honesty or the validity of his accumulating love. More than that, he felt entitled to hold that his love was far truer, far better informed, and far less reserved than those feelings which David Lydyard was doubtless pleased to call 'love'.

In his growing love for Cordelia Lydyard, in fact, Jacob Harkender was convinced that he had found something quite new in the range of human experience, far better than anything of which ordinary men would ever be capable.

The occasional painful experiences which he shared with the object of his affection only redoubled this conviction – and not, he felt sure, because of any sordid or commonplace masochistic predilection.

His other seers, of course, were occasionally injured and sometimes ill, and Harkender shared their pain as he shared Cordelia Lydyard's. They felt exactly as much hurt when they were cut, bruised or sick as anyone would; but their reactions to pain were uniformly and wholly cowardly. Luke Capthorn and Mrs Murrell sought with all their might to avoid pain or, when it could not be avoided, to quell it with unguents or laudanum. Neither of them had any interest in the phenomenon of pain save to minimise its effect. Perhaps, Harkender thought, it was because of this they had each taken the trouble to anaesthetise their emotional sensibilities, with such success as to have thoroughly insulated themselves from any possibility of feeling grief, regret, or anxiety on another's behalf.

Although Cordelia lived what the other two would have sneeringly called a comfortable life, surrounded by all the trappings of modest wealth, she knew real pain far better than they did. She had suffered, and had sometimes been afflicted with excruciations more vigorous and plenteous than Mrs Murrell or Luke Capthorn had ever been forced to bear. Nor had she contented herself with fleeing from the effects of her suffering; she had tried to face up to her pain, to study it as she suffered, to bear it with authentic fortitude. In her own small and thoroughly secular fashion, she had trained herself in the artistry of martyrdom.

Cordelia Lydyard, like Harkender and her husband, was prepared to look the Angel of Pain in the face, and to labour to understand what was written in those angry features. The resolve to do so came, in part, from her love for her husband, for whose afflictions she felt such powerful pity that she sometimes longed perversely for the opportunity to share his pain, though she understood perfectly well that she could in no way lighten his burden by so doing.

But it was not only love that made her strong in the face of pain. There was also a kind of inquisitiveness, which seemed to Harkender even braver and more noble. Her father's pursuit of the answers to the Sphinx's riddles had made her curious about the supposed oracular rewards of the way of pain, and Harkender was pleased to see that in this connection she often thought of *him*, with a fascination that was by no means wholly hateful.

Cordelia was never encouraged by these meditations to imitate the experiments which Harkender had taken up in adult life, but that was hardly necessary. Just as Harkender's best opportunities to court the Angel of Pain had come about entirely naturally, when he had been cruelly and frequently beaten as a boy, so her best opportunities were offered up by circumstance.

Three times while she served as Harkender's seer Cordelia was to undergo the pain of childbirth, the first time shortly after he first became a partner in her life. He shared the savage pangs of each birth with her, intently fascinated by her attitude. She was, on each occasion, agonised yet expectant; she was brave because the pain was a gateway to joy and hope, a beginning and an end instead of a haphazard misfortune. Harkender, observing, had no choice but to apprehend – and thus to share – the joy and the hope. That sharing helped him, more than any effort of his own ever had or could have, to preserve the hope that his own unremitting agony might prove to be significant of something similarly fruitful.

Cordelia was open to the full experience of childbirth in a way that neither Mercy Murrell nor Luke Capthorn ever could have been to any of their afflictions. Mrs Murrell had once borne a child, before Harkender met her, and the memory of it was old when he first gained access to her thoughts, but he was still able to see that her attitude had been very different. For her, the child had been a misfortune, like any other life-threatening disease, and she had sweated to be rid of it in exactly the same spirit that she might have sweated out a fever. She had given the child away, with less compunction than the mothers from whom she was later to purchase surplus offspring; Mercy Murrell had never been any more willing than Luke Capthorn to offer a hostage to fortune by daring to love another. Cordelia Lydyard was made of better stuff, and in spite of the fact that Jacob Harkender had never made any substantial investment in love before his soul was joined to hers, he thought that the investment he had made in pain entitled him to be counted her equal, and gave him the right to salute her as a kindred spirit.

The same openness which showed in Cordelia's attitude to childbirth was manifest in all her experience of emotional pain. Harkender shared with her the bottomless grief she suffered in connection with the death of her beloved mother, the sometimes agonising pity which she felt while her husband's disease took an iron grip upon him, and her inexpressibly fierce anxiety when one or other of her children fell ill.

All these pains – so different from any in his own experience – amazed and fascinated him. At first they were so alien that he could not properly appreciate them, and in the later years of their association the fact that her husband was the principal target of Cordelia's distressful affections made Harkender's identification with them problematic, but he was inevitably overwhelmed by the feelings which she had for her children. He drank deep of the delicious fever of her fear when Nell came close to death with the whooping cough, and knew that what he and she felt together then was a kind of pain as absolute in its own terms as anything which had ever touched his own heart, in the long-gone days when he had made himself a Devil-on-Earth in order to escape the horror of the humiliations which others sought to heap upon him.

Through the sum of these shared experiences of suffering, Harkender came gradually to understand that his investment in pain had not been as wholehearted as he had thought. He became aware of inadequacies in himself which he had not previously suspected, and could not help wondering whether these failings had made his earlier journey along the path of pain a futile one.

He realised quickly enough that there might be more than one reason why Zelophelon had given him Cordelia as a seer, and that he stood to learn far more from his association with her than the contents of overheard discussions between her father and her husband.

If anyone could have brought Harkender to a state of repentance in respect of the path which he had chosen in his former life, Cordelia Lydyard would have been the one. She might have brought him to repent not by virtue of her saintliness – for she was not a particularly saintly woman by the stern standards of official decorum – but by her demonstration of the fact that the living hell through which he had passed as a child was not, after all, so strange and unparalleled.

Through Cordelia, Harkender learned for the first time that the suffering which had been cruelly inflicted on him was not much greater in magnitude than that which some of his fellow human beings bore willingly and unresentfully. Through her he learned how much resentment could be borne patiently and secretly, out of honest affection for those who were its unwitting causes.

But Harkender did not, in fact, repent. The commonwealth of feeling which he came to share with Cordelia, and the love for her which filled up his careworn heart, never compromised his use of her as a source of information. Nor did it shame him into any reluctance to spy and feed upon those moments which she considered to be her most intimate and most secret. He took a wry delight in all her smooth hypocrisies and petty lies, all her envies and temptations, all her bad humours and splenetic impulses. He could not love her sins as much as he loved her sufferings, but her vulnerability to very common failures of moral expectation nevertheless wrought a subtle change in the quality of his affection. The inflammation of his soul by the joy of his Heaven-made union never made him desirous of becoming *good*.

Harkender knew Cordelia Lydyard far too well to idealise her after the stupid and pathetic pattern of Victorian popular mythology. He knew, better than any other man in England, how ridiculous it was to imagine that men might be redeemed from their more vicious appetites by the expansive virtue of their wives. And yet, he also discovered through her the fugitive truth which sustained that silly edifice of false belief. He came to know and understand that only the loving are truly vulnerable; that only the loving can be hurt as extremely as it is possible to be hurt; that only the loving can ever really hope to see the unmasked faces of the gods.

It was, he knew, an immensely valuable lesson.

5

The observations of Sir Edward Tallentyre and David Lydyard which Harkender was able to carry out through the medium of Cordelia Lydyard's eyes and ears were not uninteresting, but in the light of his emotional involvement with his host they soon paled into relative insignificance. Even without such a distraction they might easily have failed to live up to the burden of his expectation; he would probably have been almost as disappointed in them.

It soon became clear to Harkender that Tallentyre had contrived to retain his pose of aggressive scepticism in respect of any and all claims made upon his belief. He had, to be sure, been forced to admit into his world-view the fact that there were such things as werewolves; that it was possible for one man to have access to the private thoughts and sensations of another; and that powerful godlike entities of some sort did exist, one of which had caused his strange adventure in Egypt, when he had seen the Sphinx created, and another of which was behind his far stranger adventure in England, when he had been brought into the little Hell which Zelophelon made.

In a curious fashion, though, these concessions had actually served to make Tallentyre's scepticism stronger, extending the field of his doubts to the point where he would assert that scientific enquiry was unfortunately less potent than he could have hoped, and that the power of the human mind to discover the truth about the history of the earth and the nature of the universe was much less than was popularly supposed. He became fond of arguing that the building blocks of reliable knowledge were few and misshapen, and that the imposing edifices of theory which were built upon them were held together by the unstable mortar of fantasy. He became sorely resentful of the difficulty of knowing *anything* for certain.

Lydyard frequently accused Tallentyre of harbouring doubts so corrosive that they castrated all attempts at understanding, and might easily become a stubborn barrier to any kind of progress; but Tallentyre refused to relent in the slightest. He was ever enthusiastic to point out that the fact that Lydyard had once had a true vision did not and could not prove that all truth was in principle recoverable by visionary means. It was equally certain, Tallentyre said, that Lydyard's visions had contained a great deal of fantasy and illusion; because of that, one could never know whether what one saw in a vision was true or not until it had been checked against ordinary empirical evidence, and where no such check was possible, no item of visionary evidence could possibly be considered reliable.

By virtue of such arguments, Tallentyre dismissed virtually everything which Pelorus told him about the real history of the earth as untrustworthy fabrication, and he remained stubbornly agnostic about the materiality of his own confrontation with Jacob Harkender in Zelophelon's infernal theatre, leaning to the opinion that it had been a kind of shared dream.

Harkender had to admire the relentlessness of Tallentyre's argumentative powers, but could not see why Tallentyre failed to take his case one step further, to the conclusion that *all* experience was merely a shared dream, and that what he called 'ordinary empirical evidence' was simply a facet of that sharing. Then, Harkender thought, Tallentyre would have been forced to confront – as Descartes had been in that version of the *Meditations* which he shamefully suppressed – the awful truth that he might be the victim of some tricksterish demon whose maintenance of the consistency of appearances could at any moment cease.

Harkender realised eventually that Tallentyre's position was not as unrelenting as it seemed, but rather resulted from a role which he delighted to play – that of Devil's Advocate. The baronet's scepticism was not to be seen in isolation, but rather in the context of his ongoing debate with Lydyard, in which Lydyard's appointed role was to take the opposite seat on the argumentative seesaw.

It was Lydyard, not Tallentyre, who was supposed to push their understanding forward by producing hypotheses which Tallentyre would then refine by restraint and restriction. Tallentyre had no intention of forbidding speculation, and knew perfectly well that the truly important questions which were to be addressed had nothing to do with scientific certainty, but had instead to do with future possibility. He accepted that if fantasy was the only instrument which could be used to deal with such questions, then the task at hand was to use fantasy as sensibly and responsibly as it could be used; the questions were too important simply to be abandoned and forgotten.

Tallentyre and Lydyard were united in the hope that
what they had accomplished in 1872 might be the end
of the matter. They knew that the two entities involved,
whatever they might actually be and whatever the extent of
their power was, had been previously inactive for centuries,
and might now condescend to be inactive for ever. Being
exceptionally cold-souled men, they had no interest in the
possibility – devoutly conserved by the heretic priests of
St Amycus and others – that the power of such Creators
might intervene to make a Heaven of the world in which
they lived. Their hopes, like the Clay Man's, were all
pinned on improvements which men might make by their
own efforts; they wanted nothing from Creators except to be
let alone. But they both knew all the time that hope might
not be enough. They both knew that the matter might *not*
have ended; and thus they accepted that they must face as
bravely and cleverly as they could the question of what might
happen if the two awakened Creators were not content to
sleep.

Lesser men than they might have concluded that the
Creators were so powerful, and men so weak, that no
reasonable plans could possibly be made for human action
in the face of Acts of Creation; but Tallentyre and Lydyard
thought they knew better than that. They had already
intervened once in the affairs of the ignorant angels, and
could not now be convinced of their own irrelevance and
impotence, despite the fact that they had not an atom of
magical power between them.

Tallentyre was perfectly happy to believe, along with
Alfonso the Wise of Castile, that had he been present
at the Creation he could have offered God some very
sound advice. If Creation was to be upset in some fashion,
however localised the effect might be, he was ambitious to
seek such an advisory appointment. Harkender could hardly
blame him for that, given that the sole reason for his own
continued existence, from his own viewpoint and that of
his protector and possessor, was to fill exactly such a role.
It was not entirely vanity that suggested to Tallentyre and
Lydyard that they might one day have the opportunity to

offer advice to an angel; nor was it vanity that informed Harkender that *his* task was to take account of any advice on which Tallentyre and Lydyard became resolved, and offer better to Zelophelon.

So it was, therefore, that Tallentyre and Lydyard continued – in admittedly desultory but not unserious fashion – to play the game of deciding what the angels which watched the surface of the earth might eventually decide to do, and what they ought to do. Cordelia was not always party to the discussions, but she was always told of their results; Harkender was easily able to keep track of the game, and to add his own contributions to it, purely for the benefit of Zelophelon.

It was, thought Harkender, a very strange and amusing way to decide the fate of the world – if, in fact, that was the issue to be decided.

Long before he began to draw inspiration from the likes of Tallentyre and Sterling, Harkender had formulated ideas of his own regarding the interests and possible future action of the awakened angels. His initial resources were, of course, somewhat different from theirs. He was as little inclined as they were to trust the literal truth of the Clay Man's *True History*, but as an attempt to understand and allegorise the actual nature of the world he gave it far more credit than Tallentyre could. He had in addition the results of his own experiments in visionary enlightenment – the early trifling with the Way of Pain, which had first linked him with Zelophelon.

Harkender accepted that Zelophelon would probably never speak directly to him in order to offer him a detailed account of its nature, substance, power and ambition. He tried to feel less resentful of this than Lydyard did about his own possessor's mockingly uninformative masquerade as the Egyptian goddess Bast. However generous he tried to be in accepting the reasonableness of this secrecy, though, he could hardly help feeling a certain sympathy with Lydyard's suspicion that the angels were both afraid and uncertain. It was at least possible, he knew, that Zelophelon itself did not understand exactly what it had become in response to the underlying forces of change which were inherent in the evolution of the universe.

Perhaps, Lydyard suggested, the fallen angels were as much a mystery to themselves as men were. Perhaps they, too, were afflicted with dreams and nightmares which they could not control and whose significance they did not know. Perhaps they, too, meditated upon their own nature as Descartes had upon his, and found that they could not properly envision what they were.

Tallentyre, as might be expected, found this idea attractive.

'Science,' said Tallentyre once, 'is a map of the material world, which may be imperfect in many ways, and imperfectible in some, but still it lays out for us the forms of the earth and the universe, and the course of their past history. For all its faults, it's a very useful map. But when we try to turn the map-making eye upon our own selves, we find little that we can easily depict. The image of the mental ghost within the bodily machine which Descartes drew is unfortunately incoherent, but we've found no better representation to take its place. We are self-aware, but we have no sensible image of that self which is both awareness and its object.

'Perhaps these beings which we call gods or angels, for all their magical powers, are no better off in this regard. Perhaps, in fact, they're at a greater disadvantage, in having no bodies of their own, hence being all ghost and no machine. Perhaps that's why they've been so confused by the changes which have overtaken the appearances of the universe, not knowing what dangers and opportunities are inherent in whatever matter they now might choose to inhabit. If so, they might be very dependent upon their human agents, and creatures like the Sphinx, for it may be the case that only the senses of such limited material beings are capable of making descriptions – scientific maps – of reality.'

Harkender found such speculations mildly intriguing, but they echoed notions which he had long entertained, and he thought them insufficiently original to be dignified with too much reverence.

In the beginning, when he first set out to practise magic, he too had thought of gods and angels as Cartesian souls writ large – as huge entities of 'mental substance' which were not confined by bodies as human minds were, but free to roam at will, able to create material structures for their own habitation or to inhabit any material structures which already existed. He knew well enough, as Lydyard and Tallentyre did, that there was a certain paradox involved in trying to imagine things that were not material, and yet could exert force upon matter; but like them he could not find a better way of trying to envision them. But he had soon put such logical entanglements aside in order to concentrate on other matters. Lydyard and Tallentyre were reluctant to do that, and hence remained more deeply enmired in unsolvable enigmas. Their discussions of the conflict in which the angels seemed to be involved were therefore very tentative indeed, and Harkender believed that he had always had a surer grip on that issue than they would ever obtain.

Harkender had never taken seriously the notion that these mighty Cartesian minds were organised into great armies under rival commanders, as the dogmas of the Church tended to imply; but he had always been perfectly certain that they were engaged in some kind of eternal struggle against one another, and that the world of spirit seen as a whole was in turmoil. In keeping with the Darwinian spirit of his age he had come to envisage this state of conflict as a cosmic struggle for existence: a war of all against all in which the fittest survived by efficient predation. This seemed to fit in well enough with Lucian de Terre's account of the end of the Golden Age and the consequent Age of Heroes.

Harkender understood, though, that although it echoed the Darwinian idea of the struggle for existence rather neatly, this notion of metempirical affairs was not simply a reflection of the conflicts of living species. If Lucian de Terre's account of the Creators was to be trusted at all, the angels could not be separated out into species but were all – in spite of their powers of self-transformation – of one single kind. The contest between living organisms was essentially a contest of reproduction, each kind tending always to increase its numbers save for the checks exerted upon it by other kinds; the contest between beings of soulfire was a more straightforward matter of individual survival. The result of the competition between living species was an evolution of form, by which ancestral lines produced increasingly sophisticated reproductive machines; but the Creators which Harkender imagined already possessed unlimited plasticity of form, if they chose to use themselves up in its exercise. Thus, while the contest of living forms had tended towards variety and more efficient reproduction, the contest of the Creators had tended towards a lessening of numbers and increasing caution in the exercise of their power.

Lydyard and Tallentyre, in the course of their stumbling discussions, made these same points, but Harkender was impatient with the way in which Tallentyre hedged them around with countless ifs and buts. To him, the conclusions seemed obvious.

Harkender was prepared to accept that the Creation of the universe must have been, by definition, the single Act of a single Creator; he also perceived that one possible outcome of the situation which he now believed to exist was that the contest of the Creators would have a single ultimate winner. Thus, he saw, there might be a connection of past and future – a sealing of the circle of time; a union of Alpha and Omega – while in between there was naught but a riot of division and change, full of sound and fury but in the end signifying nothing.

If this were so, he concluded, then the ambition of Zelophelon – and of every other Creator which still existed, wherever in the universe it might be – must be to absorb into itself all its rivals, and thus become the one and only God. In the end, according to this argument, the quest for survival and the quest for absolute power were one and the same thing.

This seemed to Harkender a worthy and altogether understandable ambition. But when Lydyard produced a version of the same argument, Tallentyre was dismissive.

'I know you've seen visions of this ultimate God,' he said, 'but I'm inclined to dismiss them as hallucinations born of your early indoctrination in that faith which we have both abandoned. I see no need to suppose that because there are little Creators which have the power to defy natural law, they must have been made by one great Creator whose place they are ambitious to take. I see no reason to think that the universe hasn't always been in existence, and that these Creators, in spite of their numinousness and their seemingly magical powers, are natural products of its evolution, just as living things are. I stand by what I told the Spider years ago: the true scheme of the universe is as infinitely vast relative to its kind as it is to ours, and will always remain so. Even if we're as insignificant by comparison with it as the germs which swarm inside my bloodstream are by comparison with me, it has no more hope of becoming a real god than the infusoria have of becoming me.'

Harkender was unimpressed by this argument, which he considered to be based in a false analogy. He knew that his notion of the state of affairs in the world of the Creators must be drastically oversimplified, but he did not think it crucially mistaken.

Harkender accepted, therefore, that Zelophelon was both divinely ambitious and divinely anxious: ambitious to increase itself to authentic godhood by absorbing others of its kind, but anxious lest it should be absorbed and annihilated. He accepted, too, that such a combination of ambition and anxiety must have led to the long quiescence of those Creators which were on or in the earth. The result of their past contest had been to reduce their number to a few individuals of more or less equal power, none of which had dared to attack any of the others; all had elected instead to conserve their power as meanly as they possibly could, becoming quiescent and ultimately inert. That stalemate had, apparently, lasted for thousands of years before Harkender's daring exploit had tempted a small – and quickly aborted – investment of creative energy from Zelophelon.

Harkender assumed that there were several matters of crucial relevance to Zelophelon, the truth of which Zelophelon might or might not know. He was not surprised to find the same questions brought out into the open by Lydyard for

Tallentyre's consideration. First, how many other Creators were there which were in a position to attack it or be attacked by it? Second, what was their state of readiness to launch or withstand attack? Third, in what way could Zelophelon (or Bast) best employ its own creative powers in such a way as to seize and preserve a crucial advantage in the contest?

Zelophelon had presumably been tempted into action before because it had deduced answers to these questions on the basis of what it already knew and what it discovered from its brief mental association with Harkender. These had been hasty conclusions which it had then found to be incorrect. Tallentyre, encouraged by the Sphinx, had only had to make a vivid demonstration of the size of the universe, and the relative tininess of the earth, in order to startle Zelophelon into an immediate abandonment of the scheme which it had set in motion.

Evidently, the universe had changed while Zelophelon slept much more profoundly than it had been able to understand as a result of its original link with Harkender's consciousness. Harkender did not doubt that the extent of its present possession of his soul and senses was much more complete and much more careful. It now knew how large the universe was, and understood the significance of that fact – a significance which Harkender could only try to guess.

Had the universe, Harkender wondered, actually changed so much within the span of human history? When Aristotle described a universe with earth at its centre, while the planets and stars were carried around it in a series of crystal spheres encasing it, had the universe really been like that? Had the edge of Creation been close at hand, not much farther away from Athens than China? Had the stalemated Creators laid themselves to rest in an arena which seemed to them no larger than the Colosseum had seemed to the gladiators which fought there, only to wake up to the awful shock of infinity?

That such might really be the case, Harkender did not doubt, though Tallentyre refused to accept even the possibility. Harkender accepted much more readily and whole-heartedly than his adversaries that the world of apperances really did change, and he had no difficulty in supposing that what once appeared tiny might, on a mere whim of change, come to appear instead not merely large but infinitely large. But why should that matter to Creators, who must, after all, be masters of appearance? Why should a Creator not be able to exercise a whim of its own, to shrink infinity into a grain of sand?

For what it was worth, Harkender knew, the werewolf Mandorla had assumed that an awakened Creator could do exactly that, reeling back the ages to restore the Golden Age in the twinkling of an eye. But given Zelophelon's reaction to Tallentyre's challenge, Mandorla may have been wrong; the change in the universe could not have been merely a matter of superficial appearances. If that were so, then the Creators too must have changed while they lay quiescent. Zelophelon's essential situation must have altered in some very significant fashion.

But how was that to be imagined, given that it was so difficult to envision what the Creators were like?

Logically, Harkender knew – and knew long before he heard Tallentyre press home the point again and again – there were difficulties in speaking about a world of 'appearances' which could be altered by Acts of Creation. Such talk left unanswered, and possibly damned as unanswerable, questions about what it was that could 'appear' and 'change'. In order to be independent of the world of appearances on which they acted, the Creators themselves had to be pictured as operating outside or behind appearances – hence the idea that they were vast free-floating souls, able to alter matter without themselves being composed of it. He understood that the image of the mind or soul as an entity of pseudo-substance sitting in the brain and pulling the levers which activated the body-machine was essentially silly, no matter how convenient it might be as an analogy. But once one had admitted that it was inadequate to think of Creators as huge free-floating souls with the power to pull all the hidden levers of the material world, how was it possible to contrive a more accurate representation?

The discussions of Lydyard and Tallentyre never shed any new light on this enigma. Moreover, just as the two men found no means of issuing an accurate description of the relationship of the human mind and the human body, so they found no means of issuing an accurate description between that of angels and the world of matter. And yet – as Tallentyre was overfond of saying – the debate had to continue whether it had adequate descriptions to use or not. They all had to ponder the enigma of the angels, even in the absence of any sensible and coherent model of what angels actually were and how they related to the world of matter.

And so it was, quite probably, with the angels themselves.

Tallentyre often wondered aloud whether it would ever be possible for the human mind to discover an accurate description and full understanding of itself. He always concluded that there was no way to know. Harkender was sure, though, that even if no final answer was achievable there had been measurable progress in the philosophical quest. No correct answer had been achieved, but certain incorrect ones had been discarded.

Zelophelon, Harkender came eventually to believe, might easily be in a parallel position: incapable of understanding its own nature, but still capable of discovering errors in the imperfect images it had.

Was that, he wondered, what had happened when Tallentyre had shown it the appearance which the universe now presented to the educated eyes of mankind? Had Zelophelon suddenly realised – as the Creator of the Sphinx must have realised more quickly – that it had been mistaken in its estimation of its own nature?

Perhaps, Harkender sometimes thought, the power of the Creators really had been shrinking while the apparent universe was expanding. Perhaps Zelophelon, which had once had everything that existed potentially subject to its whim – were it not for its rivals! – could not now alter more than a tiny fraction of it. Even if that were so, and its hopes of godhood were indeed derelict, it might still have the earth for its achievable empire, if only its rivals could be conquered and consumed!

Even that, Harkender decided, would be a victory worth winning. Even that was an end which might justify the sacrifice of his former life in the hope of a future reward – for he had never, in all of this, forgotten himself.

Harkender was by no means as proud as Tallentyre, who waxed interminably lyrical on the subject of his refusal to worship gods even if they had the power to possess, madden and destroy him, but he was not without ambition. He desired to be the loyal servant of his master precisely because he believed that he might in some inestimable fashion share in whatever godhood, however limited, his master might one day achieve.

That was why Harkender continued for seventeen years to give his full attention to the task of trying to discover a way for Zelophelon to win its war, and the corollary task of trying to ensure that it had protection against the possibility of defeat and destruction.

These were the problems upon which Lydyard and Harkender – each of them preserved, possessed and carefully tormented – were condemned to exercise their captive minds, while Tallentyre played court jester to the pair of them.

At the same time, Harkender asked similar questions on his own behalf. Could he ever recover a better kind of life than the one he now had? Dared he aspire to something better than the merely human? And if nothing better were possible or attainable, could he – could he bear to – preserve what he had indefinitely?

No doubt, he thought, Lydyard asked the same questions incessantly of himself.

And they both, in their not so very different ways, had Cordelia to succour and console them.

6

It was his attendants, not Harkender himself, who first became aware of the fact that his wretched cinder of a body had begun to repair itself. He had long since ceased to make any significant effort to understand the distorted voices which buzzed and gibbered in his ruined ears, or even to judge their tone; nor was he alert to the returning sensations of sight, whose first signals he took to be mere phosphenes or surreal hallucinations. He had grown used to ignoring the meagre phenomena of his own existence, whenever he was forced to experience them instead of sharing the eyes and mind of one or other of his seers, and it was understandable that the change in their quality should elude his perceptions.

As soon as he did become aware of the change in his condition, though, he was able to detect all its sensory consequences, and to realise how his circumstances had changed. Once he had realised that the light which he could now glimpse was indeed light, and that the murmurous sound afflicting his ears could be decoded into words, he began to strive with all his might to see and to hear.

He learned to listen again, and discovered from the talk of those who cared for him that he had been a topic of discussion and controversy for some while.

He heard the two doctors who had charge of the asylum – unaware as yet that his hearing had returned – discussing the apparent miracle of his unexpected improvement. He heard the ambition of one to give publicity to the event quashed by the other, on the grounds it would only arouse enmity from those of their peers who would be reluctant to concede that such a thing could happen.

'We must be all the more careful,' said the senior physician, 'because of his identity. This is a man who posed as a magician, and has not been forgotten by those credulous enough to believe in his imposture. You and I know well enough that it must have been a near-miracle which kept him alive after suffering such burns, and we have some cause to be grateful for the fact that he has lain here helpless for twenty years, unseen by the world and unable to claim credit for his achievement. There are too many halfwits abroad these days who might take this evidence of belated resurrection for proof that he is indeed the Anti-Christ he once set out to be. If he becomes capable of making such claims on his own behalf, let him; but let us steer clear of it if we can.'

He would have laughed at them, but he had as yet no voice. When the power of speech did return, he was careful to be as meek as he was cunning, for he knew that it might not be easy to recover control of his own affairs. As soon as he could, he enlisted the younger doctor as an ally, and took the trouble to be excessively grateful to those who had fed and cleaned him for so many years. He promised them all rewards, and made good his promises as soon as he was able to reassert his authority over the lawyers who had held his estate in trust.

He was glad to find that he was richer now than he had been before the fire, though he did not know whether he ought to thank his trustees for that, or Zelophelon.

The road to recovery was slow, and there was no release from his pain; if anything, his agonies increased as his senses grew sharper. He was still glad to escape, whenever it was permitted, into the visionary world, to seek the comfort of his seers, and he never relaxed his vigilance over those he had been set to watch: Sterling; Hecate; Lydyard and Tallentyre. Indeed, he searched assiduously in his vicarious experiences for clues to the reason which Zelophelon must have found for re-equipping him with powers of real perception and movement.

He had often prayed, of course, for just such a release, and had always dared to hope that he might become so precious to his master Zelophelon that the angel would consent to restore his freedom. He had felt free to imagine that he might be trusted to take charge of Hecate once her undoubted powers had begun to come under her conscious control instead of responding waywardly and inefficiently to her more primitive impulses. But there was as yet no detectable sign that Hecate could direct her power, and so he looked elsewhere for reasons.

Eventually, he saw a distinct possibility that it might be Jason Sterling rather than the crippled whore whose activities might warrant action on his part.

Sterling's researches had become rather less fascinating to Harkender as the years had gone by, partly because of the increasing intimacy of his parallel involvement with Cordelia Tallentye, but partly because the scientist's work had ceased to yield much in the way of new results. For the first five years of Luke's association with Sterling, simple curiosity had been easily adequate to sustain Harkender's interest in the man; there was so much to learn about him, and Harkender's means of learning were so indirect. But as the five years had become seven, and then ten, Harkender had become aware of the fact that Sterling had ceased to make any significant progress.

The scientist had not lost his alchemical touch; his electrical experiments were still producing new species, but Sterling was not the kind of man to be content with purely quantitative achievements, and nor was his patient observer. They both knew that these additional items of evidence were bringing him no nearer to his true goal, and he had for some time been casting about desperately – but fruitlessly – for some new discovery to lend impetus to his real quest.

Harkender had known for some time before his regeneration began that Sterling might well stand to benefit from a particular imaginative stimulus which, ironically enough, Luke Capthorn could have provided, if only he had thought of it. Inevitably, this awareness had brought a gnawing but sullen frustration to Harkender's contemplation of Sterling's activities, which was further fed by the blind alleys into which the scientist's work increasingly took him.

More than once Harkender had shouted a desperate instruction to Capthorn's unhearing ears, knowing that he could do no good but unable to bear the burden of inaction; often and anon he prayed to Zelophelon, urging the angel to risk some trivial fraction of its godlike power in offering a sign.

When the sign was eventually offered, Harkender had no way of knowing whether Zelophelon had indeed contrived it, or whether mere blind chance deserved the credit; but he watched with profound relief as the chain of events unfolded, and he could not help wondering whether his own recovery was connected with it.

*

The seed of Sterling's new adventure was sown in one of the least promising of the second-hand bookshops in the Charing Cross Road, where the scientist and his servant had been driven to take shelter from a shower. While browsing, Sterling discovered the four volumes of Lucian de Terre's *True History of the World*. Unperturbed by the dust which clung to them, the scientist was inspired by the title to inspect the first few pages, and was then sufficiently intrigued to want to read the whole. The title sparked no immediate echo in Luke Capthorn's mind, but when Sterling had read the first volume he could not resist the temptation to tell his assistant what manner of story was there told.

It was, inevitably, the mention of the werewolves of London that attracted Luke's attention and made him tell his master – for the first time in any real detail – what he remembered of Jacob Harkender's interest in the same story. In the absence of the book, Sterling would have thought it a fine farrago of nonsense, but he had as much respect as any learned man for cold print, though he was far too sensible to believe more than a hundredth of what he read.

Once the beginning was made, the temper of Sterling's mind ensured that everything which Luke could be induced to remember would be drawn out of the dim recesses of his memory and displayed to the fullest extent that the servant could contrive. It was a slow and untidy business, but it proceeded inevitably to the climax which Harkender easily foresaw, and whose crucial importance he had long ago realised.

Luke Capthorn told Jason Sterling that in the days preceding the fire at Whittenton, Jacob Harkender had discovered where the man who wrote *The True History of the World* had been buried, and where he presumably still lay. And Sterling, inevitably, reasoned that if there was any truth at all in the *True History* which Adam Clay, alias Lucian de Terre, had written, then the man who lay in that tomb was only apparently dead.

Sterling did not believe it – how could he, given that he was the kind of man he was? – but he saw that the proposition might easily be put to the test, and he knew what a huge

difference it might make to his quest and to the possibility of
its success if he could bring immortal flesh into his laboratory
to be studied.

In time, therefore, Jason Sterling and Luke Capthorn set
out with Richard Marwin to exhume the man which the angel
named in the *True History* as Machalalel had forged, many
thousands of years before, out of clay.

Harkender watched them at their work through Luke
Capthorn's eyes, and saw what happened when Austen came
to challenge them. He understood far better than Luke what
the intervention of the bats must signify, and like Luke he was
at first content to assume that they had been sent by the angel
which Luke called Satan and he called Zelophelon.

It was natural enough for Harkender to guess that Zelophelon
had restored his own flesh in order that he should go to help
Sterling in his researches. The coincidence of timing seemed
to favour the hypothesis, in that he was now able to see
clearly, and hear perfectly well, and had taken complete
charge of his own affairs. While Sterling and Luke were
transporting the Clay Man to Richmond, Harkender was
already preparing to leave his asylum for the last time. He
was in the process of renting a house near the Botanical
Gardens at Kew, less than three miles from Sterling's house,
and had begun to hire servants.

He had by no means recovered the full bloom of health;
when he looked at himself in a mirror he could hardly
recognise himself, and he appeared almost as ugly and
grotesque to his own once vain eye as Hecate. His flesh
was unnaturally white and it clung very thinly to his bones,
but it had sufficient strength in it to let him stand and walk
– painfully, but effectively.

The doctors had made every possible effort to assist him,
desiring to see the back of him as soon as it might be
humanly possible; he was equally anxious to be gone.
They had put away their capacity to be amazed by his
recovery, and pretended that they had always believed in
its possibility; he pretended to take their word for it. They
spoke enthusiastically, if slightly uneasily, of his return to

normal life; he never yielded to the ever present temptation to taunt them with an account of how abnormal his life was and would for ever remain.

Although he was now awake and active for eight or ten hours a day, he slept far longer than ordinary men, and at irregular hours. He still had his seers; he had to make time for his visions. No one thought this unusual; it was obvious to all who saw him that however alert his mind was, his body would always carry the terrible scars of his ordeal.

When he lay down to rest on the afternoon of the day which followed the night of Adam Clay's exhumation, he already knew that it would be the last time he would sleep upon the bed in which he had lain for more than twenty years. His new carriage was due to collect him that evening.

Even if he had not made such arrangements, he would have had to depart; what he saw when he closed his eyes and slipped into his customary trance, spurred on by the pain still roiling in his soul, made it clear to him at last why his master had condescended to make him the gift of that common clay which men call flesh.

At first he thought that the dream in which he found himself must be a dream of his own. It was so strange that he even wondered whether it might belong to that random and untrustworthy kind which kept ordinary men incessant company when they lay in the arms of Morpheus. He had not experienced a dream of that arbitrary nature for many years, but it did not seem inconceivable that he might have recovered the privilege, along with the privileges of sight and hearing.

It slowly dawned on him, however, that he was seeing through another mind's eyes, and sharing another mind's dream.

It was Mercy Murrell's dream, and, in spite of the fact that she had not an ounce of visionary power, it was anything but a random affliction of her sleeping mind's idleness.

Mercy Murrell was dreaming that she was Eve, in the Garden of Eden.

She was dreaming of the perfect happiness of innocence, which was Eve's by virtue of her birthright, and which she felt with astonishing clarity.

While she lay supine upon the grass, in the shade cast by the boughs of a huge tree, Eve was deluged by sensations which awoke in her an entire and vivid spectrum of joys and exaltations: the coolness of the earth upon which she lay; the softness of the grass which cushioned her; the warmth of the light which filtered through the leaves to bathe her naked body; the gentleness of the caressing shadows which mediated that light; the thrilling lightness of the air which she drew into her lungs; and above all else the luxurious sensuality of a living body with a beating heart, which had never known pain.

The felicitous force of these sensations was awesome. This kind of rapture had not the ethereal refinement and ataraxic intellectuality which Harkender had always associated with the idea of Heaven; it was much more animal and physical than that, asexual but nevertheless implicitly bound up with the possession of flesh. It was a very particular kind of ecstasy, of which Mercy Murrell surely could never have dreamed without some kind of special inspiration.

Eve was still lying on her back, lost in the secret business of savouring her sensations, when the serpent came to her.

The serpent was an extremely strange creature, which moved by the beat of its night-black wings, and was not snakelike at all. Harkender understood this, remembering the statement of the scriptures that it was not until God spoke to the serpent *after* the temptation and the fall of man that the creature was cursed to go upon its belly and eat dust.

Here and now, before the fall, the serpent wore the coloured jewellery of glory upon its handsome body, and its face was incredibly beautiful.

Eve, who was innocent, looked up into the face of the serpent and smiled. She loved beauty, and trusted it implicitly. She had no concept of deception, no notion of anything which might be other than it appeared. She knew, beyond any shadow of a doubt, that the serpent meant only to do her good, to add to her pleasure in the fact of existence.

But Jacob Harkender, looking through Eve's eyes, could see all too clearly that the face of the serpent was a face he knew very well.

It was the face of the Angel of Pain.

He heard, with a dreadful feeling of foreboding, what the serpent said to Eve, in a voice whose melodies filled her head with exhilaration: *There is a fruit in this garden which thou hast not yet tasted, which is as sweet as all the rest, and yet distinct. Until thou hast tasted it, thou hast not felt all the ecstasies which flesh can sustain. Until thou hast eaten of it, and united its succulent flesh with thine own, thou art not complete. Thy heart yearns for this new delight with ever hungry beat, though it knows not what it needs to soothe its appetite.*

Eve, who had never been forbidden anything, and would not have been able to understand a threat of death had one ever been made, replied in the only way she could: *O lovely serpent with night-dark wings, tell me what name my beloved Adam, man of clay, hath given to this untasted fruit?*

None, answered the gorgeous serpent, radiant with reflected light. *To this fruit alone he hath given no name; but I call it KNOWLEDGE, and I hold it to be the last and best of all the myriad delights. I could not bear to hoard its glories to my own experience, when there are beings in the world which have not yet felt its unparalleled excitement. Taste it, I beg of you, beloved Eve!*

Eve, who had no concept of a lie, believed what the serpent said to her, and she reached out her hand to take the fruit which the serpent offered her.

Harkender would have cried out, if he could, to warn Eve (whose true name was Mercy) not to take the fruit. He would have howled as loudly as he could that the name of the fruit was POISON, and that its legacy was PAIN; but he was condemned to silence. This was not his dream, and he was not its dreamer.

He watched, through Eve's eyes, as she took the fatal fruit into her hand and raised it to her lips. He felt her bite into it and draw a piece of its flesh on to her tongue. He felt the gulp with which she swallowed it down, in advance of any evident sensation of taste.

And then, as he had known that he must, he felt her pain.

He had felt his own pain for so long, and had so confidently believed that he had known worse pain than any other man alive – by virtue of the miracle which had allowed him to live when any other man would have died – that he had not thought himself capable of further shocks.

He was wrong.

Probably, he thought, Eve's pain *was* far gentler than his, and would not have been exceptional at all, had he and she been able to judge it in purely objective terms; but Eve, being pure and innocent, had never been in Hell. Eve had never known what it was to feel anything but the lovely spectrum of the pleasures. To her, the pain which took possession of her unready body was something unimaginably hideous; the direst stress of which any creature ever made had ever been capable.

Because it was her pain, not his, Harkender felt it as she felt it, and nothing which he had previously undergone prepared him for that unprecedented martyrdom.

He knew that this trap, unsprung, had been incarnate in Eve's flesh from the moment of her creation, waiting for the moment of her betrayal. God had made her innocent, and made her pure, and made her vulnerable, and had decreed in His infinite wisdom that this should be the penalty of her innocence, purity and vulnerability. This moment, God had decreed in his mysterious fashion, was to define the substance of her enlightenment, by which she learned the terrible truth of His nature, His Creation, His *goodness*.

Eve screamed.

Eve screamed, for ten seconds which might have been ten thousand years or ten billion years, or ten eternities.

Her scream filled the nascent cosmos and echoed from the placental walls of infinity.

When she had screamed, Eve looked into the beautiful face of the Angel which had tempted her, and saw it change into a looking-glass, in which she saw herself.

Eve, whose dreamer's name was Mercy, could not recognise her own face, though she knew it well enough. But Jacob Harkender, sharing her sight, knew it immediately. Mercy, he knew, would grant herself the mercy of forgetfulness, but he had no such resource, and could not even wish that he had. He was a man who valued knowledge, no matter how poisonous it might be to the hopes and ambitious of the soul.

Harkender recognised the face, and knew what it meant.

The mirror which had been a serpent held the image of Hecate.

The Angel of Pain was Hecate.

The fruit of the tree of knowledge had been consumed by Hecate.

Harkender knew, without even needing to awake from the dream which had turned into the ultimate nightmare, that he had misread the intentions and designs of his master Zelophelon. He had been set to watch over Hecate not because Zelophelon thought that she might be useful, but because the fact of her existence gave Zelophelon cause for fear.

Now, that fear had come to fruition.

7

It was already late in the evening when Harkender arrived at Mercy Murrell's house. Cloudy night had descended on London like a musty cloak.

His carriage had travelled as fast as the traffic would permit, although his new coachman had not been entirely happy to be urged to such speed, nor with the discovery that the first destination to which his new employer required him to go was the most notorious brothel in the city. The journey had been uncomfortable in the extreme for Harkender, but in the wake of such a long confinement the mere fact of being outdoors was wondrous enough to compensate for the jolts and the bruises he received.

When Harkender entered the little theatre, the evening's entertainment was already half over, but he quickly decided that as far as his own purpose was concerned, he was in time.

Nothing disastrous had happened yet. Hecate had only dreamed of what she was, although the magic of her dream had been powerful enough to overwhelm the mind of at least one other sleeper. Harkender dared not hope that the witch girl would be as slow and silly in her awakening as Gabriel Gill had been; he knew that he might have to confront her with the power of her maker before the night was through.

When he saw Mercy Murrell sitting alone, he could not resist the temptation to go to her. She looked at him in a markedly indifferent fashion, and he knew her well enough to imagine the cold hostility behind her greeting; but he understood that he must look very ugly in his present state, and that there was not the slightest chance of her recognising his face.

By virtue of his long association with the bawd, Harkender recognised her version of *The Lustful Turk* immediately. He watched Sophie's fake flagellation diffidently, waiting for the quiet scene which was to follow, when he would see Hecate.

When she made her entrance he was initially disappointed, because she seemed so very awkward, but he fixed his renewed gaze upon her and studied her with the utmost care. He watched in fascination as the deformed girl played at comforting her fellow whore, and recognised the sincerity which blossomed as she warmed to her work. As the element of pretence was left behind by the increasing enthusiasm of her playing, he began to sense the magic that was in her: the heat of her soul. He could see – though he doubted that the nearer watchers could – how wholeheartedly she was living her part, and how real her unfeigned emotion was.

He did not start or laugh when something offstage fell over. Instead, a little shiver ran down his back as he felt the palpable force of the magical undertow which surged and eddied beneath the emotional tide of her performance. Then he relaxed again as the lights came up.

When Mrs Murrell offered him a drink, he refused, but he quickly repented of his shortness. He had come here on an urgent mission, but that did not free him from commoner impulses and temptations. This woman had been his friend once, and although he had used her quite cynically, it was good to hear her voice again.

He did not want to frighten her, so he picked up the conversation again by asking her in a politely innocuous fashion to confirm her identity; then he asked an equally innocuous question about the girl. She knew immediately which one he meant, and was easily drawn to tell him the story which he already knew.

It was unexpectedly pleasant to hear her talk, and Harkender wondered whether his unconventional love affair with Cordelia Tallentyre had softened his heart towards all women. But their conversation was inevitably cut short.

While he watched the rest of the play, left utterly cold by the inefficiently simulated acts which were its climaxes, he wondered whether he ought to bid in the auction for Hecate, in order to earn a private audience with her. He decided against it. He knew the interior of the house very intimately, and he knew not only how to find her but how to watch her without being seen himself. Mrs Murrell was more than happy to pander to voyeurs, and her rooms were liberally equipped with concealed closets and spyholes. He slipped away before the auction even began, and went upstairs to secrete himself in the place where he could look out from hiding into Hecate's room.

He knew that she would not be alone when she returned, and he also knew that if she were on the threshold of discovering her true nature any intense experience might be enough to trigger her awakening. He did not want to be the cause of that awakening, but he did want to be on hand when it happened, and the opportunity seemed invaluable.

He did not have long to wait.

Hecate came back to her bedroom in the company of a short-statured man at least sixty years old, whose eyes were remarkably bloodshot. His hair was quite white but it had not begun to recede, and he had a lean frame innocent of any rotundity.

The man commanded Hecate to undress herself, and surveyed her very steadily when she had done so, measuring the twisting of her spine with his hands as well as his eyes. He made her lie supine while he inspected her malformed face and tiny breasts, and then he shoved his fingers rudely into her vagina, pushing and poking in a purposeless fashion which she endured with perfect fortitude.

He would clearly have preferred it had she reacted, for he scowled and instructed her to smile. She tried, mechanically, but it was a very poor performance and he slapped her for it, hard enough to bring tears to her eyes.

Then he undressed himself, taking great care to lay out his garments neatly. When she turned away momentarily he instructed her harshly to watch him, and not to take her eyes from his face.

When he finally stood naked he was not a pretty sight. His skin was white and freckled with ancient pockmarks, and a great flap of it hung loose about his waist, giving evidence that he had once been much stouter than he was now. His shrivelled prick showed no sign of excitement.

He sat down on the bed and turned the whore over so that he could trace the line of her disfigured spine with a bony forefinger, jabbing at it occasionally. Once he paused to separate her buttocks so that he could look at her anus. Then he began to tell her, at great length, how ugly and disgusting she was. The words poured out of him in a vituperative torrent, sounding as if they had been spat out rather than spoken, the meaningful phrases punctuated by randomly grouped obscenities. The recitation had a certain rhythm, and it spilled out so easily and automatically that it quickly revealed itself as a practised ritual. Whether Hecate had heard it before, or whether it had been practised exclusively on others, the watching Harkender could not tell.

The girl made no sign that she understood what was being said. It was as though the verbal torrent ran over and off her, without ever really touching her; as though it were addressed to someone else in whose stead she served as a scapegoat.

This lack of response annoyed the man – or perhaps was exactly what he required – and the stream of abuse became even more insistent, even more obscene, until the man reached forward and grabbed Hecate by the hair, and pulled her head up and back before wrenching it first to one side and then to the other, roughly and rhythmically.

It must have hurt a good deal, but the girl did not cry out, and she controlled her tears. The man got up on the bed to kneel astride her while he pulled her head back and forth. It was as though she were a horse which needed cruel treatment in order to be broken.

His prick was erect now, though it was still somewhat lacking in rigidity, and he was beginning to find a kind of fever: an extreme of arousal which he reached only with the utmost difficulty. His face was like the mask of some vicious cur enduring a whipping from its master: feral and fearful and full of angry pain.

Harkender pulled back from the spyhole into the comforting darkness. His heart was hammering, but he had not the stomach to watch the completion of the act of degradation.

He found himself taut with excitation, but it was not lust or anything like it. Inside himself he was screaming at Hecate, urging her to break out and to fight back. He was willing her to become what she truly was, to take the sick and wicked thing upon her back and break it into a thousand pieces, and make a bloody feast of it fit for the werewolves of London or the rats which thronged the dank, dark cellars of the capital.

Harkender had not thought himself capable of such disgust. He would far rather have experienced cynical amusement, and he was sure that when he had last gone abroad in the world that would have been his first and only reaction.

What have you done to me, Zelophelon! he wailed, silently. *Have you given me Cordelia's soul instead of my own? Where is my strength, which should have been so precious to you? Where is my power to endure the sickness and the shabbiness of the world?*

No hint of soulfire reached him where he cowered. There was nothing in the room into which he now refused to look but sweat and sadness; nothing was happening save for a ridiculous act of fornication, of the kind which could still be made possible by calculated brutality and deliberate perversity when all natural impulse had faded away.

No supernatural force took hold of the desperate roué; no power awoke in the tormented flesh of the unsuspecting witch.

When Harkender finally brought his eye to the spyhole again, Hecate was alone, lying flat on the bed, prone and perfectly still. She might have seemed dead, save for the faintest rise and fall of her twisted shoulders, which provided evidence that she was still breathing. There was no blood, and little enough bruising.

The house was silent, and remained so while half a dozen minutes slid by.

Then, from the room on the far side of Hecate's, Harkender heard the muffled sound of a whip rhythmically falling on flesh. He knew from the texture of the sound that it was being plied with great force, and he was not surprised to hear suppressed moans of pain, which would surely have been screams had they not been stifled by a gag.

At first, Hecate did not seem to hear the sounds at all, but suddenly she seemed to realise what they signified, and she sprang up into a crouch like that of an alarmed animal. Her hand, with its fingers splayed as if they were talons, raked the air as she quivered. It was, thought the watcher, as if she did not know for the moment whether she was a human being or a wild thing – nor did he think of wolves or cats, but of something far wilder and more fabulous.

When she leaped from the bed and ran for the door, scuttling like a giant spider, Harkender knew that the moment had come. He felt a great hot wind blowing through him, and he staggered back from the spyhole, gagging as a wave of nausea thrust up through his gut. His vision blurred, and he could not immediately get a grip on the catch which secured the door of his hiding place. By the time he had fumbled his way out into the corridor and taken his first stride towards the room beyond Hecate's, the door of that room was already open and she had disappeared inside.

He heard her howl, like some angry monster of legend.

When he reached the doorway and looked in, he immediately slid sideways to take up a position flat against the wall, just inside the door. He could go no farther.

Sophie, bleeding from the effects of the whip, had fallen heavily to the floor and was writhing like a worm, unable to find sufficient presence of mind to raise herself and escape.

Hecate no longer had the appearane of a wild beast. She had recovered her composure and now seemed utterly calm, even serene; but her eyes were as hard and cold as flints, blind to everything but the face upon which they were fixed. She reached out with her hands as though to help Sophie, but without the guidance of her eyes she could only grope ineffectively. Her eyes were intent on other work.

Sophie's flagellator was floating in midair, held as taut as he could be by some invisible rack. His eyes were imprisoned by Hecate's gorgon stare, but his body had begun to rotate, cruelly twisting his neck. The cane in his hand had begun to writhe as though it were alive, like Aaron's rod transmuted into an asp.

Mrs Murrell arrived then and tried to come into the room, but Harkender was quick to take her arm and hold her back; he did not know what Hecate might do to her if she tried to interfere. Together, they watched the torture continue. Harkender was as numbly horrified by this as he had been by the lecherous activities of the man with the bloodshot eyes, though he could not for the life of him understand why.

I must be stronger! he told himself. *I must take control of this stupid, pitying flesh which has grown like fungus on my raddled bones. I must school its impulses, as I schooled those of my former flesh, to conserve the useful emotions and condemn the soft and weak. I must, or how shall I be worthy of Zelophelon's trust?*

By the time that Sophie had finally contrived to move away, blood from the decapitated body was already staining her legs, and she was now hysterical with terror. Mrs Murrell helped the panic-stricken girl to her feet and thrust her through the doorway, where other hands were waiting to receive her.

Harkender continued to support Mrs Murrell for a little while longer, until Hecate turned her gaze upon them. Then he let her go, and encouraged her with a gentle thrust of his hand to turn and run; but he stood his own ground, and was glad to find himself becoming calmer. He had found the trick of indifference, at least so far as Hecate's torn-apart victim was concerned.

Without taking his eyes off the witch girl, Harkender carefully closed the door, sealing the two of them in with the severed head which floated in midair, eight feet from the ground. The bloody cane still clung to it, writhing like a snake.

Hecate smiled beatifically, like an innocent who had just that moment eaten of the tree of knowledge and was in the process of digesting the whole great cataract of human wisdom and understanding.

'Possess my soul,' said Harkender in a very level tone, knowing full well that he spoke now as Zelophelon's avatar. 'I give it to you freely, that you might understand. One thing and one thing only I ask you to know, and accept, and comprehend: *Where there are two, there is only mistrust; but where there are three, none dare try to stand alone.* Destroy whatever you please in the world of men, but stay your hand against the angels. I know what must and might be done, because I have long prepared for this moment. Only possess my soul, and you will see; all understanding is there, waiting to be plucked and consumed.'

Harkender had not known, until his leathery tongue had pronounced the words, what he would say. He had not known, until he heard his mouth speak, exactly what Zelophelon's purpose was. He thought that he understood, now, how David Lydyard felt in being a mere instrument, untrusted and uninformed; but he accepted the necessity. He did not rail against the vanity and cruelty of his possessor. Instead, he listened.

He listened, and he understood what Zelophelon was doing, and why.

I am the fruit of the tree of knowledge, he thought. *I am the instrument charged with informing her that she is naked and not alone. And I am the hostage, offered to her as an earnest of Zelophelon's sincerity, in the hope of making an alliance instead of an enemy.*

He understood also, and only too well, that it might not work; he knew that he risked destruction. Everything was balanced on a knife edge – *everything!*

A hot wind seared his soul, moving through him like an arrow carving a way through his lights.

'What do you propose?' asked Hecate, staring into the depths of his soul while she spoke in measured fashion. It was not her own voice – not, at any rate, a voice which any mortal ear had ever heard from her lips.

It was too early to be relieved, far too early to think of triumph. But it was one step forward, and a vital one.

'One thing only will suffice,' said his mouth, speaking of its own accord. 'An exchange of hostages and a combination of wills. We three must forge an oracle, and leave its revelation naked to one and all. We cannot any longer be content to play with deceits. *Where there are two, there is only mistrust; but where there are three, none dare try to stand alone.* The world has changed, and there is too much emptiness and too much darkness and too much strangeness in it. If we cannot pledge our bravest and our best, all that we have gained will soon be lost. Only possess my soul, and you will see it; only give yours to me, and the other will give hers to both of us. It is the only way, for where there are three there must be more, and only in alliance can there be safety. This above all I have learned; this above all I offer for sharing.'

There was a storm inside him, harrowing the most secret recesses of his soul, scouring him clean of memory and understanding. The claws of the Angel of Pain were raking his heart.

He stood firm before it; he was stronger now. That untamed pity which had fluttered briefly in his flesh could not turn on itself. He stood firm, as befitted the messenger of a god.

'On my ground,' she said, bleakly, 'and in my time. I will do it, on those terms.'

The relief which swept through him was not his relief; the triumph which surged – so weakly! – in his sluggish blood was not his triumph. The plan had not been his plan, and he was but a counter in the game, a piece which would have been sacrificed, if only she had not consented to possess his soul, and had not seen what Zelophelon had inscribed on the many facets of his being.

The ignominy of it did not matter in the least, because he found himself free at last . . . at least for a little while. When he opened the door and stumbled out, he did not know what to do or where to go, and so was free to choose, free to make whatever foolish choice might motivate his heart or salve his conscience.

He ran down the stairs, knowing that he must make his escape from the house, though there was no escape from his destiny. And as he ran, the very first thought which fell freely into the luxurious void of his uncertainty was that Cordelia must at all costs be saved; and when he had found that thought, he needed no other to tell him what to do.

He had not the slightest idea whether it was possible or not, but for that brief moment of freedom, it was all that he could bring himself to desire.

Impelled by love – or, at least, by pity – and by the exhilaration of knowing that he was himself again, he threw open the door of Mrs Murrell's ruined house, and ran into the night.

Somewhere far behind him, he knew, the witch girl was similarly free. She was free to turn her deadly stare back to the ghastly severed head which she still held aloft by the power of her will: the precious trophy of her first intervention in the stupid and wretched world of men.

8

When Harkender had drunk from the fountain of youth and found himself reborn, astonishment drove everything else from his mind. Time passed while he did not know who or what he was. He stared at his hands and touched his fingers to his cheek, but it was not his appearance which was so utterly unexpected; it was the absence of pain.

He had never known that it was possible to feel as he now did. Never.

Once before, he had been young and strong and healthy, fitter by far than the great majority of his kind; but such pleasure and comfort as he had then been able to take in the sensation of inhabiting his own body had always been ameliorated by some deep and constant malaise. In all his life he had never known what it was to live without a tangled knot inside him, which for ever forbade him perfect ease.

Now, the knot was gone. He had not merely been restored to the full bloom of youth and health, but made whole.

He looked up at the man who was watching him. He too had changed, but not so profoundly.

'Where are we?' he asked, uncertainly.

'I think we're in a parody of the Garden of Eden,' Lydyard told him, 'but I suppose that it's just one more threshold on which we must wait for a while. I dare say we won't be here for long.'

He looked about, alarmed at his failure to take note of their surroundings. He had been aware of a vague green background, but now – as though some optical instrument were being brought into focus – he saw the myriad leaves in all their different aspects, and the thin rays of the sun which penetrated the canopy, and the many-coloured flowers.

He saw eyes, too: the staring froglike eyes of strange creatures which hid among the leaves, watching the invaders of their forest Paradise.

He looked for fruits, but saw none. Here, as in the Eden of legend, there would only be one poisoned tree. Whatever the angels made for their human victims, they made from images which they found in human minds. Somewhere hereabouts there would be the tree of life and the tree of knowledge of good and evil, and the fruit of the latter tree would be poison and pain.

But there is no innocent Eve! Harkender thought grimly. *And we need no serpent to tell us what to do.*

Lydyard must have been thinking along similar lines, for he said, 'Whatever we're here to learn, it won't be what Adam and Eve learned, for we're already clothed. We know the meaning of nakedness.'

It was a joke. Harkender did not laugh, but he saw the reasoning behind its telling. Fight back against fear; shame the Devil with sarcasm.

'We're uncomfortably clothed,' he agreed, wiping perspiration from his brow. He knew that he did not have to explain to Lydyard that the nakedness which Adam and Eve discovered was not the nakedness of their bodies but the nakedness of their souls, and that when the time came, they would indeed have to stand naked before the Creators. Lydyard knew all that.

Harkender removed his outer garments, folding them neatly as he put them aside, though he knew how absurd it was to take the trouble. When his shirt was loose and his belt had been let out by a notch, he felt more comfortable. He went to the nearby pool and looked at his own reflection in the water. It was his old face, as handsome as it had ever been.

What a beautiful thing I still was, he thought, *long after I had learned to cherish spoliation.*

'This was not an easy place to reach,' said Lydyard tentatively. 'It was a journey that I wouldn't like to undertake very often.'

Harkender consented to laugh. He stroked the back of his right hand with the fingers of his left, and then put both his palms to his cheeks.

'Blame the one who sent you,' he answered drily. 'It might have been easy enough, if your possessor had cared to make it so.'

'Why are we here?' asked the other bluntly.

Harkender looked around, meeting the eerie gaze of one of the creatures which hid among the leaves. It had the skin of a frog, but it stood upright on a bough, grasping a higher one with pulpy fingers.

'We're hostages,' Harkender said, not for the first time. 'Others must be brought here, too. No doubt they could be snatched from the four corners of the world and whirled through time to arrive at the same instant, but our masters are respectful of space and time, which are not bent or broken without cost. They'll choose their moment carefully, and if we must wait in the meantime, wait we must.'

'I've seen them take other hostages,' said Lydyard bitterly. 'Your efforts were in vain, it seems.'

Harkender looked at him sharply. 'Cordelia?' he said. 'You saw them take Cordelia?'

He knew immediately that he had misread the implication of Lydyard's words, and he saw from the expression on the other's face that Lydyard was angrily fearful of the implication which might be taken from his.

Lydyard must have guessed, by now, that his wife had been used as a seer; he knew it by deduction, but he still refused to accept it, still dared to hope that it might not be true.

'We're all hostages,' said Harkender tiredly. 'Wherever we are. It won't matter, in the end, who is brought on to this petty stage, and who isn't. No one is out of reach.'

'They've given my children to the werewolves,' Lydyard replied.

'I doubt that the werewolves will hurt them,' Harkender replied, genuinely desirous of reassuring him. 'If we play our part, they'll be safe.' He tried to sound certain, but Lydyard had collected himself now, and had begun to understand what was happening.

'That will surely depend,' Lydyard said, 'on what our flight into the further reaches of enlightenment reveals. If it should transpire that we are bearers of bad news . . .'

It was true, and Harkender did not trouble to deny it. Everything depended on the outcome of their coming oracular adventure. He could not begin to guess what the angels would do until he knew what truth would stand revealed when it was finished.

Lydyard followed Harkender's example, stripping to his shirt and breeches. His shirt was already wringing wet with moisture from the air. There was too much heat and humidity beneath these trees for this to be reckoned a true Garden of Eden. He felt very hungry, but there was no sign of any ordinary fruit with which his hunger might be appeased.

'It seems,' said Lydyard slowly, when he had cooled himself a little, 'that we're in the same situation. Could we not pretend to be allies instead of contestants? Need we be enemies, simply because we're pawns of rival Creators?'

Harkender was slightly surprised by the overture. 'I couldn't imagine Sir Edward Tallentyre saying that,' he said, seating himself in the shadow of a thicket and fanning his face with his hand. 'We could have been allies once before, you and I. Had you done as I asked, and come to Whittenton, all this might have been avoided. I admit that I had no inkling then of what the future would bring, and I know that you hadn't, but looking back, I think that fortune might have made a better fist of things had the Sphinx and the Spider only contrived to be allies then, instead of adversaries.'

Even while he said it, though, he remembered the words he had spoken to Hecate. *Where there are two, there is only mistrust; but where there are three, none dare try to stand alone.* There was some truth in them, despite the fact that they were only an argumentative ploy. The Creators were not of a kind which easily made alliances, unless they were driven to it by fear.

Lydyard squatted down so that he could confront Harkender on the same level. Harkender studied him idly, comparing the face he now saw with the one which he had seen through Cordelia's eyes during the last few years. The pain was gone, but there was a curious sense in which Lydyard had been more handsome when his features were straitened by stress. Now he looked too soft and too innocent.

'We needn't be enemies,' Lydyard said simply. 'Whatever we must do, we must do together.'

Harkender condescended to smile, very slightly and very briefly.

'You may be right,' he admitted. 'We have more in common than either of us might care to admit. But there's as much of Zelophelon in me as there is of Jacob Harkender, no matter how perfectly my old appearance has been restored; and there may be more of Bast in you than than you think.

'We're to be used in concert, to produce and share a common vision – but we'll see what we see through our own eyes, and each of the three which will leech upon our enlightenment will hope to see just a little better than the rest; even in alliance, they'll never cease to strive for any and every advantage. And when it's over, if we're allowed to survive, we will again be separated, and set to scheming one against another. If I said that I'd be your friend, Lydyard, or even that I wanted to be, I would be lying.'

Lydyard turned away, seemingly disgusted as well as disappointed.

'I know what discussions you've had with Tallentyre,' said Harkender. 'It doesn't matter how I know, but the fact is that nothing you have said aloud has been in secret. I don't think that you've ever quite grasped the substance of what happened in that little Hell which Zelophelon made. You've never quite understood the impact which Tallentyre's vision had.

'Tallentyre believed then – and seems to have believed ever since – that the persuasive force of his communication was the revelation that the true size of the universe made even an entity of Zelophelon's powers insignificant. He sought to demonstrate that the universe was far too vast a thing to be remade by such petty powers of re-creation as Zelophelon has. He did indeed raise that possibility, and it's a possibility which may have caused Zelophelon a little anxiety. But I believe that it was a different question, also implicit in Tallentyre's vision, that really gave Zelophelon pause.'

He stopped and waited. Lydyard stared at him uneasily, but eventually condescended to say, 'Go on.'

'Until that moment,' Harkender said calmly, 'Zelophelon must have assumed – as had I – that all the rival Creators which had inhabited the Earth in the days when the rest of the universe had the semblance of crystal spheres, were still intimately associated with the Earth. Tallentyre, in raising the possibility that there might be humanlike life on the worlds of countless other stars, also raised the possibility that Zelophelon's rivals might in fact be scattered far and wide across unbelievably vast distances.'

'Why should that matter?' asked Lydyard.

'For one simple reason,' Harkender said. 'Zelophelon assumed when it first awoke, and found itself apparently alone, that all its rivals must be inert. Thus it – and I – formulated the scheme to make an oracular instrument out of soulstuff plundered from one of them, as a prelude to a campaign of predation.

'The scheme went wrong, of course, but all might not have been lost had Zelophelon and Bast been able to follow the rational course and form an alliance against the still-inert others of their kind. That's why I say that you and I might have saved ourselves a deal of trouble, had we been able to meet before the affair got out of hand. Alas, the practicality of any such alliance was called into question by Tallentyre's tacit claim that the other Creators left over from the time which the Clay Man called the Age of Heroes might not be on Earth at all, but on other earthlike worlds separated from this one by a vast gulf of emptiness – where they might already be awake, making their own alliances.

'It's by no means obvious, of course, that Tallentyre is right. It's only his imagination that credits the worlds of other stars with life, and we must not lose sight of the fact that this huge cosmos filled with sunstars is itself no more than an appearance. You may have little sympathy with me, but I am quite happy to believe that the focal point of the universe is still to be found here on Earth, and that the universe which Tallentyre believes to be an uncontestable discovery of modern science is naught but an illusion caught in the magical crystal of the heavenly sphere which confines us. A man like Tallentyre could see no sense in debating how many angels might dance on the head of a pin, or how many Creators might be confined within the fabric of the world on which we stand, but Zelophelon sees things very differently, and so must Bast.

'The two awakened Creators dared not enter into any conflict *or* alliance until they had found out more about the puzzling nature of the universe. That, as you and Tallentyre easily deduced, is the task which has occupied them during these last twenty years. You've probably helped them more than you suspect by undertaking your own enquiries, and I know that I've been a significant instrument of Zelophelon's observations.

'I can't tell what Zelophelon has concluded, but I infer from the fact that the Age of Miracles has once again returned to disturb the Age of Reason that some vital watershed has been reached.

'We now know for certain that there's at least one other Creator awake and prepared to act on the surface of the Earth. There may be others, able to conceal their presence temporarily by virtue of their greater understanding of the appearances which the world currently presents. They may have an alliance of their own, or they may not, but if they have it's probably fragile and would be subject to disintegration if the Creators involved should judge that their interests have changed.

'That's what we're charged with finding out, by the only method which the Creators trust. We must find out how many Creators there are on Earth and what state of being they're in. We must also find out, if we can, whether there are indeed Creators on other worlds, and whether they could ever become dangerous to those which remain on Earth. Apart from that, the fate of Machalalel is of particular interest to the three – for reasons you may easily guess – and the answers to the questions in which Machalalel seemingly took an interest. The nature of man is still a riddle, so far as the angels are concerned; so, for that matter, is their own nature. All this we must try to see, if we can.

'As I said to you before, the others who'll be used have far less hope of understanding than you or I. What we see may be shared while we see it, but afterwards, when all meanings have to be disentangled, all conclusions drawn, all plans made and hatched, then we'll be enemies again, no matter what we might desire.'

Lydyard ran his hand reflexively over his renewed body. 'And we'll be restored to our former condition, I suppose?' he said. He seemed to find the thought uniquely horrible.

'You have less to lose than I,' Harkender reminded him quietly. 'But you may hope, if you like, that there's an opportunity in this for us. If we're fortunate in what we find,.

it may be that our possessors will find it to their advantage to
use us more kindly in future. However uncongenial you find
the notion, you ought to hope that we'll serve our masters
well enough to warrant a reward. If that offends your pride,
remind yourself that whatever the state of the world, still we
must live in it.'

Lydyard did not seem amused to have Tallentyre's favourite dictum quoted to him by Tallentyre's chief adversary.
But his curiosity was more powerful than his sense of injury,
and he was too hungry for information and reassurances to
turn away.

'Do you think we might be given back our health and
strength?' he asked, unready to take the implication without
a straightforward statement.

Harkender shrugged. 'How can I tell?' he said. 'But there
are two things of which I'm certain. One is that I can't be
condemned to any fate worse than the one I've suffered
during these last twenty years. Having lived through that,
there's no need now for me to fear the future. The other
is that so far as the world of men is concerned, it doesn't
matter overmuch whether the fallen angels elect to act in
concert or fall to fighting among themselves; in either case,
their power would be unleashed, and the world might be
changed out of all recognition. I do not say *destroyed* but I
do say *changed*. After the Age of Reason there may come an
Age of Unreason: a new Age of Magic, stranger even than
the last. I hope so, more devoutly than you can imagine.'

'Tallentyre would not agree with *that*,' Lydyard retorted,
although he must have known how lame it would sound.

'You know as well as I do how little that matters,' said
Harkender, with wry vindictiveness. 'Tallentyre is blind, but
he thinks that he sees more clearly because of it. I hope to
see him here; this time, I think, he can take no one by
surprise with the magnitude of his visions or the extent of
his conceit. This time, he has no move to make which can
force the players of the game to rethink their strategy. Nor
have you.'

As he pronounced the last few words he came to his feet.
He had said enough. He looked around, wondering whether

there was any reason to choose one direction rather than another. He had no doubt that he would be brought to the tree of knowledge soon enough, but he wanted to walk, if only for the pleasure of walking. It might also be pleasant to get away from Lydyard, to savour in solitude the pleasure of being alive and alone in a place outside the world.

This was merely a stage, where a group of ragged players would in time be assembled to take roles which were far beyond the range of their miserable talents, but that did not mean that he should not take what delight he could in the scenery.

He walked away, not caring in the least whether David Lydyard would rise to chase after him or not.

They would meet again, soon enough.

SECOND INTERLUDE
The Seed of Order

We need not doubt that the evolutionists have proven the most fundamental parts of their case. All the living species which now exist are related, having descended from relatively few common ancestors of a very simple kind. The simplest organisms of which we are presently aware – and it is reasonable to believe that there are some which are too tiny to be perceived, even with the aid of our most powerful microscopes – may have descended from those remotest ancestors with relatively little modification; the most complicated, man and his cousins among the higher mammals, are the result of a marvellous sequence of transmutations.

The evidence for these facts is overwhelming.

The question which next confronts us, when we have accepted this conclusion, is one of explanation. Given that this has happened, we must ask how. What mechanism has driven the process of evolution which has produced, by slow degrees, men from microbes?

It is generally believed that Charles Darwin has supplied the answer to this question, but it is not at all clear that his answer is complete. His fine books *On the Origin of Species by Natural Selection* and *The Descent of Man* present us with a wealth of evidence and argument, but the evidence which is cited, while providing excellent proof of the *fact* of evolution, is less clear in sustaining the Darwinian account of how evolution has happened.

One thing which is made abundantly clear by Darwin's

arguments is that the selection of particular individuals from a population for use as breeding stock can be a powerful agent of change. His observations on the breeding of domestic animals for particular traits are easily sufficient to sustain this case, given that we have before us a vast range of types of dogs, cats, poultry, cattle and sheep. We are, however, free to doubt whether it its equally clear that the divergence of types in nature has occurred by virtue of some parallel process. Can we really conclude that a process of 'natural selection' has been responsible for the vast spectrum of natural species? Can the struggle for existence, which is supposed in the Darwinian scheme to take the place of an actual selector working towards a predetermined goal, provide a sufficiently powerful motor for the constant divergence of new species?

The strongest evidence which Dr Darwin has to support this contention, supplemented by evidence of the same kind provided by Alfred Russel Wallace, concerns the diversification of related species in archipelagoes of islands. The most striking case of all is that of the finches of the Galapagos Islands, which Darwin observed when he served as a naturalist aboard HMS *Beagle*. Each island of the archipelago has a population of finches. All these populations, we may presume, are descended from a small ancestral population which reached the islands from the South American mainland in the distant past. In each case, however, the finches have adapted themselves physically and behaviourally to follow a particular way of life uniquely suited to the opportunities which the different islands offer.

The key concept here is adaptation, which has figured large in earlier evolutionist accounts than Darwin's. The Chevalier de Lamarck also argued that the diversification of species was a result of their continually adapting themselves to new and different ways of subsistence. The difference between the two writers is that Lamarck imagined creatures engaged in an active and effortful process of experiment and innovation, while Darwin rests his case on the notion that members of a population which are slightly different from one another may be better or worse equipped to survive and breed successfully, and that the calculus of probability is sufficient to ensure a gradual and directional shift in the capabilities of a species over the course of many generations.

There are certain severe difficulties which lie in the way of accepting any extreme version of the Lamarckian hypothesis. If we are required by that hypothesis to credit living creatures with an inbuilt determination to evolve, we must ask why primitive types of organism survive alongside more advanced forms. If we are required to accept that characteristics acquired by the striving of individual organisms are handed down to their descendants, we must ask why so many sons of skilled fathers show little natural aptitude for the work which their parents strived so long to master.

In spite of such qualms, however, we need hardly doubt that in its more modest formulations the Lamarckian hypothesis is correct. Some measure of active experimentation is certainly necessary on the part of individuals which are to be parents of new species. Had the Galapagos finches whose offspring are now so very various in habit not been enthusiastic to attempt new ways of life, natural selection could not have favoured those individuals best fitted to the various life styles which they adopted. Without flexibility of behaviour, and some impulse towards innovation, there is no scope for adaptation. Natural selection can only mimic artificial selection if organisms possess the inclination, as well as the capacity, to explore different possibilities.

It must be admitted that there are other difficulties which must be overcome before Darwinism is to be accepted as the true explanation of evolution. The whole world is not like the Galapagos Islands, rigidly divided into small, isolated compartments which offer distinct and very different opportunities for subsistence. It is easy for the human selector of domestic animals to isolate those breeding pairs whose particular attributes he desires to preserve and exaggerate, and the sea which separates the islands of an archipelago may easily be imagined to serve as an equivalent isolating barrier, but we must assume that by far the greater part of the evolutionary process has taken place in the ocean depths and on the continental landmasses, where isolation is much more difficult to achieve. It is not easy to explain how the natural variations which occur between members of a species become concentrated in particular groups of individuals, in the way that Darwin's theory requires.

It seems inevitable, bearing this in mind, that the pressure to adapt – and hence to evolve – will be greatest at the borders of the territory occupied by a population, especially when such borders involve altered physical conditions. In such conditions the isolation of a breeding group is most likely to occur, and the rewards of successful innovation are likely to be greatest. If we suppose that the main thrust of evolutionary change is associated with such conditions as these, it seems all the more necessary to hypothesise that there is some impulse towards experiment and innovation on the part of those individuals which must conquer new and different territory.

We must remember, when we speak of 'adaptation', that what organisms must adapt themselves to is an environment whose nature is largely defined by other species, which are themselves constantly busy in adapting. Every change in the numbers or capabilities of one species alters the spectrum of opportunities which all the other species have, thus altering the probabilities which are supposed to favour the 'fittest' members of each generation. Although the interdependence of living species tempts us to speak of the 'balance of nature', we should rather think in terms of a permanent imbalance in nature, whereby the challenge of adaptation which confronts each species in turn is constantly changing.

The idea that there is a 'harmony' in nature is foolish; if it really were the case that there was a place for every species and that every species was in its place, there would have been no evolution.

The fossil record informs us that there have been countless lines of descent, extending over millions of years, which have simply run into dead ends: lines where the improving refinements of natural selection – if that is what really determined the patterns of change which we see in those lines – were in the end insufficient to adapt the organisms concerned to further changes in their environment. Although a few extant species do seem to have descended from remote ancestors very similar to themselves, having apparently secured places in the scheme of things which freed them from the necessity of further adaptive responses to circumstance, the vast majority have not; they have been for ever innovating.

We can hardly doubt that the single trait most favoured by the vicissitudes is the impulse to innovate; thus the conditions under which natural selection can operate are also to be numbered among its results. This is, to be sure, a circular argument, but it is a productive circle which explains how evolution is an accelerative process, in which change is the parent of further change.

A further problem with the Darwinian account of evolution by natural selection is that it requires us to accept that there is some spontaneous source of physical variation in populations. It is unclear whether we must take it for granted that these variations are entirely random, but we must certainly refrain from assuming that there is some kind of calculated strategy involved.

Some such variation is certainly necessary to differentiate the probabilities of survival and breeding success of each individual within the population, but its inclusion in the theory requires some cause or mechanism, and we cannot dismiss that requirement by talk of spontaneity. Just as organisms must have some inbuilt impulse to behavioural innovation if natural selection is to work, so they must have some inbuilt impulse to physical innovation.

We cannot hope to solve the puzzle of spontaneous variation until we have a competent account of the way in which organisms reproduce themselves. We do not yet know how the egg cell of a particular species carries the design of the organism which it will become. If we accept the relatedness of all life, we must be prepared to imagine some fundamental process which is at work in the propagation of plants from seeds and cuttings, and in the binary division of protozoa, as well as the fertilisation and development of egg cells in animals, but of what that process consists we have as yet no notion.

Until we have a competent account of the process of reproduction, it will be impossible to decide whether Darwin's theory is true, because the theory will remain crucially incomplete. Until we discover the chemical nature of the fundamental process of reproduction, we cannot imagine how that process might be disturbed by the forces of change, and until we can do that we cannot pass final judgement on any theory of the evolution of species. There are, however, certain observations which we may make on the basis of logical extrapolation of the alternative possibilities.

It seems highly likely, if not indubitable, that some kind of natural selection does occur, but whether such a process is solely responsible for the pattern of evolution as it is mapped out in the fossil record and the variation of extant species is certainly open to doubt. In any case, we must recognise that the true driving force of evolution is not natural selection *per se* but rather the impulses to innovate, physically and behaviourally, which allow the selection to take place. An argument of this form may seem to carry an unfortunate echo of outmoded vitalist ideas, but some substitute for the traditional notion of *anima mundi* must be incorporated into Darwinian theory if we are to consider it effective.

This carries implications not simply for the natural philosopher but also for the practical scientist. In the past, men have contrived to alter the forms of domestic animals by selective breeding, accepting the bounty of nature regarding the innovative capacities of the organisms with which they worked. In the light of our present understanding, might it not be productive to redirect our attention to the elementary forces of change on which selection operates?

If, by whatever means, the impulses to innovate physically and behaviourally could be amplified, the power of both natural and artificial selection as forces of change would be amplified in proportion.

We are fully entitled to regard the human species as the most advanced on Earth and the one which is most rapidly evolving. In our own species, if in no other, we can readily identify the impulse of behavioural innovation which is so important in allowing natural selection scope in which to operate, and we can see how marvellously that power has in turn been increased. The power of conscious, rational thought has been the outcome of this productive circle of causality.

It is the amplification of the impulse to innovative behaviour that has allowed human beings to usurp the privileges of natural selection in respect of all our dependent species – and to insulate ourselves, in large measure, from exactly those forces of natural selection which shaped us. But we are not yet masters of our own future evolution. It is plain that the impulse of physical innovation within us has not been exaggerated to the same degree as the impulse of behavioural innovation; but there is no reason to assume that this could not be done, if we could discover a means of doing it.

If a way could be found to increase the force of that other impulse, and thus to increase the plasticity of human flesh and human form, a further acceleration of human evolution might be possible. Then, the empire of consciousness might be extended to its proper bounds, and the human species might legitimately claim to have come into its inheritance.

Until we have achieved an amplification of our powers of physical innovation equivalent in magnitude to the amplification of our powers of behavioural innovation, we cannot claim to be lords of creation or masters of our own being, but there is no reason to think that such mastery may not in time be possible.

As a species, sentient man is still in his infancy, but if Dr Darwin's theory allows us to understand how we came to be, perhaps it can also allow us to imagine what we will become, tomorrow or in the fullness of time.

(Passages from 'The Competence of the Theory of Natural Selection as an Explanation of the Origin and Evolution of Species' by Jason Sterling, *Quarterly Review*, June 1881.)

THREE
Obdurate Pride and Steadfast Hate

1

Jason Sterling lowered the pocket telescope from his eye, collapsing it to the size of a cigar. He placed it carefully on the windowsill. Then, unobtrusively, he put his hand into the pocket of his jacket to reassure himself that the derringer was there and positioned in such a way that it could easily be drawn out, ready to fire.

He bit his lower lip, more contemplatively than anxiously.

'Luke,' he said, speaking calmly enough, although he was very conscious of his subdued agitation. 'There's a man standing beside the grocer's shop on the other side of the road. You can't mistake him; he's exceptionally handsome, with fair hair and piercing blue eyes. Would you ask him, very politely, if he'd care to come into the house for a few minutes? I doubt that he'll try to harm you, but be careful of him, and promise him that we mean him no harm.'

Luke looked at him curiously, but left the room to do as he was told. When he had gone, Sterling turned to the man who sat in the armchair beside the hearth. The man was still pale and frail, but his thin face was alive with intelligence now, and he held himself well though his borrowed clothes did not fit him. He was reading a book. It was a book that he himself had written, though the expression of concentration on his face suggested that he did not remember it as well as he might. He looked up when he became aware that Sterling was staring at him.

'If the man will consent to come in,' said Sterling, 'I think you might recognise him. I'll be glad if you can identify him, for it will help to confirm what I was told earlier today by the man I went to see.'

The man in the armchair shook his head, very slightly, to signal puzzlement. 'If what you have told me is true,' he said softly, 'and I do not doubt your word, I have been absent from the world for more than thirty years. I doubt that I could easily recognise anyone that I knew then.'

'If Lydyard told me the truth,' said Sterling, 'this man will have changed very little.'

He watched carefully to see what effect that hint might have on his guest, who seemed to have collected his scattered wits well enough by now, but Adam Clay was not much given to starts of surprise. He merely smiled, and looked down again at the book he had written, more than a hundred years before, and published under the name of Lucian de Terre.

Sterling had always thought that it was a book of startling lies and hidden meanings, but what Lydyard had told him had sown a seed of doubt. He was beginning to wonder whether he could possibly be the one sane man in a company of lunatics – for Luke Capthorn was surely as mad as any of them – or whether he might be no better than the alchemists of old after all, unwittingly dabbling with the unholy.

Either way, he thought, it would be very interesting to meet a shape-shifter. Was it not the whole object of his work to give men conscious command over the properties of their bodies?

He watched while Luke approached the blond man, and held his breath until the man nodded his head, consenting to be led into the house.

Adam Clay laid down his book when he heard the front door open and close, and waited for the apparently young man to appear. He put a name to the newcomer without any hesitation: 'Perris! Has Mandorla sent you to watch over me – or to lie in wait for Pelorus?'

Perris bowed to him, and smiled ironically. He was trying to pretend that he was in complete control of the situation, but could not quite conceal his unease. He turned to face Jason Sterling, and said: 'I am at your service, sir. Why have you asked to see me?'

'I'd like you to carry a message for me,' said Sterling, trying to match the other's matter-of-factness. 'I would like to speak to your mistress, if that's possible.'

Sterling was glad to see a faint doubt creep into the werewolf's expression as the uncanny blue eyes stared at him appraisingly.

'I will be glad to take a message for you,' Perris answered. 'But I do not think that she will come.'

'Why should she not?' said Sterling. 'She has nothing to fear from me, but if what David Lydyard has told me is true, we may all be in peril. You may be in greater danger than I.'

Perris scowled resentfully and opened his mouth to reply, but before he could begin Adam Clay leaned forward and spoke.

'Peace, Perris,' he said. 'If this man is right, then circumstance might make allies of us for once.' To Sterling, he said: 'I think you should explain what this Lydyard said to you that has troubled you so much.'

'He brought me to his house to pepper me with warnings,' Sterling replied, as lightly as he could. 'He told me that the werewolves of London were watching me; that is how I guessed what this man was when I had studied him through my spyglass. He also told me that we are all under observation by others more powerful than they. He claims that the beings which that book of yours calls Creators have recently awakened from a far longer sleep than yours. He believes that one of them has guided my work and intervened to help me when I was nearly apprehended bringing you from your grave. He says that Pelorus has disappeared, and that he himself was wounded by a werewolf which attacked him at his home.'

'That is not true!' The exclamation came from Perris.

'I believe that much, at least,' said Sterling soberly. 'The man was certainly hurt, and I think that he was sincere in trying to warn me. He said something about a murder which will be reported by the evening papers, but he didn't say that it was done by one of the werewolves.'

Perris seemed perplexed by all this, and if appearances could be trusted he surely knew nothing about these incidents. His gaze flicked from Sterling to Adam Clay and back again, and he licked his lips nervously. Sterling felt absurdly proud of himself; here was an authentic werewolf, in his smoking room – and the werewolf was afraid! But he knew how paradoxical his feeling was, for if the werewolf had cause to be alarmed by these revelations, how much more cause there must be for the merely human among them to be anxious!

'Lydyard told me that we were all in dire danger,' said Sterling, re-emphasising the point in the hope of obtaining a more informative reaction. 'He included the members of his family, everyone in this house, and the remaining werewolves, too. If he's right, we can only waste time by keeping watch on one another. Perris, if you can find Mandorla I wish you would bring her here. She may know better than Lydyard what's happening. If you can't find her, then you must confer with those of your kinfolk who are left about what you wish to do; but I ask that you or one of the others will return here, to give this man your own account of what's happened during these last thirty years.'

Perris looked at Adam Clay, but not as a man might look to a friend for advice. Sterling knew that if *The True History of the World* could be trusted – and he was inclined to trust it a little better now – there had always been bad blood between Mandorla's pack and the man which Machalalel had made from clay.

'Dr Sterling has not had time to tell me very much,' said Adam Clay, mildly, to Perris. 'Nor do I really know what manner of man he is. But he knew enough to take me from my grave, and if this other man has contrived to frighten him, there may be good reason to be frightened, even for the likes of you and me. Go now. See if you can find Mandorla. If you cannot, I too ask you to come back, or to send one of the others.'

'I was told to watch,' Perris countered, though not with any determined stubbornness.

'Tell me one thing,' said Adam Clay softly. 'Is it true what this man says, that some among the Creators have awakened from their long sleep?'

Perris hesitated only for an instant before saying: 'It is true.'

'Then what Sterling has said to you is news that Mandorla would want you to bring back. We have sometimes been enemies, I know, but this is a new and strange world, and we may yet find a common cause. Go on, Perris, I beg of you.'

The werewolf seemed glad enough to have been convinced, and nodded. Then he turned on his heel. Luke Capthorn opened the door for him, but did not follow him into the hallway.

The three who remained said nothing until they had heard the front door close. Then Sterling said: 'We'll dine at eight, Luke. Please attend to all your usual duties. I can't tell what may happen, but I ask you to be on your guard.'

Luke frowned, evidently feeling that he was entitled to a much fuller explanation; but Sterling was not at all sure that he could offer one, and contented himself with waiting until his order was obeyed. After a second or two, the servant's frown melted, and Sterling saw a calmer expression take its place. He had seen that expression before, in the graveyard at Charnley Hall, and he wondered exactly what grain of conviction it signified. Although he was an uneducated man, Luke nevertheless seemed content to believe that he knew as well as anyone what kind of mystery was unravelling here, and had some reason to think that he was more likely to be protected than destroyed. Sterling guessed that Luke thought that his master was of the Devil's party without knowing it, as Lydyard also seemed to do. But Luke appeared to believe that the Devil was his friend.

When Luke had gone, Sterling sat down. He removed the gun from his pocket and placed it on a small side table. Adam Clay reached over to pick it up, and he inspected it closely before replacing it.

'It is neater than the ones I know,' he said.

'The world has made more progress in the last thirty years than in the previous hundred,' said Sterling. 'Nothing is improved faster by an increase in human ingenuity than engines of destruction.'

'So I had observed,' said Adam Clay, grimly. 'When I wrote this, I hoped that men had learned to put folly behind them. I remember now that no sooner had I committed to cold print my celebration of a coming Age of Reason than the path of history wriggled out of my grasp like an eel, avid to seek out an Age of Madness. The Terror in France was only the beginning.'

'Indeed it was,' said Sterling. 'I would tell you, if we had all the time in the world, the history of the Paris Commune of 1871, and that of the American Civil War. Everyone believes that Britain must soon be embroiled in another war, more destructive than any seen before. But there are more problematic questions to engage our interest, and I hardly know where to begin.'

'Who is this man Lydyard, and what did he tell you?' asked the other. 'That seems an adequate point of departure.'

Sterling inclined his head in agreement, but was still forced to pause in order to find the best way to set out the story. Since the sleeper had revived, he had had no chance to offer him an elaborate account of the events leading up to his awakening, and now his own ideas had been thoroughly confused. The plans he had made for the study of Adam Clay's immortal flesh had been called into question by all this talk of diabolical angels, and Lydyard had been so intense that he could not ignore it.

'Luke was once the servant of a man named Jacob Harkender,' he said eventually. 'I had the story of it from Luke, and thought him grossly mistaken, but now I've had the same account from Lydyard I suppose there must be some truth in it, however heavily disguised.'

'Tell me,' said Adam Clay. 'I will probably find it easier to believe than you did.'

'Harkender was apparently a magician, who tried to raise the Devil, or something like him,' said Sterling cautiously, 'and, it seems, succeeded. Then, with the aid of that powerful being, Harkender caused the birth of a miracle-child, who was to become his apprentice in magic, and his instrument. But in doing that, a second being – angel or devil or Creator, call it what you will – was also awakened. The first had Harkender for its eyes and ears, and the child too; the second quickly gathered in what pawns it could, including this man Lydyard. There was nearly a conflict between the two Creators, and the werewolves of London took a hand in the affair, too, but somehow the conflict was averted. All that was twenty-one years ago, and when Luke came to me he thought it over and done with; but he had found out while he was with Harkender what you were and where your body lay, and this he told me once I had found and read your book. I revived you for my own purposes, because I believed that you could and might help me in my work.

'Now Lydyard has accused me of being an unwitting pawn of the thing which Harkender roused, a thing which he names the Spider. He says that it is spinning another web, ambitious to carry forward the conflict from which it earlier withdrew. He says that there is another wonder-child in the world now, perhaps more powerful than the other and more carefully controlled. He may, of course, be insane – or, if sane, may have misunderstood the situation completely. Ill and hurt as he is, he did not present to me the image of man entirely in control of his faculties.'

After he had finished, there was a pause. Sterling could only guess what impact the story might have on his guest, but he knew that Lucian de Terre had expressed the fervent hope in the final volume of his book that the ancient Creators might have been rendered impotent by time, and his optimism regarding the possible perfection of the world of men had been partly based in that hope.

When Adam Clay finally spoke, it was to say: 'The priests of St Amycus have always claimed that the Creators would return, and that the world of men would come to an end when they did. I had convinced myself that they were foolish, but so much else of what I prophesied has been betrayed by experience that I can readily admit that I might have been wrong. It was the followers of Amycus, after all,

who dedicated so much time and effort to the mortification
of their flesh by scourging and starvation, in the hope of
distilling what meagre rewards there are in the visionary
powers of the cold human soul. I relied on reason alone,
which I thought the better guide. Perhaps they saw more
clearly than I thought.'

This speech was a disappointment to Sterling, not so much
for its content as its despairing tone. He had expected better
of the author of *The True History of the World*, whose
vaulting imagination had seemed to him to harbour a bold
spirit of adventure.

'Lydyard was not so despairing,' said the scientist. 'Although he was in a good deal of pain, there seemed to be
considerable courage in him. He told me that these beings,
no matter what awesome magic they have, have no more
power of reasoning than ordinary men, and that they are
badly handicapped by their ignorance. Could that be true?'

'Oh yes,' said Adam Clay. '*That* was always true. Even
Machalalel, who may have been the wisest of them all, was
much more a creature of vision and inspiration than logic
and theory, and his failure to understand the world drove
even him to despair. The world which spawned the Creators
was not a kind of world conducive to the accumulation of
reliable theory, for it had only just begun to incorporate
causality. It is *this* world that holds the opportunity for the
triumph of reason, or seemed to hold it once. Perhaps, in
time, the Creators will overcome their ignorance, but even
if they do not, what can mere reason do against the might
of raw power? What defence have we against casual Acts of
Creation which defy and sweep aside the petty dominion of
causes and effects? The appearances of the world are, after
all, mere appearances; its order is an arbitrary thing, which
may vanish or fall apart upon the instant. If the Creators are
as stupid now as they were before, that may be all the more
reason to fear them.'

'I don't believe that,' said Sterling flatly. 'Whatever these
Creators are, if they belong to the Earth I cannot conceive
that they have the power to upset the universe. I don't
know what little miracles they worked twenty years ago,

but I do know that they were very *little* miracles, which did not much disturb the world. I'll accept, if you like, that these magical beings can play tricks with appearances, and might muddy the thoughts and dreams of men sufficiently to madden them, but I will not believe more than that until I see it.'

'You do not know them,' said Adam Clay, with a sigh. 'I do.'

'But I know the world,' Sterling countered. 'And I'm not so sure that you understand it as well as I, even if the underlying message of your book is true. Nor am I sure that your Creators can grasp that understanding securely, even if they do have the power to look into the minds of men like me and David Lydyard. That, I think, is what Lydyard also believes. He seems to hold to the opinion that we are not entirely lost, even though he acknowledges that the ancient gods are loose again in the world which men have built.'

'Perhaps it is good that he holds to that opinion,' said Adam Clay. 'Where else could he find hope? But that does not mean that he is right, or that there *is* hope.'

'We've come so close to an authentic Age of Reason,' said Sterling, 'that I won't easily consent to believe that anything can stand in the way of its attainment. You despaired too soon. That's one of the things I desired to tell you when I planned to bring you back from the grave: Clay Man, you despaired too soon!'

'I hope with all my heart that you are right,' said Adam Clay, in a voice hardly above a whisper. 'But it is pride that I hear in your words, not wisdom. If the Creators are awake again, I can only conclude that all this has been for nothing. The whole history of man has been nothing but an empty jest, or a negligible experiment, and I wish that you had let me sleep until the end of time.'

'Your reason and your faint heart may agree on that,' Sterling answered coldly, 'but your flesh did not. It began to quicken the moment I wrested the lid of your box away. If that Creator which made you decided that it had made a mistake, it was wrong. Yours is the heritage that should belong to all men. It will, if I'm only given time to discover its secret. *If I only have time!*'

As he said it, he jerked his head upright and turned towards the window. In the street, a newsboy had just reached his pitch, and had begun to shout. 'Murder!' he was crying, with the extravagant glee typical of his breed. ''Orrible murder in East End brothel! Read all abart it! Murder!'

'If you only have time,' echoed Adam Clay, so softly that he could hardly be heard.

2

Sterling held the mouse aloft by its tail while he carried it to the tank. It squirmed angrily and tried to curl itself around in order to bite his finger, but it could not reach. He slid the roof of the tank aside with his other hand, and dropped the mouse into the water. It began to swim furiously, thrashing its legs in a most untidy manner but somehow keeping its head above water.

It did not swim for long. The sleek creature which had waited quiescent upon the sand at the bottom of the tank sailed aloft, snaking through the water with an astonishing, sinuous grace. Its bloated head struck like an arrow at the flank of the struggling mouse, and seized hold with rasplike jaws. The flattened vermiform body coiled around the mouse as though the creature were indeed the python which its colouring recalled.

The struggles of the victim ceased almost instantly, and with the folds of its killer cocooning and compressing it, it began to sink into the depths of the tank.

'It'll be drained of blood in a matter of minutes,' Sterling said. 'But that won't be the end. The leech will replace what it takes, and its powerful throat will act as a substitute heart, to pump its own blood substitute through the mouse's vessels. The substitute contains powerful digestive juices which, over time, will liquefy the greater part of the animal's tissues, so that they too can be drawn off as nourishment. It is, I think, a way of feeding which has no precise parallel in nature.'

'It is a leech, you say?' said Adam Clay, while he watched the two creatures settle on the sand. The victim was quite anonymous now, completely enwrapped by the mottled coils of its captor, and the object resting on the floor of the tank looked for all the world like a bird's egg, so nearly elliptical had it become.

'I call it a leech,' said Sterling, 'but its forefathers were not leeches; they were planarian worms, and very tiny. Giantism is not always a consequence of induced evolution, of course; my gaudy little manikins are no bigger than the frogs and toads which were their ancestors, and have much the same dietary habits. But increase in size is such a spectacular advance that I have sought to produce it in many of my new species. Huge insects become very ungainly, but such creatures as these have remarkable scope for enlargement.'

Adam Clay looked away from the tank, where nothing now seemed to be happening, and Sterling tried anxiously to fathom the expression in his eyes. Others to whom he had shown his pets had been repelled; most had found the whole idea of what he was doing loathsome. Many men seemed to feel a particularly acute sense of threat in the revelation that flesh was so easily mutable. It was not simply the idea that what he was doing was in some way blasphemous, for the unease seemed to affect hard-headed evolutionists almost as much as devoutly religious men. It was genuinely a sense of threat, a curious sense of violation. It was as though the knowledge that such things could be done might be enough to transform the observers into monsters.

The Clay Man, however, claimed that he had once lived in a world where all was mutable and nothing fixed: a world in which the infinite duplication which was now the universal pattern of reproduction had been a novelty and a strange aberration. If there was anyone in the world, Sterling reasoned, who might feel an instant sympathy with what he had achieved and was trying to achieve, it would be Adam Clay.

Even had he not been so ardently desirous to study the flesh of the immortal Clay Man, in order to investigate its differences from merely mortal flesh, there would have been reason enough for Sterling to revive the man who had written *The True History of the World*. Even if the memories recorded in the book were false, as the Clay Man admitted that they might be, the fact that a man could imagine and cherish such ideas seemed ample evidence of a ready-made sympathy for Sterling's work.

His guest looked around, slowly, at all the things Sterling had shown him. The electric light – of a kind which Adam Clay had never seen before – probably added somewhat to the bizarrerie of the scene, but Sterling was nevertheless disappointed to see the evident discomfort in the other's expression.

'This is no magician's den,' said Sterling, feeling that he had to press the point home, 'no matter what resemblances you see between my apparatus and that which medieval alchemists used. There is no magic here, no matter what Lydyard suspects. All this was done by science, by patient trial and error. It was no magic wand that made that wondrous new leech, but careful method and hard work, extended over many long years. I couldn't begin to guess how many egg cells I've wasted in bringing forth a dozen new species, although I'm certainly no more profligate in that regard than nature.'

Clay returned to look at the first vivarium which he had been shown, where hundreds of strangely delicate creatures roamed the surfaces of broad green leaves. Sterling knew that they seemed to the uninformed eye to be made of glass, though the transparent mineral from which they formed their delicate exoskeletons was not in fact a silicate.

'They do not resemble Crosse's drawings of his own acarids,' Clay observed.

'Crosse's specimens were monsters of their own kind,' said Sterling. 'The grotesque tangles of filaments were an aberration. Had he known what kind of eggs had been unwittingly admitted to his apparatus, he would have had more success in repeating his experiments, and might in time have perfected his methods to the point of producing true-breeding specimens. Alas, he was mistaken about precisely what it was that he had achieved, and so his achievement was wasted. Did you know him?'

'No,' said Adam Clay. 'I heard of him, of course, as all England did. I knew Faraday slightly at the time when the controversy blew up, and I heard him talk about the affair, but I never met Crosse.'

'I find it slightly unusual that you didn't seek him out,' said Sterling, slightly vexed by the other's failure to react according to his hopes. 'Of all the men in England, surely you knew better than any other what his results might signify?'

'You mistake me,' Clay answered, uncomfortably but quite plainly. 'My championship of the Age of Reason, in that silly book I wrote, was not the hymn of praise for what you call science that you have taken it to be. It was a celebration of the power of human hands, organised in association to carry out great tasks. The examples uppermost in my mind were the pyramids of Egypt and the Colossus of Rhodes, and great cities like Paris and London. Those were wonders which needed no particular ingenuity to design or construct, but only the combined efforts of legions of men. I sought to find virtue in what was to me the strangest aspect of mankind – the sheer numbers generated by duplicative reproduction – and the Reason in which I found hope for the future was not the cunning which has made so many new machines, but the sanity which proclaimed the ideals of Liberty, Equality and Fraternity. You seem to think that I should understand and applaud what you have done, but if you had read my book more carefully you could hardly have overlooked the fact that I am no evolutionist. Unless, of course, the words on the page are no longer those which I wrote. That is entirely possible.'

Sterling frowned. He was disappointed, but not downcast. He was sure that he could explain to his visitor, if he only had the time, exactly what the import was of all the things he had achieved. Yes, he had hoped to find the Clay Man better disposed towards the march of science, but he had also hoped that the immortal might see another and altogether different significance in his work. He had wondered whether the dim and distorted memories which the Clay Man had of an Age of Miracles might not refer to an era of very rapid evolution, when the impulse to physical evolution had for some reason been much stronger than it was now. With the Clay Man's help, Sterling had thought that he might find a better version of the allegory of the *True History* – one which had no room for magic, but only for natural process. There seemed little prospect of that now.

'Let's go up again,' he said, suppressing a sigh. 'It's more comfortable in the smoking room, and there is a great deal that I want to tell you. I'm not convinced by Lydyard's warnings, but I have my own sense of urgency too. We all grow older with every day that passes, and face the risk of death. If immortality is indeed an achievement that can be gained, every day that is lost in the search for its secret is a risk that can hardly be justified.'

'Immortality is not quite the happy state that you imagine,' said Adam Clay quietly. 'The werewolves, at least, have no doubt that it is better to live as a mortal wolf than to be eternally human.'

'But they see your state as something final and unalterable,' Sterling countered. 'All their ambitions are directed towards a past which is dead and gone, and whose loss makes them irredeemably miserable. Even you, although you know what a deceiver memory is, and although you found some hope for the future in your imagined Age of Reason, are still weighed down by the burden of the past which you imagine you've lost. But I see immortality as a beginning, not an end. I believe also that conscious control of form would be a leap forward in the pattern of evolution. If you'll allow me to do it, I think I might persuade you that it's my way of thinking, not yours, which is the better one.'

Adam Clay shook his head slowly, and implied by the gesture that it could not be done, though what he actually said was: 'You are most welcome to try.'

'Neither your *True History of the World* nor the history which modern science infers,' said Sterling patiently, while he watched the swirling clouds of smoke ascend from his cigar, 'can offer a complete interpretation of the world of appearances in which we find ourselves. Both testify to the inescapable limitations imposed upon us by our senses and our memories. When philosophers go in search of absolute certainty, they're quickly reduced to a curious solipsism of the moment. If I'm determined to be extreme in my doubts, I can be certain only of the fact that I exist at this particular instant in time, enjoying the particular sensation, alloyed with the particular thought, which is the present state of my stream of consciousness. All else is conjecture and conviction: the universe, and the past, are simply hypotheses recruited to explain the moment. Agreed?'

'Agreed,' said Adam Clay, with a slight inclination of his head. He was not smoking, and the glass which he held in his hand contained water.

'I admit that I read your *True History* through the lens of my own understanding,' Sterling went on, 'but I don't think that I mistook its import. It's in part a book of lamentations, exploring the misfortune which has given you a memory of the past which is very different from the past whose record is written in the rocks of the Earth and the implications of astronomical observations. The appearances which the Earth and the cosmos now present to human understanding say that the universe is vast and very old, and that the age of the Earth must be measured in millions of years, if not thousands of millions. Your memories, on the other hand, assure you that the Earth and the cosmos which contains it are little more than ten thousand years old – that time itself is little more than ten thousand years old – and that before there was an Earth, or time, there was a mysterious and unimaginable flux of pure Creativity, which had not yet given birth to cause and effect.

'You take from this contradiction of appearance and experience the inference that it makes little sense to speak of a single true history of the world. You suggest that all the conceivable pasts which might have produced this fleeting moment of the present, whether preserved in the memories of immortal beings or in the objects of the world of appearances, might somehow be real. You go on to argue, though it seems now that you were not as wholehearted in the argument as I thought, that it is futile to worry overmuch what the truth of the past was, and that men should concentrate instead on that which is both intellectually graspable and by our own efforts controllable: the future. I know that you may not agree with my emphasis, but have I the substance of your argument?'

Adam Clay nodded again and said: 'Go on.'

'Where we differ, I think, is in that you make no distinction between different kinds of imagined past. You see your account of your own remembered history as one more in a series of stories about the way the world may have been created and organised; you set it on a par with the mythology of the Bible or the folklore of the ancient Greeks. I don't; I compare it with the notion of universal history adopted by the evolutionists, whose more extreme exponents attempt to discard the idea of a Creator altogether. This leaves the universe without a point of origin or any divine hand to ordain the particular laws acording to which it seems to work, but I'm not among those who find that state of affairs inconceivable.

'In a curious sense, your account too has an absent Creator, because it begins with a description of a Golden Age already well tarnished, in which a host of subsidiary Creators has emerged. None of these subsidiary Creators can be conceived of as having the power to have created the entire universe, because they're mere parts of it. Despite your apparent suspicion that any one of them might bring about a radical reordering of the perceived laws of nature, I can't believe it; it seems to me that their power must be severely limited, partly on purely logical grounds but also because the evidence of your account suggests strongly that there's some kind of fundamental pattern of change which affects and includes them along with all other entities, and which is very puzzling to them. You – and, presumably, they – agree with religious men in seeing these puzzles in terms of the ordinance of some hidden and almighty Creator-of-Creators into whose design everything else fits, but as there is nothing you can say about this ultimate Creator save that he is unidentifiable and incomprehensible, it is easy enough to replace him with a natural process very different in kind from the powers of those you call Creators.'

Adam Clay shrugged his shoulders while Sterling paused to draw on his cigar and sip his wine.

'It seems to me,' Sterling continued, 'that in your history and mine – and all other conceivable histories – there is but one fundamental question. How does change happen? What shapes the history that is? The moment which is all I truly know is for ever on the threshold of becoming a different moment, and it does so with what seems to me to be a measure of inevitability slightly modified by the action of my will.

'Common to your history and mine is the notion that whatever exists changes; there is less difference than one might at first suppose between your conviction that the ultimate motor of change is that Creativity which was unfettered during your so-called Golden Age, and my assumption that all change is cause and effect. Even cause and effect, you see, requires some kind of initial impulse, or some kind of spontaneous input which feeds the system. In my evolutionist writings I speak of an impulse to innovation characteristic of all life, but there must be some such impulse even in the realm of the non-living. Lucretius calls it *clinamen*: the tiny, spontaneous swerve of an atom which sets in train the vast chain of collisions and interactions which brings difference and change out of uniformity. You use the word yourself in the *True History*.'

'I remember,' said Adam Clay. 'Out of respect for the old atomists, I conjectured that the Creativity of the Creators might be regarded as a kind of *clinamen*.

'Good,' said Sterling. 'Let us call it *clinamen*, then: this source of the chain of cause and effect. Lucretius imagines it as a single event which only happened once, but you and I agree that is not necessarily the case. It might instead be something which for ever feeds the universe with potential change: a persistent and ever present element of randomness in the behaviour of atoms; a continuing impulse of innovation. I have been very interested in this impulse, and the role which it plays in the evolution of living things. If Darwin is right, you see, it is that continual flow of tiny differences which provides the raw material with which natural selection can work.

'My experiments, building on work done by Crosse and others, have been directed to the end of trying to increase and concentrate the effects of elementary change – of *clinamen* – on particular entities which are especially vulnerable to change: the egg cells of animal species. I've succeeded, as you've seen. I have, in the most successful trials, speeded up the ordinary rate of evolution by a factor of several million. Nor are the effects which I have contrived entirely confined to eggs and embryos. Even developed organisms, so long as they're capable of further growth, might under the proper conditions be enabled to undergo processes of metamorphosis.'

'Like the werewolves,' said Adam Clay reflectively.

'Like *you*,' said Sterling. 'Your defiance of death is a kind of reproduction, a kind of continuing metamorphosis of the flesh. What you and the werewolves lack is conscious control over the metamorphoses of which you're capable, but you have time to discover and develop that, if you'll only consent to try. You have all the time in the world! What Machalalel did for you is a beginning, not an end.'

Adam Clay was silent while he absorbed the consequences of Sterling's argument; at last, the scientist thought, he was making progress.

'What you are saying to me,' said the Clay Man, eventually, 'is that your science, and the kind of magic which Machalalel had – and which the other Creators still have – might both be capable of attaining the same end, and might therefore be regarded as the same thing.'

'Yes,' said Sterling. 'If I'm to be required to believe in magic at all, or in the power of mysterious Creators, then I must fit it into my own natural philosophy. Magic, if it exists, must involve control of what we have agreed to call *clinamen* by a particular kind of consciousness.

'I don't pretend to know what is meant by the mysterious heat which possesses the souls of those who can allegedly do magic, nor can I begin to understand why the experience of pain is correlated in such beings with supernatural powers of vision, but much else that you describe in your book can be accommodated to my way of thinking.

'I have found ways of increasing, concentrating and directing the flux of *clinamen* by means of electricity, in a purely mechanical fashion. By this means, I hope one day to achieve the same ends that powerful magic is said to have achieved. I hope that I may be able to make men immortal, and perhaps give them the shape-shifting powers which the werewolves have.'

'And would you also be able to make immortals mortal?' asked the Clay Man.

It was a surprising and rather disappointing question. 'Perhaps,' Sterling answered, 'although I can't see the advantage in that.'

'The werewolves might, if you can explain to Mandorla what you have tried to explain to me. You would not have needed me, had you been able to find her as easily as she has found you.'

'I'll be glad to have the werewolves as collaborators,' said Sterling, 'if that is their desire.'

'And what of the others?' aske Adam Clay quietly. 'What of the one which – according to Lydyard – has been your collaborator all along? Are you really so sure that it was electrically stimulated *clinamen*, and not borrowed magic, that helped to produce your monsters?'

'They're not monsters,' said Sterling. 'They're merely new species. Nor does it matter in the least what label we attach to the means by which they were created; what matters is whether the process is consistently controllable. In any case, if we accept Lydyard's account, we must conclude that no Creator could have intruded its magic into Crosse's experiments, for none was then awake.'

'None,' said Adam Clay contemplatively, 'that Lydyard knew of.'

As he spoke, the quiet of the night was suddenly split by the long, loud and eerily echoing cry of a wolf. The beast could not have been more than a dozen yards from the window of the room where they sat, and it brought Sterling instantly to his feet, full of foreboding.

3

As the howl's echoes died away, Sterling went swiftly to the door. He did not need to call for Luke Capthorn because Luke was already hurrying along the corridor, equally anxious.

'Is all secured?' Sterling demanded.

'As tightly as it can be,' the servant replied. They both knew, however, that the house was no fortress; the windows at the front of the house were tall and unshuttered.

'Tell Mrs Tolley to remain in her room,' said Sterling. 'Then fetch a shotgun to the smoking room.'

'What about Richard and the lad?' asked Luke. Marwin and the boy who tended Sterling's horses slept above the stables, which were at some little distance from the house and on the far side.

'They must have heard the cry,' Sterling said. 'If they have the sense to keep their own doors locked, they should be as safe there as we are here. Perhaps they'll be safer, given that the werewolves have nothing against *them*.' He wondered, as he said it, what the werewolves of London could possibly have against *him*, but he no longer dared assume that they bore him no malice.

Luke nodded, and moved off to carry the instruction to the cook. Sterling went back to the smoking room and picked up the small pistol from the side table where he had laid it down. Then he looked up at Adam Clay.

The Clay Man did not seem at all frightened. That was not in itself reassuring. The Clay Man, he knew, had no particular cause to be frightened; even death held no terrors for him.

'What might it signify,' Sterling asked him, 'that their emissary has returned in wolf form and not in human guise?'

'If that is Perris,' said Adam Clay, 'he can no longer be counted an emissary. You have read the book, and I need not remind you that while the werewolves are wolves they retain only the smallest vestiges of human reason and human purpose. While they are wolves, they hunt as wolves. Do not open the door, unless you are ready to face a wild beast.'

Luke returned then, carrying a broken gun. While Sterling and the Clay Man watched, the servant inserted two cartridges into the barrels, fumbling as though his hands were trembling a little. When he looked up at his master, though, his gaze was steady. The three of them remained still for a few moments, listening. Nothing could be heard.

'I doubt that there is any danger,' said the Clay Man evenly. 'If the wolves intended to kill us, they would not have paused to warn us with their howling.'

As if to prove him right, the doorbell sounded. It was its ordinary sound, but Luke did not move an inch in response to the summons. Sterling could not blame him, though he knew full well that only a human hand could sound the bell; a wolf could not have grasped it.

'Stand beside me, Luke,' Sterling said. 'Keep the gun ready, but don't fire in panic, and be careful with your aim.'

When Sterling left the room, Luke obediently fell in beside him, and Adam Clay also rose from his seat. Together, the three of them went to the door.

'Who is it?' asked Sterling loudly, before laying a hand on either of the bolts. He had no intention of touching them unless he heard a human voice in reply.

The answer that came was by no means expected.

'Sir Edward Tallentyre and William de Lancy. Let us in, Sterling, I beg of you! There's something dangerous out here, and I would far rather hide from it behind your door than stand here unarmed in the shadows.'

Sterling could not contain his astonishment; he turned and met Luke Capthorn's eyes, glad to see that the servant was as startled as he was. But Capthorn's eyes narrowed again, and Sterling too was tempted to disbelief.

'Forgive me my caution, Sir Edward,' Sterling replied, 'but it seemed to me that I heard the call of a wolf only a few minutes ago, very close to the house.'

'I heard it too,' said the voice from beyond the door, 'and that's why I beg you to hurry. Be assured that legend lies when it says that the werewolves of London can only be hurt by silver bullets. Strange flesh they may be, but they are only flesh, and they bleed when they're hurt. I have no gun to ward them off, but you must have one in the house.'

Sterling drew his pistol and signalled to Luke to be ready, but before he could open the door, Adam Clay stepped past him.

'Stand well back,' said the immortal. 'Let me do it. I will come to no harm, whatever happens.'

Sterling did as he was told. The Clay Man drew back the bolts one by one, then turned the key in the lock and drew the door open.

Two men stood on the step, neither young nor unduly handsome. Sterling did not know how cunning the shape-shifting powers of the werewolves might be, but he reasoned that it did not matter whether these were wolves or not, given that they wore human guise and must therefore be possessed of human reason.

The two men came in, and Adam Clay shut the door behind them, turning the key in the lock again and drawing the bolts.

Sterling stared at the older of the two men. He was in his sixties, but he stood straight and tall. He was not powerfully built but he was all muscle and sinew. His skin showed all the usual signs of aging, but seemed hard in texture. His companion, though he seemed to be somewhat younger, appeared much the frailer and wearier of the two; his eyes were wild and haunted, and he was breathing raggedly.

'My friend has recently been injured,' said Tallentyre, who seemed to be appraising Sterling as carefully as he himself was being appraised. 'He is not himself, but he would not be left behind in Kensington. May we sit down?'

Sterling put the derringer away in his pocket and led the way back to the smoking room. There the younger man lowered himself thankfully on to the sofa, and closed his eyes as if to shut out the horror of the world. Tallentyre remained standing, waiting for introductions to be made.

Sterling announced his own name, and added: 'This is my servant, Luke Capthorn, and this is Adam Clay, who once styled himself Lucian de Terre. I believe you've heard all our names before. Is Lydyard not with you?'

If he had hoped to take Tallentyre by surprise, he was disappointed. The man had been told what company to expect.

'I had hoped that I might find David here,' Tallentyre told him. 'When I arrived at my daughter's house, I found that he had gone out with a man who would not give his name, and he had not returned before I left. My daughter is very anxious. She told me what passed between you earlier today, and that you had urged him to come here. She was annoyed by her inability to give me a better account of what's happening; I came to you in the hope that you might have an explanation.'

'I fear not,' said Sterling, acutely aware of the inadequacy of his reply. 'Wherever Lydyard went – and I'm surprised, in view of his condition when I saw him, that he went anywhere at all – he didn't come here. If your daughter told you what passed between us, you'll know that he summoned me to Kensington in order to give information to me, not to ask for explanations. Until he told me, I didn't know that the werewolves of London really existed, let alone that they might have any interest in me. Now, as you've seen, we're easily frightened by sounds in the night.'

Tallentyre turned suddenly to face Luke Capthorn, and said: 'Where can I find your erstwhile master, Jacob Harkender?' Sterling knew Luke well enough to see that he was genuinely surprised by the question.

'As far as I know, sir, he's dead,' the servant said. 'I haven't seen him for nigh on twenty years, and I know that when they found him in the ruins of his house he was horribly burnt and barely alive. They took him to an asylum in Essex, but I can't believe that he has survived until now.'

'He had a protector, had he not?' Tallentyre asked sharply, but Luke only flushed sullenly in response.

'Luke is telling the truth,' Sterling intervened. 'I'm sure that he knows nothing of Harkender's fate. Have you any reason to think that Harkender is involved in this?'

'I'm sure that his protector is,' Tallentyre countered.

Adam Clay took half a pace forward and said: 'With due respect, Sir Edward, you cannot know that. Even I do not know how many of Machalalel's kind are bound into the surface of the Earth, but I do know that any one of them might be at work in shaping these events. Possibly there is more than one.'

Tallentyre turned again to study the man who had spoken. 'You're the man who was in Austen's care so many years ago,' said Tallentyre, meaning it as a question although he did not frame it as such. 'You're Pelorus' friend. According to his testimony, you're the one creature still alive who existed before he was given human form.'

'I am,' said Adam Clay.

'But you don't know what's happened to the world while you slept in the grave,' Tallentyre went on. 'Are you really so certain of what's happening now?'

'Not certain at all,' said the other frankly.

Tallentyre looked down at his companion, who was showing no sign of recovery. De Lancy was slumped in his chair as though he were quite unconscious of what was happening around him. Evidently, Sterling thought, their journey from Kensington had been more hurried than they would have preferred.

'If anyone should have been able to unravel the mystery, it was poor de Lancy,' said Tallentyre. 'Lydyard and I were briefly used by the Sphinx as its instruments, but de Lancy has been its intimate companion for twenty years. It seems, however, that the Sphinx has been destroyed and de Lancy casually cast aside. He's badly hurt, exactly as poor David was once hurt, and his senses are still scattered. He could easily have been killed, but he seems to have been preserved upon a whim. Something seems to be playing with us, gentlemen, as a cat plays with a mouse, for amusement. I think Jacob Harkender might do that, or something which learned to see the world through Harkender's eyes.'

As if to emphasise his conclusion, there came again the ululating howl of a wolf, quickly taken up by other beast voices. The cries came from somewhere close at hand, as though the wolves were gathered in the street beyond the railings which guarded the front of the house.

Sterling hesitated for a moment, then he went to the window and drew the curtain aside so that he might look out.

As he did so, he felt his clutch upon the cloth draw tighter, though there was no conscious intention in the seizure. His heart, which had been beating unusually quickly before, now became painful as its pace surged. He could not believe his eyes, and in the helplessness of his unbelief it seemed that his thoughts seized up entirely, leaving him incapable of emotion or response. He could not even contrive to be afraid.

He must have seemed quite calm to the others, for they did not immediately become alarmed. Some seconds passed before Tallentyre said: 'What do you see, Dr Sterling?' Even then, the baronet's tone suggested that he expected a calm and ordinary answer.

Outside the house, the street should have been lit by gas lamps. The buildings opposite should have loomed in silhouette against the night sky, their many windows glistening in the reflected light. There should have been lights at several of those windows, where his anxious neighbours had come to peer out, frightened by the howling. There should have been a host of sharply delineated shadows cast by walls and railings, lampposts and gables.

In that wholly constructed landscape, the werewolves of London could only have seemed alien and out of place. They would have been strangers in a world which they had not made, where they never could be truly at home. Had there been a whole pack of them gathered in the street, they might have seemed menacing, but they would also have seemed oddly forlorn, like strays.

Alas, the landscape upon which Sterling found himself looking out was not the one that should have been there. The environs of the house had been changed completely in the few moments which had elapsed since Tallentyre had come in.

The only visible source of light was the moon, which hung close to the distant horizon, seemingly bloated and uncannily coloured. Its light was brighter than the light of any moon

Sterling had ever seen through the smoky London air, and was multiplied ten- or twelve-fold in forming what seemed for a moment to be a vast liquid river spilling like milk from the distant world to the Earth below. The apparent river of light was a reflection in the surface of a vast and calm sea, whose waves lapped very gently upon a barren strand which extended as far as the street should have extended from the door of the house. The railings which normally protected the front of the house were gone, replaced by the dark foliage of alien trees.

Standing or squatting patiently upon the sand, watching its windows with faintly glowing eyes, were five enormous wolves. They were pale and grey in the moonlight, and their dark tongues lolled out of their gaping mouths, as though the beasts were cooling themselves.

They did not look out of place at all; it seemed to Sterling that they belonged here, even though he knew that earthly wolves were creatures of the cold north, not the fevered tropics.

As soon as he thought of the tropics, Sterling became conscious of the radiant heat streaming from the window glass. Outside, he knew, it must be very warm.

'Sir Edward,' said Sterling, wishing that he could sound calm but knowing that his terror was evident in his half-strangled tone. 'Look!'

Tallentyre came quickly towards him. So did the others, except for the semiconscious de Lancy.

Belatedly reasserting control over his hand, Sterling swept the curtain aside, so that all of them could bear witness to the miracle which had befallen them.

Sterling was glad to find that even Tallentyre was speechless for a few seconds. Adam Clay was the first to speak. 'You are right, Sir Edward,' he said quietly. 'Whichever Creator has us in its power is certainly determined to astonish us, and to play games with our fears and expectations. They always had a certain childlike pride in their showmanship, and it seems they have not lost that while they slept.'

At least, thought Sterling, *we may hazard a guess that this playful fallen angel will not cut its entertainment short by feeding us to the werewolves.* But he knew even as he formed the thought that it was a stupid and petty response to a challenging situation, and he fought against his instinctive refusal to accept what had happened, in the hope of finding a saner one.

'If this is the Spider's doing,' said Tallentyre, with a calmness which Sterling could only envy, 'it's not the first time that it has done something of this kind. Then it built a little Hell and drew us into it; now it offers us a tropical coast. It's strangely reluctant to meet us face to face in our own surroundings. Do you think we might find David *here*?'

Sterling found himself wishing, churlishly, that something might happen which would shake Tallentyre's composure as rudely as he himself has been shaken.

'Is this some kind of dream?' he asked gruffly. 'Or has my house in truth been snatched into another world?'

'It's a truth which I once tried hard to disbelieve,' said Tallentyre, with just the trace of a tremor in his voice, 'that the world is not as solid as men of science would wish. It can take on the nature and disorder of a dream, and when it does, there's little sense in asking what is real and what is mere appearance. Yes, certainly this is a dream; but while we're trapped in it, everything we see is as real as any appearance of the material world. I've always known that what had happened once could – and perhaps must – happen again.

'It seems that we've been drawn together, Dr Sterling: you, the Clay Man, de Lancy and I. Perhaps we're about to be put on trial, as David and I were once put on trial before. This time, perhaps, we might hear the Spider's calculated response to the truth which I once forced it to accept.'

'I'm grateful for your quickness of mind,' Sterling said, wishing that his voice might be less grating. 'Perhaps you might advise us as to what we should do.'

Even while he was speaking, one of the wolves which watched them from the beach was changing its form. With unbelievable quickness it became a crouching human being, who then stood up, stark naked. The silver sheen which dressed the sea was behind her, so that she showed up only in silhouette, but there was no mistaking that it was a woman.

'Is that Mandorla?' asked Tallentyre of Adam Clay.

'I cannot tell,' the Clay Man answered.

Sterling expected her to come forward, to speak to them through the window and deliver some portentous message, but she did not. Instead, she raised her hand and beckoned. She was not beckoning to the watching men; Sterling realised immediately that she was signalling to someone else, who must be hidden among the trees which stood between the wall of the house and the beach.

Three figures ran forward from concealment, on to the sand. They ran towards the werewolves without any sign of fear, very eagerly. They were all human, but none of them full-grown.

Children! Sterling thought pronouncing the word in the privacy of his own skull as though it were as sinister as it was absurd.

He thought at first, though he had no basis whatever for the assumption, that they were infant werewolves. Then his earlier wish was granted, and Sir Edward Tallentyre cried out in anguish, his awesome composure having been stripped away upon the instant. The cry was very strange, to have come from a human throat; it was like the cry of an animal in pain.

Sterling remembered that David Lydyard had three children, who were Sir Edward Tallentyre's grandchildren.

The werewolf in human form reached out her arms to greet the running children, and gathered them in maternally. And then, with the same astonishing suddenness as before, the human silhouette dissolved and became a crouching wolf again.

The three children, who had kept their ordinary form only long enough for Tallentyre to recognise them, changed too. They were, it seemed, infant werewolves after all.

When the entire pack came upright and loped away across the sand, leaving moist footprints behind them, the children went too.

'For the love of God!' whispered Sir Edward Tallentyre –
who was, Sterling remembered, one of the most renowned
atheists in London. 'Teddy! Simon, Nell . . . my poor
Cordelia!'

4

Tallentyre thrust Luke Capthorn rudely aside and ran
to the door of the room. He turned the handle and
pulled the door towards himself. There should have been
light beyond – the light of the electric bulb mounted in the
wall of the corridor – but there was only darkness.

Tallentyre staggered back, as though he had been buffeted
by a sudden rush of wind. It was not so much a wind, though,
as a wave of moist heat which swept into the room, carrying
with it a strange admixture of sweet and foetid odours: the
exaggerated scents of a lush tropical forest. Although he was
as far away from the door as it was possible to be, Sterling felt
himself assaulted by the odours and the avid humidity which
hastened to possess every corner and cranny of the room.

The house, he realised, had not been moved at all. Only
the room in which they were standing had been translocated
into this alien place, only the appearance of the walls and
windows, the carpet and the furniture.

That appearance was dissolving already. The curtain which
Sterling still held was changing in his grasp, becoming warm
and leafy. The paper on the walls, ironically patterned with
exotic flowers, was fading into spreading canopies of green.

They had all turned to watch Tallentyre as he ran to the
door, and now Adam Clay went to take the baronet by the
arm, while Luke Capthorn fell backwards clutching his gun,
seeking support from the back of the chair where de Lancy
was still slumped. But the chair was solid no longer, and
Luke fell to his knees while de Lancy sank to the ground.
The harsh electric light, which had illuminated the room
but a moment before, flickered and faded as it dissipated
into a tiny cloud of fleeing fireflies. Sterling lost sight of

all his companions, and although he reached out towards them as the forest closed in, his hand met only hanging branches.

The window by which Sterling had been standing was no longer there, but the heavy moon still shone through a gap in the trees, and the beach beyond was still visible, patterned with the pawmarks of the wolves. He moved forward on to the open sand, where he could see the moonlight on the water and the star-filled sky above. His eyes, so unexpectedly denied the glare of the electric bulb, were still adapting to the dimmer light, but he was sure that he would be able to see more clearly in a moment or two where his companions were.

'Luke!' he cried. 'Come on to the sand.'

But Luke did not come, and as Sterling's eyes grew accustomed to the dimness he saw that the place he had come from was now a dark and shadowy wall of trailing tree branches hung with creepers. All of his erstwhile companions, he knew, must be behind that cloak of vegetation, but none of them came forth in response to his cry. It was easy enough to imagine that they too might have been transformed, like the children who had run across the sand, into wolves or other beasts.

Sterling looked down at the sparkling sand and saw the marks which the children had left. Human footprints headed towards the disturbed place where the wolves had waited; animal tracks continued from there, extending into the darkness.

'I'm here!' he shouted. 'Come to me, if you can, any of you.'

After a moment or two, an upright shadow detached itself from the great confusion and came towards him; a second followed. As soon as the first man was clear of the overhanging branches, the moonlight caught his face and Sterling saw that it was Tallentyre. Adam Clay was close behind him. Sterling was pathetically glad to see them, and to know that he was not to be left entirely alone. He swallowed hard and wiped the sweat from his brow with his sleeve. He expected to see Luke too, but no one else came out, and he knew how hopeless it would be to plunge into the darkness in search of his servant.

'Where are we?' he whispered. 'How did we come here?'

'We were brought,' the Clay Man said. 'Something reached out and snatched us up like a handful of insects. We are outside the world.'

Sterling saw that the Clay Man was surprised and frightened, in spite of what he knew about the Creators and their ways, but that he was fighting to regain his composure. Sterling expected nothing less of himself, but the shock had been almost too great to bear. A shudder of terror was trying to take possession of his body, and he had to force his dizzy mind to fix itself on a further question.

'Why?' he asked, knowing that the word must sound like a cry of pain.

'That,' said Tallentyre, whose own voice was held level only by the utmost effort, 'is what we must discover.'

The baronet was looking down at the footprints in the sand, as Sterling had, evidently wondering whether he should follow the trail which led away into the distance. He too put up an arm to wipe moisture away from his forehead; then he took off the coat which he was still wearing, and threw it down. He took off his jacket, too, and his tie. Sterling, after a moment's hesitation, followed suit. He guessed that the temperature was in the high eighties.

'What will it be like when the sun rises?' he asked, glad to find that he could now keep his voice steady while he spoke the words.

'In dreams,' Tallentyre replied bitterly, 'the sun is not obliged to rise at all. We're awake and can be hurt, but we're nevertheless in a kind of dream. You may find that you feel more at home here than you might expect, Dr Sterling. You've lived a greater part of your life in dreams than your waking brain can remember.'

Then, without asking for the advice or consent of his fellows, the baronet began walking away. He was following the tracks made by the wolves. Sterling wondered briefly whether they might be led into a trap by the trail, but quickly realised how absurd the thought was. They were already entrapped, as completely as they could be. He looked back at the dark forest, still hoping that Luke might step forth, but no one came, and it now seemed probable that that no one could or would. Tallentyre seemed to have accepted that, or else he had ceased to care even about his friend. He had barely glanced at the wall of shadow before setting forth.

Sterling shrugged his shoulders and fell meekly into step with Adam Clay, who was already hurrying to keep up with Tallentyre.

When they had gone a little way, Sterling moved alongside Tallentyre. He felt a desperate need to talk, to search for explanations. 'Tell me what's happening,' he begged. 'Dream or not, we must decide what to do.' As he formed the words he felt his anxiety ease a little; as Tallentyre had suggested, he had less difficulty in adapting his attitude of mind to their situation than was altogether reasonable.

'The decision is unlikely to be ours,' said Adam Clay. 'I doubt that it is worth our while to make plans.'

Tallentyre rounded on their companion. 'No,' he said. 'We mustn't think like that. Whatever power our captors may wield, we're not mere clay to be moulded. Even the angels are prisoned by time and space and substance. They may steal the senses of others, and leech upon the intelligence of others, and plunder the dreams of others; but in the end, each and every one of them stands in confrontation with the universe outside itself, and must make its own reckoning of what it is and what ends it has, and what schemes it must make in order to pursue those ends. We are men, and may do the same.

'Twenty years ago, David and I persuaded the entity which we call the Spider that it didn't know enough about what manner of being it had become, or what manner of universe it confronted, to determine what ends it ought to have or how to achieve them. I knew even then that it had resources enough to make investigation of all the questions which lay open and unanswered before it; I always knew that it would grow wiser, and that one day, it might be persuaded by its acquired wisdom that there was something to be gained by working further miracles. For twenty years, I've known that this moment might come, and have tried to be ready for it. No matter that it has the power of life and death over all of us, no matter that it hates us, and terrifies us for its pleasure, we need not yield. We must do what we can!'

Tallentyre had stopped in his tracks, and now that he had let his pent-up anger out, he did not seem ready to stride purposefully on. It seemed to have come home to him how futile it was to chase across the sand in search of a party of wolves. Sterling still had his own gun in his pocket, but Luke and the shotgun were somewhere else.

'We have no quarrel with one another,' said Sterling breathlessly. 'There's no need for accusations and recriminations.'

Tallentyre hesitated for a moment, then he nodded. 'Of course,' he said. 'I'm sorry.' As he spoke the latter sentence, he nodded to Adam Clay, who acknowledged the apology graciously.

'Do you believe this being which you confronted before holds you in sufficient esteem to tell you the results of its deliberations?' asked Sterling, as reasonably as he could. 'Do you think that it feels obliged to give you a second chance to overturn its conclusions?'

Tallentyre was not in the least dismayed by his sceptical tone. 'You're a scientist, are you not?' he said. 'You see with your own eyes where we are. Whatever will confront us will confront us in its own time and for its own reasons. The important thing is to respond as sane and reasonable men, do you not agree?'

'It's not easy,' said Sterling, in an aggrieved tone.

'No,' Tallentyre admitted, 'it isn't. But you must decide whether you will approach whatever has kidnapped us with the attitude of a brave man or a coward. If you're a coward, you might fall down on your knees and pray for deliverance; if not, you must cling to the power of reason. Say this to yourself: if there truly are such beings as gods, or angels, or Creators, they are after all merely beings like ourselves. They're very different from us, undoubtedly more powerful, and perhaps they are to us as we are to little insects; but that doesn't mean that we should fall down before them and plead for their favours.

'If a scientist ant which had a conscious mind found its nest idly trampled underfoot by a human being, it ought not to waste its time in fruitless prayer or despairing lamentation. It ought to say instead, "This is a being, like me. It's so huge that it pays little heed to my own kind, and cannot care about me overmuch, but still it's a being with which I might communicate, with which I might dispute, and with which I might even reach agreement, given that we must both be obedient to the same principles of reasoning." And if the ant should ever succeed in establishing a means of communication with the unwitting and uncaring trampler of its nest, do you not think that the man in question – if he were a man of science – ought to be very interested to hear what the ant had to say?

'In answer to your question, yes, I do believe that the being which I startled twenty years ago owes it to me to tell me the result of its deliberations. If it is wise, that is precisely what it'll do.'

'I think you misjudge it,' said Adam Clay softly. 'As flies to wanton boys are we to the gods . . . I wish that it were not so, but it is.'

Tallentyre's face softened slightly, and he nodded again. 'You might easily be right,' he conceded. 'If the priests of St Amycus are right in any of their beliefs, it is probably the belief that the fallen angels hate us, and that our terror is their pleasure. But if that's true, it only proves that these godlike things are *not* wise. If that is so, they're certainly not entitled to our awe, our humility or our worship. If their only purpose in bringing us here is to torture and kill us, they're not even worthy of our respect.'

'Those whom the gods hate,' said the Clay Man, 'are rarely allowed to die but once. I remember the Age of Heroes, when they were more generous with the gift of immortality, and ingenious in their punishments.'

While this argument continued, Sterling thought hard about Tallentyre's parable. A host of possible questions and contradictions entered Sterling's mind, but he did not know whether it was worth arguing over a metaphor.

'If this thing has really brought you here to dispute with it,' he said, 'why has it brought me with you? Am I merely another ant, with bolder ideas than the rest, brought to stand beside you?'

'I dare say that you are,' said Tallentyre. 'But it may be that you have served a more specific purpose than that. The Sphinx enlisted enigmatists to help her unravel the mystery of the world; I've been one of them, though I think she has studied me from a distance, using David Lydyard's eyes. No doubt the Spider did likewise. I suspect that you've been the Spider's instrument, and that your experiments in evolution have been part of the Spider's quest to understand the nature of the world. You've been an instrument within your own laboratory.'

'Then why do we not stand before the throne of this arachnid angel?' Sterling asked. 'Why are we walking along an infinite beach, following the footprints of a pack of werewolves which may or may not include your grandchildren? I've heard that gods are disposed to work in mysterious ways, but such perversity can hardly encourage your hope that they're scientists like you or I. If an ant were to make itself known to me and suggest that we discuss the nature of things, I would receive it more straightforwardly than this.'

'So would I,' said Tallentyre sadly, looking at the dark waves beating on the shore. 'The Clay Man may be right in his assessment of the strange stupidity of the Creators.'

Sterling followed the direction of the baronet's gaze, and examined the face of the moon, which had sunk so far in the sky that only three-quarters of its disc was still visible above the shadow line of the horizon. The night was growing darker, and it was clear that the path of light which extended itself across the surface of the sea would soon dwindle away. The tracks extending before them still seemed endless.

'I think I might be very interested in the sentient ant,' said Sterling, almost absent-mindedly. 'So interested that I might want to know far more than what it felt inclined to tell me.

I might want to see what it could do if placed in a maze, or confronted by many different kinds of puzzle. I might think that it was, after all, naught but an ant, and need not be given the same consideration I would extend to a man, or even a cat. And then again . . .'

Tallentyre had taken a hesitant step forward, as if to continue on his former course, but he paused again, presumably wondering whether it might not be better to rest and wait. 'You may be right,' he said. He looked at the Clay Man. 'One thing we do know about these angels, if *you* can be believed, is that they are ever eager to cannibalise one another. They can only nourish their powers of Creativity by predation. They move in such mysterious ways in order to confuse one another. The Sphinx may have been destroyed, but it may not, and these beings know far better than to trust to appearances. Either way, the maker of the Sphinx is probably still alive, and still awake. Nor, as you tried to remind us, can we be certain that there is no third party involved. All the angels might be fighting among themselves to use or to hide or to possess us.'

As Tallentyre finished, he began to walk again, but this time he moved away at a right angle to the tracks in the sand, towards the place where the gentle waves lapped at the beach. Despite the movement of the moon against the starry backcloth of the sky, the strand had not altered its dimensions at all; there was neither ebb nor flow of the tide. The baronet reached the water's edge and knelt down. He caught a little of the sea water in his cupped fingers and lifted it to his lips. Sterling wondered what he expected to taste.

'Brine,' said Tallentyre, spitting it out and looking back at him. 'Ordinary brine.'

Sterling licked his lips, realising that he was very thirsty. The sweat on his face was salty too, as sweat ordinarily was.

'The angels will surely provide,' said Sterling ironically. 'Whatever the beings which brought us here from Richmond intend, I doubt that they'll simply let us die of thirst.'

'No,' said Tallentyre grimly. 'It cannot intend that we shall die.' The way he said it was intended to imply that there might be another possibility, almost as dire.

Pain! Sterling thought, remembering that in the true history of the world, according to Lucian de Terre, pain had a very special place. For some – even, if they had the trick of it, some of those with cold, blind souls – pain was the gateway of vision. It would be ludicrous to think that he and Tallentyre and Adam Clay had been brought here only to die, but it was by no means obvious that they had not been brought to suffer agonies of deprivation.

All their clever philosophic talk of sentient ants had skated over the most vital question which the metaphor threw up: how, after all, might an ant contrive to talk to a man? Sterling could see no reason why an angel should not come to stand before them, in human guise, and say to them whatever it cared to say, but it was easily conceivable that the angel might seek a different kind of confrontation, in which it might appear to the sight of the inner eye rather than the outer ones.

Sterling was not comforted by his own ability to reason thus. He wished, now, that Luke was still with them. Why, he wondered, had the dark forest swallowed the servant up, preventing him from responding to the summons? Was he still with de Lancy? Had this dream-world rejected the two of them, spitting them out into the room which they had left behind on Earth?

The moon was still sinking. The brightness of the stars was more noticeable by contrast, but, when the moon no longer spread its silvery sheen across the water and its fainter glitter across the sand, it would be very difficult to follow the footprints any farther.

'Perhaps we should rest,' said the Clay Man, 'and wait for the dawn.'

'Perhaps,' Tallentyre agreed. 'I wonder if David is here. Even if he is, we probably won't find him unless we're allowed to do so. As for the children which turned into wolves . . . perhaps that was only a lure to draw us forth.'

'It was an illusion sent to try you,' said Sterling, wishing to reassure himself by reassuring the other. 'Your grandchildren are safe at home, I feel certain of it.'

He knew, once he had said it, that it sounded foolish. He did not feel any such certainty. How could he?

'There is no safety,' Tallentyre replied, with sad conviction. 'There is no safety anywhere for creatures like us, or for our children, while things like the Spider are prepared to exercise the power of their dominion. Make no mistake, Dr Sterling, our purpose here must be to persuade these beings that it's against their own interests to waste their power in use. At the very least we must convince them that their magic is better spent in ways which leave us unharmed, to live our lives as we would wish.'

Sterling saw that Tallentyre expected him to agree, and for a moment he was so caught up by the pressure of that expectation that he almost did. But then he saw how different Tallentyre was from himself. He saw that the summit of Tallentyre's ambition really was to have the world left alone to the inertia of its innate order. And he understood for the first time something which Luke Capthorn had tried to explain to him, but had not been sufficiently articulate to make clear: why Jacob Harkender had hated and despised his adversary.

Jason Sterling was suddenly and uncomfortably certain that he knew how Jacob Harkender would have responded to Tallentyre's statement of purpose. Harkender would have said that only a man like Tallentyre – not merely a rich man, but an aristocrat – could so casually take it for granted that the world of men was best left as it was.

Harkender's purpose, he knew, had been very different; now he realised for the first time that it might not have been entirely selfish or entirely destructive.

Sterling found himself confronted then with a question which he had never asked himself before, even though he had read *The True History of the World* with all the fascination which was due to such a bizarre and adventurous text. If he were, indeed, to be confronted by an angel which had the power to change the appearances of the world, what might he ask of it?

Absurd as it was to think that any such request might be granted, still he felt that the question was an important one. Ought his purpose in this to be the one which Tallentyre declared so confidently? Or might he, on reflection, come to a very different idea of the end most devoutly to be desired?

As he asked himself this, he felt almost inclined to laugh, for he felt that Harkender was not the only one whose reported conduct he now understood a little better. He remembered too what Lucian de Terre had written about Mandorla and the other werewolves. They had been cursed by one Creator, and their most desperate desire, unweakened by ten thousand years of life as nearly human beings, was to persuade another to lift that curse.

And why not? Sterling thought, playing Devil's Advocate. *Why should they not want that for themselves, while caring not at all what might happen to those whom they were made to parody?*

Even as he cherished that heretical thought, however, he could hear other words echoing in his mind. 'They hate us . . . our terror is their pleasure . . . as flies to wanton boys . . .'

He realised that Tallentyre was right. It would be better by far to have been let alone.

Alas, it was now too late to hope for that.

5

Dawn's light filled the sky with brilliant blueness long before they saw the sun itself, whose rising was obscured by the crowns of the trees which fringed the beach where they had lain down to rest.

Long before he saw the sun, Sterling had concluded that this place was nowhere on the surface of the Earth he knew, but as soon as he had stepped backwards on the sand in order to see the sun's disc above the trees, the fact became manifest. This sun was greater than the sun he knew, and yellower in colour. Its radiance did not seem quite as intense as the tropical sun of Earth, but its hugeness compensated for that.

Tallentyre seemed quite unperturbed by this new mystery. Indeed, the baronet, like the Clay Man, gave every indication of having slept peacefully, which Sterling had been quite unable to do.

'We must go into the forest,' said Tallentyre. 'We must find fresh water.'

Sterling's thirst had by now been magnified into a dull burning sensation in his gut. It was difficult to moisten his tongue, in spite of the humidity of the air. He nodded, but as he came back towards his companions he suddenly stopped, having caught a glimpse of eyes among the foliage. As soon as he had noticed one pair, he saw others. He recognised immediately the kind of creature to which they belonged.

He had been their creator; they were climbing toads with front-facing eyes.

Adam Clay had seen them too, and he reached up to pluck something from the underside of a broad leaf. He brought it, cupped between his hands, to show Sterling. It was a glasslike acarid.

'A compliment of sorts,' said the Clay Man softly. 'If you still hoped that you came here by accident, this tells you otherwise.'

Tallentyre looked at the insect uninterestedly, but took more notice of the staring amphibians. Sterling explained, very briefly, what they were.

'But there was no magic in their making,' he said defiantly, when he had finished. 'Or, if there was, it was a magic that men can hope to master, like any other practical science.'

'I suppose there's little point in wondering why we find ourselves beneath an alien sun,' said Tallentyre obliquely. 'Or why the world is populated with things whose like you've made in your laboratory. It may be a compliment, as the Clay Man has said, or it may be a way of mocking you with the notion that your discoveries were not your own at all. Think of all this as a terrarium, like the ones you use to house your creations, and of yourself as a captive in it. The sun and the sea are the products of artifice; they're mere scenery, like the trees and the sand. Even the seeming dimensions of the island are probably illusory.'

Once they were within the forest, partly shielded from the enormous sun, Sterling felt a little more comfortable. His eyes adjusted to the filtered light and he looked about for more fauna. He could see none that he did not know already, and he wondered whether these froglike things fed only on acarids, or whether their Creator had taken the trouble to provide a more varied diet. Their presence here seemed so evidently a jest aimed solely at himself that it did bring home to him, forcefully, the fact that this whole world had been made for the habitation of a few particular individuals, carefully crafted for their containment. Even if it were carved from the stuff of dreams, he thought – even if it were to be reckoned a mere stage for the setting of some strange drama – it was still a considerable compliment.

It could not and would not have been done without a reason.

Sterling still carried his jacket, though Tallentyre had abandoned his. Caution had made him pick it up; he felt compelled to guard against the possibility that he might need the gun which was still in its pocket. Adam Clay still had the coat which he had borrowed; he too had little enough faith in providence.

They found water soon enough. It was a little stream quite free of salt, from which they were able to quench their thirst. They washed the sweat from their faces, and were thankful for such respite from the heat as they could obtain while the water evaporated from their cheeks and brows.

'That's better,' said Sterling, gratefully, 'but now my thirst is eased, I know how hungry I am. There are flowers on the trees, but I've seen no fruit to eat. I would have thought that an obliging angel would have placed it ready and ripe upon the branches, even if it had no other purpose but to feed the three of us. But then, an *obliging* angel would certainly have made it cooler; if this was an attempt to build an Eden fit for men, I am inclined to judge it a failure.'

'If this were Eden,' Tallentyre countered, 'the fruit might not be entirely safe to eat. Should you have cause to converse with a serpent, think hard before you follow its advice.'

Sterling studied the older man carefully. There was

something different about him now that he was more brightly lit. He seemed harder and fitter than he had appeared under the electric lights in Sterling's home. It was as though he had shed some outer skin which the real world compelled him to wear, to become a creature of purified purpose.

'You don't seem to me the kind of man who would refuse to eat of the tree of knowledge, even if God had commanded that you refrain,' said Sterling.

'I didn't tell you what you should do,' Tallentyre reminded him, still trying to make light of everything, 'but only to think hard about it before you do it. Alas, I can't believe that this is Eden, and I doubt that we'll be fortunate enough to find knowledge so easy to obtain. Which direction do you favour now?'

'Do you want to go back to the sand, to follow the tracks the wolves made?' asked Sterling.

'I see little point,' the baronet answered. 'If the island's maker is disposed to play Circe, and turn my grandchildren into animals, it will presumably keep them safe in that guise. What could I do if I caught up with them?'

'In that case,' Sterling opined, 'we might as well go inland.'

Tallentyre looked at Adam Clay, who simply shrugged. The baronet nodded, and set off to lead the way. Sterling followed, and the Clay Man brought up the rear. They moved unhurriedly, and the undergrowth was so thick that they were forced to make slow progress. Sterling would gladly have traded his derringer for a machete, but he did not want to stop. While they were moving, there was always a chance that they would arrive somewhere, or find food.

'Your daughter said that I'm very much like you,' said Sterling to Tallentyre, after a little while. 'Did she tell you that?'

'She didn't mention making such an observation,' Tallentyre answered. 'There was too much urgency in her manner, and she was very anxious about David. But she told me what you said about the purpose of your work. That – and certain other things – led me to think that you had more in common with Jacob Harkender than with me. I may have been mistaken.'

Sterling was not particularly displeased by the comparison, but he was glad that Tallentyre conceded the possibility that he had been mistaken. 'I'm no magician, Sir Edward,' he said. 'Although my views on evolution diverge sufficiently from the Darwinian to seem heretical to some, and despite my having read and understood *The True History of the World*, I'm a man of science. It was not a superstitious turn of mind that sent me questing after a means to make myself immortal, but the power of reason, which said it might be done. The very existence of this man behind me surely proves the point. If immortals exist, you can hardly claim that my search is sure to fail.'

'I concede the point readily,' said Tallentyre. 'My earlier judgement was hasty, and based in part on the company you choose to keep. I have no reason to like Luke Capthorn, who once conspired to deliver my daughter into dire danger.'

'He has been a good enough servant to me,' said Sterling flatly. 'And a useful one. He told me where to find Adam Clay's resting place.'

'You can't expect me to admire him for that,' Tallentyre answered. 'I dare say you think that you did him a service by hauling him out of his grave, but Pelorus would not have seen it thus. Has he thanked you himself?'

'No,' said the Clay Man, 'I have not. But I understand why Dr Sterling did what he did, and I cannot condemn him for it.'

'Given time,' said Sterling, grateful for the tenor of the immortal's response, 'I believe that you and I, working in concert, could have found an answer to the question of how your flesh differs from ours. I'm disappointed, Sir Edward, that you never tried very hard to do likewise, given that you've known the werewolf Pelorus for twenty years. Can you really be content to accept death as your destiny, when you know that there are beings in the world which are like us in form, yet need not die?'

'I have not your optimism regarding our power to penetrate the mysteries of our own being within the space of a single lifetime,' Tallentyre replied. 'I was born and educated, you'll remember, in an age when the first faltering steps in organic chemistry had yet to be taken. One day, I know, we'll know better what we are made of and how we reproduce ourselves, but for the time being we've only just contrived to ignite the flame of understanding. Perhaps my grandchildren will live to see the day when human immortality becomes a realistic goal of science, but for myself, it never seemed . . . But perhaps I'm simply rationalising my failure. It might be closer to the truth to admit that I thought of immortality as a magical end: a whimsical gift of the Creators, for which I refused to beg, just as I refused to worship.'

'I doubt that I could be so proud,' said Sterling honestly.

'That may be another reason to beware of silver-tongued serpents,' said Tallentyre. 'Whatever it is the Spider wants from you, it may try to buy with false promises. I have little enough in common with the followers of St Amycus, as I've said, but I know that they're not entirely misguided in their convictions. I sympathise with the mistrust which makes them identify the earthbound angels with the Father of Lies.'

'I know nothing about the Order of St Amycus save for the hints given out in the *True History*,' said Sterling. 'And they are few enough.' He turned to the Clay Man and added, 'Presumably because you had some respect for their desire for secrecy?'

'It was not my purpose to reveal their secrets to the world,' Adam Clay agreed.

'It's a matter of little importance,' said the baronet dismissively. 'They're a sect of gnostics who think that those the Clay Man calls Creators are demonic beings, whose master created the material universe while the true God was responsible only for the creation of souls. They assert that the recent awakening of the Creators is the prelude to the destruction of the material world – or, at least, of humankind – but hope that faith in the power of Christ may still be the salvation of our poor cold souls. I suppose that according to *their* doctrines, this inefficient Eden would be a seductive trap made by a minion of the Devil for the purpose of temptation; I don't know how they would explain the fact that it has taken the trouble to bring us here, given that we're presumably damned already, and not worth the trouble of tempting.'

'Perhaps we're to be sent back to our lives better armed to carry forward the work of the Anti-Christ,' Sterling suggested lightly. 'Indeed, if your heretic priests have the right of it, perhaps we've been summoned here so that one or other of us might be appointed to *be* the Anti-Christ.'

'If we ever return to our own world,' said Tallentyre colourlessly, 'it might be better not to spread such rumours around. David assures me that the English followers of St Amycus are good and amiable men, but it is not unknown for men to have been burned at the stake by well-intentioned fanatics who were otherwise as good and amiable as men ever are.'

Sterling could not tell whether the other man was serious or not, but decided that it was a matter of no importance. They were simply filling in time, waiting for they knew not what.

They soon stopped to rest for a while. Sterling had already become so thirsty again that his unappeased hunger seemed dull and unimportant, but there was still no sign of fruit on the branches, and they had not found another spring. He looked up through the greenery at the bright-blue sky. He wondered whether they were being silly in refusing to be still; they were, after all, at the beck and call of whatever had brought them here, which could probably transport them wherever it wished in the blink of an eyelid. Why should they tire themselves out instead of simply waiting to see what would happen?

'This is a waste of time,' he said to Tallentyre, eventually. 'Why is nothing happening? Surely whatever brought us here wants something more from us than the sight of us wandering thirstily and hungrily through this interminable forest? Or is it simply that we've been thrown together so that the Devil's minion can eavesdrop on our conversation?'

'I doubt that,' said Tallentyre. 'It could have watched us easily enough in Richmond; it must have a reason of some kind for bringing us here. It might be observing us in the hope of discovering whether we are only what we appear to be, or something more.'

'What's that supposed to mean?' Sterling asked, a little intemperately.

'It means that you or I – probably without even knowing it – might be possessed by one of its rivals. I've been possessed before, you see, by the creature which we called the Sphinx. I took some of the Sphinx's power into the heart of the Spider's dream. I consented to that, and knew that I was doing it, but it might easily have been done without my consent and without my knowledge.

'Whatever else we can guess about the nature and motives of the being which has seized us, we can be reasonably certain of one thing. It is afraid. In order to do what it's doing, it's using up some tiny fraction of its store of Creativity, making itself weaker. No matter how tiny that fraction is, it might conceivably make sufficient difference to render our captor vulnerable to the others of its kind. That's the chief reason that it moves in mysterious ways: it seeks to conceal its plans, motives and resources from the prying of others of its kind.'

Sterling tried to work saliva around his dry mouth, and tried to borrow moisture from the air, which was still very moist though they had climbed some way above sea level. He glanced uneasily at the Clay Man, but then looked back at Tallentyre.

'But you and I are only human,' he said finally, 'are we not?'

'Perhaps,' Tallentyre answered. 'And perhaps not. Not all of those who are possessed are aware of it. Be patient, Dr Sterling. I can't promise you that all will be revealed, but when the time comes, something will happen. I dare not promise you, either, that it won't hurt; I can only ask you to think on what I said last night. Be brave, and whatever may befall us, try to understand.'

I am dead, Sterling thought suddenly. *I am dead and on my way to Hell. This is indeed temptation, and a test of virtue. I am on trial, for my immortal soul, and the Devil is chuckling with glee to see me flounder in uncertainty.*

He could not believe it; it made no more sense than anything else that had been guessed. All he knew for sure was that the world which he had trusted had betrayed him. The only certainty was that nothing was certain. He had lost sight of truth, and beneath the aching of his thirst and his hunger he felt another craving: a craving for some miraculous renewal of his faith in the order of things. He bowed his head, tiredly.

What has become of my impulse to innovate? he thought. *Where is the courage of my soul?*

He felt a hand fall upon his shoulder, and he looked up to see Adam Clay.

'Tallentyre is right,' said the man he had brought alive from the grave. 'This is the world in which we find ourselves, and we must do what we can. If there are more things in Heaven and Earth than we have so far contrived to dream, then we must learn to be more accomplished in our dreaming. What else can we do?'

Sterling nodded. 'What else?' he agreed.

6

They came to a small hill where the trees grew farther apart, from whose crown they were able to look out over the forest canopy. They could see the sea in the distance, but in other directions the forest seemed limitless.

The air was somewhat fresher here, but Sterling had become very thirsty again, and he looked desperately about for water. Tallentyre pointed to an interruption in the leafy canopy some little distance away from the course they had been following. They were not high enough to see whether there was water in the gap but it seemed worth investigating, and so they set off in that direction.

The pool which they found was some forty or fifty yards across at the widest stretch. It was almost a lake. Trees clustered about its banks, forming a dense wall, but they found a gap where one man could kneel and take up water. Sterling fell to his knees immediately and cupped his hands, lifting the lukewarm liquid as carefully as he could and delivering it into his mouth. It had a slightly sulphurous taste, but it was fresh enough. When he had drunk his fill he dipped his head down, closer to the surface of the pool. He scooped up water as fast as he could, wetting his face and his hair. Then he stepped back, apologetically, to let Tallentyre take his place. Adam Clay waited patiently to take his turn.

The baronet drank as daintily as Sterling had, but quickly moved aside, sitting down with his back against the bole of a tree and his knees drawn up. The Clay Man, with no one waiting to follow him, took a more leisurely approach. Sterling, meanwhile, moved restlessly within his clothes; the heat of the sun had made him very uncomfortable.

'We might take time to bathe,' said Tallentyre. 'The water is not very cool, but it seems clear enough to wash us clean.'

Sterling shrugged. He had grown weary of the trek, now that they had seen that there was nowhere to go. There seemed little point in continuing to beat a track through the undergrowth. The strangely bloated sun, which was still approaching its zenith, promised that the day would become even hotter. 'Why not?' he said. 'If whatever brought us here desires us to be elsewhere, no doubt it can transport us there as easily as it snatched us out of out own world.'

'No doubt,' said Tallentyre drily. He looked up at the alien sun, shielding his eyes with a bony hand, and frowned deeply.

'I have not yet abandoned the hope,' said Sterling grimly, 'that this is but a dream from which I'll soon awake. I dare say that it would evade the sieve of memory as cunningly as other dreams, and leave me none the worse.' As he spoke, he caught sight of the staring eyes of a half-hidden batrachian homunculus, whose steady gaze was fixed upon his face. He stirred restlessly under that peculiar gaze, and wondered whether the presence here of his own creations might not be taken as proof that this was but a dream.

'While the Creators haunt it,' said the Clay Man, 'the whole world is but a dream, whose reality might at any moment be forfeit.'

'They would like us to think so,' said Tallentyre. 'I dare say they would like to think so themselves. But we have not yet seen their powers of miracle-working extended to the full, and until we have we're entitled to be sceptical of their wilder boasts. All this is persuasive in its way, but it's a very modest illusion. I couldn't be convinced that its maker could sensibly lay claim to godlike power until I had counted the stars in its sky, and convinced myself that they were distant suns like the stars which light our own skies, massive and newly minted.'

'The stars are points of light,' the Clay Man countered. 'What you read from their appearance by inference is but one more illusion. You know that the Creators exist, and what they can do. Can you doubt that they could produce the image of an infinite sea of stars where none existed, if they were so disposed? Do you really imagine that your refusal to worship them is sufficient to deny them the power of their godhood?'

'They are beings,' said Tallentyre flatly. 'They're very unlike us, but they're relatively tiny and relatively impotent in a universe which is vast beyond their imagining. They may have thought themselves gods before, but they know now that they were wrong, and no matter how they may resent the fact, a fact it remains.'

'You say that,' Sterling put in, 'and yet you also say that they can possess us, hear the thoughts inside our heads, and move us from the world we know to some parallel fairyland like this. If they can do all that gods and angels are supposed to do, what good does it do to deny them the title? How *should* we think of them, if not as gods or angels?'

Tallentyre looked up at him. 'Do you know Flammarion?' he asked.

'The French astronomer who believes that our souls can fly between the stars after we're dead, faster than light itself? I've certainly heard of him.'

'I spoke to him a few days ago. I can't share his faith in the survival of the soul after death, despite the attractions of his notion that it may be reincarnated as often as it pleases on any of the worlds of the infinite universe, but I am fascinated by some of his ideas. As an evolutionist, you should be interested in his essays about the forms which life might take on worlds where the physical conditions are very different from our own.'

'There's a certain fascination in reading his speculations,' Sterling admitted. 'There's some merit in what he says about our experience of the world being shaped by our senses, and his insistence that creatures with different sensory apparatus would perceive a very different universe.'

'What he has to say about serial reincarnation might best be seen as a metaphor,' said Tallentyre, 'although he certainly doesn't intend it thus. The real beauty of his argument is his insistence that intelligence might find a home in creatures adapted by natural selection for very different ways of life. For the most part, it is true, he speaks about planetary surfaces where the physical conditions are very different from those pertaining to the surface of the Earth, but he goes beyond that to suggest that souls – for which we may read "sentient intelligences" – might inhabit physical systems of any magnitude and any kind. I don't know what the Creators are made of, or how it comes about that they can work the kinds of magic which they do, but when I try to imagine what they are, it's in ideas like Flammarion's that I seek inspiration, rather than in the vocabulary of churchmen and mystics.'

'Labels do not matter,' said the Clay Man dismissively. 'The only thing that matters is the reality of their power. While they were inert, men were free to dream of the Age of Reason. Now, it is the Creators who will determine the shape of the future.'

'You're wrong,' said Tallentyre. 'Labels do matter. Labels allow us to make correct distinctions, and we must try as hard as we can to make sure that we know exactly what we mean by the words we use.'

Neither Sterling nor the Clay Man replied to that, but the silence which fell was an uneasy one. Tallentyre may have felt that he had been too brutal in concluding the argument, because he was the one who broke the silence, changing the subject abruptly. 'I think,' he said, 'that the pool is too inviting to ignore. My clothes and my skin alike have picked up an uncommon burden of grime and sap from the low branches and those infernal creepers which impeded our progress. I'm in dire need of a wash.'

Sterling could agree with that, but did not immediately move to imitate the older man when he stood up and began to strip. His thoughts still dwelt uncomfortably on the thorny question of where they were and why. *We are castaways,* he thought. *Crusoes marooned by the flood of history.*

He could no longer refuse to believe what Tallentyre and the Clay Man had told him, but he had only just begun to try to imagine its consequences. He wondered if the island and the forest might be seen as a kind of experiment, and the engorged sun as a kind of microscope which focused upon him – upon them all – in order that their movements and transactions might be closely observed. If his life and all his discoveries really had been prompted and guided by some curious angel, perhaps his carefully cultivated wisdom was now to be harvested.

But how?

The water which he had swallowed lay like fire in his belly, and he wondered whether there was real brimstone in it. His thirst had been quenched, after a fashion, but he did not feel well, and he was desperately hungry. The pangs of his hunger were genuinely painful.

Is it merely to suffer that we have been brought here? he wondered. *Are the angels unsatisfied with their ordinary ability to share our thoughts and our sight? Do they seek to purify the knowledge that we have, and extrapolate it by the methods in which they place their faith? Will they drive us mad with thirst and poisonous water, in the hope that the extremes of our madness will reveal to them something which our waking thoughts cannot?*

Tallentyre now stood unashamedly naked, and Sterling idly studied the contours of the old man's body. Despite the wrinkles at his neck and the weathering of his face, Tallentyre seemed to be well preserved. He had lived an active and disciplined life, and his muscles had not wasted.

As Tallentyre waded into the water, Sterling began to unbutton his shirt. As an atheist, he had always valued cleanliness above godliness, and although there was something undeniably bizarre about the notion of washing his body here, in this covert outside the world, he too felt dirty. He was slow, though, in removing his shirt; some instinctive reluctance held him back. It was nothing as simple as embarrassment or shame; there was a lurking unease which he could not quite bring to consciousness.

Then, all of a sudden, he was struck by a frightful premonition of disaster.

'Tallentyre!' he shouted, with such urgency that the baronet turned instantly, desperately alarmed. But he automatically looked behind Sterling, at the trees, searching them for the danger against which he was being warned.

Sterling snatched up his jacket from the place where he had laid it down, grappling his gun from the pocket. He knew even as he did so how useless the weapon would be, and yelled: 'Get out, man! *Run!*'

Tallentyre, who was waist-deep in water, could not run. He could not even turn before the thing was on him.

Had he been a little further in, neck-deep instead of waist-deep, he might have been dragged down in an instant, but as things were, the advantage of leverage was still with him, for the creature which came to savage him had no skeleton to bear its weight. Even so, it reared up out of the water to strike with its appalling head, while its flattened body was rapidly coiled about its victim's legs.

Sterling did not hesitate, but immediately ran into the water. It was not so much his sense of duty towards the baronet which impelled him as his sense of responsibility, for this creature, albeit on a vaster scale by far, was an avatar of a form of life which he had created.

He fired the derringer at the greedy mouth with its three flailing rasps, just as those rasps fastened themselves upon Tallentyre's chest and bit deep into his flesh.

Tallentyre gasped as the shots were fired. One bullet went home, and then the other. Sterling was no marksman but he had fired at such close range that he could not miss. Both bullets tore through the leech's body behind the head, and left exit wounds spouting red ichor; but the redness of the fluid was donated, at least in part, by the blood that was flowing from Tallentyre's wounds.

The splayed jaws of the vampiric worm covered an area of Tallentyre's body which extended from shoulder to waist, and their multitudinous teeth were tearing into him with a fury which would have been astonishing had Sterling not seen the like of it so many times before. He knew, though, that the monster could not use its strength to the full while it was half out of its natural element, and, having thrown the little gun aside, he did not hesitate to grab at the head with both his hands and try to yank it back, away from the wounds which it had inflicted.

Adam Clay, who had leaped into the water just half a stride behind, went to pull Tallentyre in the opposite direction, catching and supporting him as he keeled over.

Tallentyre thrust with all his might at the loathsome thing which had fastened itself upon him, and the Clay Man's support lent valuable strength to him. Between the three of them they contrived to wrench the old man free from the tearing jaws.

'Stand firm!' Sterling cried, knowing that they must at all costs keep the fight above the surface. It was not easy advice to follow, because the writhing of the worm threatened to pull the Clay Man and Tallentyre off balance, and drag them both down into the dark water; but the fact that they were two and not one, and had Sterling to help them, spread the burden of resistance and gave them the advantage.

Sterling was astonished to find himself trying to tear the worm apart with his bare hands, and equally astonished to find that he was succeeding. The leech's power was dependent upon the turgor of its body, and the gaping wounds behind its head had deflated its most dangerous part, shocking the smooth muscle into submission. The rubbery outer tegument was elastic, but not as tough as he might have expected, and the jagged rips which his shots had inflicted gave him a starting point for tearing. One of the three jaws lashed back at him, ripping the skin from the back of his left wrist and forearm, but the shock of the pain only made him redouble his desperate effort to render the mouthparts impotent.

As the three men wrestled with the monster, its thrashings became more furious, but the increased ardour was coupled with a gradual failure of the reflex by which it tried to wind itself about their legs and topple them. Sterling was swayed

by the blows but did not fall, and all the while he continued
to hurt the creature with his hands.

But the worm was not the only one which was weakening;
Tallentyre's chest and belly were a mass of ugly wounds,
and blood was pouring from him into the water. His ribcage
showed in three or four different places, and at least one
of the gashes in his abdomen was deep enough to have cut
into his entrails. He could not remain in the fight, and as he
sagged in his supporter's arms the Clay Man was forced to
stagger away; in so doing he lost his balance and was knocked
sprawling upon the surface of the water.

Tallentyre fell away from his would-be rescuers, face
down, and blood spread out around them all like a great
cloud.

The worm was defeated now, and it too was leaking
fluid copiously. Its whole body was beginning to go slack,
and its head seemed no longer to be capable of seizing
and gripping. Sterling threw it aside, and went to pluck
Tallentyre up before he drowned. Adam Clay was already
floundering back to his feet, ready to lend what assistance
he could.

The baronet was a tall man, by no means light in spite of his
slender build, and his two companions could not easily pick
him up. They dragged their burden half floating to the bank
of the pool, only taking care that the man's nose and mouth
were clear of the bloody water.

Once they had reached the side, they hauled Tallentyre
up on the rock and turned him on his back. Sterling was
grateful to find that the stricken man was still breathing;
the greater number of his evident wounds were superficial,
but they were so many that the loss of blood had been
profuse, and still the life was ebbing out of him. Sterling
used his fingers to close the deepest cut of all and hold it
closed, but Tallentyre was losing consciousness. The Clay
Man seized the baronet's shirt from the place where it had
been put down, and they used that as best they could to stem
the flow.

At last it seemed that the worst was over, and the flow of
blood was stemmed by clotting. Sterling could not estimate

how much blood the other had lost, but did not think that the loss would have been fatal under ordinary circumstances.

Alas, the circumstances were far from ordinary.

Sterling was suddenly struck by the thought that if all this were naught but a dream made solid – if this world had a maker who must be assumed to be immanent in every part of it, attentive to every event which occured here – then Tallentyre might be made whole again in a single instant, by casual decree. With that thought in mind, Sterling looked up at the sky, at the violent sun where he imagined the godling's eye to be. He was giddy from his own exertions, and any urge to beg or plead which he might otherwise have entertained was utterly drowned out by wrath and resentment.

He addressed no words at all to the vivid sky. What purpose could possibly be served by howling abuse at the author of this atrocity?

The brightness blinded him, and he looked down again at the ground, closing his eyes against the afterglow and the injustice of his predicament.

As flies to wanton boys . . . he thought again, bitterly. He did not complete the silent sentence, because he was interrupted by a small sound. It was the sound of a boot scraping on the root of a tree.

Sterling opened his eyes and looked round. Adam Clay had turned too. The face of the newcomer was obliterated for a moment or two by the bright blur which still lingered in Sterling's eyes, and he had to blink furiously before he could make out that the man who stood nearby was Luke Capthorn. Oddly enough, there was no one he would rather have seen; he was a man who knew the value of a faithful servant.

Unfortunately, the expression on Luke's face was not that of a servant eager for orders, and he was still carrying the double-barrelled shotgun which he had fetched to defend them all against the werewolves of London. De Lancy was with him, but he looked even worse than he had done when Tallentyre brought him into the house in Richmond; he was plainly exhausted, and so dazed it was impossible to believe that he knew what was happening

'Leave him,' said Luke, in the tone of one who had the right to give orders rather than receive them. 'Stand back.'

Sterling still felt slightly giddy, and shook his head to clear it.

'Luke?' he said, not knowing why he doubted the other's identity, but knowing that he did. There was something strange about Luke's eyes, as though they were not eyes at all but pits of shadow.

'Stand back!' said Luke again, with such ferocity that Sterling fell back a little way, though he was still on his knees. Adam Clay, moved by a similar instinct, did likewise. The way between them was barely clear, but Luke did not hesitate; he raised the shotgun to his shoulder and fired, at a range of six or seven yards.

The shot took Tallentyre full in the wounded chest, and the baronet's body convulsed with shock. There was no room for doubt that the shot had killed him; his wounds opened up again, far worse than before, and Sterling could see the awful wreckage of his ribs and pulverised heart.

'Dear God!' cried Sterling. 'Why?'

Luke fixed him with the dark stare of those uncanny eyes, and giggled. 'I had *permission*,' he said. 'He's not necessary, and my master didn't want him. My master prefers de Lancy.'

As he spoke he gestured with the gun, pointing its twin barrels back over his shoulder at de Lancy, who stood quite still, lost in a dream and utterly unaware of what had just occured.

'You should have let the leech do its work,' said Luke to Sterling, with appalling certainty. 'We're all here to do the Devil's bidding, whether you know it or not.'

Sterling came slowly to his feet, wishing that the wetness which made his clothes cling to his body were not so stickily tainted with Tallentyre's blood and the ichor of the magical leech. Adam Clay did not rise, but simply stared numbly at the dead body of the man he had just risked his own life to save.

'What do you mean?' Sterling demanded breathlessly. 'Are you mad?'

Luke giggled again, as though to lend force to the argument that he was mad. 'You shouldn't say so,' he said. 'I know what's happening, and you don't. I *know*, for I have ever been a more faithful servant of our master than you.'

Sterling shook his head. 'No, Luke,' he said. 'Indeed you do not understand!'

Luke laughed again, more softly this time. 'Shall I show you?' he asked, with an ironic tone which Sterling had never heard him use before. 'Shall I *show* you?'

He pulled the barrels of the gun back towards himself, and calmly inserted them in his mouth. His arm was fully stretched, but his finger was still awkwardly wrapped around the second trigger.

'*No, Luke!*' said Sterling again, hearing his voice rise eerily into a scream; but Luke had already pulled the trigger.

Sterling saw Luke Capthorn's head explode. He saw the back of the skull blown off and blood-red tissue hurled away in a great ragged cloud.

And then, impossibly, he saw the explosion reversed. He saw the scattered fragments of brain and bone sucked backwards in time, converging and uniting again.

When Luke removed the barrels from his mouth, he was whole and alive and standing steady. He was smiling.

'It's only a dream,' he said, smugly and mockingly. 'Did you think that it was real? It's only a dream, sent to tease us by the Devil.'

Sterling shook his head numbly. 'It was not the Devil who brought us here, Luke,' he said, in an incongruously meek and level tone. Despite what he had just seen, he believed what he said; he felt that he had to explain to Luke how badly he was mistaken, even though he had no proof to offer that could possibly compete with the proof which Luke had just offered to him.

Luke shrugged his shoulders disdainfully. 'The world we knew has ended,' he said offhandedly. 'This is a second Eden, where all begins again. But this is Satan's Eden, not the one to which he came crawling as a serpent. This is only a dream, but when we wake, it will be to the Devil's world.'

'Did you believe that all along?' asked Sterling.

'I knew it,' Luke confessed. 'I always knew.'

Sterling wondered, madly, whether Luke might not be right – not about the Devil, which might as well be called by that name as any other, but about the world having ended. He remembered what Tallentyre had said about the priests of St Amycus, patiently waiting for the end. But he could not believe it; though he and his companions had been snatched out of time and space into a cocoon of dream-stuff, the world *must* be going on without them, as it always had.

'And now,' he said, his voice still embittered by shock and horror, 'you hope for your reward. I take it that you no longer consider yourself to be in *my* service?'

'We are all the Devil's servants,' Luke answered, colourlessly. 'There can be no other master in a world which is his dream.'

When Adam delved and Eve span . . . Sterling thought, strangely glad to be able to find a fugitive irony in the situation.

Luke reached into the pocket of his jacket then, and brought out three little objects. They were shaped like apples, but they were violet in colour. Sterling had never seen fruits like them. Luke reached back to hand one to de Lancy, who took it automatically and held it ready.

Sterling became suddenly aware of how horribly hungry he was.

Luke came forward towards him, holding out his hand, and said: 'Eat. You have only to eat, and you will awake, understanding everything.'

Fighting temptation, Sterling said: 'There are three, but we are four.'

'The Clay Man will wake, too,' said Luke flatly. 'But our understanding is not for him. Eat.'

Sterling looked into Luke's eyes as he came farther forward, bearing his gift in the palm of his left hand. Luke's eyes were orbs of jet black; they were utterly featureless, and yet Sterling did not doubt that they could see him. He did not doubt that they could see into his very soul.

He accepted the fruit; and when the others put theirs into their mouths, so did he. He wanted to wake up, and he wanted to understand, and although he knew full well that there must be some trick or treason in the offering, he took it.

What else could he do?

The Price of Progress

For ten thousand years men have laid responsibility for the shape of the future at the doors of their various temples. Powerless to redeem themselves from the rigours of everyday existence, they have not been ashamed to crave redemption from their multitudinous gods. Their priests have been appointed to pray to those gods that the world might be kept safe from catastrophe, and little changed. Sometimes, for the sake of their children, men have pleaded also for more bountiful harvests, for an end to war, or for greater equality and justice in the affairs of men; but they have usually accepted that the worst oppressions of earthly existence are unlikely to be lifted.

When men have been hopeful about the possibility of a better future, they have usually set that future outside the world, in the eternity which they imagine to lie on the other side of death. There, if nowhere else, the men of the past felt free to imagine an eternal paradise; but they have always reserved such paradises for the deserving few. Men have, for the most part, been exceedingly jealous of their most hopeful dreams, and have rarely hesitated to make for those whom they hate an alternative eternity of punishment and pain.

It is not surprising that men who have found the world in which they live to be hostile and ungenerous should be as miserly themselves in hoarding the treasure of the imagination for the favoured few, reserving misery for the many. Earthly existence has always been a kind of Hell for the mass of men, and their venomous hunger for retribution against those whom they hate is born from the savage ache of their own misfortune.

With the hindsight of history to guide us, we may say unhesitatingly that the prayers of men have been utterly futile. Such gods as there are have no love whatsoever for men, and none for the world which men inhabit. While men were content to look to the gods for the protection and the preservation of all they owned and built, their hopes were always certain to be dashed.

The greatest triumph of mankind over the evil circumstance of earthly existence is to be observed in the fact that the men of today no longer go to their altars to beg on bended knee for their world to be preserved as it is. The Age of Reason began with the realisation that, if the world is to be kept safe for the generations which are to come, then men must keep it safe by their own efforts, and with the corollary assertion that the world might yet be made better if men were prepared to improve it. There is infinitely more hope in that realisation than in all the wasted prayers of ten thousand years, for it is parent to the knowledge that wars might end, harvests might increase, and justice and equality might be brought to reign over the affairs of men, if men will that it should be so.

The men of the Age of Reason have elected to take responsibility for their own future, and for the future of their children and their children's children. The prophets of the Age of Reason have laid down this challenge for their fellow men: that if men desire Paradise, far better that they should strive to build that paradise on earth, and furnish it by the efforts of honest toil, than pin their ambition to the tail of a stupid and paradoxical dream which asks them to wait until they are dead before they may truly live.

The happy wisdom of the Age of Reason is that this can be done, if men will only join together in the great work of making it happen. Men may end war by laying down their arms. Men may increase their harvests, by applying their best cleverness to the skills of tilling and planting, and to the improvement of their stocks. Men may have justice, if they will only consent to treat one another justly; and all men may have an equal chance to make what they can of themselves, if they will only consent to concede such opportunities to one another.

These ends cannot be attained unless a certain price is paid, for there is one thing that they must abandon for ever in order to make a paradise of Earth; but if the age which is dawning is in truth an Age of Reason, men will gladly surrender that which must be surrendered.

The price which must be paid for this paradise on Earth is Hell, for if there is to be paradise on Earth it must be a paradise for all, and not for the few. If wars are to end, if all harvests are to be bountiful, if justice is to reign and men are to have equal opportunities to be what they may, then none must be eternally punished and none must be eternally damned.

Some might think that this is a trivial price to pay for Paradise; but ten thousand years of history, ten thousand years of misery, and ten thousand years of anguish provide powerful evidence to the contrary. No man has ever sought Hell for himself, but few indeed are those who have not asked it for their enemies. It has made no difference which gods the men of the past have chosen to follow; whether they have been gods of terror or gods of mercy, gods of wrath or gods of justice, uncaring gods or fatherly gods, they have all been jealous gods.

Those men who have taken into the very heart of their faith the commandment to love one another have been more generous with their hatreds than any others; they have been the makers of the most vivid hells of all. There are no untarnished gods, and if men truly desire paradise on Earth they must give up *all* their gods, and give them up for ever. To those who would argue that if gods did not exist it would be necessary to invent them I have this to say: if the gods had not absented themselves entirely from the world of men, it would be necessary to banish them; and if that could not be done, there would be no hope for humankind.

Some might suppose that it ought to be easy enough for men to give up the bitternesses and resentments of the past in exchange for the promise of a better future, but it is not. The past is where every living man has dwelt and suffered;

the past is real to a man in a way that the future can never
be. The pains and humiliations which men suffer as they live
from day to day are graven on their bodies and minds alike;
the past is writ in livid scars which can never truly be healed,
but the future is yet to be writ and cannot easily be read.
There is no act so difficult for a wretched man to perform as
an act of forgiveness.

Because of these things, I do not hesitate to say that
the true test of the Age of Reason will not be found
in the accumulation of knowledge or the cultivation of
cleverness, but in the capacity to generate forgiveness. If
Liberty, Equality and Fraternity are indeed to be enshrined
at the heart of the Commonweal, they must first displace Hell
with the charity of forgiveness. History has shown that even
men who follow a god whose creed is based in forgiveness
cannot learn to do this; if the men of the future are to learn
it, they must forget their gods.

The present revolution in France may be the greatest event
in human history. Its promulgators are ambitious to take
responsibility for the remaking of the world, and they may
well have the means to achieve that end in their own country,
thus to set an example before the entire world. One barrier
and one only stands before them, but it is neither the walls of
the Bastille nor the luxury of Versailles; it is the shadow of
the guillotine. The true test which the Revolutionaries have
to face is this: can they forgive? If they can, they will surely
win; if they cannot, they will surely fail, and will live to see
their ideals turned to the cause of hate and hell and horror.

I, who have lived ten thousand years and will live ten
thousand more, declare without hesitation that the Age of
Reason must eventually dawn, if the intellect of man has any
purpose other than to torture him. If such an age were never
to arrive, then all human history would have been without
meaning or direction. I, who have looked into the faces of
such gods as there truly are, can say with certainty that
there never was any hope for mankind to be found in their
benevolence. Those gods are gone now, and the best hope
of man is that they are gone for ever. I, who have languished
ten thousand years in the dark despair of ignorance, can say

with authority that enlightenment is the most precious gift which life has to offer; to understand the world is to obtain dominion over its affairs. It is enlightenment that gives me the courage to hope.

In the end, men will accept responsibility for the future; in the end, men will build a paradise on Earth; in the end, men will surrender that burning hatred whose name is Hell, and proudly proclaim the treaty of Reason and Amity. In the end, this *must* come to pass, for any other end would be naught but a carnival of destruction which would obliterate mankind and send the world entire into eternal darkness.

If, in the end, what I have dreamed must come to pass, then let it be now. I ask only this of my fellow men: turn away from your departed gods, and cease to pray; embrace Reason and renounce Hell.

Let it be now that we begin the work of building paradise on Earth.

(From vol. IV of *The True History of the World* by Lucian de Terre, London, 1789.)

FOUR
The Unconquerable Will

1

As David Lydyard watched Jacob Harkender walk away into the forest, he had to fight an impulse to run after him, begging to be allowed to keep him company. It frightened him to think that Harkender understood far better than he what was happening. But he held his ground. He did not move until the other man was out of sight.

What should I do now? he asked himself. *How may I use the health which has been given back to me?*

He did not have time to search for answers. From a place very close to the point at which Harkender had disappeared, another creature emerged from the greenery, heading straight towards him.

It was a wolf, as huge as the one which had attacked him in his garden.

As the animal came closer David tensed his newly obedient muscles, but the expression in the creature's eyes did not seem hostile at all, and the beast did not crouch down as though to spring. David stood still, with his back to the pool whose magical waters had returned to him his youth and his health, and met the wolf's stare as bravely as he could while it came to him.

When the wolf licked his hand, as meekly as could be, he laughed.

'Perhaps this is Eden, after all,' he said aloud. 'If there are lions here, they must lie down with lambs, and even wolves can be trusted to be loyal.'

The wolf looked up at him, almost as though it expected to be recognised.

'Pelorus?' he said hesitantly.

The wolf made no gesture of assent that a human might have understood, but it touched him lightly on the thigh with its muzzle, and he crouched down to play with it as he might have played with a huge hound. His fear was gone, and he was suddenly certain that this was Pelorus though the beast's eyes were a dilute brown and not the vivid blue of Pelorus' human eyes.

The wolf accepted his fondling for a while, then it pulled away and went four paces off. It looked back expectantly. David frowned, wondering why, if this was Pelorus, it did not change into the man he knew. But he remembered the eager way in which Mandorla, in her wolf form, had leaped into the illusion which had appeared in the mirror in his bedroom, and her earlier assertion that Pelorus had been taken. If he and Harkender had been restored to their ideal state, why should not the werewolves of London have been restored to theirs?

'You want me to follow you?' David said, although he no longer hoped for any readable reply. The wolf merely waited.

David had not forgotten that the visions which came to him under the spur of his illness had lately been redolent with alarmist intrusions of the idea of Eden, all of them insistent that Eden was to be reckoned a kind of snare. He had been amused and intrigued by such notions at first, thinking them an ironic gloss on the Bible's account of the temptation of Adam and the Fall of Man, but they had saturated his visionary odysseys in exotica to such an extent that he had been unable to avoid the conclusion that they were an urgent warning. Now that he was no longer under the spur of his sickness, he realised, he might be insulated from the attentions of the Sphinx and her mistress for the first time since the euphoric days of health and happiness which had followed the conclusion of his first adventure outside the Earth.

If this was a trap, though, he was well and truly in it, and there was no obvious way out. When the wolf moved off into the forest, therefore, David was content to follow.

As they walked, David studied the trees. He could not recognise any species that he knew, but that was not entirely surprising, given the heat and the humidity. The leaf litter over which he was walking was moist and pulpy, and he knew that if any semblance of biological order had been incorporated into this dream-world such detritus must rot down very quickly, without ever forming a stable humus. The trees which grew here should be adapted to the circumstances which pertained here, if the Creator which had made this Eden had been able to draw upon the intelligence of men like Sir Edward Tallentyre and Jason Sterling.

With this thought in mind, David searched the branches for signs of life: for birds, monkeys or lizards. There were none at all, and he could no longer see any of the humanoid toads. The forest was, in fact, uncannily silent. Nor were there any fruits hanging from the branches, though there were florets clustered on dependant stalks, and lesser flowering plants clumped wherever the sunlight could reach the ground in full enough measure to nourish them.

All men everywhere dream of Eden, David mused. *Of all human myths, the nostalgic longing for a pastoral place of peace is the most persistent. But Eden never existed; like all nostalgia, the longing for it is a tired malaise of the mind.*

He remembered something which Tallentyre had said, when he had first mentioned the invasion of his visions by the idea of Eden, and the corollary conviction that it was some kind of trap. 'It is an idea which the Scriptures might support,' the baronet had opined, speaking lightly but earnestly, 'if one were to take a sceptical view of the true import of the Creation myth. Eden might justly be considered a place where God laid a trap for Adam, in order to justify an eternity of punishment. One who read the Scriptures without being blinded by faith might easily conclude that the God described there never intended to love and cherish his children, but took care to ensure that they would fall into disobedience, in order that they might not only be made to suffer but be made to feel deserving of that suffering, through thousands of years of cruel and brutal use.'

The wolf led David to a place where the ground began to rise quite steeply, although the slope was as densely forested as the level ground. They ascended only a little way before they came to a crevice let into the side of the hill. The opening was narrow, but when David followed the wolf into the passage he found that the walls quickly drew apart again to make a descending corridor where a man might comfortably walk. He hesitated to follow the animal when it vanished into the gloom, but after a moment's pause he found that his eyes were adapting to the darkness far better than he might have expected.

The wolf's eyes glowed greenly as it looked back at him, waiting for him to continue. They moved on together into the darkness, and David's enhanced sight soon picked up the ghostly flanks of the beast as it slid between walls of rock which were limned in dull red.

The air in the passage was drier than the forest air, but it was still warm, and the rock to either side was so warm to the touch that it did not seem like rock at all, but more like the kind of tough tegument which overlaid the flesh of elephants or African cattle.

They had gone less than forty yards when the corridor opened up into a broad cave, floored with fern leaves brought down from the world above. There, waiting for them, were many other wolves: an entire pack.

David stepped back involuntarily as soon as he saw the beasts, all grey as ghosts with emerald, reflecting eyes, but his alarm faded quickly enough. The animals made no move to fall upon the man who had been lured into their den, but simply looked at him blandly.

Pelorus – if, indeed, it was Pelorus that had guided him to the lair – moved to join the other wolves, turning about to face them as he took his place by the side of the beast which seemed to be the leader of the pack. David studied the company uneasily, wondering why he had been brought here. He counted the wolves and found that there were thirteen in all. He could not tell how many were male and how many female, but he did see that three were younger than the rest, two of them hardly more than cubs.

David felt a nauseous knot growing in his stomach, and found that he was nearly trembling with anxiety.

Ignoring the larger beasts he stepped forward, reaching for the cubs. One – the smallest – leaped immediately into his arms, and he cradled that one in the crook of his left elbow while he squatted down. The second of the three leaped up also, and he changed his position, seating himself with his back against the stone wall, so that the third could climb on to his lap. Then, with all three of his mutated children gathered in, he felt an unexpected relief creep over him.

The cubs were warm to the touch and very soft; they caressed him with their bodies, and he felt a wave of pure peace wash over him from his inmost heart to the periphery of his flesh.

The adult wolves moved restlessly, but not in any menacing way. If anything, they made as much effort as they could to give him room, and although they looked at him very steadily there was nothing in the least threatening in their stare.

His eyelids felt very heavy, and the relaxation of his muscles made him feel like a dead weight. The three wolf cubs continued to move over him, stroking him with their flanks and ears, but he could no longer hold them. He was slipping helplessly into a deep sleep, and could not find the strength of will to fight it.

He knew that he was falling asleep, and beginning a new dream within the dream.

In this unlooked-for dream, he seemed to be in the room where he worked at the hospital. He recognised the ana-tomical diagrams on the walls, and the desk where he worked; but he had his back to the door and he was facing the desk from the wrong side. Someone else was sitting at the desk, writing with his pen.

He did not recognise the person at the desk until that person paused in his writing and looked up. Only then did he see that the other wore his face, as lined and careworn as it ought really to be, but smiling.

'Do not be afraid,' said the doppelgänger. 'This is merely a dream within a dream. Nothing here can harm you.'

David could only stare, dumbly, at himself.

'The world of dreams is labyrinthine,' said the other calmly. 'Once it has claimed us, we can never really be sure that we have emerged again into the true world, or whether any true world really exists to welcome us. Nor can we ever know when we have reached the heart of the maze: the axis upon which all the world's confusions hang and turn. But that does not matter. Because you and I know full well that this is but a dream within a dream, we need no longer confuse ourselves with conundrums. We may speak clearly to one another, may we not?'

'If you wish,' said David faintly, glad to have found his tongue.

'Very well,' said his other self. 'Firstly, the children will come to no harm. Pelorus and Mandorla will guard them as if they were their own, and Zelophelon will not try to hurt them now. Cordelia was never in danger, and may yet be freed from her unwitting bondage.

'Secondly, you have more power than you know, and will have still more when you have seen what the Creators are anxious to see by the light of your imagination. The being which you call Bast can snuff you out like a candle, but she will never dare to do it now. While Zelophelon has Harkender and Hecate's maker has Sterling, she must have you. She is fortunate, for you are the best of the three. The others may think that they see as clearly – even poor Luke Capthorn is convinced that he knows the wicked ways of the world as well as any – but, in truth, you are the only one who has a real chance of understanding. It does not matter that Zelophelon has kept Tallentyre out and demanded de Lancy in his place; *you* are the one who matters.

'You will see further and better than all the rest, if you only have the courage; and when you have done that, you will be far too valuable to Bast ever to be discarded. Use that advantage, David; make demands. She will not grant them all, but she will grant some. The angels are already afraid, or they would never risk this bold experiment; when they know the result, their fear will be increased. Never underestimate them, David – they are horribly dangerous – but the one which possesses you needs you, not as any mere instrument but as a genuine oracle, and you may make it pay for what it needs. Demand what you will, and whatever Bast gives you, continue to demand more. In time, she will be forced to give you some of what you ask.'

'Why?' asked David bluntly.

'No questions, David. You must remember that this is only a dream within a dream. It is a time for advice and reassurance. All will be well, if you do what they demand, as freely as it requires to be done. Accept this pain, David, and it will never again be as bad. Never – I promise you that.'

'How can I believe you?' said David, whispering. 'How can I believe you when you wear such a deceitful disguise? This is all mockery, all trickery.' Even as he said it, though, he felt that this was different, like no dream he had ever had before.

'It does not matter what you believe,' said the doppelgänger, in a voice he could hardly recognise as his own. 'This is only a dream, and you may take from it whatever reassurance you will. The news is good: you will emerge from this stronger than before, with an opportunity to set some things right which have long been wrong. I only urge you to remember that, and to be prepared to make the best use you can of your opportunity. Make demands, David. If they are unanswered at first, repeat them. Even if they are answered in the meanest possible way, nothing is lost; you can only gain by being assertive.

'Of course you cannot believe what I say, for I am only a figment of a dream, but that does not matter at all. The children will be safe; so will Cordelia; so will you. Demand better treatment for the future, and you will get it, however grudgingly.'

There was an air of finality about the way the last words were spoken, and the image of the man at the desk seemed to quiver in the lazy air.

'One question,' said David, hurriedly. 'Only one. Make demands, you said; this is my first!'

The man behind the desk smiled silkily, but his face was almost transparent.

'Very good,' he said. 'One question; one answer.'

'Who are you?' asked David. 'And don't dare to tell me that you're David Lydyard, or that names don't matter. Tell me your true name!'

The other was still smiling, but his body had begun to lose its apparent substance. The entire room was fading into ghostly insubstantiality, as though it were dissolving back into the darkness whence it came. David had an awkward and sickening conviction that the last thing to disappear would be the mocking grin, and that he would be left without his answer. What justice, after all, could he expect to find in the labyrinth of dreams?

But he was wrong. He got his answer. As the image faded away, the lips spoke; and the sound, though faint, was quite audible.

'I am Machalalel,' said the ghost, as darkness claimed him.

He awoke in the same dark cave which he had left behind, but the wolves were gone now; it was empty. The walls appeared ruddy to his enhanced vision, as though it were their warmth which he could see. He got up, went to the passage through which he had entered the cave, and followed it up towards the light.

Outside, someone was waiting for him.

She wore the appearance of Cordelia, but not even for the merest instant did he suppose that she was actually his wife. Nor was it the fact that she looked twenty years younger than when last he had seen her that convinced him that she was someone else; he knew, after all, that he looked twenty years younger than when she had last seen him. It was her expression that told him that she was merely some mischievous spirit which had chosen to play games with him.

She held out her hand. There were two little violet apples, each no bigger than the ball of his thumb, lying on her open palm.

'It is time,' she said. 'Eat.'

He took the apple. 'I know who you are,' he said. 'And I know that the fruit is poisoned.'

'Would you rather I had worn the appearance that was given to me while I lived in the world of men?' she said.

He shook his head. 'Appearances are not important here,' he said. 'Within your own illusion, you may contrive whatever you please. But this will dispel all illusion, will it not? This will free our inner eyes from all the webs of delusion which imprison and confuse them.'

He thought that she frowned, very slightly.

'Not immediately,' she said. 'The exchange of hostages is not yet complete. It is a delicate affair.'

'It must be,' said David, 'given that the angels hate and mistrust one another so much, and given also that they must be desperately afraid of what they might see, when they dare to look out instead of in. Will you also feel pain, or is that reserved to us?'

'I am a creature, like you,' she said. 'It is my soul's heat which will give us all the power to see. We will all suffer in the same degree. If you know who and what I am, you know what kind of existence I have had. Do you really think that you have had the worst of this?'

He remembered what she had been. He remembered, too, what Jacob Harkender had been during these last twenty years. He smiled thinly, and said: 'You were made to be what you were and what you are, like the Sphinx and Gabriel Gill before you. Gabriel rebelled, and if you do not like what you are, you have your own power now, and may do the same.'

'I have the power,' Hecate agreed. 'But I know better what I might do with it. It is time, now. Eat.'

David took the little apple and swallowed it whole. He felt it stick briefly in his throat, but it began to dissolve instantly. Hecate's dream-world dissolved with it.

He found himself inside a large house, which he had visited many times before; but this time, it was different, because he was not in his own body and he looked out upon its dusty corridors from unfamiliar eyes. Usually, he could see nothing in the mirrors which surrounded him, but this time they reflected a dozen images of the same human figure: it wore the face of the young Cordelia, but it was not Cordelia. It was Hecate, about to undertake the journey to Bast's pyramid in his place.

The landscapes of the dream were the ones he knew, but Hecate's sight was at once more curious and more confident than his own. She found nothing threatening in the ticking of the clocks; nothing confusing in the labyrinthine sprawl of the corridors, nothing oppressive in the starry sky.

She walked with easy grace for a while, then floated upon the air as though flight were second nature to her. She flew through the shadowed canyon fearlessly, and felt no sense of desolation in the ruined city with its huge fallen statues. She flew steadily and patiently, untouched by unease until . . .

Until she saw the pyramid.

The edifice was as gloomy and fearful to her as it had ever been to David when he was summoned to it in his own dream-form. The arched portal and the catacombs behind it induced in her the same sense of imprisonment that they had always induced in David; and the yellow light, which he always found mildly reassuring, seemed to her to be ablaze with menace.

She walked into the chamber of the cats, knowing that if there were to be treachery now, she could not escape it. Like Gabriel Gill in Zelophelon's Hell, she might have destroyed herself but she could not save herself. Like a defeated wolf, she had bared her throat in a gesture of submission, placing herself at the mercy of her maker's rival.

Only once before had David's heated soul shared the consciousness of a creature like Hecate: a magical being whose human form was but a costume. That was poor Gabriel, who did not know what he really was, and had little power. Hecate, by contrast, had come smoothly into her inheritance. She was more powerful than Gabriel, and more enlightened, and yet there was little enough in that part of her intelligence which she shared with David that seemed truly alien to him.

Is it only the limitations of my sight, he wondered, *that make her attitude seem so similar to mine? Or is it that when they elect to take human form, even the angels and their minions must think and feel as humans do?*

He looked at Bast through Hecate's eyes, and found her terrifying; but Hecate's attitude was no more worshipful than his had ever been.

'I am here,' said Hecate. 'This exchange is completed.'

'And the other,' the cat-headed goddess replied, looking down from on high.

Walking forward from another corner of the room was Luke Capthorn, the hostage offered to Bast by Zelophelon. He walked unsteadily, as though half drugged. Hecate had evidently been forewarned of this, but David was surprised. He could not believe that Luke was of any real value. What had Bast traded for him? He remembered that someone had told him, at some point in time which he could not quite pin down, that Tallentyre had been kept out and de Lancy – the pawn of the sleeping Sphinx – put in his place. Luke Capthorn for de Lancy seemed a more equitable trade.

Whereas I, David realised wryly, *have been traded for a little angel! Which of us would be the more expendable in that exchange?*

Bast stared down from her huge, slit-pupilled eyes at the two tiny figures which stood before her throne.

'Are you willing to be hurt?' she asked, as she had asked before. David, sharing Hecate's sight, knew that the question was addressed as much to himself as to his temporary host; he did not waste time in wondering whether Harkender was sharing Luke Capthorn's vision.

'I am,' Hecate replied.

'Aye,' replied Luke Capthorn, speaking with another's voice and not his own. It was as though he had no choice at all.

Having received that answer, Bast looked deep into Hecate's eyes, dissolving Cordelia's borrowed body with the acidity of her gaze. David felt himself drift free, a disembodied presence. He had ceased to feel alarmed about any such transition, and made not the slightest effort to resist as darkness rushed in to claim him.

When David could see again, he was standing at the top of the pyramid, in a simulacrum of his own body, in its natural condition. All the old aches and pains beset him, but they seemed almost comfortable in their familiarity.

Bast stood with him, face to face. She was no longer a giant, though she still had the body of a woman and the head of a cat. The stars above were extraordinarily bright. The dead and desolate city below filled the plain as far as David's human eyes could see, in every direction.

'David,' she said gravely, as a human being might speak to an old friend. He tried to remember whether it was the first time she had ever spoken his name, but he could not.

'If you wish to tempt me,' he replied, injecting as much contempt into his tone as he could, 'show me the kingdoms of my own world, not the shattered ruins of a world that never was.'

'I have tempted you before,' she reminded him. 'I know how to do it.' Her voice was sonorous and silky; the sounds could never have been made by the throat and mouth of an ordinary cat.

'If you wished to beg my forgiveness,' he said ironically, 'you might have done it a long time ago.' He was convinced that he had the upper hand, and was determined to show it.

'Our kind needs no forgiveness from yours,' she told him evenly.

'As ours needs none,' he replied, 'from our beasts of burden or the animals we eat for meat. But sometimes, we must ask a favourite horse to grant us a little more effort; and sometimes, we condescend to shed a tear for a pretty lamb delivered to the slaughterer.'

'What we shall do now,' she told him, 'might be as useful to you as to us. At the very least, you will share the enlightenment which we seek; at best, your most devout wish might yet be granted.'

'What wish?' he asked suspiciously, not certain what she meant.

'To be let alone,' she answered. 'Your family and your world. If you are fortunate enough in what you find, you may prove that we have nothing more to gain by any interference in the affairs of men.'

'But if I'm unfortunate,' he countered, 'I might prove instead that your interests would best be served by its destruction.' He knew that he had been told not to worry about that, by one who already knew, but here – for the moment – he could not quite remember who it was. He was sure that he would remember it in time. For now, the point had to be made.

'To seek enlightenment,' said the goddess, still staring him frankly in the face with her beautiful cat's eyes, 'is always dangerous. There is always the risk that the truth might be unpalatable.'

'I know it,' he said bitterly. But then he added: 'Although I ought to be glad that he won't share the hurt, I wish that Tallentyre could be here.'

'So do I,' answered the angel. 'But he was not acceptable to Zelophelon. None of this was my design, David; it was Zelophelon who proposed it, but I cannot and dare not stand aside. Had I contrived to forge an alliance with Zelophelon many years ago, before the other awakened, it might not have come to this, but all is changed now. We must act as cleverly as we can in our own interests, and in order to do that, we must discover certain things that we desperately need to know.'

'All is certainly changed,' he agreed bitterly. 'For twenty long years you've afflicted my dreams, playing with my soul as a cat plays with a mouse, never deigning to stand as we stand now, face to face. Now, I have suddenly become your champion in a collective enterprise. I'm your racing horse, or your fighting dog, and so you condescend to come to me at last as one thinking creature to another, and face me with eyes which are suddenly earnest and warm. You have used your whips and spurs to the fullness of their effect, and now you're pleased to add a cajoling voice and faint promises of reward to your urgings. But you're too proud to beg my forgiveness, of course; you're far too vain to admit that the way you've used me has been unnecessarily cruel and undesirably dishonest.'

'Those men who expect better from their gods are fools,' she answered. 'We both know that.'

'If I thought that you could pay it,' David said, with carefully contrived contempt, 'I would ask a high price for the service which I am now to be compelled to offer. But I've never believed that you're a true god, and I suppose that I'll have to content myself with lesser demands.'

'If I could have told you all that you desired to know,' she replied soberly, 'I would not have needed to use you as I have used you so long, or as I must use you now. It is because I did not know – and because the only other of my kind who seemed to be awake knew no better – that I have schooled you to be my instrument and my seeing eye. I have already said that you will share whatever enlightenment you discover on our behalf, and that you might find a reward in it, if you are lucky.'

'You seem very certain that it'll work,' said David, in a lower tone. 'But we're only human, despite the heat which you and the others will breathe into our souls to help us see. Even Hecate is only a little more than human. Our hurt may only be torture, and what it brings in its wake might be anything but the truth. The last of the ancient oracles died with the Age of Miracles, and you can't be sure that you can forge a new one now.'

'We must try,' said the goddess. 'If we have learned nothing else from our dealings with men, that much we know. We must try.'

As she spoke, she vanished into darkness, and he felt the fruit in his throat, still dissolving. He found that his eyes were closed, and forced them open, half expecting to find himself back in Hecate's makeshift Eden; but there was no bright sky or vivid foliage to be seen. The light was much softer, and it was difficult to focus on any visible shape.

Even now, he dared not hope that the dream was over, or that the coming enlightenment would be easy to attain.

2

The soft, subdued light was gentle on his tired eyes. A cool, calming breeze blew through his anguished soul, like the smothering mercy of laudanum.

He was still in his own body, seemingly awake and in the real world, echoing with the constant pulse of pain which was the summary effluvium of the multitude of little aches afflicting his backbone and his joints.

He was standing in one of the rooms beneath the hospital where he had worked for many years. It was not the private lair where he kept his books and his writing table, but one of the dissecting rooms nearby, where cadavers were laid out for their organs to be probed and displayed.

David had sometimes wondered, as he watched students delving with their scalpels, how it would feel to be under the knife, apparently dead but in fact alive and awake, feeling every movement of the blade and yet unable to indicate by the merest whisper of the voice or twitch of the features his state of awareness. Is that, he wondered, how what was to be done to him would be represented to his consciousness? Could that be the particular nightmare plucked from the gallery of his most intimate horrors, chosen to hurl his soul into the furthest reaches of visionary consciousness?

He looked across the room at the door to the corridor, and remembered what he had momentarily forgotten. He remembered that he had been in his own room – had dreamed of being in his own room – and had met someone or something disguised as himself.

He had met Machalalel, maker of the Clay Man and the werewolves of London. Machalalel had told him that all would be well. Machalalel had promised him, in effect, that the truth which he had yet to discover would be to his advantage.

David hurried out of the dissecting room and along the corridor to his private place, where he had so often hidden from the world. He rushed in, closing the door behind him, and stared at the empty chair behind the desk. He was alone.

And yet, he did remember. It had only been a dream within a dream, but he remembered.

He looked around the familiar room. The high, frosted windows and the shelf-decked walls were exactly as they should be, and so were the bottles and jars upon the shelves, the coloured pictures on the walls, the blackboard and the small chest of drawers full of instruments. Everything was the same.

Then he turned round and looked at the door through which he had just passed, on the back of which was mounted . . .

The face of the Egyptian coquette stared back at him, as it always had, but it was not now a painting done on cloth. Now it was inscribed on the lid of what seemed to be an actual mummy-case. The doorway was no longer a rectangle, in spite of the fact that it had been a rectangle when he had come through it. Now there was only the curved lid of the mummy-case set in the wall.

He knew that it was not really a mummy-case. He recognised it for what it was, and understood which of his myriad nightmares had been chosen to serve as the Gate of Ivory or Horn through which he must go.

There was no one else in the room. No one would seize him, drag him to the curved door and open it to put him in. He would have to do it himself. He understood that: this he must do willingly, if he was indeed to see what there was to be seen. He had to consent. He had to consent to the nightmare, to the pain, to the fusion of his powers of inner sight with those of his five companions.

You are the only one who stands a real chance of understanding, Machalalel had said. Did that mean that Machalalel – who was, after all, only a dream within a dream – already understood? Or did it only mean that Machalalel knew how little the three contending angels understood?

There was no purpose to be served by hesitation; the apparent passage of time was irrelevant. Equally, there was nothing to be lost by slowness. He was free to stand and wait, until some kind of goad urged him on: hunger, thirst or merely the creeping agony in his spine, which felt as though a corkscrew were being turned inside his vertebrae. He knew well enough, from experience and scientific observation, that there was a certain pitch of pain-induced frustration when a person nagged by a dull pain might seek a sharper one, by way of relief. In such a moment, he knew, a man might smash his fist or his face into a brick wall.

No such goad assailed him yet. The god which had him in her untender care required the fullest measure of collaboration of which he was capable. She wanted him – needed him – to walk into the embrace of the Angel of Pain by his own volition.

He was free. How many times had he insisted that he was free?

The image on the outside of the box was a very poor portrait of the Angel of Pain. Had he been a painter, how glorious a countenance might he have given her! The dead, flat eyes which stared into his own so blankly were not even a shadow of the bleak and wrathful eyes which he had so often confronted.

How it would startle the world, he thought, *if the crowds which hurry to see the annual exhibition at the Academy were to be confronted with an honest portrait of the Angel of Pain! How they would recoil under the ferocity of her gaze . . . and yet, even as they fled, would they not see how very beautiful she is, how absolutely imperious in her implacable wrath, how magnificent in her incapacity for kindness?*

David remembered Satan as he had first seen him, suffering in Hell with seven great nails driven through his body.

But I, he thought, *am Satan. I was always Satan, in my dreams. My names were Prometheus and Tantalus and David, and I still carry the stigmata of those cruel nails wherever I go. I am free, but I cannot choose the circumstances of my freedom.*

He walked forward, lamely, to draw back the lid of the casket and display the nails which were beneath.

In medieval times, they had called this device an iron maiden. They did not know the Angel of Pain as he knew her, or they might have named it differently.

He studied the seven nails behind the lid and the clasps in the rear of the case which would hold him in place to receive them. This time, they would be differently placed. Two would enter his eyes, two his abdomen, one his groin and two his knees. None was long enough to deliver an instantly fatal stab; the victims of this machine had been intended to die slowly.

David studied his hands, brushing them lightly together to savour the sensation of touch. There was nothing dreamlike about it; only cold logic told him that he was not really awake, not really in this room in the underworld. Every appearance said to him that whatever else was false, the flesh which he wore was real: solid, frail and indubitably his own. Only his intelligence said to him: You are in the hands of the gods, and this is not the world in which you live the life to which you were born. You are in the hands of the gods, and whatever befalls, you can be remade, remoulded, restored.

There was no one to force him into the narrow space, no one to hold him while the clasps were sealed. He had to step into the machine himself and hold his position while the spikes impaled him. He would feel them entering his body, exactly as if this *were* the underworld and he a prisoner of some heresy-hunting maniac. He would feel them; and even though the visionary flood which would assault him as his own eyes burst would blast him out of this shabby imitation of space and time, into the vastness of eternity, he would continue to feel them grinding away inside him, mauling his guts with slow and careful claws. Even though the Angel of Pain would fly down from the stars as she had so often done before, to pluck him into the air and soar with him into the kaleidoscopic sky, he would feel the cruel solidity of the nails inside him, pressing upon him by virtue of his own sagging weight: raping, spoiling and polluting him.

He would feel everything, as the Promethean Satan – his other self – had once felt the eagles tearing at his flesh, devouring his heart again and again and again, with no prospect of release . . .

Freely, he had to accept the caress of the spikes.

Freely, he had to accept the embrace of the Angel of Pain.

Freely, he must roll the dice of enlightenment, without any certainty that what he saw would be to his own advantage, to the advantage of his children or to the advantage of mankind. That was the bargain which he had made with the gods; the only bargain which they had offered him.

Slowly, almost reflexively, he made the sign of the cross, touching his head and heart and both his shoulders. Although he had long since ceased to be a Christian, there was no mockery or irony intended. Once, he had seen an infant angel crucified; and he had seen that angel descend from his cross to work a little miracle of kindness. He was not scornful of that example, and sought to borrow a measure of strength in remembrance and recognition.

Then he stepped into the iron maiden, positioned himself carefully, and pulled the lid towards him.

His courage failed at the last, but that did not matter. It had needed only the slightest pressure to set the lid in motion, and inertia completed the task, sealing him in total darkness.

For just an instant, the sensation of the spikes entering his flesh was absurdly devoid of pain, and he wondered madly whether he had somehow cheated those which sought to use him by rediscovering the art of anaesthetic shock which humankind had lost . . . but he had not.

The pain came, unbearably, and with it came the light.

Never having been involved in any communal worship of the Devil, Luke Capthorn had never built an altar to Satan. He kept no icon of the one he had appointed to be his Lord. Nor was he any kind of scholar; his notions of what Satan looked like, and how to worship him, were all inherited from others.

From the nuns at Hudlestone, from Jacob Harkender and from Jason Sterling – none of whom had known, at the time, to what purpose their ideas might be put – Luke had assembled vague visions of Sabbats at which the Lord of Hell was pleased to meet his loyal subjects, receiving blood sacrifices and favouring their arses with diabolical sodomy. He imagined that the Devil sometimes wore the head of a ram and sometimes a bat, that his tail was forked and that his shanks were shaggy. He imagined also that the Devil's eyes were like coals of fire, burning furiously.

None of this was in the least confused by his brief experience of Hecate's false Eden, nor by his deliverance into the hands of cat-headed Bast. Unlike David Lydyard, he was quite prepared to believe, as soon as that was all behind him, that it had been some kind of drunken hallucination. Unlike David Lydyard, he was entirely convinced, when he was returned to apparent corporeality, that he was in the one and only body he possessed, in the ordinary world.

Strangely, the one thing which disturbed him about what he took to be a dream was the fact that he had shot and killed Sir Edward Tallentyre. He did not regret having done so, because he knew that in a dream one can shoot and kill whomsoever one pleases without being held culpable, but he was puzzled by the fact that he had taken the trouble, given that the man was so sorely hurt anyway, and that his master – for whom he had a sincere respect – had been trying hard to save him.

His mild disturbance did not last long. It was quickly replaced by puzzlement regarding his surroundings. He was in the laboratory where Sterling kept his electrical apparatus, and he was not sure how he came to be there, or what he was supposed to be doing. He was fully dressed and standing up, and clearly had not woken that very instant from his tangled dreams, but he was not sure what task he had been about when he lost track of time.

He looked around, trying to find some clue to what was happening. When he caught a glimpse of movement in the shadows, he realised that one of Sterling's animals must have escaped. Perhaps it was one of the frog things or one of the mice which the scientist fed to his leeches. He grasped the supposition that he was here to catch the creature, and he immediately moved over to the place where he had glimpsed movement.

There was nothing to be seen, and he was suddenly afflicted with a profound frustration. Silently, he cursed the invisible creature. Then he cursed his vile position and his vile employer. Then, having invited his true Lord and master to claim the souls of all those who had temporarily vexed him, he turned on his heel and started towards the door.

He stopped dead when he saw what was waiting for him there.

It had neither the features of a ram nor those of a bat, but it had horns and it gathered about itself a cloak which looked strangely like a bat's folded wings. It was not cloven-footed, nor had it any evident tail. But its eyes were like coals of fire, burning furiously.

'Your wishes are granted,' it said. 'Your master is damned and all is changed. Your servitude is at an end, and I have come to reward my loving son.'

Its face was bronzed and metallic, but not unhandsome. Its tongue was forked, like a snake's, but when it gently licked its black lips it did so with such grace that Luke found a sinister pleasure in the anticipation of that tongue licking his own lips and probing within his mouth. The eyes which burned so brightly were like the eyes of a little child.

Purged as they were by the corrosions of nostalgia, Luke's happiest memories were of Hudlestone, where he had first learned to satisfy his lusts with the children in his care. He had used the boys more often than the girls, because the boys knew better how to endure mistreatment, and he was always afraid that the girls might be weak enough to confess his sins to the nuns. Nowadays, although he sometimes used a portion of his wage to buy the services of prostitutes, his satisfactions seemed so much more meagre. All the magic had been lost from them; all the beautifully impure joy.

'Who are you?' asked Luke, in a whisper whose awe revealed that he knew what answer to expect.

'I am the maker of the material world,' the other replied. 'I am the designer of the flesh and all its appetites. I am the architect of lust and avarice, sensation and ecstasy. I am the Lord of the Free, the Answerer of Curses; and you are my loyal servant, my own true flesh, my son.'

'Are you real?' asked Luke, meaning: *Are you material? Are you here in the flesh?*

'Ever and always,' the Devil replied. 'I do not hide in light or traffick with the canker-worms which men call souls. I am in and of the flesh, and I come to my loyal subjects in palpable form, to show them what I am. My love is honest and material, not cold and ghostly. My son, do you desire my love?'

Luke knew that he was free to say 'I do'. He knew that he desired to say 'I do'. He knew that he *must* say 'I do' lest his master's generosity be turned to injured pride.

Somehow, though, he could not quite pronounce the words.

He was grateful, therefore, when the Devil seemed to understand what he meant. When he saw the Devil smile at him, he felt only relief. And when the Devil moved towards him, he felt only the ecstasy of surrender: the knowledge that it was not necessary to speak, but only to be taken.

He knew how huge and cold the Devil's member was, but he did not care. He knew that there would be pain in being taken by such an instrument, but he was certain that he could bear it. The virgins he had taken in the golden days of his youth had accepted the pain, though some had had to bite their lips to stifle screams, and he saw the justice and the propriety in what he had to do. The pain, he knew, would be soon enough dissolved by pride and joy, that he might yield himself to his own true father, the author of his flesh, the master of his senses.

Freely, he offered his flesh.

Freely, he freed the Devil's prick from its cladding; freely he warmed its head with his mouth; freely, he played with the Devil's serpentine tongue. Freely he turned, and drew in his breath, tensed for the moment of entry, expecting pain but expecting ecstasy, too . . . expecting to discover love at last . . . expecting that the climax of his life would be an explosion of pure sensation that would set his flesh alight . . .

But he had underestimated the probable pain.

He had spun himself a cocoon of fond illusions, which could not in the end contain the shaft which struck into his body, tearing and scathing and seething inside him like a white-hot spear, turning everything to searing, blinding light.

William de Lancy started suddenly, as though he had caught himself on the brink of falling asleep, and brought himself fully awake with a convulsive jerk. His pipe, which must have been in his hand, clattered on the bare rock as it fell and skittered away.

He had the most peculiar sensation of having lost consciousness not for an instant, but for an eternity. He felt, though he did not know quite how he was able to feel such a thing, that *years* had passed – years in which he had lived a fantastic and astonishing life, of whose details he could not now remember a single one.

But it was still 1872; he was still in Egypt, in the desert south of Qina.

He could see shadows moving inside both the tents. Lydyard was quiet now, but Tallentyre was still keeping vigil over him; de Lancy was glad that the crisis semed to have passed and that the boy would live. The Jesuit, meanwhile, was moving restlessly back and forth, in the grip of some anxiety of his own; he was seemingly unable to calm himself, even to kneel down and pray.

De Lancy still made occasional attempts to pray, but they always decayed into mere pretence. He was miserably incapable of faith, whether that faith be in the existence of a benevolent God and a saviour, like Mallorn's, or in the nonexistence of any kind of God at all, like Tallentyre's. De Lancy was a doubter, ever fearful of the things which he doubted. That there was something supernatural about the world in which he found himself he was perfectly convinced, but what form and identity it had he could not begin to guess.

If the shadows which crowded around him had begun to move and had proceeded to drag him down into some mysterious abyss of darkness, de Lancy would have been terrified; but he would not have cried out, as Tallentyre surely would, that it was impossible and could not be admitted.

Here, in Egypt, he felt the closeness of the other world. He wondered what it had been like to live in the land of the pharaohs, when the world was young and the gods walked the earth with the heads of birds and beasts, and a man might go into the great wilderness beyond death with his servants to keep him company and money to buy a proper place in Heaven. De Lancy could not see himself as a pharaoh, but he could easily imagine himself a priest or a merchant. He could fancy himself a master of slaves, braver and more cunning than the rest of his kind. He might have been a builder of empires then, instead of what he was: a traveller, gawking at the wonders of a world which was far too large and far too various. He had no more faith in the colonial service and the future of Victoria's empire than he had in God.

He almost drifted off to sleep again, but caught himself up as suddenly as before. To his astonishment, there was a man standing nearby, silhouetted against the stars: a man of mystery, who could only have come from the desert.

'It can be done,' said the man softly, as de Lancy struggled to make out his shadowed features. 'Time cannot bind those who know its secrets. But there is a price to pay. Those who turn their backs on the future cannot live in it, and must appear to die. Would you trade the future for the past, if you could?'

Tallentyre, de Lancy knew, would have said contemptuously that it was impossible and could not be admitted; but de Lancy felt curiously intoxicated, as though he had been granted special powers of comprehension which allowed him to see that the shadowy man spoke the literal truth, and that this was an opportunity which had to be accepted on the instant, or lost for ever.

'Yes,' he said, immensely proud of his own bravery. 'I'd risk the world itself on the turn of a card, if there was a chance that I might find a better and bolder life than this.'

'To die,' said the shadowed man, with pity in his voice, 'is not without pain. You are free to refuse.'

'I am free,' de Lancy agreed. 'And that is what I desire above all else: to be free!'

He had not known, until he said it, that it was what he desired most in all the world. Nor did he know, even after he had said it, why he desired it so devoutly. But it was true.

Suddenly, for no particular reason, he reached down to pick up his pipe, reaching into a crevice in the rock where it had fallen. When the scorpion's sting first penetrated his skin, he thought that it was only a pinprick – but then he felt the venom enter his bloodstream like a tide of fire, and he whispered 'Thank you' as the world dissolved.

He had underestimated the pain that he would have to suffer as the future was torn from his living flesh. He had not had sufficient imagination to make him properly afraid; and as the poison sent him sprawling and vomiting, writhing insanely upon the jagged rocks, he found that he could not, after all, bear what he had consented to have done to him.

But it did not matter, by that time, whether he could bear it or not. It was done to him anyway, and all the world was turned to unbearable light.

Jason Sterling woke up by slow degrees, feeling his whole body descend into a morass of discomfort. His limbs ached – as well they might, given that he seemed to have been sleeping fully clothed in a lumpy, leather-clad armchair – and his head was thick with befuddlement. His mouth was dry and his tongue seemed unnaturally large.

He opened his eyes to look around, but he had some difficulty in recruiting the surprise appropriate to his surroundings. He was in his library, staring at the spines of the books arrayed on the shelves. He had no memory of having gone to sleep there, but there was an empty decanter on the table beside his chair, with a brandy glass and a book. The sour taste in his mouth as he tried to moisten his tongue with saliva assured him that he had been drunk, but he searched his memory in vain for traces of yesterday. The thought that he would have to summon Luke Capthorn in order to discover what day it was annoyed him sorely, and he dismissed it from his mind in favour of a stern resolve to pull his scattered wits together.

He stood up, stretching his cramped limbs. Then he went to the window and drew back the curtain to let in the morning light. The day was bright, but there was a mist still lingering and there had been a heavy dew overnight; the bushes in the garden were sparkling with little droplets of water, which caught the hazy sunlight and displayed a thousand spiderwebs which could not normally be seen.

He went back to the table and picked up the glass, turning it between his two hands as though to conjure up the lost memory of the last time he had played with it between sips of Armagnac. It stirred no recollection, and so he set it down again and picked up the book instead. It was a cheap yellowback: a railway novel of the kind which sold in huge quantities at the London stations. it was called *The Elixir of Life*, but it was not the Harrison Ainsworh novel of that title; it was signed instead Lucian de Terre.

At the sight of the book, Sterling's heart leaped with excitement. It triggered a whole chain of associations which, though vague and uncertain, reminded him not merely of the day before but of a project which had occupied him for many years, and whose culmination was at last close at hand. Something in the novel, he knew, had helped him to place the last piece in an intellectual puzzle which had troubled him for the greater part of a lifetime; while he had been turning its pages in search of idle amusement, some insignificant incident of the plot had triggered the vital inspiration which had intoxicated him even before he had drunk to his success.

There was a horrible moment of suspension when he tried to bring the vital inspiration to mind and failed. He recalled anecdotes of other famous men who had waked from dreaming convinced that they had solved the great riddle of existence, only to find in the morning that they had forgotten it, or had written down gibberish when they thought they were inscribing the vital formula.

Those recollections filled him with such a black rage of frustration that he would have howled aloud, had the secret not at that very moment returned to his mind with precisely the same intuitive force with which it had first struck him. He was only amazed that he had been able to remain in his chair when he read it, and had even managed to close the book and lay it down, before drinking brandy after brandy, instead of rushing downstairs to his laboratory to do what needed to be done.

He went now, not too hastily but with the purposeful stride of a man about to achieve his destiny. As he walked, the jumbled memories of his years of endeavour seemed to stir and bubble in his brain: the cauldron of his past, his growth, his intelligence, his identity, coming at last to the boil.

A rhyme possessed his thoughts, not banishing the storm of memory but making the images dance: *Fillet of a fenny snake, in the cauldron boil and bake; eye of newt, and toe of frog, wool of bat, and tongue of dog, adder's fork, and blind-worm's sting, lizard's leg, and howlet's wing . . . scale of dragon, tooth of wolf, witch's mummy, maw and gulf of the ravin'd salt-sea shark, root of hemlock digg'd i' th' dark . . .*

His footfalls fell in with the unfolding rhyme as he descended the stairs to the den where he had worked his alchemy since that discovery in an old vellum text of the first clue which had set him on the road to the elucidation of the greatest secret of them all. Ever since that crucial moment the highway of his life had led inexorably to the crossroads which faced him now: the crossroads by the gallows tree, where one road lead to Paradise and another straight to Hell.

All the necessary equipment, he possessed. All the necessary knowledge to apply it, he now had. All the discipline required of him, to make his body a fit recipient for the fluid of life, he had endured.

For twelve long years he had plundered the lightning and stored its magical force in his mighty engines of Sheffield steel, hoarding it against the day when he would know how to use it. Now, thanks to some indefinable coincidence of his own intuition and the hint casually thrown out by the innocent and unknown Lucian de Terre, he knew what to do.

The arrangement of his various machines took him an hour or more. It would have been much easier with another to help, but it never entered his head to call his servant. Luke was in any case a simple and superstitious man, who might consider the entire proceedings diabolical.

When he was ready, Sterling took his position nakedly between the anode and the cathode of his great circuit, and he began to fasten the electrodes to the two sides of his body: two to the eyelids, two to the thumbs, two to the abdomen, one each to heart and groin. Thus aligned with the secret pathways in the body, whose course he alone knew, they would channel the force of life into a state of perfect balance, filling him with a miraculous energy which would transform and revitalise the four humours, infusing the very atoms of his being with a magical resilience which would restore his youth and give him immunity from death.

When he was completely ready he stood stock still, arms displayed and head thrown back, savouring the moment. All his life, every waking moment he had spent during these last forty years, had been dedicated to the achievement of this instant of time.

Then, without further ceremony, he reached out and flicked the switch that would set the whole apparatus to work.

Its effect was not instantaneous, but it was rapid. No more than seven seconds passed between the activation and the discharge; but seven seconds can accommodate a good deal of anxiety and apprehension, and while they passed Sterling found himself seized by a very peculiar and terrifying sensation that he was somehow not where he thought he was, nor *who* he thought he was, and that all the images which had danced to the pipes of remembrance mere minutes before were only silly phantoms and grotesques sent to make a mockery of him by turning upside down his desires and ambitions, his ideas and achievements, his knowledge and his methods.

So urgent was this appalling claim upon his imagination that he had to resist it very fiercely, crying 'No!' with all his might.

I am a free man! he howled into the empty darkness where his mind was, filling the emptiness with echoes. *I cannot be denied the force and fabrication of my own will! I am who I am!*

Then the life force of the captured lightning flowed into him, searing a path along the secret channels, coursing through the conduits of his very soul, burning and burning . . .

He had not known – how could he ever have guessed? – that it would hurt so much. The first sensation was a mere pricking of the thumbs, but from that infinitesimal seed grew an awful crescendo of pain which went on and on and on, gaining intensity not in any merely arithmetical fashion but compounded and compounded, until the acceleration of his agony became seemingly infinite.

I live! he screamed inwardly, to fill the infinite darkness with the intensity of the wish. *I live, and cannot be confined! I am the alkahest, dissolving time and space themselves!*

But he could not stop, or even contain, the agony which flooded him . . . or the *light.*

*

For Jacob Harkender it was different.

Harkender knew exactly what was happening, and he needed no cunning seduction or deception. He had passed through the fire already; he had given all that he had to give, and was not sorry to have the chance to give it all again.

Even so, he had to return from the Eden of dreams. He came back to the precarious discomfort of the flesh.

He felt that Zelophelon trusted him well enough to give him charge of his own reincarnation. He assumed that he could have placed himself in any moment of his arduous existence. He could have placed himself under the multicoloured dome of his strange house at Whittenton, where he had used Mercy Murrell's whores to dispatch him on his boldest journeys into the ecstatic realm. He could have gone back to his boyhood, to the time when he was first forced by continuing cruel circumstance to find some magical release from the round of petty abuses, beatings and rapes. He could have gone to Egypt, to relive the fabulous experiment by whose means he had stolen a soul from a sleeping angel and placed it in the womb of Jenny Gill.

He could have chosen any of these moments out of time, he thought, because he alone – *alone*, although Lydyard and Hecate knew what was happening as well as he did – had not the slightest fear or apprehension in regard to the odyssey which he was about to undertake. For him, and him alone, it was an opportunity without risk or cost.

He feared nothing, not even the possibility that the revelation might show him the falseness of all his earlier beliefs and hopes. He no longer cared about that.

He alone had true freedom of choice in selecting a gateway to the vision. He alone could exercise true perversity.

He chose to dress himself, not in his own flesh, but in the flesh of another. He felt fully entitled to do so, having lived nearly half his adult life with his own flesh in ruins, sharing the flesh of others. He chose the flesh whose sensations he loved best, the flesh which felt easiest to bear. That he would be a prisoner in that flesh until the oracular journey began did not seem to matter at all, because he had learned long ago that the power of intention was not always a force to exercise with pride.

He could have selected for reliving any of the countless moments which he had previously shared with Cordelia Lydyard. He could have shared the birth of any one of her children, or bathed in the luxury of her lovemaking, but he did not want to focus his attention and emotion quite so sharply. He chose instead to forge a new link, with whatever moment passed for the present in the world of appearances from which he and all the others had been withdrawn. He chose to return to reality upon the hazard of chance, to visit the flesh which he loved best for what might be the last time.

He found Cordelia sitting in her dressing room, alone. She was staring at her image in an oval mirror set above the table where she usually set her hair, inspecting the tracks of her tears.

Harkender was astonished by the frightful void of her feelings, which had been driven to the edge of anguish and beyond, into a desert of utter desolation.

Her children were gone: taken.

Her husband was gone: taken.

Her father was gone: taken.

Her world was gone. The core had been cut out of her very existence. She had even been cheated of her grief; she had not even their deaths to mourn. She had nothing. The walls of the world had simply blurred, and all that she loved, all that gave meaning to her daily existence, had fallen through. There was no ambition, but only loss. There was no hope, but only emptiness.

Jacob Harkender looked at the reflection in the mirror: the reflection of a woman nearly forty, aged but handsome, alive but so weakened and ravaged by shock and stress as to seem more nearly dead.

If he could have done it, he would have changed that reflection to the face of another, who could offer her some message of consolation; not his own face, which might have made her briefly savage with hate and rage, but the face of her husband or one of her children. It would only have been an illusion, and she would have known it, but whatever words the illusion had uttered, or had seemed to utter, would have struck her mind with all the force of a divine covenant. She would have believed, in spite of what she knew.

But he could not do it.

Despite what he had thought when he chose to visit her, Harkender found that it was *his* helplessness rather than the extremity of *her* despair that pricked his conscience. He had played the voyeur within her thoughts for a long time, and had easily grown used to his impotence. He had thought that it could not possibly trouble him now, but he had underestimated his own empathy. He felt for her more strongly now than he had ever done before, even when he first told himself that he loved her.

Even now, he was not sorry that he had asked Zelophelon to refuse her father as a hostage. He could not regret his insistence that it should be de Lancy and not Tallentyre who would take part in their adventure. But if he had been able to make Sir Edward Tallentyre's face appear in Cordelia's mirror and say 'All will be well, my child', he would have done it.

Then the reflection in the mirror moved. Cordelia was reaching out with her right hand to pick up a long and sturdy pin of the kind she sometimes used to secure a bonnet on top of her gathered hair. She held it for a moment between her thumb and forefinger; then, quite carefully and delicately, she changed her grip so that she held it like a dagger. Her eyes studied the reflected bosom of her dress.

Harkender found his thoughts suddenly congealing with horror – horror that stabbed him with astonishing force.

'No!' he said, very quietly.

'No!' he screamed with all his might, as though by the sheer force of his effort he might compel her to hear him.

But she could not hear him, and all that she could see through the mist of her exhausted tears was her own reflection.

She put the point of the pin to a place beneath her left breast, feeling for the gap between the ribs. She changed her grip again, so as to place the full weight of her hand behind the rounded head of the pin. Then she pressed as hard as she could, and kept on pressing.

It did not hurt at all.

It did not hurt Cordelia at all.

But Jacob Harkender, who had once turned the panoply of his emotions into a great cataract of hate, was scalded and burned and blasted by a fit of anguish which possessed his soul and made him understand that there is a kind of pain which is outside and beyond the flesh, which might in its own way become unendurable.

And then, mercifully after its own peculiar fashion, in harness with the pain there came the light.

For Hecate, before she came into her magical inheritance, flesh had always been a burden. It was not simply that her body was misshapen, ill-designed for the commonest of human activities; her deformity was by no means confined to her limbs and back, but extended into the minute organisation of her tissues and organs, perverting every level of her being.

Her thoughts had always been slow, her ideas primitive, her ability to articulate limited. She was not so far beneath the common run of mankind to be reckoned an imbecile, but she was rightly thought foolish.

Had she had better command of her powers of thought and forethought, she might have found a way to make an earlier contact between her consciousness and the magic which was incarnate in her, growing as she grew. She would not have understood those powers, but she might – like Gabriel Gill before her – have found a way to think about them, to study them, and to begin the business of subjecting them to discipline and conscious command. As things were, she could not do that.

While she was a child, her magic remained as wild and mercurial as the dreams which possessed her mind by night, overflowing from time to time to disturb her environment in some petty and random fashion, but never subject to the direction of her will. Her removal into Mrs Murrell's establishment, and the education given to her there, made no difference at all, until the time came when her destiny was rudely thrust upon her. Her metamorphosis from ugly nymph to angel was accomplished in the space of a few hours.

She had been created as she was for a purpose. Her maker had carefully withheld the sufficiency of intelligence which would have given her a measure of control over her powers while she was still a child, and might have allowed her to arrive at a realisation of what she really was. It is not only those whom the gods destroy whose sanity they steal, but those for whom they have specific and narrowly defined uses. Hecate had been crafted as a plane lens upon the human and material worlds: an eye with only a minimal intelligence to interpret what it saw. She was given potential to be something very different, but that potential was locked up until the moment when it had to be released.

The maker who designed her had paid no attention to the irrelevant by-products of its scheme. The fact that her inability to discipline her magic was reflected in a similar inability to discipline her thoughts and feelings was of no consequence. It did not matter that the deformed girl was a helpless slave of her moods, ever subject to seemingly random surges of feeling which she experienced, without knowing why, as affection and fear, pity and petulance, pleasure and misery.

What the pressures of these various emotions made of her attitudes and responses was not important to her maker; nor did it matter in the least that in the brief interval of her metamorphosis, the flood tide of these emotions drove her to murder.

Mercy Murrell had induced in Hecate that particular alloy of gratitude and fear which can lead to the most acute kind of dependence. Sometimes Mrs Murrell scolded her fiercely; at other times she was kind; but always hers was the power to determine the pattern of events. In her house, she was an indomitable empress, and her whims dictated the distribution among her subjects of pleasure and pain. She commanded from Hecate an anxious craving to obey. Most of the whores who worked in the house were inclined to scold Hecate all the time, and mock her in addition; all they inspired in her was bitter hatred, for they had not sufficient power over her to temper her loathing with fear, nor sufficient inclination to tempt her with occasional acts of kindness to make her anxious to win their approval.

Only one or two of her partners in vice, chief among them Sophie, treated her gently enough to win her affection. Even Sophie was moderate with her kindness and occasionally impatient, but in the main she treated Hecate tolerably well. She did so not because she had a heart of gold, but rather because she was fortunate enough not to be horrified by ugliness. Sophie never found Hecate's appearance disgusting, nor her presence discomfiting; and because Hecate was always mild with her, she was always mild in return. It all came quite naturally to Sophie; there was no virtuous motive involved. Nevertheless, such treatment brought about a rapid focusing of raw emotion in Hecate's attitude to Sophie.

Hecate loved Sophie, and that was why she destroyed the man who overstepped the limits of her tolerance on the night that he had won the auction for the privilege of using her. It gave Hecate a great deal of pleasure to squeeze the life out of him with invisible hands, to press and crush his well-formed flesh until it was as sore and useless as her own, and above all else to pour the pain into his brain to make him suffer and suffer more. Fifteen years of thoroughly human anguish, pent up in her like a huge, ugly knot, came unwound in that moment of triumph, that moment of achievement, that moment of fulfilment; and Hecate was later to remember it as the one true moment of her entire existence as a creature of flesh and bone. It was not merely the climax of her brief human career but its justification, its redemption from awful confusion.

It was, inevitably, that moment to which she chose to return, in order that the angel to which she had been given as a hostage could bind her into the prophetic wheel which pain would spin.

Mrs Murrell was in the doorway, staring at her.

Sophie had gone, hurried away by someone else.

The headless body on the floor was leaking out blood from the twin arteries in the neck, and blood was dripping, too – though much more slowly – from the severed head which remained upright in midair, its eyes bulging out with shock and its tongue, engorged and discoloured, projecting from its silently screaming mouth like the head of a lizard.

Hecate was smiling.

Hecate looked Mrs Murrell in the eyes, and she smiled. She laughed. In returning to this form, she had surrendered those powers of thought and imagination which she had acquired in metamorphosis. Like a werewolf returned to its animal shape, she had acquired the limitations of the appearance to which she had reverted. Delight welled up inside her, shaking her with uncontrollable giggles.

She pointed to the head and cried out in glee, too excited to grope for actual words: 'La! La! La!'

She watched the horror in Mercy Murrell's eyes, which had made her whole face liquid, harden by degrees into flinty wrath.

Hecate could not understand why.

Once, Mrs Murrell had staged the story of Salomé – in her own version, of course. Sophie had played Salomé, and the whore who had played her tormentor in the Turkish travesty had played John the Baptist, tortured by Herod's minions and lasciviously pawed by his temptress before yielding up his head so that Sophie might use it as a dancing partner. Hecate had also been allowed to dance with the fake head, after her own shambling fashion, in order to add a touch of burlesque to the penultimate act. It had been the most important part she had ever played, and she had been warmed by the laughter of the crowd and the cheers, whose irony she had not been able to perceive.

Mrs Murrell had been pleased with her then; but the bawd was by no means pleased with her now.

This time, Mrs Murrell picked up the birch rod with which the luckless man had beaten Sophie too long and too hard, and slashed Hecate across the face with it. Then she slashed her again and again and again, in a blind fury which admitted neither logic nor moderation.

It was a mad thing to do. Even Hecate had some vague understanding of that. Hecate knew that what she had just done to the man who hurt Sophie she could just as easily do to the woman who was beating her, but she did not. She could have torn Mrs Murrell limb from limb and scattered her quarters to the corners of the room, but she did not. Nor did she flinch from the blows of the rod. Instead . . .

The pliable wood flayed the skin from her cheeks and skin. It scarred the eyes which she would not deign to close, and blinded her. It ripped the hair from her scalp in little hanks which fluttered to the ground.

And it hurt her; it hurt her hotly and dazzlingly; it gave wings to her soul.

And so she laughed, and laughed, and laughed, while the light bathed her in its glory.

Meanwhile, Eve – who was innocent – looked up into the face of the serpent and smiled. She loved beauty and trusted it implicitly. She had no concept of deception, no notion of anything which might be other than it appeared. She knew, beyond any shadow of a doubt, that the serpent meant only to do her good, to add to her pleasure in the fact of existence.

She took the fatal fruit into her hand and raised it to her lips. She bit into it and drew a piece of its flesh on to her tongue. She swallowed it down, in advance of any evident sensation of taste.

She looked up into the serpent's face, gratefully.

The face changed, and in its place she saw a severed head, miraculously suspended in midair, gouting blood at the neck. She saw the expression on the face of the severed head, bloated by the effects of strangulation and the experience of utter horror.

Then she saw the light.

Then, and only then, did she realise who she really was.

Then, and only then, did she realise what a mockery her innocence had been.

Then, and only then, did she realise that the face of the serpent which had tempted her, beautiful though it might have been, was the face of the Angel of Pain.

3

In the beginning, there was only the light and the pain; it was as though he had been plunged into that lake of fire in Hell where the souls of sinners were destined to roast eternally. But he suspected already that the notion of eternal suffering was stupid; he could only suppose that in time, whatever was constant had to fade into the background of consciousness, provided only that consciousness could be maintained. Eternal pain would simply become a condition of sensation.

That was what happened; the pain which was at first unbearable became bearable, and by degrees it ceased to trouble him at all. What had been pain was transmuted into a kind of sight, or at least into *some* kind of sensation. The light eventually ceased to blind him, and it became possible to apprehend the world which its fervour had hidden.

Because he was who he was, he found himself capable of understanding what had happened, or at least of putting it into words. Perhaps it was only a tale that he invented, to impress the stamp of meaning on something essentially inchoate, but it allowed him to subdue his experience by naming and organising and analysing it.

There was, he knew already, a distinction to be made between the physiology of pain and the consciousness of pain. He knew that the one inevitably gave rise to the other: that the transmission of certain kinds of signals through the nerves to the brain evoked the conscious experience which men called pain. But he also knew that the flow of causality could sometimes be reversed. He knew that emotional anguish could begin the chain of circumstance and excite the nerves.

He knew that the consciousness of pain might be induced by some cause other than the excitation of the nerves, and therefore understood that if the consciousness of a man could somehow be linked to the greater universe as well as to the body which housed it, the flood of alien sensation might assault the mind like a torrent of unbearable pain.

Knowing that, he was able to believe that if a man were brave enough to endure such pain, he might in time transcend the agony of it, and begin to use that new power of sensation.

This, David realised, was what the angels did when they possessed human victims and intruded into their dreams. The angels were entities which could touch the consciousness of a man in such a way as to extend the reach of his consciousness beyond the limits of his body. It was a kind of sharing or overlapping: the forging of a link between a human mind and a mind of a very different kind, whose natural existence was on another scale, and whose sensory apparatus was different.

It was not, as the Clay Man had supposed in trying to interpret the nature of the Creators, that ordinary pain conferred the gift of sight; the truth was that the human mind so resisted the dubious gift of new sensation that it reproduced all the mental elements of pain, until – for those who had the courage to endure it – the mind yielded to its change and allowed the pain to fade away into the background of sensation.

The sense by which the angels apprehended the universe was not really sight at all. It was an unhuman sense which had no name, and resembled touch or hearing as closely as it resembled the sight of the eyes of men. It still made sense, however, to think of it as a kind of sight belonging to an inner eye. It made sense because human consciousness itself regarded sight as the primary sense, so that the 'magical' powers which the angels could confer upon those which they possessed – to make dreams take on apparent materiality or to build a bridge between the consciousness of two human minds – were inevitably construed as visions. It made sense, too, because humans, for exactly the same reason, made 'seeing' synonymous with 'understanding'.

As David learned to use the sensorium of the angels, he could not give any other name to what he did but to say that he *saw*. There was no other word he could put in its place; but the imprecision of it was less important to him than the fact that it gave him a means of grasping what had been done to him. Once he had grasped that, he had increased his own freedom to make use of the opportunity which the linkage of human and alien senses offered him.

Because he was the kind of man he was, his intellect could begin to unravel the significance of what he saw. He knew that the perceived nature of the world which he inhabited – the real world of material objects – was to some extent an artefact of his senses. He knew that the world must appear very different to a bat or a bee, let alone a barnacle or a bacterium.

He knew, too, that what appeared to the human eye as emptiness was not necessarily empty at all. He knew that the invisible atmosphere which he breathed was a great riot of many different kinds of atoms and molecules; and that even the vacuum between the worlds was filled with gravitic and magnetic fields, and was continuously flooded by the paradoxical disturbances of light and other radiations. He knew that the material world was bracketed by the infinite and the infinitesimal, and that all talk of 'objects', perhaps even talk of matter itself, supposed a particular kind of viewpoint.

That was not the viewpoint of the angels, and their senses revealed a very different universe.

The universe of men was unimaginably vast and desolate; the stars were very numerous, but the distances between them were so huge as to defy the human imagination; and to the human sensorium, those distances seemed utterly dark and empty. The universe of the angels, on the other hand, was full; it was a fervent, turbulent, liquid confusion with no emptiness in it at all, but only furious activity.

To the angels, matter was the nearest thing to emptiness they could conceive, because matter was lumpen and leaden and torpid and unspirited; even the heart of a sun was to the angels a stagnant swamp of serenity. To the angels, the universe was certainly vast, and growing explosively, but it was still a unity; it did not seem to *their* senses that Creation was a vast emptiness strewn with lonely objects, but a vibrant, restive flux in which matter was the heaviest and coldest and dullest of all the games which its true substance played.

But matter was nevertheless important to the angels; the materiality of the universe was significant; it *mattered*. (The words which David was forced to recruit could not do justice to the sensations, having been evolved to describe a very different order of things, but even their unaccidental ironies were helpful.)

From the viewpoint of the angels it was all too obvious that the universe had been different in the past. Like humans, they were prisoners of time, but their lifespans were not nearly so ephemeral, and their consciousness of time was very different: constricted, straitened, collapsed. The angels could see that their world was changing, qualitatively; they could 'see' its explosive evolution quite plainly. Nor could they doubt that they were changing with it, inevitably but not entirely helplessly.

Because the angels had minds, they had a measure of control over their 'bodies', but because they were not objects – unlike stars or particles of dust or human beings – the control which they had was not mechanical in kind. David had no other word for it but 'magical' and did not hesitate to invoke that word, but he knew that the supernatural qualities which the angels had were not really outside the nature of the universe at all; they simply belonged to an aspect of it which human senses could not directly apprehend.

The angels intersected the world of lumpen matter, and belonged to it in their own fashion, but they were not confined by it. Somewhere in the world of unspirited matter each and every one of them had an anchorage. That anchorage was not an object of a particular kind, like a stone or a tree or a statue, but it was nevertheless something possessed of position.

The angels were not 'made of' matter in the sense that men were; they could 'possess' matter, including the matter of which men were made, in which case their minds could interact with the minds of the men whose bodies they possessed, but they were never entirely confined by the matter which they possessed. The 'selves' of the angels were extended, in a very complicated fashion, into that marvellous ebullient confusion which mere men could perceive only as emptiness and absence.

The angels, David thought, were more like patterns than people; they were more like magnetic fields than objects. But in spite of their intangibility they had the power to act and alter their environment in ways which were – viewed by human senses, from the torpid world of matter – strange and incomprehensible.

Everything that happened in the world of men and material objects, David knew, was weighted down by the particular paces of time. Even light had to move at its own allotted speed, taking years to travel between the stars. In the world of objects, causes and effects flowed at what seemed to human senses a very fast pace, but the magnitude of the empty distances between the stars made even the quickest rush of cause and effect seem very slow. From the viewpoint of the angels, it was different. Their universe was vast, to be sure, but it was also a coherent whole in which every point of action was somehow linked with every other. The angels had powers of action which transcended the limits of material cause and effect: powers of Creativity; godlike powers.

But they were not gods. As David and Sir Edward Tallentyre had always been enthusiastic to insist, they were not gods.

What the angels could do was still bound by certain definite limits of possibility. They could affect and transcend the limits of material action, by playing with the forces beyond and beneath the level of material interaction, but they were bound by the fundamental laws of their own peculiar existence.

They were not gods, but only thinking beings, trying as best they could to comprehend the strange and wonderful universe in which they found themselves. Meanwhile, they also tried as best they could to understand themselves, and plan their lives to the best possible advantage. They had lives of their own and projects of their own; they could be hurt and destroyed; they could cooperate with one another and compete with one another; they knew fear, and they knew hope.

Despite their very different physical nature, their minds were not so very unlike the minds of men. Although their powers of perception and their powers of action were awesome, the fundamental aspects of their existential plight were very similar. An angel, like a man, might say *cogito, ergo sum*, but once it had said that, all else remained to be discovered by reason and plagued by doubt. Like men, the angels could be clever or stupid, honest or deceitful, bold or cowardly. Like men, they could make mistakes; like men, they had the utmost difficulty in understanding their own mental nature.

In some ways, they were very much greater than men; but in some ways they were less.

The angels were limited, as men were. Whatever powers they had, there were others they had not. In the same way that men, avid to understand themselves and the world in which they found themselves, had sought to enhance their powers of sensation, so too had the angels.

In one way, it had been simpler for the angels. They had other minds ready to hand, already 'inside' them, easily possessed by them. It had been easy enough for the angels to use the senses of men, and to find in those senses a kind of window – or perhaps a microscope or a spectroscope would be a better analogy – through which they could look upon a very different world.

David realised that in one important respect, using the sight of another thinking being had to be very different from augmenting sight with a microscope or telescope. The sight of a living being was active; it was something that already embodied an understanding. Human eyes were *not* mere windows from which the soul looked out, because vision was not separable from understanding. The human eye recognised objects which it knew; it paid attention to some things and ignored others; its responded as it scanned and shifted to all kinds of interpreted stimuli. In that respect, human eyes were not at all like microscopes or spectroscopes.

The angels which had learned to see with human eyes had, perforce, to endure the filtering of information through the sieve of human understanding; their use of such 'instruments' was dependent upon the competence which the instruments already had.

Because of this, the angels' second-hand understanding of the human world was very vulnerable indeed to the dangers of human misunderstanding.

David already knew how the angel which Harkender now called Zelophelon had been betrayed by Harkender's particular vision of the world; it had accepted, along with his sight, his theories and his emotions. He already knew how Sir Edward Tallentyre had exposed the limits of Harkender's understanding, and had shown the angel how much more there was which needed to be seen and understood.

Now, he began to understand what had happened before that – ten thousand years ago, and perhaps much earlier. He understood why the Clay Man's *True History* was not a true history at all, but why it had seemed to be true, not only to the Clay Man but also to the angel which had, presumably with difficulty, moulded him from the matter which it possessed.

When the angels had first borrowed human senses, in order that they might look into the material world and see it as men saw it, they had inherited all the idols of the primitive human understanding. They had seen the universe which primitive – newly conscious – men had seen, and had understood it by means of the same rough-hewn notions. They had literally *seen* the world as an animate thing full of spirits, made by strange and perverse Creators. It had seemed to the angels, as it had seemed to the men who inhabited the material world, that the Earth must have fallen away from a state of earlier perfection to its present ruination; they had inevitably come to imagine the universe in much the same way.

The angels had really believed in the Golden Age which the Clay Man had tried to describe, but they had inherited that belief, unwittingly, from the misunderstandings of men.

The angels had accepted all that they had learned from the men they possessed; they had been unable to separate truth from illusion. It was not so very foolish of them. If the lenses of microscopes were afflicted with the disease of faith, confounding the reality of what was seen through them with all manner of false idols, how could the scrupulous human scientist separate truth from illusion? The only guide he would have would be the degree to which microscopes agreed and disagreed with one another, but if all microscopes held certain false idols in common, how extraordinarily valuable an atheist miscroscope would be!

Was that, David wondered, why Tallentyre had shocked Zelophelon so profoundly? Was that why Machalalel, if he were *not* just the figment of a dream within a dream, had taken the trouble to communicate with him?

The angels were not gods, but as soon as they had linked their own intelligences to those of the primitive men they first possessed, they had inevitably come to see themselves as gods. That was the only way in which primitive men had been able to name them and fit them in to their own model of the universe.

Names did matter, because names helped to form images and in the end became the controllers of those images.

Primitive men had tried to understand the angels which possessed them by distorting them into the images of gods. Perhaps, for a time, the angels really had repaid the compliment. Perhaps, briefly, there really had been an age of little miracles, when at least a few of the gods which men had made had responded to their expectations and their urgings.

Even so, David knew, Lucian de Terre's *True History* was simply a catalogue of myths. It was a human interpretation of a story concocted by the angels out of human interpretations of their own nature and descent: a vicious circle of mistakes and illusions.

There could be no further doubt as to the truth of certain matters, David decided, in spite of what the *True History* argued about the mutability of the world of appearances and the deceptiveness of apparent relics of past eras. The world was ancient; it had existed for thousands of millions of years before the evolution of human sentience had created the conditions which allowed a number of angels to possess their new senses and become persuaded that they were gods. And it had been that conviction of their own godhood which had made the angels fearful of a God of gods; a mysterious ultimate Creator who had made the universe of matter and set them to preside over it.

For all that he was only a man, very tiny compared with the angels and utterly impotent to wreak the kind of havoc and destruction which they could wreak, David was convinced that he saw more clearly with the aid of the new sense which he borrowed from them, and the power of his own intellect, than the angels themselves had ever seen – or ever could have seen – by means of their parasitism of the senses of primitive men. It was not that his intellect was greater in power than the intellect of the angels; perhaps, indeed, it was because his intellect was less powerful. The simple fact was that his was the frame of mind which *could* understand, given only the right point of view and the right imaginative lever.

David *saw* and understood what the angels were, as best he could within the limits of his understanding.

He saw, too, what the others saw.

He now understood, or thought he did, why the angels had not contented themselves with an oracle based in a single human consciousness. They knew how fallible and how very various human understanding was, and so they had sought to possess six minds, bridging them all as intimately as they could, in order to filter out their idiosyncrasies by combining their insights. He also understood, or thought he did, why that had simply been one more mistake. Two eyes see better than one, but only if they are in harmony. The compound eye of a fly, he supposed, must work well enough; but he took leave to doubt that the mere multiplication of images was an adequate substitute for proper focusing.

David knew that what the others saw, when added to his own vision, might only create confusion upon confusion; and he had reason to suspect that there was one among the greater company of angels who had known this even before the present experiment had begun. That fact alone, he knew, must be enough to terrify the three collaborators. The knowledge that whatever they learned Machalalel knew already – and that Machalalel had taken care to make sure that they discovered it – would certainly spoil any victory they believed they had attained.

In spite of his conviction, also endorsed by Machalalel, that he alone saw clearly what there was to be seen with the aid of the angels' own power of sight, David was very interested in what the others could and did see. He was not so vain as to think that his own understanding could not be further enhanced, and now that the pain of alien perception had faded into background noise, his curiosity had become powerful.

While he built his own understanding from what he saw, he looked into the minds of his companions. While he did so, they looked into his; but what he borrowed from them, and they from him, remained a matter of individual inclination, confused by the baleful influence of particular idols of false belief. The six humans had to share their insights, because they could not conceal them, but there was nothing to compel them to attain any unanimity of understanding.

De Lancy was the one who saw least and understood least. He had been used by the Sphinx as a virtual slave, forbidden by her to see or remember anything but what she had wanted him to see and remember. Since that evil night in the Egyptian desert he had virtually ceased to exist as a free and rational being. He had no resources at all which he could profitably bring to the task of making sense of his experience.

To de Lancy, the alien sensations which flooded his intelligence remained incomprehensible, and the fact that he was potentially capable of sharing the instruments of understanding which his companions had made no difference. When the pain ceased, eventually, to ravage his soul, de Lancy was content to drift into a kind of limbo: a numb state of peace which actively refused all possibility of sensation.

David was surprised by the capacity which de Lancy had for refusal, and by the strange contentment which the other found in the suspension of all sensation. It was, he saw, a kind of bliss; and he realised that such an ability to transform Hell into a vapid, colourless kind of Heaven might be reckoned a gift by people of a certain turn of mind. He realised, too, that his own lack of interest in such a prospect might not necessarily be echoed by the angels, and that there might be grounds for hoping that they were far more intrigued and tempted by it.

Perhaps, he thought, de Lancy might be reckoned to have found nirvana – and if only the angels could be persuaded that it was a worthwhile end or ambition, they too might condescend to accept a similar numbness and passivity.

Perhaps, David thought – although he knew how futile it was to manufacture lies – de Lancy had the best attitude of all; perhaps de Lancy had found the only kind of paradise which intelligent minds could ever reach.

He tried to be modest about his own determination to avoid such an end at all costs.

Luke Capthorn was probably less intelligent than any of his merely human companions, not having had the benefit of any but the most rudimentary education, but he had not de Lancy's crippling disadvantages. He had been alive and alert these last twenty years, and he was by no means so stupid as to have learned nothing from his long association with Jason Sterling. His secret Satanism, however absurd it seemed to the critical eye, had at least served to equip him imaginatively for extraordinary experiences.

Thus forearmed, Luke came through the initial barrier of pain with difficulty; but when the effect of it began to lessen he greedily embraced the conviction that what had happened was that the god he had chosen had brought him through the fire, to live in Pandemonium as a favoured servant instead of a mere victim.

Thus, where de Lancy found a particular kind of Heaven, Luke found a particular kind of Hell, and nothing he saw in the minds of his companions was adequate to shake his faith in it.

Luke never lost consciousness of his pain, even when it became bearable and might have been ignored. Deliberately, he clung to it, not out of any masochistic perversity but for an oddly philosophical motive of which David was mildly surprised to find him capable.

In Luke's rudimentary philosophy, the whole world – the whole universe – was perpetually saturated with pain. Like Schopenhauer, of whom he had never heard, Luke had seen the incontrovertible truth that for living things, the universe has far more misfortune in it than happiness, and that the will to survive at all costs is in a way perverse, always wagering against the odds. But Luke had not allowed his appreciation of this fact to make him miserable, even though he had never conceived in his own mind the Schopenhauerian enterprise of substituting the power of an Idea for the force of the Will. He had no need to, having followed the simpler strategy of accepting the duty of worshipping evil and taking the Devil for his god.

Luke had steeled himself to bear misfortune, misery and the fundamental discomfort of life, asking in exchange only that he should see how much greater were the misfortunes and miseries of others. He was prepared to suffer with Lucifer in Hell, in exchange for the power to inflict torment himself: that was his dearest and most secret desire – and that was what he was delighted to discover in the universe revealed to him by the alien sense which was given to him to share.

Luke saw the fervent and frantic universe of action and confusion as an illimitable fiery furnace, embracing everything with its sound and its fury. He saw it as a laughing thing, mocking the feeble pretensions of cold and lumpen material beings which hoped to find any kind of peace and solace outside the grave. De Lancy's limbo Luke saw simply as voluntary nonexistence: the ultimate cowardice. The angels, of course, he saw as the vast company of Satan, cast down from some still-mysterious Heaven by the armoured hosts of God, but given the material universe by way of compensation, as their torture ground for making merry.

David's ideas were as open to Luke's inspection as Luke's were to his, but Luke took no account of them. Unlike David or Harkender, Luke had been tricked into this experience; he had not come armed with curiosity, or with the special courage required to sharpen curiosity. He had made a choice of sorts in yielding himself up to the oracle, but the choice itself had embodied idols of false belief which now grew so huge and powerful that they could not be broken.

David was as anxious that the angels should ignore Luke's perverse fantasy as he was desirous that they should take heed of de Lancy's; but he realised that no matter how confident he was of the truthfulness of his own vision, the angels might not have sufficient power of discrimination to acknowledge his correctness. There was, he had to suppose, a real danger that one or more of the angels might find a destiny in what Luke Capthorn offered.

In the real world, there was no Devil – but there might be, if one or other of the angels were sufficiently beguiled by the possibility.

David tried with all his mental might to condemn Luke's idols and call them stupid. While he was doing it, he cried out to the observing angels that they must have heard *that* interpretation of the world before, in ancient times – and must therefore have set it aside then, even before they withdrew from the world of men. Alas, that only made him realise that there were still questions left unanswered, enigmas not yet understood.

Why, he wondered, had the angels 'gone to sleep' ten thousand years ago? And why were they 'awakening' now?

In Hecate's vision, perhaps surprisingly, he found a very different set of interpretations.

David had already formed certain hypotheses regarding the reasons for Hecate's placement within the human world. Her maker, to whom he had not yet been able to attach a name, seemed to have been attempting to bracket the gamut of human experience in possessing Sterling and creating the crippled girl. The angel had moved Sterling very subtly, taking great care not to let him become aware of the fact that he was influenced from outside; it had used and valued him as a man of bold intellect and considerable insight, much as Bast had used Tallentyre or as Zelophelon had used Harkender. Hecate, on the other hand, had been deliberately formed to be slow and stupid, innocent of preconceptions; she had been made in order to be an outsider within the human community, unable to share in any but its meagrest rewards, but able to bear witness to its horrors.

David could only wonder at the fact that Hecate did not, like Luke Capthorn, see the greater universe as a pit of suffering constantly teased and tormented by the imps of Hell.

Instead, Hecate saw the greater universe as a kind of theatre.

David had briefly shared Mercy Murrell's world-view, and knew what a deep contempt the bawd had for the emotions and impulses of men, which, in her view, took their honest form only when the most restrictive shackles of morality were temporarily shed. That was what her brothel had been designed to permit; although it had limitations of its own, it stood in the relation of a moral utopia to the tyrannies of Victorian society, allowing a few concealed desires to find a kind of expression. Mercy Murrell was fiercely cynical about those covert desires, having seen their elaborate expression in violence, abuse and calculated perversity, all of which made victims of the members of that sex which men were supposed to revere, protect and love. David could hardly have blamed Hecate if she had formed a similar opinion, but she had not.

Hecate had *not* learned to see the world of men as a seething cauldron of repressed hatreds and evil impulses; Hecate had selected a single facet of her not quite merciless experience on which to build a personal philosophy. She saw the world of men as a theatre writ large: as a place of pretence and a place of drama.

Within the space of her miserable existence, the parts she was given to play in Mrs Murrell's pornographic dramas had been the only things Hecate had ever truly understood. They were the only active responsibilities with which she had ever been trusted. Those trivial mimes, whether comic or pathetic, had been the intervals of her existence in which she seemed to *live*, instead of being merely a misshapen lump of human clay, pummelled and pounded by constant misfortune.

Now, released from a brief period of more absolute servitude in which she had been her maker's hand and voice, she had been given another standpoint from which to look out upon the whole of Creation, and she had imposed upon it the same frame of reference.

Hecate endured with consummate patience the interval of blind agony, and in coming to herself again had little difficulty in perceiving and recognising the innate theatricality of the universe entire. The excited plenitude of the sense-world of the angels was to her the purest confusion, yet she did not for a moment presume that it was actually chaotic; she merely accepted that it was beyond the reach of her poor powers of comprehension. The duller, slower, colder world of matter, which was in and of that buzzing and booming maelstrom and yet was free of some of its awful turbulence, she saw as a play – a mode of activity bound by a kind of script which made it infinitely safer and more certain, and essentially manageable.

Because she saw it as a play, she never doubted for a moment that the world of objects had a plot; that its history had shape, meaning and purpose; that it was intended to evoke particular effects and emotions upon the minds of hypothetical observers. She did not doubt that the world was possessed of narrative tension and suspense; that it would have some kind of climax and denouement; that it would be guided from beginning to end by the fictive principles of melodrama. She did not doubt that the desolation of space was but a stage, on which many plays might be staged in their turn, each and every one partaking of the same qualities and yet being individual.

David understood how similar this pattern of metaphors was to the notion of the world which the angels had once acquired from newly sentient men. He remembered that the notion of a series of Creations was fundamental to many myth systems, and that each one could indeed be imagined as having the qualities of a drama enacted upon the universal stage.

He realised, too – coldly and fearfully – that beings like the angels had the power to make it so. The world of matter was, in the end, governed by the complicated transactions of the molten hyperreality which lay behind and beneath the emptiness of space and the orderliness of time. The angels, operating in that hyperreality, had the power to alter the world of matter: the world as it appeared to men and all the other inhabitants of planets. The angels were capable of planning planetary histories, of writing scripts which whole species – even whole life systems – might be recruited to enact.

There was small comfort in knowing that the angels were not gods, if they were capable of doing all that gods were supposed to do, in respect of the inhabitants of one tiny worldlet – or a dozen, or a thousand tiny worldlets – briefly crystallised out of the cosmic alkahest.

Hecate, David realised, offered the angels a way of life, a possible *raison d'être*, which they might conceivably take. They might, if they saw their way clear, decide to appoint themselves godly overlords and make the Earth their puppet theatre, as some of them might, perhaps, have done once before, if there ever had been an authentic Age of Miracles or Age of Heroes.

Except, David reassured himself, that they seemingly had more urgent concerns. The angels had fears of their own, and they apparently had the utmost difficulty in combining their efforts in any collective enterprise. Drama, in order to be properly executed, required leisure. He was not certain that the angels *had* leisure, and harboured a strong suspicion that they did not.

In the enmity and confusion of potential gods, David saw, might lie the real hope for human freedom and human progress. Given that the universe did contain beings which might be capable of planning human history and forcing the world to conform to their plan, it was best to hope that they could not spare the time or coordinate any such effort.

Even so, he realised, the heretic priests of the Order of St Amycus – who believed in the existence of such a drama, and had spent centuries trying to divine the twists and turns of its plot, and to anticipate the scheme of its denouement – might not be such fools after all.

Sterling, of course, saw things very differently. Like Luke Capthorn, he had been tricked into participation in the oracle, and very casually tricked, but once enlightenment became possible he had no idols of false belief to screen him from the truth. All his life he had tried to cast down such idols; all his life he had been curious to see what lay behind and beyond the sturdiest pillars of man's belief.

Sterling was not so confused as to refuse the power of David's vision; nor was he so modest as to refuse the assumption that he might enhance and improve it.

Sterling's understanding of what was happening was so close to David's, and so enthusiastic to borrow from it, that it was not until David came to interrogate and reassess what he had gained that he realised how much the other had contributed to the resources of his own understanding. What he had first thought of as *his* vision was really *their* vision, to a considerable extent.

As a man of science, Sterling recruited similar words in order to get a grip on what he saw, and because he had access to David's own thoughts he was able to borrow whenever his own inspiration was momentarily lacking. There were slight differences, however, between the overlapping interpretations which they synthesised. Sterling's essential interests were different from David's, coloured by his own particular history and his own theories. He had not had David's long and intimate acquaintance with the angels, and was far less inclined to dwell upon the detailed implications of the revelation of their nature, or to compile a commentary on the puzzles and challenges which knowledge of their existence had posed to David. He was much more interested in the astonishing universe which was revealed to him by the magical extension of his mind to include a sixth sense, and much more interested in the processes of evolution that went on within it. Sterling it was who strove with all his might to build an understanding of universal change and process.

Like David, Sterling knew that he might only be inventing a story, using fictions and misleading words to paper over the abundant fissures in his understanding, but like David he was not discouraged by that knowledge, only trying all the harder to do the best he could. He, moreover, had actually read *The True History of the World*, and believed that he had a better understanding of the allegory which it contained.

Sterling found, in the present state of the evolving universe, many evidences of its past. He understood that the world of matter must belong to a late phase of the universe's development, and that there must have been a time before it, which he likened in his mind to Lucian de Terre's Golden Age.

After the the beginning of time, he supposed, everything must have been in flux; there would have been no atoms to begin with, and no order; there had been energy, but its effects had been quite random. It must have been a nascent, pregnant kind of chaos, but all potential, with nothing in it of decay. Even when atoms were first born they would not have been eternal in existence or in kind; in those days they came into being and were lost, and they changed constantly without ever achieving identity; while they existed, they were in a perpetual state of *becoming*.

Clinamen, which name he naturally elected to apply to the seed of order, must have been a special kind of change. Of all the infinite changes which the atoms explored with their being and becoming, some were inevitably of a special kind which generated patterns and sequences, and it was these emergent patterns that became the basis, not only of entities and objects, but also of forces and relations. Collectively, he decided, the seeds of order might be seen as an array of diseases which were ultimately bound to consume chaos, converting it into scheme, pattern and system – but the process could not be a smooth one, because the patterning influences were in competition, contradicting one another. This process of ordering was by now well advanced.

It must have been in an earlier phase of this ongoing conflict, Sterling concluded, that some kind of consciousness had first emerged. Perhaps long before there were stars and planets, while the universe was still very young, there had been minds of some kind. These must have been the remotest ancestors of those beings which Lucian de Terre called Creators: bred from the conflict of the different kinds of *clinamen*, diffuse and disembodied but nevertheless able to exert the pattern-making forces which had given birth to them and were the essence of their existence.

When the first galaxies of stars began to form, Sterling guessed, the war between the proto-Creators would already have been in full swing. Long before there were worlds which could be cradles for organic life, there were probably minds, and long before there were molecules which could build the fabric of organic entities, there were things which might have been reckoned to be alive.

The history which the Clay Man had written contained, Sterling believed, not only the story of the Earth but that of many other worlds. It was, in its rough-hewn fashion, an allegory of how life came down from the spaces between the stars to colonise the waters and the rocks of worlds. It was likewise an allegory of the evolution of life on worlds, from proto-cellular entities to bacteria to protozoa to plants and animals, and from animals to man. It was the story of the creation of all things, but it was inevitably told as if it were simply the story of the making of mankind, to whose emergence all else was subsidiary.

Like David, Sterling found it difficult to find ready answers to such questions as what were the Creators made of. He could only take recourse in dubious formulae. He understood that they had no particular substance of their own, although they could not have existed in their present forms, had there been no substance to inhabit. He decided that the best way to grasp what they were was to think of them as concentrations of *clinamen*: as agglomerations of order-creating potentiality, capable of intention and strategy, in themselves immaterial but not independent of matter. The words he found to allow him to imagine what the angels were argued that they had no forms which were uniquely their own, but were instead pure formativeness.

By this means Sterling sought to understand what the *True History* meant when it stated that many Creators had exhausted their Creativity, and that others had become very anxious to conserve theirs lest they be exhausted in their turn. He supposed that the angels were indeed at war with one another, and had been from the very beginning; and that the ability to prey on one another – to absorb and corrupt one another's pattern-making potential – must have been something which emerged from the process of their own mental evolution.

Sterling decided that there must be in worldly life, and in the kind of intelligence which eventually evolved within it, a pattern-making tendency which was not unlike that which the angels had – or, more precisely, that which the angels *were*. It operated, he presumed, at a very different level. What the Creators did worked at a fundamental level, more elementary than the level of the atoms of which all physical things are made; but the patterning which living things did – and which, by the same token, they might be reckoned to *be* – operated on a much cruder scale. The work of the Creators could, obviously, have effects at the scale on which life operated – effects which would necessarily appear to human beings miraculously uncaused – but those effects were achieved in a fashion which was very different from the fashion in which living things, including men, transformed their environment.

Like David, Sterling was content to call the power of the angels 'magical', but he was equally cautious in doing so. Because he could not say what was meant by magic except that it interrupted and subverted the patterns of cause and effect, he felt that it must be deemed a purely negative term signifying a void of understanding; but he felt an urgent and passionate desire to fill that void.

Sterling was not content to know that magic was workable, and yet be unable to master it; what he desired, more than anything else in the world, was to have the alchemical power to defeat the threat of death. As soon as he understood what it was that was happening to him in this strange, shared dream, the principal focus of his effort to understand became concentrated on that one goal. Although he did not become as completely bound up in his own particular interpretation of the hyper-world as Luke Capthorn, he became selective in what he attended to. He borrowed from the sight of the others with whom he shared the dream only that which complemented and completed his own obsessive quest.

In his way, Sterling saw as far as David – perhaps even farther – but his was still a partial experience, in which much that he might have taken heed of was ignored. He was by no means ashamed of that, being of the school of thought which held that a good memory was one adept in forgetting, and that a sharp eye was one which knew how to screen out everything but the object of concentration. Sterling actively tried to cultivate dreams: dreams of future possibility; dreams of the potential evolution of mankind and all organic life.

David could appreciate the virtue of that attitude, but he found greater fascination in certain questions which Sterling was content to dismiss as irrelevant. He wondered whether Tallentyre, if he had been allowed to take part in this adventure, might have done as Sterling did, and perhaps extended the boundaries of their collective experience even further.

The overlapping vision which David Lydyard and Jason Sterling shared was not entirely a two-way collaboration. It was also fed and shared, albeit in a peculiar fashion, by Jacob Harkender. Harkender's contribution was, however, far more interesting to David than to Sterling, and David felt that he had borrowed more from Harkender in formulating his own reactions than Sterling had in formulating his.

Harkender had formed his own ideas of what the angels were long before David had first been possessed. He had learned by his own efforts to isolate his consciousness from the stream of earthly events, and from the temptations of self-supplied delusions, sufficiently to interact with the minds of the angels. He believed, still, that it was his probing which had awakened Zelophelon from inertia. He believed that he had found the angel rather than the angel finding him. Perhaps it was true.

Harkender, stimulated by the particular alloy of pain and humiliation which had at first been thrust upon him, and which in time he had learned to cultivate, had already caught fugitive glimpses of the reality which lay on the far side of the blinding light. He had already mastered certain tricks of a magical kind, discovering ways to use a little of the potential inherent in the interpenetration of the world of matter by the consciousness of the angels. Like Mandorla's magic, Harkender's was very feeble, but it was real.

For nearly twenty years, Harkender had lived hardly at all in the realm of his own senses; he had given himself over as far as he possibly could to the sight of the inner eye, managed and motivated by the angel Zelophelon. He was far better adapted to sensory symbiosis with the angels than any of his companions – even David, whose dreams had been so sorely troubled for so long.

As they passed through the blinding light, therefore, agonised by the flames of supernatural awareness, only Jacob Harkender believed that he already knew what was happening, and what they would find on the far side of that vivid fire.

Harkender took it for granted that of the six of them, *he* would see farthest and clearest; that *his* would be the vision which would concentrate and unify the oracle. He fully expected that Sterling and David Lydyard would learn the folly of their former ways of thought, and be irredeemably infected with his esoteric wisdom. He had no doubt that his own world-view was right, but he thought that even if it were wrong, his authority would be amply sufficient to impress its stamp on the entire company. This was something he was desperately ardent to accomplish; it was a salve for his pride which he had sought all his life. Only Tallentyre, he imagined, might have had stubbornness enough to stand him off – and Tallentyre had been deliberately excluded from the oracle.

In all this, Harkender was mistaken. He found the world beyond the light far more difficult of apprehension and comprehension than he had ever imagined, too slippery to be grasped by his imagination, in spite of all the tempering to which his rebel soul had been subjected.

It might have been better, in a way, had his idols of false belief been as jealous and as powerful as those which Luke Capthorn had, or which de Lancy quickly contrived to erect as a shield. That way, at least, he might have clung to his illusions. He was, however, an essentially honest man and he knew far too much about the world and its ways to make himself stupid by self-deceit.

Harkender quickly realised that it was David Lydyard and Jason Sterling, reinforcing and amplifying one another's insights and constructions, who were efficiently coming to terms with the produce of their enhanced vision. He could neither deny nor defy what they were doing, nor wrench it out of shape to suit his own vocabulary of images and ideas. He could not hide in innocence, as Hecate, Luke and de Lancy could. He learned, and felt himself punished in being forced to do it. And what he gave to them in return – what he, in his own particular fashion, contributed to their joint enlightenment – was as unexpected to him as it was to David.

Had David been alone, or had he had only Sterling to help him build his understanding, that understanding would have been essentially clinical. It could never have taken on the emotional coloration of Luke Capthorn's demonic dream, because that was so obviously false. But Harkender did insert into their vision a powerful emotional charge, because he understood what they came to understand, and became a true collaborator in its making, and his reaction to it was far more corrosive and subversive by virtue of that fact.

Harkender, when he was finally forced to see the true import of what men like David and Sterling – and Tallentyre – believed, could not refuse it. He saw the sheer intellectual power and glory of what they were doing, and could not close his inner eye against that enlightenment. And in seeing that, he was forced also to see that his own carefully erected edifices of imperfect wisdom had been built on the treacherous sand of his frustrations, his resentments and his all-consuming lust for revenge against the world which had treated him so cruelly.

He understood that the calculatedly heretical beliefs which had been part and parcel of his pose as a magician had, as he had always thought, arisen out of the enlightening force of the pain of too many beatings and too many rapes; but he understood, too, that what he had made was fashioned far more by the power of desire than by the power of clear sight.

As a child, impotent in the hands of callous torturers, all the desire of which he had been capable had been refined into a longing to be able to strike back: to bring down the wrath of the gods upon those who abused him. What he had looked for and lusted after, when he made himself a magician and went in search of the gods, was their wrath – but the wrath which he had so confidently expected to find, and so desperately hoped to control, was only his own wrath, hugely enlarged by the optimism of his will.

What Harkender had hoped and expected to find on the far side of the blinding light was not simply a realm inhabited by gods, but a realm infused with the searing heat of vengeance, which might arm him with thunderbolts to aim at all his enemies – which category included, in his thinking, all the men in the world; for behind his particular tormentors, lending tacit endorsement to his ill-treatment by commending the system which sanctioned it, stood every man on Earth.

Now, Harkender realised belatedly how childish that had been; how literally childish all attempted magic was. He realised that the seemingly boundless ignominy which had been heaped upon him, spoiling his life and spoiling the universe apprehended by his senses, had, after all, been mere bullying. At the time, it had seemed to be a concatenation of events as frightful as the Apocalypse, and he had never outgrown the horror which had been scored and rammed into his very soul, but he saw now that in the scheme of things, it really was trivial and temporary. Now, seeing as David Lydyard and Jason Sterling could see, he understood that the brave thing to do – the sensible thing to do – would have been to wait for its inevitable end, and then to put it behind him in order to live as best he could.

Harkender had not been able to do that. He had never before thought of that inability as failure; he had always thought of it as an awakening to the frightful reality of human injustice, as an unquenchable ambition to achieve righteous revenge; but he saw it as failure now.

He could see it as failure now not simply because he was able to look into the minds and hearts of David Lydyard and

Jason Sterling, and understand their attitude to the world, but also because the groundwork for such a fall had been laid during the many long years of his servitude as a master of seers.

David, sharing Harkender's dream, saw and understood what he had already guessed: that Jacob Harkender had used his wife Cordelia as a seer. He also saw and understood the curious and perverse love for his wife which Harkender had cultivated, nurtured and savoured. Harkender, in his turn, saw and understood David's love for his wife, and understood David's reaction to the knowledge that Harkender knew Cordelia far more intimately than he ever could.

It was a very strange experience, for both of them.

Harkender had previously taken pleasure in David's ignorance, but he found it impossible to take such pleasure now. When the opportunity arrived for him to be cruel, he shirked it; there was not sufficient evil in him to let him gloat. Even without that extra twist of the knife, Harkender could have understood it if this particular revelation had been the nearest thing to Hell which David had encountered in the realm of the angels; but David had been educated by Sir Edward Tallentyre, and he reacted to this ugly fact as he had been trained to react to all discoveries: if it were so, then he must live with it. David Lydyard had what Harkender had never had: the courage to accept that although events could hurt him, he must never despair.

On the other hand, David was surprised to find consolation in what might have been the most painful aspect of the confirmation of his suspicion. He found that the fact that Harkender had learned, in his fashion, to love Cordelia did not add a further dimension of offensive insult to the injury, but made it instead more easily bearable. David had always loved his wife, and he understood that if that were so, he must consider her worthy to be loved. He could not blame Harkender for making that discovery, any more than he could blame Harkender for what Zelophelon had made him. So David forgave Jacob Harkender for knowing what he should never have been permitted to know, and Harkender accepted David's forgiveness.

That was the beginning of their mutual understanding, but not the end.

It was the chastened Harkender, not either of the mentally stretched men of science, who infused their vision with an acute sense of emotional significance. He it was, after all, who had hoped to find in the fervent confusion of plenitude a massive charge of righteous wrath, and had found nothing of the kind; he it was who felt the absence of that wrath, and anything else which might have stood in place of it.

The angels, Harkender realised, and communicated to his cooler fellows, *could* if they so chose become godly overlords of mankind; but if they did they would not be, and could not be, either of the kinds of god in which men had so long tried to believe. They would not be, and could not be, righteously angry, carefully punitive gods; and they would not be, and could not be, moral, merciful and loving gods. They would be callous, arbitrary, exacting gods from whom neither favour nor fairness could be expected; they would be bullying gods. They might, if they saw fit, condescend to play games with mankind, writing scripts for the race to perform, but such games and scripts would be essentially careless of human needs, desires and ambitions.

As flies to wanton boys . . .

It was through Harkender that David came to realise that Luke Capthorn was not quite such a fool as his view of the angels implied. If the angels decided to play at being gods, they would indeed be Satanic. Although they had never in fact been cast down from Heaven, and had no ready-made interest in tempting and torturing human beings, the effects which they had on human existence would be very similar.

Harkender imparted to his companions the appalling dangerousness of the universe which they had discovered by sharing the angels' powers of sight. He made them see and feel the horror of the fact that all the angels – including, and especially, Zelophelon – could be reckoned devils.

And Jacob Harkender, now that he had truly passed through the flame and come into his heritage of wisdom, belatedly discovered that he was not of the Devil's party after all.

That was almost the whole of the vision which David and his companions had – *almost*. The rest of it was very difficult indeed to demystify; but at least he understood why it was so nearly incomprehensible. The participants in the vision were, after all, nine in number and not six. While the humans donated their powers of thought and sight to the angels, the angels by necessity imparted theirs.

Alas, the thoughts of the angels were so very alien as to lie almost entirely beyond the limits of human comprehension.

But the angels were not gods; they were beings, like men, which had plans and projects, anxieties and fears, and things which they devoutly desired to know.

One question, more elementary than the rest, David had already posed for them: *How many angels could dance on that infinitesimal pinhead which was the Earth?*

How and why it was that they required the effort of combined human and angel senses to answer that question David could not quite grasp, but he grasped the answer.

The number of the angels which were anchored in and to the Earth was seven.

Six other beings like Bast were anchored to the bubble of lumpen matter which was the Earth; two of them were Zelophelon and Hecate's maker. Of the four others, he could put a name to only one: Machalalel.

David was not certain of the exact and full significance of this revelation, but he took comfort from one aspect of it. The three angels which had conspired to seize and use him were outnumbered, even on Earth. That fact should inspire them to caution, and certainly did not encourage recklessness.

That, he thought, must be reckoned hopeful; he was very enthusiastic to find *something* hopeful to carry back to the world of men.

David was certain that there were other Creators associated with other worlds, and probably others anchored in the stars and in the dust between the stars; the total number of such beings, though undoubtedly finite, must be very great. Any one of them probably had power enough to annihilate all life on Earth, if it were so disposed, but such an act would probably never be risked by any single angel; such an expenditure of its creative potential would surely weaken it so drastically as to open the way for its own destruction by its fellows.

What he had learned of the angels before and during his experience encouraged David to think that the possibility of their forming an alliance to destroy the world in concert might be remote. He was, in any case, forced to hope so.

But there was one more possibility which he and Sterling had discovered in the course of their oracular vision, and which must now be known to the three angels, even if one or more of them had not realised it before. Each Creator might, if it were clever enough, work upon earthly life in a subtle and magically inexpensive fashion, introducing potential for change which might then be amplified by the patterning potentials inherent in life itself.

This, David guessed, one or more of the Creators which inhabited the Earth might already have done, perhaps at various times in the distant past. Machalalel had seemingly attempted tentative ventures of some such kind, among whose results were Mandorla's werewolves and the Clay Man. If the three Creators which had used him had not known this until they received the intelligence from the oracle which they created, they certainly knew it now.

How they might use that knowledge, and to what ends, he could only guess.

4

David found himself standing in the gloomy interior of the great pyramid. Bast was on her throne, as huge as she usually was. Her cats moved restlessly back and forth on the cold stone floor.

David reached down to pick up one of the animals. He cradled it in his arms, stroking its golden fur. It purred.

He looked up into the gloom, and met the staring eyes of the pretended goddess.

'You don't need this any longer,' said David harshly. 'These trappings – that awe-inspiring ruined city – are meaningless now. You have nothing to gain by showing yourself to me in this fashion, and you can't need it as a mirror of your own being. In the *true* history of the world, there are no gods. The shadows cast on the walls of the cave by the flickering firelight are only shadows, after all. We have climbed up to the light at the mouth of the cave, you and I. We have looked out into the world beyond, together.'

'Would you have me come to your house in Kensington?' asked the goddess. 'Would you have me dress in crinoline and lace, and leave my motor car with your respectful servant? Would you have me take tea with your wife? Or should we meet as gentlemen, at your club, to sit before the fire in the smoking room? If this is all unnecessary pretence, what would *that* be?'

As she spoke, he felt a curious sense of triumph swelling within him. She had never condescended to trade defensive sarcasms with him. He wondered whether the fact that she had chosen to resume her gargantuan status might be symptomatic of her unease.

Make demands, Machalalel had said.

'All this has served its purpose,' David said dismissively. 'In the theatre of dreams, even fantasies have meaning, and there are meanings which can only be conveyed in fantasy. But we understand one another far better now than we did before. Perhaps we can't meet as equals, but there is nothing any longer to be gained by maintaining your pose as a mighty god. You're an aspect of the evolution of the universe, as am I; together we're cleverer than either of us could be, were we apart. You need me now more than you did before; my senses and intelligence have been well educated, and your rivals have Sterling and Harkender. I don't ask to be released, but I have conditions to make for my continued servitude.'

She leaned forward on her clumsy and uncomfortable throne, and her eyes gleamed. 'Whatever I am,' she said, 'I have the power of life and death over everything that you hold dear. Everything!'

'You have the power to torment and destroy me,' David agreed. 'Just as I have the power to agonise and amputate my own right arm. Would you blind yourself to spite a rebellious eye? How you might delight Zelophelon or Hecate's maker by so doing! You need me – not any man chosen at random, but *me*. Without human senses and human intelligence you can't even begin to understand what you are, and nothing but the best-educated human intelligence will suffice. You were misled before, but you know better now; and you must realise that a much finer understanding will one day be possible, if only you'll wait for the explorations of human science to proceed. You have the power to annihilate the human race, but that would be a very stupid thing to do, would it not? Far better to protect it, to urge it on to greater efforts of the collective will. We're very tiny and very weak, but we are necessary.'

'I can wipe that knowledge from your mind,' said the goddess. 'All this was but a dream, and is easily forgotten.'

'Certainly,' said David. 'If you dare not pluck out the eye which has offended you, at least you might blindfold it. If only you could agree with your collaborators that Sterling and Harkender should be blindfolded too . . . if only you could trust them to do it!

'We both know what the truth is, and from now on, I shall have propositions to put which may be to our mutual advantage. Now that we've been allowed to see ourselves and to know what we really are, I believe that we have a clearer idea of what we might do for one another. Let's forget threats and entreaties, and deal with one another as intelligent beings.'

Nothing changed. She still sat on her enormous throne, looking down at him from a great height; but it seemed to David that her eyes did not gleam so brightly with inner fire.

'What is it that you want me to do?' she asked, in her low and intense voice. 'Your children have already awakened in their beds, and their dreams of being wolves are beginning to fade away from the grasp of their waking minds. Your wife is awake and perfectly well. She is no more than usually anxious for the fate of those she loves. You have been ill with a fever, and are asleep in your bed, but you are soon to wake. No one has called at your house – no one at all. Nor were you ever bitten by the werewolf, although you have been more than usually troubled by the effects of your illness, and of the laudanum which you use to counter it. It was all a dream, you see. It was all a dream within a dream!'

The world of dreams is labyrinthine, David remembered, *and we can never really be sure that we have emerged again into the true world, or whether we have reached the heart of the maze.*

'You're more than usually tidy,' he said. 'What about Tallentyre and de Lancy? Did they ever leave Paris?'

'They are in London, but Tallentyre has not seen you yet. De Lancy is recovering from the injuries which he sustained in the shipwreck, but he too has been taking laudanum and has suffered a grave loss of memory. He remembers very little of what befell him after his accident in Egypt twenty years ago, and almost nothing of his more recent experiences. I doubt that he will ever recover his memory.'

'And Tallentyre is well, despite the trick which Zelophelon played on him in Hecate's Eden?'

'Perfectly well,' she said. 'The nightmare of his murder will not trouble him at all, for he will have more to remember than his death, if he remembers anything at all. But you still have not told me what it is that you want for yourself. Do you propose to wake up having enjoyed a miraculous cure? Or will you boldly ask for immortality?'

'I believe that can be left to your own judgement,' said David casually. 'It's for you to decide the point at which you might dare to cast me aside in favour of a cleverer substitute. I will have more demands to make, in time, but there's one more thing I must ask for Cordelia without delay. I want her protected from Harkender's prying eyes.'

'How would you ever know?' she countered. 'Do not suppose that what you have just done will ever be done again.'

'For your own good,' he said patiently, 'you should protect us all, as Zelophelon and Sterling's master will take care to protect *their* protégés.'

'Is that all, for now?'

'Not quite. It seems to me that if you can do it, it might be wise to free the werewolves from the curse which forces them to be human more often than they desire to be. Give them the power to choose. Not as a gift to me, but out of simple prudence.'

'What interest have I in the werewolves?' she asked.

'You have an interest in Machalalel. If your fragile alliance with Zelophelon and Hecate's maker can be held together, fear of what Machalalel might know is the most important bond which will secure it. You must be careful of the werewolves – and the Clay Man, too – simply because they exist and you don't know why. If you can help them, do it. If you can't, you'll know that they are, and always have been, the eyes and limbs of your most dangerous rival.'

Silence fell when David had finished speaking, but he would not be disconcerted; he continued to stare as levelly as he could into the great cat's eyes which loomed so high above him, glowing softly viridian in the dim light.

She did not promise anything, but he had expected that.

She had listened, and he knew that she would not have deigned to do even that, had she not felt it necessary to hear what he had to say. He knelt down to release the cat which he had been holding in his arms, stroking it gently all the while. Then he stood up again. He had not taken his eyes off hers for an instant.

'I can see you,' he said, very softly. 'I know you. I alone can look you in the eye, and know what lies behind whatever appearance you choose to present to me. You're not human, I know, but you are a thinking person. Aren't you lonely for the sight of eyes which may look into your own and have some inkling of what you are?'

She did not answer him.

She did not say anything at all.

But her silence no longer seemed eloquent; it merely seemed forlorn.

In Eden, Sir Edward Tallentyre awoke from a dream of darkness and desolation. He was lying beside a pool of water, but it was not the same pool in which the leech had attacked him. There was more shade here, because the pool was surrounded by trees bearing luscious red fruit; it was fed by a tiny waterfall whose soft sound filled the humid air.

As he sat up he realised that he was still naked, but there was no visible wound on his chest. He touched his fingers to his forehead and found it slick with sweat.

It was only then that he saw the woman watching him from the shade of the nearest tree. For a moment, in spite of her unusual clothing, he thought that she might be his daughter Cordelia, but then he saw that her face was actually quite different. Instinctively he moved to shield his groin with his thigh, made anxious by his nakedness.

'What happened?' Tallentyre asked, more harshly than he had intended. 'Where am I? Where is Sterling, and Adam Clay?'

'You are in Eden,' she replied.

'And you, no doubt, are Eve,' he said testily.

'No,' she answered, in a slightly mocking fashion. 'There is an Adam here, but no Eve.' Nevertheless, she plucked one of the fruits from the bough above her head, and tossed it to him. He tried to catch it, but it fell to the ground. He picked it up and looked at it suspiciously, as though expecting to find it riddled with worm holes. It was the size of his fist, but not very heavy.

'It is not poison,' she told him. 'Indeed, its sweetness is very pure and precious.'

He bit into it, and found that she spoke nothing less than the truth.

'I was wounded,' he said, 'or thought I was. But I've been in a place like this once before, and I remember how easily a wound may be healed in places of this kind.'

She smiled, but again he had the impression that she was laughing at him.

'Even death counts for little in Eden,' she told him. 'Here, injury is nothing and pain everything. But you feel no pain now.'

'I feel no pain,' he admitted. He bit into the fruit again, and ate it ravenously before looking up.

'It's sweet enough,' he said. 'But I learned nothing. I already knew that I was naked.'

She was joined then by a second person. It was a man, dressed far more incongruously than she, in clothes so ill-fitting that they might have been borrowed from another. She picked another fruit and gave it to him. 'This is my Adam,' she said to Tallentyre. 'Once fallen, now redeemed. You have met him before and you will meet him again, in a very different place, quite soon.'

Tallentyre and Adam Clay exchanged glances. Adam Clay did not seem astonished to see him fit and well again; Tallentyre guessed that the other man had arrived, as he had himself, at that state of mind where nothing was surprising. *In a certain sort of dream*, he thought, *one expects everything and nothing; there is no occasion for astonishment. Then, when one wakes, one has a frustrating sense of having lost a means of perfect understanding of the world and its ways*.

He looked the woman in the eye and said: 'Who are you?'

'That does not matter,' she told him. 'You will probably never see me again. What I shall be in future I do not know, and as for what I was before . . . I was a whore; only a whore.'

'Lilith,' said Tallentyre, as though he had been asked a riddle and was hazarding a guess. 'Your name is Lilith.'

'One name is as good as another,' she said. 'There is no power in names, until one knows exactly what they mean.'

'I am not so sure of that,' said Adam Clay. 'To give something a name is the beginning of the road which leads to understanding. Every further revelation of what the name implies is a step along the road. One day, we will find out how to name you properly, and know exactly what we mean when we speak of you. You may not always be able to change your names as easily as you change your appearances, in order to to hide from our understanding.'

Her only response to that was to laugh. But then she turned, and touched the Clay Man on the forehead. He became as still as a statue, robbed of life and time. She came forward, reaching out the same hand to Tallentyre's head.

'You ought to present yourself as an angel with a flaming sword,' he told her drily. 'Have you no sense of theatre at all?'

David had no sensation of a gradual awakening; his return was abrupt. His eyes were open, already adapted to the faintness of the flickering nightlight beside his bed. Nell was sitting in the chair, as though keeping vigil over him. She was wearing her nightgown.

He looked at her and felt the loving smile which was already engraved upon his features.

He was not entirely without pain, but the pain had abated. The ache in his back and the sullen burning of his joints had eased considerably. The sense of relief which swept over him drowned the residue of discomfort, and left him feeling giddy with joy.

'I had a dream,' said Nell tentatively.

'Did it frighten you?' he asked, still luxuriating in his freedom from pain.

'No,' she said. 'It wasn't a horrid dream, but I wanted to tell you about it as soon as I could, in case I forgot.'

'I think I can guess what you dreamed,' said David lightly. 'I think you dreamed that you were a wolf, and that Teddy and Simon were wolves too, and that you belonged to a pack of wolves who had a dark lair in a great forest.'

He watched the amazement in her eyes, taking a curious pleasure in his power to evoke it. 'How did you know?' she asked. 'Did you dream it too?'

'Yes,' he said. 'I think my dream and yours must have got mixed up. It happens sometimes.'

'I could see that you were dreaming,' she said. 'That's why I waited for you to wake up. You were making strange noises, the way you do when you're hurting. But you're better now, aren't you?'

David struggled to a sitting position, unhandicapped by any agony of movement but no less clumsy for that.

'Yes,' he said, revelling in the truth of it. 'I feel better. What day is it, Nell?'

'Monday,' she said, but then she paused. 'Well,' she amended, 'it *was* Monday. Now we've woken up, it must be Tuesday.'

David looked at his arm, which was unwounded and unbandaged. *It is all so easy!* he thought. *All the ills of the world might be cancelled out at a stroke, if only the angels cared enough to do it. Alas, they do not care at all.*

'Daddy,' said Nell, 'why do we dream?'

'Because we aren't machines,' he said softly. 'Because we have to think in order to live, and we have to feel in order to think. Dreaming is how we reach out with our minds to explore the unreal. Dreaming is to remind us that what our senses tell us about the world isn't the whole story, that what we see with our eyes is only the beginning of understanding.'

'I think it was nice to be a wolf,' she said. 'But I'm not sure. Now I'm awake, I don't know what it was like, but in the dream, it felt . . . as though nothing could hurt us.'

'I know,' he said. 'I know what you mean.'

'But you were hurting in your dream,' she said. 'I could see that. Why did your dream hurt when mine didn't?'

'Sometimes it's difficult to get away from hurt,' he said, 'even when you sleep. That's why I sometimes have to take medicine. It's the illness I have, you see.'

He showed her his hand, intending to let her see the swellings which marred the joints. The swellings were not as pronounced as they had been before, and the joints were not as painful.

'Why do we hurt?' she asked, with a frown of perplexity on her face. 'Teddy says that's what your work is – to find out why we hurt.'

'Pain is part of the price we pay for being able to think,' he told her. 'To be able to think and talk, we have to be conscious, but we can't just decide what to be conscious of, or we'd surround ourselves with lies. Pain is just part of the package. Particular pains tell us about particular injuries, but that's not all there is to it; pain reminds us that the world wasn't made for our convenience, that life itself is a struggle against hostile circumstances. Pain is a spur which urges us to see more clearly, to understand more fully.

'But one day, Nell, people will be masters of their pain instead of slaves to it. One day, people will figure out how to come to terms with pain, not by dulling it with laudanum,

...ut by taming it and making it harmless. *One* day, we'll find out how to lift all the curses that afflict us. *Then* we'll really be free. My work is part of that. It's only a small part, but because there are so many millions of men, the collective effect of all the small parts they play is potentially very great.

'I can't do very much myself, but there are countless others to take over when I can't do any more. Together, they can do *anything*.

'One day, people will have learned to live with pain, and then they'll understand their dreams.'

She didn't understand him. She wasn't old enough. But one day, she would be. One day, everyone would understand.

Later that same Tuesday morning, Nell greeted the arrival of her grandfather by leaping into his arms and confiding to him that she had had a dream of being a wolf.

'Did you dream it too?' she asked.

'No,' he said. 'People don't often dream the same dreams. But I spent a most uncomfortable night aboard the train from Dover, and I had some very strange dreams of my own.'

'Daddy can tell you what they were,' she said confidently. 'Daddy knew what I dreamed before I told him.'

Tallentyre looked quizzically at his son-in-law, who was bathing in the sunlight which streamed through the window of the sitting room, watching them.

'You dreamed of the Garden of Eden,' said David, with the confident smile of a clever performer.

'So I did,' Tallentyre admitted, with a slightly harsher expression on his face than the occasion warranted. 'Perhaps you could tell me more about the peculiar things which befell me there. I fear that they are slipping from my own memory like water through a sieve.'

'I'm not sure that I know all the details,' said David, 'but there's a great deal that I *can* tell you. You may find your memory revitalised when we go out. We have to go to Richmond, to call on a man named Jason Sterling. It was he who stole the Clay Man from Austen's burial ground. I think he has succeeded in waking him up, but whether he has or not, he has some experiments which you'll undoubtedly

find interesting. I can't be absolutely sure that he'll
when and how we met, but I know that he won't tur

'I know the name,' Tallentyre answered with
sure that I've met the man, but when and wh
dire thing, David, to grow old and find that
is disposed to play tricks on you.' He lowe
ground and patted Simon on the head b
embrace his daughter. David waited patien
time for the baronet to come to him and

'You seem a little better,' said Tallen
David's face and then at the hand which
the pain eased?'

'I'm a good deal better,' David co
how long the remission will last, bu
blessed relief it is to be comforta
memory has played me some curi
settled now, and I remember all t
to see you again.'

'And of what,' Tallentyre ask

David knew that his friend
question, but he permitted h
smile.

'I dreamed that I was
lightly. 'At first, it was unu
passed, the cold became a mere fa
was able to study the storm of which I was
frightful storm: terrible and wild and beautiful. bu
better than Eden . . . And in spite of all the wildness o
storm, I was convinced, as I suppose a snowflake has to be,
that it's no bad thing to fall.'

the next twelve months, or twelve years, if only the clock
could be put back and the murder undone?
The absence of a murderer would be a nine days' wonder in
life, but still it would be a nine days' wonder. News meant no
a nine days' wonder in the newspapers' wonder. Everything
and the sellers of news were ever avid to hurry hist
always pleading with their gods for the precious gi
more murder, one more catastrophe, one more
would greet the last trump with cries of delig
only that they could publish the news of its a
Pennies out of pockets. Those were the coins which
value of the world's suffering, the wo
for scandal to feed the appetites of
excitement, pennies to soothe the
those who dared not visit whores
into the turbid water, dealer in bank
Mercy Murrell, as it danced over swirling s
of a wide-bellied rowboat
alike.   She weighed the
parapet and into the
attractive, not bec
had happened las
position so com
priate climax
intention to
too bad-te
She w
How
not

without
It was all
She could hear
near the station. Already
of a horrible murder, trying to
their predatory cries. What was fatal
temporarily good for theirs: a headless corps
was worth pennies in their pockets.

Pennies! What were pennies compared with the flood o
sovereigns which would have flowed into her house during

She did not turn when the carriage drew up beside her. She knew by the sound of its wheels upon the road that it was not a police vehicle, but she probably would not have moved in any case. She was locked into a private confrontation with her misfortune, and was not in any mood to run away. When a naked hand was placed upon her own gloved hand where it rested on the parapet, she was suitably surprised, but she did not start and she was slow to turn. She would have wagered confidently that there was no face on earth whose sight could have wrung more out of her than a bitter frown.

But she was wrong.

'For the love of God!' she whispered, though it was not an oath she used frequently.

To see the face itself would have been astonishment enough, because she had seen the wreck which had been made of that face half a lifetime before. Burnt faces, she knew, could not be remade; they never healed. But there was more, because this face had the bloom of youth upon it. It had fewer blemishes upon it than it had before the fire.

She would have sworn that the Jacob Harkender at whom she was staring was not a day older than twenty-five. That was why she asked, with an edge of taut alarm in her voice, 'Who are you?' although she did not doubt that he was exactly what he appeared to be.

'Come with me, Mercy,' he said, in a gentle tone which was almost as bizarre as his appearance. He spoke to her as if she were his aged mother, tenderly – but he had never been a tender man.

For a moment she had no answer at all, but then she found one. She laughed excitedly, and said: 'Dorian Gray!' She was, after all, a woman of letters, and knew Wilde well enough to steal his themes. Long ago, when she had been a regular visitor at Whittenton, she had seen more than one flattering portrait of Jacob Harkender, including one which he had painted himself; she had presumed that the portraits had burned with the house, but now she was struck by the fantastic notion that one must have survived, and that Harkender's diabolical magic had at last succeeded in trading its appearance for the burnt, blind wreck which he had been.

'Not quite,' he said to her. 'There's one, at least, who'll be unshakeable in his conviction that it's the Devil's work, but he's another man's servant now, and I don't want him back.'

'Of all the men who might deserve a miracle . . .' she murmured, fighting to suppress another laugh, which might have sounded uncomfortably mad.

'I'm the least,' he agreed. 'But you've known the world well enough to know how much more irony than justice is in it. If my master is the Devil, I've surely served him well enough to be his favoured son.'

'He did me an ill turn,' she observed, suddenly vituperative, 'when he foisted that accursed witch girl on me. It's a poor reward for all my kindness, that she should ruin me! Nor will she ever hang for what she did, the bitch, for there's not a court in the land would believe that she could do it.'

'*Caveat emptor*,' said Harkender, whose hand still lay upon her own, waiting for hers to be lifted. 'When you spend sixpence for a fallen angel's spawn, you can't expect to buy a saint.'

She looked at his carriage then, and at his patient coachman. She did not recognise either of them. 'Where are you taking me?' she asked, admitting that she could not possibly do otherwise than what he asked of her. He was, after all, a thing of miracle and magic.

'We have a place to live,' he said, 'with furniture and servants. There's much to do of a very ordinary nature, and there's also much to do which is of a very different nature. Do you remember, Mercy, how I told you long ago that I had found a way to knowledge and power which none but a few could follow? Do you remember how I swore that I would find the means to disturb and hurt the world of comfortable men?'

'I remember,' she said.

'It was a more difficult path than I thought,' he told her soberly, 'and its end was not what I expected; but I'm not sorry that I followed that path, nor that I've reached the place at which I find myself. Come into the carriage now, and let's be on our way.'

Again there was that frightful tenderness in his voice, which she could not begin to explain, given that he had not seen her for twenty years and had not liked her overmuch before.

Perhaps, she thought, as she consented to be taken by the hand and lifted into the carriage, he was really some deceptive minion of Satan come to ferry her across the dismal river to the nearer shore of Hell, and thence to the Lake of Fire which had so often been prophesied as her ultimate doom. Even with that thought in her head, though, she did not recoil from him. Was she not made of stone? Was she not immune to all the restless affections and afflictions which were the curse of womankind? Was she not the keeper of the finest house in London, and a dramatist, too?

When the horses set off and moved through their easy paces to a rapid trot, she did not care at all where they might be going, but only that she was on her way. It was enough that *someone* had come to collect her, whether he be a beautiful magician or the Devil in disguise.

When the door opened, David was so intent on what he was writing that he did not look up immediately, but continued doggedly until he had reached the end of his sentence and the end of the thought that he was shaping. It was so good to be able to write freely, and it seemed that his thoughts now flowed with quicksilver lightness from his mind to the page.

When he did look up he was only mildly surprised to see who it was. He was glad, too.

'I had expected Pelorus,' he said.

'He has gone to your house,' she told him. 'I dare say that he will be glad to see Sir Edward, and he has always liked your pretty wife, has he not? I knew that I would find you here; you are a creature of habit, after all.'

She was standing in front of the picture which was tacked to the back of the door, obscuring its disconcerting eyes. Her own eyes were less disconcerting than they had been.

'How are you, Mandorla?' he asked. 'Has anything changed since we last met?'

She shook her head slowly, and he could not tell whether she knew what he meant.

'How are *you*?' she asked. 'You look better.'

'I'm a great deal better,' he assured her. 'I've made my peace with the Angel of Pain, and have become more adept in the art of dreaming.'

'I kept my promises,' she said gently.

'I know,' he said. 'You have my gratitude.'

'We are friends now,' she agreed. 'I hope we may be friends for ever, but who can tell what the future may bring?'

'No one,' he said. 'We can't tell what Machalalel might do, or any of the others. They're subject to the whims of their own fate, just as we are subject to them.'

'They hate us,' said Mandorla. 'You may think that what you have now is a gift, but it is simply another kind of curse. I know whereof I speak. They hate us, and their one delight is to make us miserable.'

David shook his head. 'That's not true,' he said. 'Our ancestors helped to make them what they once were, but they're not so innocent now. They have their own anxieties, frustrations and resentments, but they are beings like us. They can hate, but they may also learn to love, in time.'

'I cannot help but feel that your lesson is intended for my ears as much as theirs,' she replied wryly. 'And I am suitably flattered. But you must not allow yourself to be carried away by optimism simply because the ache is gone from your bones. You will find a full enough measure of suffering in what is to come; I am sure of that.'

'Perhaps,' he admitted. 'But there's cause for hope, even for you. One day you'll be a wolf again, if that's what you desire. One day, Pelorus will be reconciled with the pack. One day . . . you may decide that it's not such a dire punishment to be human, some of the time.'

'You have beautiful children, David,' she said. 'It is more unfortunate than you could ever imagine that they were wolves for such a little while. They can never be truly content, you know, now that they know what it really is to *be*. Although they may have forgotten already, the knowledge will always be present, deep in their minds; and if ever they hear the werewolves of London calling in the night, their hearts will ache for what they once had, but lost for ever.'

'All men must sacrifice their dreams of Eden,' he told her. 'We emerge from the dark, warm womb into the harsh light of the world, where we learn to think and to feel. Our hearts ache, but we can bear it. You can learn to bear it too, Mandorla. Whatever you believe, you're more human than wolf, and if you were ever to achieve your most fervent desire, you too would find that the forgotten secret of humanity would trouble your dreams and set an ache in your heart. For creatures such as you and I, there's no freedom without pain; and now that you've tasted freedom, I can't believe that you could ever happily endure the prison of wolfish instinct.'

She smiled wanly.

'I wonder what you will say to me in a thousand years' time,' she said, 'when you have tasted death and returned to life a dozen times or more, and all those you once loved have mouldered to dust in their graves.'

He met the solemn gaze of her violet eyes without flinching at all, although he knew that such *might*, if a certain angel willed it, be his fate.

The only answer he gave her was an echo.

'I wonder,' he said, as bravely as he could.

Not for a moment did the Clay Man doubt his memory of the paradoxical garden which he had visited with Jason Sterling and Sir Edward Tallentyre, although he knew full well how fallible an instrument memory was.

He knew that all of them had been involved in some adventure of the Creators', but that was not a new experience for him. He remembered – and trusted the memory, within appropriate limits – the long-gone time when the Creators had last been eager to dabble in the affairs of men: the Age of Heroes, he had been ironically content to call it; the age of seers and oracles, of sports and marvels, which still survived in myth, though not in any firmer evidential record.

It might be interesting, he thought, were that kind of era to dawn again; but he fervently hoped that it would not.

He did not know whether to be more or less optimistic in the aftermath of what had happened. In the the wake of the Terror and Napoleon's wars and the failure of the Chartists, he had lost faith in the possibility of an Age of Reason; it would not be easy to renew that faith, especially now that he must take account of the Creators again.

From the window of Jason Sterling's smoking room, where the shared dream had begun, he studied the street outside. He was not searching for the prying werewolves or anything else, but simply marvelling at the trivial details of the world: at the gas lamps which were folding back the gathering darkness of the evening; at the gay clothes which the women wore; at the press of the carts and carriages which testified to the increase of trade and wealth; at the newsboys hustling in fervent competition, trying to curdle the blood of passers-by with their promises of gruesome intelligence.

There had been a horrible murder in some fashionable brothel in the East End. When he had last been awake and alert all the fashionable brothels had been further west, within a stone's throw of the Palace of Westminster; they had had their own division bells installed, to summon the Members back whenever it was required that they should vote on the fate of the realm. The Houses of Parliament had been rebuilt since then; times were changing.

The stink of the streets seemed worse than it had been thirty or forty years before, but that might have been an illusion caused by the fact that he had not become used to it. There were more horses, to be sure, and there was more litter, but London had ever been a dirty city, and Richmond had to be reckoned part of London now. The city was spreading, greedily swallowing up towns, villages and green fields, expanding at a desperate pace, and there would be no stopping it while the ends of prosperity were served.

It had all been very different a hundred years ago. What he saw now differed more from what he had seen in the eighteenth century than the eighteenth century had differed from the eighth. Change was more rapid now than ever before.

He had dared to hope, in 1789, that change had come under human dominion and human control. Perhaps, he thought, he had been wrong even then. Perhaps the Creators had already begun to awaken; or perhaps they had been stirring in their sleep. If the Terror had only been a fragment of *their* nightmares, and not a human thing at all, the thought of it might be easier to bear. On the other hand, even if it had been a venting of human spite, perhaps there were still grounds for hope. Human lifetimes were short, and every new generation had the chance to repent of the worst follies of the last.

'Where are you, Machalalel?' he whispered, half aloud. 'Why have you forsaken me? Why have you forsaken all those you made? You died, I know, but I have died myself so very many times, and I know now that your death was only one more performance, one more deceptive jest.'

He would have been happier by far had he known that all this was Machalalel's doing, but he could not believe it. If that petty Eden had been Machalalel's, he would surely have known it; and if Sterling's work had been guided by Machalalel, it would certainly have proceeded further and faster than it had done so far.

'Why should I care,' he asked himself, 'what the Creators do? What does it matter to me what men make of their world, when I can outlast all their follies? Why should I puzzle over dreams, however real or false they might be?'

There was no use in pretending. He did care, and he always would. Pelorus, not he, had been forced to hear and bear the will of Machalalel; but he had needed no such imposition to make him fascinated by the world and its inhabitants. Machalalel had not succeeded in making a true human being from the callow clay he chose to mould, but he had not omitted curiosity from the creature he had shaped.

The Clay Man did not know whether that curiosity was a curse or a gift, but it was inescapable.

I must write another book, he thought. And another, and another, until I write one which will do the work which I intend it to do. But first, I must find the kind of truth which will not decay, and I must find the kind of hope which will not be so easily betrayed. Next time, I will not be forced by irony or despair to sign myself Lucian. Next time, I will speak plainly, and *I will be heard*.

Later still, David Lydyard lay back in his bed, glorying in the softness of the sheets and the delicious warmth within his own body. For a moment he stretched himself out, letting the cool air play with the heat of his flesh; then he turned back to his beloved Cordelia and wrapped her in his arms. There was no flinching from one another now, no sense of separation between them, no unease in the way they looked into one another's eyes. They were *together*.

'Whatever happens,' he whispered, 'we'll have this moment and a thousand like it. Whatever happens, we have had joy, affection and the best rewards of life. Whatever happens, I will always love you.'

'I know,' she answered.

He knew that it was true. She did know. So did he.

Brian Stableford
The Werewolves of London £5.99

The mournful howling of wolves echoes through eternity. For when they are not wolves they must bear the image of man . . .

In 1872, David Lydyard accompanies his guardian to Egypt. Lured into a search for the 'real' Egypt by a priest they encounter a land of tombs and snakes and fiery desert demons . . .

David now finds himself possessed by uncanny visionary powers. At the same time Gabriel, a foundling boy brought up by nuns, experiences a mysterious force developing within him.

Others covet these powers for their own purposes . . . the heretic priests of the secret Order of St Amycus, the occultist and reputed Satanist Jacob Harkender . . . and the legendary werewolves of London.

'Truly magical' FEAR

'By far the best book he has ever written, a scientific romance of very great scope . . . the most intelligent novel yet published in 1990' INTERZONE

'So absorbing . . . you're in for some surprises, right up to the last page' LOCUS

interzone

SCIENCE FICTION AND FANTASY

Monthly   **£2.25**

- *Interzone* is the leading British magazine which specializes in SF and new fantastic writing. We have published:

BRIAN ALDISS	GARRY KILWORTH
J.G. BALLARD	DAVID LANGFORD
IAIN BANKS	MICHAEL MOORCOCK
BARRINGTON BAYLEY	RACHEL POLLACK
GREGORY BENFORD	KEITH ROBERTS
MICHAEL BISHOP	GEOFF RYMAN
DAVID BRIN	JOSEPHINE SAXTON
RAMSEY CAMPBELL	BOB SHAW
ANGELA CARTER	JOHN SHIRLEY
RICHARD COWPER	JOHN SLADEK
JOHN CROWLEY	BRIAN STABLEFORD
PHILIP K. DICK	BRUCE STERLING
THOMAS M. DISCH	LISA TUTTLE
MARY GENTLE	IAN WATSON
WILLIAM GIBSON	CHERRY WILDER
M. JOHN HARRISON	GENE WOLFE

- *Interzone* has also introduced many excellent new writers; illustrations, articles, interviews, film and book reviews, news, etc.

- *Interzone* is available from good bookshops, or by subscription. For six issues, send £14 (outside UK, £17). For twelve issues send £26, (outside UK, £32). Single copies: £2.50 inc. p&p (outside UK, £2.80).

- American subscribers may send $27 for six issues, or $52 for twelve issues. All US copies will be despatched by Air Saver (accelerated surface mail).

- -

To: **interzone** 217 Preston Drove, Brighton, BN1 6FL, UK.

Please send me six/twelve issues of *Interzone*, beginning with the current issue. I enclose a cheque / p.o. / international money order, made payable to *Interzone* (Delete as applicable.)

Name _____

Address _____

_____

All Pan books are available at your local bookshop or newsagent, or can be ordered direct from the publisher. Indicate the number of copies required and fill in the form below.

Send to: Pan C. S. Dept
           Macmillan Distribution Ltd
           Houndmills Basingstoke RG21 2XS
or phone: 0256 29242, quoting title, author and Credit Card number.

Please enclose a remittance* to the value of the cover price plus: £1.00 for the first book plus 50p per copy for each additional book ordered.

*Payment may be made in sterling by UK personal cheque, postal order, sterling draft or international money order, made payable to Pan Books Ltd.

Alternatively by Barclaycard/Access/Amex/Diners

Card No.   □□□□□□□□□□□□□□□□□□□□

Expiry Date   □□□□□□

———————————————————————————

Signature:

Applicable only in the UK and BFPO addresses

While every effort is made to keep prices low, it is sometimes necessary to increase prices at short notice. Pan Books reserve the right to show on covers and charge new retail prices which may differ from those advertised in the text or elsewhere.

NAME AND ADDRESS IN BLOCK LETTERS PLEASE:

....

Name _____

Address _____

_____

_____

_____

6/92